The Other Emily

BARBARA FREETHY

Fog City Publishing

PRAISE FOR BARBARA FREETHY

"Barbara Freethy's suspense novels are explosively good!" — *New York Times bestselling author Toni Anderson.*

"A fabulous, page-turning combination of romance and intrigue. Fans of Nora Roberts and Elizabeth Lowell will love this book." — *NYT Bestselling Author Kristin Hannah on Golden Lies*

"Powerful and absorbing...sheer hold-your-breath suspense." — *NYT Bestselling Author Karen Robards on Don't Say A Word*

"Barbara Freethy delivers riveting, plot-twisting suspense and a deeply emotional story. Every book is a thrilling ride." *USA Today Bestselling Author Rachel Grant*

"Freethy is at the top of her form. Fans of Nora Roberts will find a similar tone here, framed in Freethy's own spare, elegant style." — *Contra Costa Times on Summer Secrets*

"Freethy hits the ground running as she kicks off another winning romantic suspense series…Freethy is at her prime with a superb combo of engaging characters and gripping plot." — *Publishers' Weekly on Silent Run*

"PERILOUS TRUST is a non-stop thriller that seamlessly melds jaw-dropping suspense with sizzling romance, and I was riveted from the first page to the last…Readers will be breathless in anticipation as this fast-paced and enthralling love story evolves and goes in unforeseeable directions." — *USA Today HEA Blog*

PRAISE FOR BARBARA FREETHY

"Barbara Freethy is a master storyteller with a gift for spinning tales about ordinary people in extraordinary situations and drawing readers into their lives." — *Romance Reviews Today*

"Freethy (Silent Fall) has a gift for creating complex, appealing characters and emotionally involving, often suspenseful, sometimes magical stories."— *Library Journal on Suddenly One Summer*

"If you love nail-biting suspense and heartbreaking emotion, Silent Run belongs on the top of your to-be-bought list. I could not turn the pages fast enough."— *NYT Bestselling Author Mariah Stewart*

"Hooked me from the start and kept me turning pages throughout all the twists and turns. Silent Run is powerful romantic intrigue at its best."— *NYT Bestselling Author JoAnn Ross*

"An absorbing story of two people determined to unravel the secrets, betrayals, and questions about their past. The story builds to an explosive conclusion that will leave readers eagerly awaiting Barbara Freethy's next book."—*NYT Bestselling Author Carla Neggars on Don't Say A Word*

"A page-turner that engages your mind while it tugs at your heartstrings ... DON'T SAY A WORD had made me a Barbara Freethy fan for life!" —*NYT Bestselling Author Diane Chamberlain*

"On Shadow Beach teems with action, drama and compelling situations... a fast-paced page-turner." —*BookPage*

ALSO BY BARBARA FREETHY

Mystery Thriller Standalones

ALL THE PRETTY PEOPLE

LAST ONE TO KNOW

THE OTHER EMILY

Off the Grid: FBI Series

PERILOUS TRUST

RECKLESS WHISPER

DESPERATE PLAY

ELUSIVE PROMISE

DANGEROUS CHOICE

RUTHLESS CROSS

CRITICAL DOUBT

FEARLESS PURSUIT

DARING DECEPTION

RISKY BARGAIN

PERFECT TARGET

For a complete list of books, visit Barbara's Website!

THE OTHER EMILY

For more information: http://www.barbarafreethy.com

CHAPTER ONE

LIGHTS. *Camera. Action…*

Words I'd said before as a film director. Words that were going through my head now as an honoree for the prestigious Top 30 Under 30 List by *VIP Magazine.*

I wasn't ready for the lights, the cameras, or the action. But as I looked out the window of the limo, which was crawling through the heavy Los Angeles traffic, I realized I needed to get ready fast. I could see the bright spotlights surrounding the entrance to the Excelsior Hotel in Hollywood, where the red carpet was set up, and photographers were waiting to snap photos of me and the other twenty-nine rising stars.

I couldn't believe I'd made the list.

Me, Emily Hollister, had become someone important. It seemed impossible to believe.

I'd been born into nothing and lived a very rough and ragged life. But at twenty-eight years old, I'd scratched and scraped my way into a senior producer/director role at Holly Roads Productions, where a freak accident had led to me directing what had turned out to be the movie of the year. The sequence of events that had brought me to this moment was nothing I could have imagined.

I should be feeling cocky and excited to celebrate, but my palms were sweating and I was fighting back an urge to jump out of the limo and run away into the dark of the night. I'd always felt more comfortable in the shadows, but I also knew how to put on a mask, be who people thought I should be, which was what I would do tonight.

"Emily?"

I turned away from the window to meet the questioning eyes of Francine Montgomery, the vice president of Holly Roads Productions, and my mentor. Francine was an attractive blonde in her early fifties, who had been working in Hollywood for thirty years. She'd started the production company ten years ago with her partner, David Valenti, and a significant investment from wealthy entertainment lawyer, Curtis Nolan, who also was one of her ex-husbands.

"What's wrong, Emily?" Francine asked, her sharp, penetrating gaze always making me think she saw a little too much.

"Nothing." I forced a smile onto my face. "Just nervous. I'm not used to being the one in front of the cameras."

"You'll do fine. You're young, beautiful, and smart. And you just directed a blockbuster movie that brought in more money on opening day than any other film in the past year. There's already talk of Oscar nominations, for the film and for you."

"That seems impossible to believe. I can't see the Academy giving me the nomination when I only ended up directing because Mitchell was injured, and we were in a remote location. There was no time to get anyone else to the other side of the world to take over. They're going to take all that into account."

"Maybe. Maybe not. It's probably a long shot," she conceded. "You're young and you're female, so those are also two strikes against you, but your work was brilliant, and that may sway some voting members."

Despite her words, I wouldn't let myself even consider the possibility of getting an Oscar nomination.

"You need to stop being so modest, Emily," Francine continued. "You caught a lucky break, but when given the opportunity to shine, you did just that. I am very proud of you, and I have to take a little credit for your success. I hired you to be an intern eight years ago."

"For which I will always be grateful," I said, as we exchanged a smile.

"This honor tonight—it's a big deal," Francine said. "It not only gives you some press, it also puts our company out there, and that's always important. Your honor is our honor. Try to remember that. You're not doing this just for you, but for us, and you've always been a team player." Francine paused. "I'm glad you let Gina style you tonight. You look...perfect. And it's nice to see you out of jeans and a sweatshirt. You're a beautiful woman, Emily."

I had never thought of myself as beautiful, maybe not horribly unattractive, but when I looked in the mirror, I saw past the face that looked back at me, the face that always felt like a mask. I knew what I looked like on the inside, and it wasn't that great. But tonight, my mask was exceptionally good, with my long brown hair falling in soft waves around my shoulders, my brown eyes framed by thickened lashes, and my makeup giving a glow to my pale skin. My champagne-gold mini dress clung to my body, showing off my curves and a lot of leg. But I wasn't entirely sure I wouldn't trip down the red carpet in my ridiculously high strappy heels.

I couldn't think about that. I needed to get over my anxiety. This was a great opportunity for me and the company, and I didn't want to mess it up.

"Francine is right. You look great, Emily," Kaitlyn interjected, drawing my gaze to the seat across from me. Kaitlyn Dahl had joined the team as my assistant three months ago and was a twenty-three-year-old, starry-eyed brunette who probably couldn't wait to find herself in my position.

Kaitlyn had graduated from film school a year earlier and had little practical experience but a lot of ambitious drive and confidence. She was willing to do whatever job was thrown at her, no matter how mundane. Having been in her position myself, I knew how mundane those tasks could be. But Kaitlyn had a willing attitude and a sincere belief that every step she took would get her closer to where she wanted to be. In some ways, she reminded me of myself and how I'd felt at twenty-three. The five-year age difference between us wasn't much, but sometimes it felt huge. But that was probably because I'd had to grow up fast when I was a child, always making me feel older than my years.

"You both look good, too," I said. "I'm really glad you're with me tonight. When Ashton told me he'd have to meet me at the party, I was not looking forward to going into the hotel alone."

"Why is Ashton so busy that he can't walk the red carpet with you?" Francine asked, a note of annoyance in her voice, reminding me she wasn't a big fan of the man I was currently dating.

"He's shooting a guest spot on *The Trigger Man*," I replied. "They've had some issues and are running late, which is perfectly understandable."

"I suppose," Francine said halfheartedly.

"Ashton is a good guy. You should get to know him."

Francine gave me a somewhat odd look. "I know him, or, I should say, I know men just like him. My first husband was an actor, and I got to see his act every night until I realized he had more audiences than just me."

"I'm sorry that he cheated on you."

"You can't trust actors, Emily. They're very good at pretending to be whoever you want them to be."

Francine didn't realize that wasn't the best argument she could have used, because I was good at pretending, too. Or at least, I used to be. I was giving away far too much tonight.

"Well, I think Ashton is a dream," Kaitlyn said with a small sigh. "He's handsome and so interesting. Whenever he drops by to see you, Emily, he always takes a minute to ask me how I am. You're lucky."

I ignored Francine's eye roll and smiled at Kaitlyn. "I think so, too." I actually didn't know what I really thought about Ashton. He seemed like a good guy, but we'd only been going out for six weeks. Right now, it was fun, and that was all I was looking for. I wasn't even sure there was anything else to look for. I didn't have a high opinion of love and an even lower opinion of marriage.

"What's happening with the screenplay on *Aces High*?" Francine asked, changing the subject to the movie we would start shooting in the next few months. "How is Roy doing on the screenplay revisions?"

"After his usual tantrum, he settled in."

Roy Vignetti was a talented screenwriter but could also be obnoxious when asked to make even the smallest edits. I had to handle him with kid gloves, because he was constantly threatening to quit, and I needed him to finish the script we'd been developing for months. "I should have a new draft to look at on Monday," I added. "How are the negotiations going with Natasha Rodrigo? She's perfect for the role of Elena."

"Her agent wants double what we offered," Francine replied, her lips tightening. "I want you to come with me to lunch tomorrow at the Moonraker. Show her how well the two of you will work together."

"Will we work together?" I licked my lips as I felt another wave of nerves that had nothing to do with the party. While I'd stepped in for Mitchell Gray on the last movie after he was injured on the set, he was still our top director, with three Academy Award-nominated films to his name, and Francine had been very cagey about whether I'd be producing or directing the upcoming film.

"Yes. I need both of you for this movie. Mitchell is ready to direct." Francine paused. "And you'll be working alongside him."

"But he'll be calling the shots." My stomach twisted with disappointment.

"You did a great job, Emily, but Mitchell is one of the greatest directors of all time. There's still a lot you can learn from him. And he could use your perspective as well."

I didn't believe Mitchell was interested in my perspective. He'd barely let me utter an opinion before his accident. I'd been his gopher, not his assistant director. "Why don't you have Mitchell meet with Natasha then? If he's going to direct, she'll want to talk to him."

"Natasha actually has some reservations about Mitchell. She knows he's very skilled, but she's not a big fan of him personally. I think she may have had a run-in with him in the past, something about him casting his wife Tara over her. It happened more than a dozen years ago, but she still holds a grudge. She is, however, very intrigued by the work you did on *The Opal King*. It was her favorite movie in years."

"That's nice to hear."

"If you can assure Natasha that you'll be working alongside Mitch, I think it will convince her to come our way. Lunch is tomorrow at noon. Don't drink too much tonight. I want you fresh for the meeting."

"All right." I tried not to let my unhappiness show. I thought I had earned the directing job for *Aces High*, a project I'd been working on for months. But Francine still believed Mitchell was better than me. Or maybe it was Curtis and David who were pulling that string. They both pretty much let Francine run the company, but when it came to the big talent, the big money, they always weighed in.

I personally thought Mitchell was living off his past work. From what I'd seen before he'd gotten hurt on the last film, his best days were behind him, and mine were in front of me. I wished Francine could see how much I'd done for him even before his accident. Or maybe she knew Mitchell had used me as a crutch, but he had a bigger name than me, which meant more money, more support, more interest from everyone. It was a reality I had to live with.

The limousine finally stopped as we pulled up in front of the hotel. It was showtime.

As I followed Francine and Kaitlyn out of the limo, I was immediately hit by the hot breeze of a very warm Friday night in mid-September. There was a huge crowd in front of the hotel and probably an even bigger crowd at the rooftop party.

Before we had taken more than a few steps, David Valenti and Curtis Nolan joined us. I hadn't expected either of them to show up at a party celebrating the thirty-and-under crowd, when they were both in their fifties. On the other hand, they were always happy when our company was getting press, and there was a lot of media here tonight.

They were both good-looking men. Curtis had dark hair streaked with a touch of silver at the temples and green eyes that had made him irresistible to his three ex-wives, one of whom was Francine. Curtis was part of old Hollywood. His father had been a producer, his mother an actress. As an entertainment lawyer, he had repped some of the biggest names in the business, and several years back, at his ex-wife's urging, he had decided to invest in our company.

David was Curtis's polar opposite, with sandy-brown hair that had a touch of red in it, pale skin, and brown eyes. He was nowhere near as sophisticated as Curtis, and I'd always found him to be far more approachable. David's father had been a cinematographer, so David had also grown up in the industry, but brought a different perspective. He'd recently married for the first time and had spent most of the past few months on an extended honeymoon in Europe.

"Emily," David said, giving me a cheerful smile. "You made it. And I don't just mean you got here tonight. You're a big deal."

"Thanks."

"We're very happy to have you representing the company," Curtis added. "You've had a hell of a good year."

"I have. I didn't know either of you were coming tonight."

"We came to celebrate you," David said. "So, walk the red carpet and talk up the company, will you? We're going to meet you inside."

"I will."

"Have fun," Francine added. "Don't worry about networking. You deserve to just have a good time."

"Thanks." I turned to Kaitlyn. "Do I look okay?"

"You look perfect, Emily," Kaitlyn said. "And this is all so amazing. You're living your best life right this second. How many people can say that?"

"I know I'm lucky."

"Thanks for letting me come tonight."

"You deserve it. You've been working hard the last few weeks."

"We'll meet you inside," Francine said, urging me toward the red carpet while she and Kaitlyn headed into the hotel through a different door.

I squared my shoulders and stepped onto the carpet. A few steps later, I reached the first waiting reporter, an attractive Black woman, who towered over me by a good four inches. She asked a question, then put the microphone in my face. I was so nervous, it was hard to remember her question, something about the honor of the list.

A voice inside my head told me to get it together, to act like I belonged. If I did that, no one would question me, no one would doubt my accomplishments. That voice belonged to a man named Jimmy, a man who had known how to get exactly what he wanted and had taught me how to do the same. His methods had not always been legal or ethical. But his advice was probably sound.

"I'm thrilled to be here," I said. My voice sounded weak, so I put some energy into it. Lifting my chin, I looked directly at the reporter. "I'm proud to be in the company of the twenty-nine other amazing individuals being celebrated tonight. I can't wait to meet them."

"Some might say you're only here because of Mitchell Gray's freak accident," the reporter commented, her sharp gaze raking my face.

She was eager to get an emotional reaction from me, but I would not buy into the premise of her question.

"I'm here because I had the privilege of directing an amazing cast and crew and bringing a story to life that has resonated with audiences all over the world. *The Opal King* was truly a special story."

Flashing a smile, I didn't wait for another question but moved down the carpet, where I found a reporter who was more interested in my relationship with Ashton Hunter and wanted to know if he was coming to the party. It would have been nice to have Ashton next to me. He definitely would have taken up a lot of the focus.

But I shouldn't want that. I shouldn't want to be in someone else's shadow.

Annoyed with myself, I shook my head and continued talking up the company and the last movie as well as the next movie.

It took another forty-five minutes before I finally made it up to the rooftop bar with its amazing 360-degree view of Los Angeles. I gratefully accepted a glass of champagne from a passing waiter and downed it in a couple of big gulps as I told myself the worst was over.

Then I saw the woman heading straight for me. Her blonde hair and big brown eyes were more than a little familiar. I'd met her in high school, and for three years we had run with the same crowd. But I hadn't seen Cassie Byrne since our high school graduation, and I wasn't excited to be reunited now.

"Emily Hollister," she said with a bright smile.

"Cassie Byrne," I replied, as we exchanged a brief hug.

"It's been a minute," Cassie said. "You look stunning tonight."

"So do you. What—what are you doing here, Cassie?"

"I work for *VIP Magazine*," she said, referring to the sponsor of the list. "I planned this event."

"Really? Well, it's amazing. This venue is beautiful."

"Only the best for the best," Cassie drawled, an edge to her voice that reminded me our relationship had always been one of love and hate. We'd shared a mutual friend, Alina Price, but had never been quite as good of friends with each other. "Congratulations," she added. "I saw *The Opal King*. It was great. When your name came up for the list, I thought you were perfect for it."

Cassie made it sound like she'd had some say over the nomination, but surely that wasn't true. "I appreciate that," I said, not wanting to ask a question I didn't want answered.

"It's funny how you ended up stepping into Mitchell Gray's shoes. Although this wasn't the first time, was it?"

"Excuse me?"

"Our high school play, remember? Kimmy Taylor tripped down the stairs, and you had to take her place as the lead."

I licked my lips. "I forgot about that."

"Just saying—you often seem to be in the right place at the right time."

"Is that what you're saying?" I challenged. "Because it doesn't sound like it."

"Oh, I'm just teasing," Cassie said with a laugh and a dismissive wave of her hand. "You always take things too personally, Emily. You did a great job on that film, and you deserve all the accolades you're getting."

"Thank you. I'm surprised you didn't go into acting instead of event planning. You always had your eye on Hollywood."

"I did some modeling and acting for a while, but I discovered I'm better at planning events and parties where I get to meet interesting people and go to fascinating places." Cassie paused. "Speaking of events, our high school reunion is next weekend, and you haven't responded yet."

"Right. I can't make it. I'm really busy."

"We all are. You should make time. It will be fun."

"I'll try," I said, having absolutely no intention of going to that reunion. The last thing I wanted to do was go back to my past.

"Well, if you can't promise to make the reunion, at least come to lunch with Alina and me. We're meeting on Tuesday. When I told her I was going to see you tonight, she asked me to tell you how much she'd like to see you again."

I wouldn't mind seeing Alina. She had been one of my best friends in high school, but I'd made a point of not staying connected to anyone from that time in my life, and it seemed like a bad idea to change that now.

"Or are you too big for us now?" Cassie challenged. "I'm an event planner and Alina is a high school drama teacher. Maybe we don't have much in common anymore."

I didn't like the irritated glint in her eyes, and I didn't need someone working with *VIP Magazine* with access to reporters to suddenly feel slighted by me. "Don't be silly," I said. "I'd love to do lunch. I don't have my calendar, but I'll check it tomorrow and I'll make it happen."

"Good. I'll text you to confirm. The magazine has your phone number."

"Great."

"It doesn't feel like ten years since high school, does it?" Cassie asked.

It felt like a million years to me, but I lied again. "Not really." I grabbed another glass of champagne from a passing waiter and put my empty glass on his tray. "So, everything is good with you, Cassie?"

"Very good. I've been seeing my boyfriend for almost two years. I think he's about to pop the question."

"That's wonderful."

"Did I hear you're dating Ashton Hunter?"

"Several weeks now."

"I saw him as your guest, but I haven't seen him come in."

"He should be here soon. He had a late shoot today."

Cassie nodded, her gaze reflective. "You really do have it all, don't you, Emily? Great job, celebrity boyfriend...it's all going perfectly for you."

"I can't complain, but my life is still a work in progress."

"My life needs a bit more progress than yours," Cassie said with a small laugh.

I took another gulp of champagne as I scanned the crowded room for someone I could use to escape from this conversation. Relief ran through me when I saw Ashton approaching, moving through the room like a young, handsome prince. He was tall and lean with blond hair and striking blue eyes. Ashton never seemed aware of the wake he created, which I found to be one of his best traits.

When he reached me, he opened his arms, and I moved in for a quick hug and a kiss. He smiled at me. "How's my rising star doing?"

"Very well." As Cassie cleared her throat, I stepped back and added, "This is an old friend of mine, Cassie Byrne. She helped plan this event. Ashton Hunter."

Ashton sent his dazzling smile in Cassie's direction. "Nice to meet you, Cassie."

"You, too. I love your work."

"Thank you. How do you and Emily know each other?"

"We went to high school together," Cassie replied. "I knew Emily before she was a rising star."

"You could probably tell me some stories about her."

"I definitely could," Cassie said with a mischievous smile.

"No one is telling any stories tonight," I interrupted. "And I was not that interesting in high school."

"Emily could be boring," Cassie agreed. "But look at her now."

"I can't stop looking at her." Ashton sent me another dazzling smile.

I flushed, always feeling a little unsettled when Ashton said things like that, which often happened when we were with other people. Lifting my glass, I realized it was empty.

"Let me get you another drink," Ashton said.

"Actually, I need some food."

"Go. Enjoy yourselves," Cassie said. "We'll catch up later."

I nodded, relieved when Cassie left.

"You look beautiful, Emily," Ashton told me when we were alone, or as alone as we could be in a crowd. "I'm a lucky guy to be here with you."

For some reason, his compliment felt a little over the top, but I'd been noticing that happening more and more lately. I should be thrilled at how much he seemed to care for me, but instead, I felt unsettled by the flattery. Clearing my throat, my gaze moved to an older woman with dark-brown hair talking to a trio of men. "Isn't that Christine?" I asked. Christine Pelettier was not only Ashton's agent but one of the top agents in town.

"It is. And she wants to talk to you tonight. I promised I'd find a few minutes. Let's say hello now."

I hesitated, not sure why his agent wanted to talk to me. "She's in the middle of a conversation, and I need to use the restroom. I'll catch her later."

"Okay, but Christine wants to congratulate you, so hurry back."

"I will." I made my way through the crowd, stopping long enough to grab a crab puff from a passing waiter and pop it into my mouth. It tasted good, but it didn't do anything to calm the queasy feeling in my stomach. I really shouldn't have drunk two glasses of champagne without eating first. I moved toward the restroom, only to find a line out the door.

Sighing, I got in line, smiling at a young female influencer who I recognized from social media, one of the other honorees. She barely gave me a passing glance as she and her friend talked rabidly about some guy at the party.

"You'd think they'd have a restroom just for honorees," Kaitlyn said as she came up behind me.

I smiled. It felt good to see a friendly face. "You'd think," I agreed. "But it's moving."

"Your interviews were great, Emily. Francine and I caught them on the hotel monitor. No one would ever know you were so nervous in the limo."

"Thanks. I tried."

"Especially because you must have been a little upset from Francine telling you that Mitchell will direct *Aces High*."

"It was disappointing, but I wasn't surprised."

"Male directors always get the nod," Kaitlyn said. "It's not fair. You did such a good job, and I'm sure you want to prove you're not a one-movie wonder."

"I will prove that—at some point."

"But how long will you have to wait? You wouldn't have gotten that movie if it hadn't been for Mitchell's freak accident," Kaitlyn reminded her. "How long will he be in your way?"

I knew she wasn't trying to be mean, but her words stung, mostly because they were true. "I don't know. But I'll make it happen at some point. And now people know what I can do."

"You are really good. I would have put you in charge of *Aces High*."

I appreciated her positive words. "Thanks."

"Maybe Natasha will make having you as director part of her ask to be in the movie. You should work that angle. Francine already told you that she needs you to get Natasha on board. Use your power."

"I'm going to do my best to get Natasha on the project because she'll be great for the movie, whether I'm the producer or the director or the assistant director. Even if I'm not in the chair, I want to make good films."

"I personally wouldn't want to be in the director's chair. Producing is much more fun. But then, I'm more of a big picture person. I'm less interested in camera angles." A serious gleam entered her eyes. "There's something I should tell you, Emily."

The sudden conflicted look in Kaitlyn's gaze disturbed me. "What's that?"

"It's probably nothing."

"What's nothing?"

"You know how I said that Ashton is always friendly when he stops by the office?"

"Yes," I said warily. "Why?"

"Ashton asked me questions about the part of Dominic in *Aces High*. I think he's interested in the role. He wanted to know who you were talking to."

"That doesn't make sense. Ashton has never asked me about that part or any other. He has his own projects."

"He said he read the script and thought the role of Dominic could be an Oscar contender. Maybe I shouldn't have said anything to you about it. It was probably nothing. But I thought maybe you should know. Was I wrong?"

"No. I want you to tell me things I need to know." Had I let Ashton's sparkling smile wash away my normal wariness? Was his interest in me more business than personal?

"Ashton would probably be great for the part. It wouldn't be the worst idea to give him a shot at it."

"Maybe." I didn't want our professional lives to intersect, at least not yet, not when our relationship was still new. "I don't understand how he even read the script. Did you give it to him?"

"Of course not. I assumed you showed it to him."

I hadn't, but the script had been lying around my home. It was possible Ashton had read through it at some point. I felt a wave of uneasiness, but I told myself not to get carried away. Ashton hadn't asked me about the part, and maybe Kaitlyn had misunderstood his interest in the role. He might have just been commenting that he thought the script would make a good film.

"I'm going to skip this line and come back later," Kaitlyn said.

"Okay," I told her, watching her walk away. Worrying about Ashton having a hidden agenda only made my stomach churn. I really needed food. As soon as I got through this line, I would head to the buffet.

I was almost to the restroom entrance when one of the female servers came over to me. "Emily Hollister?" she asked.

"Yes. I'm Emily," I replied, surprised by her question.

"I was told to give this to you." She handed me a folded note card.

"What's this?"

She shrugged. "No idea."

As she walked away, I opened the note. There were only a few handwritten words on the card, but they made my heart stop: *I know what you did.*

My stomach flipped over, and an intense wave of nausea rose within me as the words blurred in front of my eyes. I stuck the note into my clutch and pushed past the two women in front of me, saying "*Emergency!*" as I almost barreled into a woman coming out of a stall.

I ran into the stall, locked the door, and threw up.

Sometime later, I heard a woman ask if I was all right. I squeaked out a few words, saying I was fine. I didn't want to talk to anyone. I didn't want to see anyone. I just wanted to run.

CHAPTER TWO

I DIDN'T KNOW how long I stayed in the restroom, but it was probably a good thirty minutes. When I returned to the party, the crowd had thinned out. I saw Kaitlyn talking to Ashton by the buffet, and I headed in their direction. I'd reapplied my makeup, so hopefully no one would notice my pale face.

"There you are," Ashton said. "Where on earth have you been?"

"I hope you didn't stand in line at the restroom all this time," Kaitlyn said.

"No. I've been talking to people," I lied. "You know how it is."

"I'll let you two chat," Kaitlyn said. "I'm going to grab a drink."

As Kaitlyn left, I gave Ashton an apologetic smile. "Sorry, I didn't realize how long I'd been gone."

"It's fine. This is your party. You should talk to people. But you missed Christine. She had to leave."

"I'll catch her another time."

"Are you avoiding her?" Ashton asked, a thoughtful gleam in his eyes.

"No. Why would I?"

"It didn't seem like you wanted to talk to her."

"It's a busy night."

"Okay, good. I want us to have dinner with her next week. Christine has some thoughts about my career, and I'd like your opinion."

"I'm sure you know what you want, Ashton."

"I'd like your input. You're clearly a very smart woman, one of the top 30 under 30."

"Which I appreciate, but I'm ready to go home." As his gaze drifted away from mine, I could see that he hadn't heard what I said. "Ashton, are you ready to leave?" I asked more sharply.

"What?" he asked, clearly distracted by someone on the other end of the room.

I followed his gaze to see Mitchell Gray talking to Francine. Damn! Mitchell was the last person I wanted to see.

"I didn't know Mitchell would be here," Ashton said. "I'd like to meet him."

"You would? Why?"

"Because he's an incredible director. You know that. You worked with him before he got hurt."

"Yes, but he's not the friendliest of people," I muttered. "And he doesn't like me. I've told you that before. He thinks I stole his thunder by taking over when he got hurt and that my success is only because of his work on the movie. I just executed, nothing more, which isn't true."

"I understand things are a little off between you," Ashton said. "But you're going to be working with him again. Might as well make nice now. Let's talk to him."

Ashton grabbed my hand and led me across the room. The last time I'd seen Mitchell had been eight months ago when I'd visited him in the hospital right before I left Australia after finishing our film. He'd been in a lot of pain then and had barely said more than a few words to me. Since that visit, I'd sent him a few emails with questions about various things, to which he'd either answered tersely or not at all. I couldn't imagine he'd come to this party to congratulate me.

As we approached, I saw him leaning heavily on a cane. Clearly, he wasn't completely recovered. When he saw me, a frown creased his already heavily lined face. He was in his mid-fifties, but he'd aged a lot since the accident that had left him with a broken back and foot, cracked ribs, and internal injuries.

"Hello, Mitchell," I said. "It's good to see you."

He nodded and simply said, "Emily."

"I was just telling Mitch about the progress you've made on *Aces High*," Francine said. "And how much you're looking forward to working with him again."

"We'll see," Mitchell said tersely.

Clearly, he wasn't any more excited about working with me than I was about working with him.

Ashton squeezed my hand, reminding me why we were in this awkward conversation.

"Mitchell. This is Ashton Hunter," I said.

"Of course," Mitchell said with a friendlier smile. "I'm familiar with your work, Mr. Hunter. Your timing is impeccable."

"And I'm a big fan of yours," Ashton said, shaking Mitchell's hand with enthusiasm. "Your vision is unmatched. The way you see a scene…all the nuances, the angles, the shadows, the lights—it's magic."

Mitchell's tension eased under Ashton's flattering words. Most directors had a big ego, and Mitchell was no exception.

"Thank you," Mitchell said. "I appreciate that."

"I would love to work with you sometime," Ashton added.

"I would like that as well."

"We should go," I interrupted, not liking the way this conversation was going. "I'm sure I'll see you soon, Mitchell, Francine."

"I'll see you tomorrow," Francine said, giving me a pointed look.

"Yes."

Ashton reluctantly left with me. "Why did you cut that off so soon?" he asked, his voice edgier than normal. "I wanted to talk to Mitchell."

He stopped walking, giving me an annoyed look, which was highly unusual. Since we'd met, I'd felt like Ashton was always happy, almost unusually happy, and eternally optimistic, but he wasn't feeling either of those emotions now.

"I'm sorry, but it's awkward with us right now," I explained. "Surely you could see that Mitchell barely wanted to speak to me."

"Which is why you need to keep talking and clear the air."

"We can't clear the air. Mitchell hates that I got credit for his film. But I have never taken all the credit, Ashton. In interviews, I have always said that Mitchell set the tone, the standards, that we'd had many discussions before he got hurt and I took over. It didn't matter. The press loves an underdog story, and when the film grossed a record-breaking amount on opening, I got the praise, and he couldn't stand that." I frowned, thinking maybe I was over-apologizing. "Not that I didn't deserve the credit. I made the decisions on the second half of the film. And I don't know what else I can do to smooth things over. Or why I should even have to do that."

"I get it. But avoiding Mitchell won't make the problem go away. You're going to work together on *Aces High*. You need to find a way to break the tension between you two, and I can be a good bridge between you two. Use me."

Ashton was very good with people. I looked over my shoulder, but Mitchell was gone, and Francine was now talking to Kaitlyn. "He's gone. But if we run into him again, I won't bail out so fast."

"You can't wait for a run-in. I think we should invite him out to dinner next week."

"Seriously?" I asked in shock. "He'd think I was out of my mind."

"Use the movie as a reason to get together. We'll invite his wife, Tara, and make it a foursome. We can go to the Soho House next Saturday night."

I really wanted to say no, but the plea in Ashton's gaze was impossible to ignore. He also wasn't wrong. I needed to get along with Mitch. While I'd rather work on my own, I couldn't afford to be sidelined completely on *Aces High*, and Francine had already told me Mitchell would be the director. I couldn't let him knock me off the film. "All right. I'll call his assistant on Monday and see if I can set something up."

"Great. Now, who else should we talk to?"

"I'm ready to go."

"Go? It's early, Emily," he said in surprise. "It's half past eight."

"To be honest, I'm not feeling very well. You stay. I'll get a rideshare home."

"Are you sure? Maybe I should go with you."

I smiled at his halfhearted offer. "It's fine. Stay. Enjoy yourself."

He frowned. "It would be more fun with you."

"Not tonight."

"Really? I'm heading to New York tomorrow. We won't see each other for a few days."

I had forgotten about that, but I was so rattled with everything going on, maybe it was a good thing he'd be gone. "When will you be back?"

"Probably Wednesday."

"We'll see each other then. It's only a few days."

He leaned down and gave me a kiss. "You look beautiful tonight. I was looking forward to getting you out of that dress."

"Another time."

"Feel better."

"Thanks." As I left Ashton, I looked around the party, wondering about the server who had delivered the note to me. She was blonde...I thought. I hadn't really looked at her. But none of the servers in view were familiar. Two were men, and the only woman I could see had black hair. That wasn't her.

I should have asked her who'd given her the note, but I hadn't thought it was anything out of the ordinary. Since I'd gotten some fame in recent months, people often slipped notes to me with the opening lines of their screenplay and their phone number attached. I hadn't expected the note to be a threat.

Feeling the return of my earlier panic, I hurried out of the party, wondering if any of the people who glanced my way was the sender of that note.

I shouldn't be reacting with fear. It was what the person wanted—to shake me up, unsettle me, make me afraid. But I couldn't shake the nauseating feeling of unease. And I wasn't even completely sure what the message was referring to.

The words rang again through my head: *I know what you did.*

They could be talking about more than one thing, and none of them were good.

I squeezed into the elevator and made my way out of the hotel and grabbed a cab. On the ride home, I took the note out of my bag, trying to find some clue in the handwriting, but it wasn't familiar in any way—not the writing, not the note card, nothing. Although there was a faint smell of perfume. I held the card up and took a deeper breath. Jasmine, lavender, something…

But the perfume could have come from the server who'd handed me the note card.

I should just throw it away.

But it felt too important to discard.

What did this person know? Was the veiled threat a reminder that my fame was only because of Mitchell's accident? Maybe he'd sent it to me to throw me off my game.

I wouldn't put it past him. He could be a vindictive man. And he loved a good mind game.

That was probably it. I felt a little better with that thought. This didn't have to be about my distant past; it could be about the last year, and that was far less dangerous.

Rolling down the window, I let the warm breeze wash over me. September was one of my favorite months of the year. My mom had loved it, too. She'd let me skip school more than once so we could go to the beach while everyone else was working or studying. We'd often go to Malibu, where there were fewer people, where we could walk along the beach and pretend we lived in one of the beachside mansions on the waterfront.

I let out a sigh, not wanting to think about those moments with my mother, because they had been too short, and far too long ago. She'd died just after my tenth birthday.

Needing a distraction, I pulled out my phone and saw a text from Cassie, saying she was sorry we hadn't had a chance to talk more. She'd heard I wasn't feeling well and had left early. She reminded me to check my calendar to confirm lunch with her and Alina on Tuesday.

I slid the phone back into my bag without answering. I couldn't deal with her right now. I didn't know if she was an old friend or an old enemy. And now, I wondered if she'd had something to do with the note I'd gotten. In fact, the more I thought about it, the more likely it seemed. She'd already mentioned that I'd gotten a break in high school when Kimmy Taylor fell down the stairs, just like I'd gotten a break when Mitch had his accident. Or maybe she was talking about something else. My life had been a series of secrets and dramas, big and small, but that was all in the past, or at least it should be.

Fifteen minutes later, I got out of the car in from my condo building in Century City, not far from Beverly Hills. I'd moved into this neighborhood of newer, luxury buildings intermixed with boutiques, galleries, jewelry stores, and juice bars four months ago after getting a bump in pay after the success of *The Opal King*. It wasn't as posh as Rodeo Drive, which was a few miles away, but it was still very nice.

As I approached my building, I saw a man come out of the jewelry store next to my building. He wore a security guard uniform, navy-blue slacks and matching shirt, with a logo on the right chest pocket. He didn't look like the guard I usually saw there, who was older, balding, and a little out of shape. This guy was young, fit, and had thick, wavy brown hair that was a little long and out of control.

He gave me a quick look, then turned as someone inside the store called his name—Ethan.

I found myself staring at the door for a long minute, which was stupid. I had a boyfriend and didn't need to be intrigued by anyone, especially not a security guard for the jewelry store.

Opening my bag, I took out my keys. I was about to move toward my front door when a man came running around the corner, jogging straight toward me at a fast clip. He wore black track pants and a hoodie. He was also wearing sunglasses, which seemed odd since it was nighttime. I moved to the side so I could get out of the way, but he was suddenly upon me.

He grabbed my arm and bag with a force that sent a shaft of pain from my elbow to my wrist. I screamed as he ripped the clutch from my hands. Then he gave me a hard shove, knocking me to the ground before he ran down the street.

I felt a sharp sting on my shoulder as my back hit the brick wall behind me.

The guard came running out of the jewelry store.

"What happened?" he asked.

"Someone just robbed me," I said in shock. "He grabbed my purse and knocked me down."

"Where did he go?"

"That way," I said, tipping my head. "But he's already gone. He was running so fast. He came around the corner and just attacked me."

He squatted down in front of me, his dark-brown gaze meeting mine. "Are you all right?"

"I—I think so." My knees were stinging and scraped from hitting the ground, and my shoulder was aching, but I was lucky that was all that happened.

The guard extended his hand, and I gratefully took it, relishing the warm strength as he helped me to my feet.

"Do you need me to call someone?" he asked.

"I guess I should call the police." I stopped abruptly. "I don't have my phone. It was in my bag. Do you have a phone? Can I use it?"

"Uh, I can call for you," he said, taking out his phone.

I leaned back against the side of the building as he made the call, my breath still coming short and fast. I couldn't believe someone had mugged me in front of my building. This was a safe neighborhood. And it wasn't even late at night. It was nine o'clock.

"The police are busy," he told me a moment later. "Dispatch said it will be a half hour or more before someone can get out here."

"Really?" I asked in surprise. "That long?"

"Muggings aren't a top priority when no one is hurt. Do you live nearby? The police said you can go home, and they'll come and interview you as soon as they can."

"I live right here." I tipped my head to the door a few yards away. "I was just about to go inside. At least he didn't get my keys." The keys were still clutched in my right hand.

The guard gave me a brief smile. "What's your name?"

"Emily Hollister."

"Unit number?"

"It's 404. Top floor."

He relayed my name and address to the dispatcher. When he hung up, he said, "The police will be here as soon as they can. You can wait in your place."

"Okay." My gaze moved back to the jewelry store. "There's a camera over the door of your store. Do you think it would be helpful in identifying the mugger?"

"I can look."

"If that guy had been fifteen seconds earlier, you would have been outside with me."

"I'm sorry I wasn't."

"Me, too." I suddenly realized what was in my bag: my wallet, my ID, one credit card, a little cash, and some makeup.

Luckily, I'd left my bigger bag at work where I'd gotten ready for the party, so not all my cards were gone. But the thief had my license and my address. That couldn't be good.

"You okay?" he asked again.

"They know where I live," I said, troubled by that thought.

"I doubt they'll be back. It was probably random."

"Was it?" I questioned.

"You think you were targeted?" He gave me a thoughtful look. "Why? Did you have something of value in your bag?"

"No. I don't know. It probably was random." But I couldn't help thinking about the note I'd gotten at the party.

"Why don't I lock up and walk you up to your place?"

"Can I look at the security camera?"

He immediately shook his head. "Sorry. We just closed, and I can't let you into the store. Let me lock the door, and I will get you safely into your place. Then I'll come back and check the video."

I thought about that. Did I want him to walk me upstairs? I didn't know him. Was I really going to let him into my home? On the other hand, he was a security guard. The jewelry store trusted him to watch over their diamonds. They must have checked him out.

I was still debating what to do when he'd locked up the store and turned back to me.

"Ready?" he asked.

"What's your name?"

"Ethan Burke."

"Do you have identification?"

He hesitated, then reached into his pocket and pulled out his wallet. He removed his ID and handed it to me.

I noted his address was in Culver City, about fifteen minutes from here. He was thirty-five years old with brown hair and brown eyes, and he was not smiling in his photo. Nor was he smiling now. He had a guarded, somewhat angry, handsome look to him, which didn't make me feel better.

"Now, can I walk you upstairs?" he asked, as I handed him back his ID. "You can trust me."

I stared back at him, his words making me realize how crazy I was being. Hadn't I learned a long time ago that words didn't mean anything?

"I don't trust anyone. I'm going to say goodnight. Thanks for your help, Ethan."

He gave me a thoughtful look, then nodded and said, "Smart. Trusting the wrong person can be dangerous."

CHAPTER THREE

ETHAN'S WORDS sent a tingle down my spine, a mix of fear and an odd attraction to his intense, dark eyes. I forced myself to turn away and move to my front door. I inserted my key with a shaky hand and then stepped inside, not letting out a breath until the door latched behind me. Then I walked over to the elevator bank and rode alone to my fourth-floor condo.

There were only two units on each floor, and as I stepped off the elevator, my heart jumped again as I heard someone walking down the hall. But when the woman turned the corner, I realized it was just my neighbor, Monica Paul. Monica was a few years younger than me, with brown hair and eyes, and a friendly smile. Her grandmother, Delores, had been living in the unit across the hall but had recently gone into a rehab center after suffering a fall and then a stroke. Monica had moved in three weeks ago.

Monica worked at a clothing boutique in Beverly Hills, and she was always stylishly dressed, as she was tonight in a faux leather mini skirt and cropped sleeveless sweater.

"Hi, Emily. You look amazing," Monica said. "Where are you coming from?"

"A party."

"Must have been a fancy one." A frown crossed Monica's lips. "You're bleeding. What happened? Are you all right, Emily?"

I followed her gaze to my scratched-up knees. "I'm okay, but I was mugged."

Her jaw dropped as her eyes widened in shock. "Oh, my God! Seriously? Where were you?"

"In front of the building. I was taking out my keys when a man came running down the street. He grabbed my bag and shoved me down to the ground."

"That's horrible. I can't believe it. This is such a nice neighborhood."

"I guess that doesn't matter."

"Did you call the police?"

"They're coming to talk to me, but they don't seem to be in a hurry. I'm not hurt, just shaken, and I lost my wallet and phone." I would need to replace my phone as soon as possible. Losing that felt even worse than losing my ID. Everything was on my phone. I felt lost without it. But I couldn't do anything about it tonight. It was late, and I had to wait for the police.

"Can I do something to help?" Monica asked. "Do you want me to wait with you?"

"No, I'm okay, and you look like you're on your way out."

"Just going to meet some friends, but I can be late."

"Thanks, but I'm fine."

"Did you get a good look at the person who robbed you?"

I thought about that for a second. "Not really. It happened so fast. It was a man. He had a hood up and dark glasses, so I don't really know that I would recognize him again."

"That's scary. You seem so calm. I'd be freaking out."

"I don't think it's hit me yet." I paused. "He has my ID, which means he has my address, but not my keys, so hopefully he can't get into the building. But if you see anyone in the hall who doesn't belong here, let me know, or call the police."

"I will. I feel a little strange going out right now."

As a worried look ran through Monica's eyes, I tried to give her a reassuring smile. "I'm sure he's gone. It was probably random. I was just in the wrong place at the wrong time."

"Well, I'm glad you're all right." Monica paused. "Was that the actor Ashton Hunter that I saw leaving your place last weekend?" She immediately gave me an apologetic smile. "I'm being nosy, sorry. You don't have to tell me."

"It was Ashton. We've been seeing each other for a few weeks."

"How did you meet him? Oh, wait, you work in the film industry, too, I forgot."

"We met through a mutual friend," I replied, not wanting to discuss Ashton. But I did want to talk to him. I'd text him from my computer. Maybe he could come over and keep me company. "You said you're going out with friends? Anywhere fun?"

"A party at my coworker's apartment. She promised to introduce me to some people. I'm new in the city and it hasn't been easy to make friends."

"That's right. You're from San Diego."

Monica nodded. "Yes. Have you been there?"

"A few times." I knew I should offer to help her meet some people, but my mind was spinning, and I couldn't focus on anything but getting into my home.

"If you ever want to get coffee or a drink sometime, let me know," Monica said.

"I definitely want to do that. Maybe next week. I need to get my life back in order."

"Of course. Take care, Emily."

"I'll see you later." As she rang for the elevator, I made my way around the corner and down the hall. I heard the elevator doors ding, and then everything was quiet.

Knowing I was alone on the floor made the hairs on the back of my neck stand up, and I ran down the hall and into my unit as quickly as I could, locking the door behind me.

I switched on all the lights as I tentatively checked out my bedroom and bathroom before feeling like I could relax. There was no one here, and everything looked exactly as I had left it. Not that there was a lot to mess up. I hadn't really decorated since I'd moved in. Aside from a few pictures and the basic required furniture, the condo was spotless and very sparse.

I knew I needed to make it feel homey, but after a lifetime of being ripped away from a place as soon as I got comfortable, I felt like moving stuff in would jinx my life. Although, after getting a threatening note and being mugged, setting up my kitchen was probably the least of my worries.

Walking over to the windows in my living room, I looked out over the street. The night had darkened, and the street was quiet. All the shops were closed. And the nearest restaurants were a few blocks away.

I needed to relax. The mugger wasn't going to come back and rob me again, although he might be pissed at how little money he'd gotten. But he had my credit card, and I needed to cancel that.

Moving to the dining room table, I got onto my computer and opened my credit card account. I didn't see any fraudulent charges yet, so I reported the card as stolen and hoped that would prevent a financial disaster. Then I opened the app to find my phone. The last known location was outside my building. Apparently, the phone was now off. I marked the phone as lost so that the thief wouldn't be able to access my data, and I immediately changed my password for the cloud, hoping that would add an additional layer of protection.

My doorbell rang, and I jumped again. As I made my way across the room, I told myself that the mugger wouldn't be trying to get in by buzzing my number. "Yes?" I asked, pressing the intercom.

"Emily Hollister? It's Officer Chu," a female said. "I'm following up on your call about a robbery."

The female voice felt comforting. "Yes. I'll buzz you in. Unit 404."

I waited by my front door, keeping it closed until I heard the knock. Looking out the peephole, I saw two uniformed officers. I turned the deadbolt and let them in.

"I'm Officer Chu, and this is Officer Dominguez," the woman said, waving her hand toward her male partner, as they stepped into my home. "Can you tell us what happened tonight?"

I went over the sequence of events, which took about a minute, and that was only slightly longer than it had taken the man to rob me.

The police officers were polite and compassionate but didn't give me the sense that they were going to rush out and try to solve the case.

"The security guard next door, the one who works at the jewelry store, was the one who called it in. His name is Ethan Burke. He didn't see the attack, but he came out right after," I added. "He said they might have surveillance video."

"We'll check on that," Officer Chu said. "Are you hurt? Do you need medical attention?"

"No, just some scrapes."

"I'm glad that's all," she said.

"You're not going to catch him, are you?" I asked.

"Probably not," Officer Dominguez interjected. "But we'll see if his face comes up on any video in the area, and if we can track him down, we will."

"He has my address."

"I'd suggest getting your locks changed," Officer Dominguez said.

"He didn't get my keys. I had them in my hand."

"That's good." Officer Chu gave me a reassuring smile. "It sounds like a crime of opportunity. You were alone on the street and well-dressed. He was probably hoping for some easy cash."

"Okay. I'm going to go with that." I escorted them out of my home and locked the door again, then returned to my computer. I sent a text to Ashton, telling him what happened and asking him if he could come over. I waited a minute, hoping to see an immediate answer, but nothing came back. He was probably talking to someone at the party and not looking at his phone.

I sent a second text to Francine, letting her know what happened but also confirming that I'd meet her for lunch tomorrow. There was no answer from her, either.

As I thought about who else I could contact, I was reminded of how few close friends I had. I'd buried myself in work the last several years, and while I knew a lot of people, I didn't have a bestie to call in a crisis. Not anymore, anyway.

A long time ago, Alina Price had been that person. Thinking about Alina reminded me of Cassie and her invitation to join them for lunch. I'd left my past behind, but I missed seeing those girls. Maybe not Cassie, but definitely Alina. It might not be the worst idea to go to lunch.

Although, the note I'd received earlier in the night reminded me that there could be danger in going back, in reminiscing about times I didn't want to talk about.

However, that note might have nothing to do with my distant past. The more I thought about it, the more I wondered if Mitchell had the server deliver it to me. He wanted me out of the way. I was a thorn in his side, and he had an eye for drama. Messing with me at a party where I was being honored was something he'd enjoy.

Shaking my head, I sighed, knowing I was getting caught up in a never-ending circle of possibilities, and just forgetting about it was probably a better idea.

Getting up, I went into my bedroom and changed out of my dress, throwing on pajamas and a robe, before stripping off my makeup and washing away the mask I'd put on earlier. Staring at myself in the mirror, I saw the fear lingering in my eyes, and I knew I couldn't chase it away.

Jimmy had always told me to be wary when things got too good. There was usually a fall coming. Things had been going very well for me lately. Was I headed toward some inevitable crash?

Shaking my head, I told myself it wasn't inevitable. I wasn't like Jimmy. I wasn't pretending. I wasn't faking my life. I was doing a job I was good at. I'd earned my success. And I would not lose it. I also would not let someone take it away from me.

Tomorrow was a new day, and I would put tonight in the rearview mirror, start fresh. I'd win over Natasha Rodrigo, and maybe that would be enough to convince Francine to give me the directing job instead of Mitch. It was a long shot. But the only odds I'd ever played had been long. *Why should it be any different now?*

I woke up Saturday morning in a bad mood. My dreams had been filled with images from the past, and I hated when that happened. I was relieved when the sun streamed through my window, and I could get up. I showered, grabbed coffee, slathered peanut butter on toast, and then walked over to the French doors that led to my balcony.

It was a sunny day, not a cloud to mar the blue sky. While my view was of the retail area surrounding my building, it still opened up my mind and my world. I needed to look forward, keep my eye on the horizon. It was only what was in front of me that mattered, not what was behind me.

When I finished eating, I checked my computer and saw a text from Francine expressing her concern and asking me if I was all right. I assured her I was fine. I would pick up a phone and then meet her and Natasha for lunch. There was still no word from Ashton, which seemed odd, so I sent him another text with a big question mark, asking him if he had seen my other text about getting robbed. Nothing came back, so I finished getting dressed and then headed downstairs.

I wished I had my car, but I'd left it in the underground garage at my office so we could arrive at the party in the limo. I would have to pick it up after I got a phone. That was my priority.

Before leaving the building, I glanced in every direction, afraid to leave the safety of the lobby, but I couldn't stay inside forever. I pushed open the door and stepped outside. It a few minutes before ten and the jewelry store next door was still closed. There were plenty of cars on the road, though, taking away the deserted feeling I'd had the night before.

I moved down the block and crossed the street. There was a phone retailer a few blocks away, and I'd found an extra credit card in my dresser so I could pay for the phone and a taxi to my office, where I could get my bag and my car.

As I went through the practicalities of replacing what I lost, I felt more in control of my life. The note was probably from some jealous person and the mugging was random. Those were yesterday's problems.

After purchasing a new phone, I hopped into a cab and headed to my office, which was located a few miles away, near the Paramount Studios lot, where we often shot our films when we weren't on location. I took the elevator to the top floor and then unlocked the glass doors leading into our office suite.

It was very quiet inside, which wasn't surprising, considering it was Saturday. But I was surprised to see Kaitlyn and Jonah Pennington, one of our associate producers, sitting in the conference room, watching something on the large video monitor. I stopped in the doorway.

"Morning," I said.

Kaitlyn jumped, as if she were guilty of something. Jonah just turned and gave me his usual cheerful smile. Jonah had blond hair, blue eyes, and a perpetual tan that came from his obsessive love of tanning.

"Hey, it's the girl of the hour," he drawled. "I heard the party was amazing."

"It was great. What are you two working on?"

"I'm editing Wilson's documentary," Jonah replied. "There's

something bothering me about it. I asked Kaitlyn if she'd tell me what she thought about it."

"Do you want me to look?"

"Sure. Do you have time?"

I suddenly realized I didn't have time. "Actually, no, I don't. I have to meet Francine and Natasha Rodrigo for lunch. I just stopped in to get my bag and my car. Will Monday be too late?"

"Monday is fine. I'm going to Newport Beach with Palmer tomorrow," he said, referring to his long-time partner. "His sister just had a baby."

"That's fun."

"Maybe. I'm not really a baby person. Kids don't always like me."

"Everyone loves you, Jonah," I said, which was true. Jonah had an outgoing personality and was always the life of the party. He was also one of the few people I really thought of as a friend. Maybe because we'd started working at the company the same week.

"You left the party early last night," Kaitlyn interjected. "Ashton told me you weren't feeling well. Are you better?"

"I'm fine. Did you stay late?"

"Until the end, and then I wound up getting drinks at Harry's Bar with Ashton and a bunch of people."

"What other people?" I asked curiously, wondering why Ashton still hadn't texted me back.

"Jackie Wills and Scott Davidson, Mari Tucker and Liam Shelton." Kaitlyn cleared her throat as Jonah uttered a little laugh.

"What?" I asked, seeing a look pass between them.

"It's nothing," Kaitlyn said.

"Oh, honey, it was definitely not nothing," Jonah said.

"Well, somebody tell me."

"I made out a little with Liam," Kaitlyn replied, her cheeks turning red. "I had a lot to drink. When he kissed me, I kissed him back."

"He's practically engaged to Ariel Stanford, Kaitlyn," I said with a frown. Liam Shelton was a very popular actor and a big player. I liked him well enough, but I certainly wouldn't date him, especially not when he was involved in a long-term relationship, although I didn't know why the pop star Ariel Stanford put up with Liam's inappropriate behavior.

"Practically engaged means he's still single enough to kiss at a bar. It wasn't a big deal," Kaitlyn said. "It's not like we hooked up."

"But you gave him your number," Jonah put in.

"You're not being helpful," Kaitlyn told him. "And I gave him my number because he's a good contact to have."

Jonah laughed. "Sure he is."

"Just be careful," I couldn't help saying. "You're new to the Hollywood scene. It's all very glamorous, but it has a dark side, and you could get your heart broken."

"You sound like my mother," Kaitlyn said dismissively. "I can take care of myself, Emily. I'm not like you. I don't take things seriously. I'm young. I'm going to have fun." Kaitlyn paused. "But I appreciate your concern. I know you're just looking out for me."

"I am. But you're right. It's your life. Anyway, I better get my bag." I left the conference room and hurried down the hall. When I got to my office, I saw the whirlwind of chaotic mess I'd left behind the night before when Gina and Connie had come in to style me and do my hair and makeup. I sat down at my desk and swept the makeup supplies into the large tote bag I'd used to bring them into the office.

As my gaze moved toward my computer, I wondered why the screensaver was on, why it hadn't gone dark. Then I noticed the green video light blinking. I turned on the computer, wondering if I'd left a video chat app on, but there was nothing open.

Why was the video light on? Uneasiness ran through me. *Was someone watching me through the computer?*

CHAPTER FOUR

"HEY, YOU'RE STILL HERE," Kaitlyn said, making me jump.

My gaze moved to the doorway. "What?"

"I thought you were grabbing your bag and leaving." She paused, cocking her head to the right as she gave me a look of concern. "Is something wrong?"

"My video light is on."

"What do you mean?" Kaitlyn came into my office to look at my computer. "The light isn't on."

I glanced back at my computer and saw she was right. The light was off. "It was on a second ago."

Kaitlyn peered over my shoulder at the now dark screen. "Are you sure?"

"Yes. I was looking to see if I'd left my video chat on, but the program was closed. How could my video be on without a program open?"

"I have no idea. But it's off now."

Was that because whoever had been watching me had realized I'd noticed the light was on? Or was I just being paranoid?

It didn't feel like paranoia; it felt like something else was going on. I just didn't know what.

"I'm going to grab those coffees," Kaitlyn said. "See you Monday."

"Yes," I said, still distracted by my computer. I waited another minute after Kaitlyn left to see if the light would come back on, but it didn't. It was probably nothing, I told myself. And I had enough to worry about. I needed to get my head together and think about how I wanted to pitch Natasha.

Francine wanted me to convince Natasha that Mitch and I would be a great package deal, but I'd love to showcase myself over Mitch. I just didn't know how to do that under Francine's watchful gaze. I couldn't go against her. She was the one who'd hired me as an intern eight years ago and as an assistant two years after that. She was the one who continued to give me breaks and opportunities whenever she could. Making a run around her would only backfire.

Frowning, I gathered my things and headed out the door. My car was downstairs in the underground garage, and the nearly empty garage did little to ease my nerves, but I got inside and pulled out without any problems. Once on the street, I felt more in control.

The drive out to Malibu and the Moonraker restaurant took thirty minutes. LA traffic was always bad, and warm weekend days at the beach made it even worse. But it was nice to be outside, with the bright sunshine driving all the dark thoughts out of my head.

When I arrived at the restaurant, Francine and Natasha were already seated at a table on the patio overlooking the ocean. They were night and day in appearance. Francine was blonde and fair, with a stylish sophistication. Natasha had dark hair, olive skin, and an exotic beauty set off by a bright, colorful dress. I felt like a pale imitation of both of them. But I wasn't here to compete in looks or style; I was a director and a producer, and I could do things they couldn't.

With that reminder, I pulled out a chair next to Francine and across from Natasha and gave them both a smile. "Sorry I'm a few minutes late," I said.

"You're fine," Natasha returned. "It's nice to see you again, Emily. I don't know if you remember meeting me at the premiere of *The Opal King*."

"Of course I do. I've been a fan of yours for a long time."

"Well, the feeling is mutual. Francine was just telling me that you were robbed last night. That must have been terrifying."

"It was very scary and so shocking. I'm lucky that the guy just grabbed my purse and knocked me down."

"That is lucky," Natasha said, concern in her dark eyes. "Did he have a weapon?"

"I don't know."

"I was wondering the same thing," Francine put in.

I shrugged. "He ran toward me like he was jogging, and then he just grabbed me." I shivered at the memory. "I don't know if he had a weapon. He didn't show it to me if he did. But it all happened very quickly. It was seconds, really."

"What did the police say?" Francine asked.

"That it's unlikely I'll get anything back or that he'll be caught. It was a minor crime in their eyes. But enough about me. How are you, Natasha?"

"I just got back from Paris. So I'm very well." Natasha paused as the waiter came over to ask me what I'd like to drink.

Francine and Natasha were drinking champagne, but memories of my champagne-fueled nausea the night before made my stomach turn over, so I opted for an iced tea.

"No bubbly for you?" Natasha asked.

"I had a lot to drink last night."

"That's right. The party for the Top 30 Under 30. I remember when I hit that list. It was ten years ago." Natasha shook her head, her dark waves bouncing on her shoulders. "I was twenty-six. I thought I'd made it. I had no idea that there was still a long way to go."

"I know I still have a lot of road in front of me," I said. "But

I'm excited about what's next. *Aces High* has the potential to be a great movie."

"I read the script, and I enjoyed it very much."

"Roy is making some changes to the script, and in those revisions, the part of Elena is being expanded. She'll be a pivotal character in the film."

Natasha nodded. "Francine mentioned that, and I was happy to hear it. I don't want to play any more characters that are one-dimensional. I like a woman who operates in gray areas."

"Elena definitely does that. I also love flawed characters faced with morally confusing choices," I said, excited to talk about something that actually mattered to me, and that was craft. "Roy will have a new draft ready on Monday. He's an amazing writer. And he gets better the more he knows the characters and the actors who will be portraying those characters. He plays to their strengths."

"That's good. I'm not that familiar with his work." Natasha hesitated. "I do love your work, Emily. I was very impressed with what you did when you stepped in for Mitchell."

"Thank you."

"It was a joint project," Francine interjected. "Mitchell and Emily worked wonderfully well together. As they will again on *Aces High*."

"Mitch is good. He has a long track record of success, but I understand he's still struggling with some physical challenges."

"He's getting better every day," Francine said. "He'll be fine by the time we're ready to shoot."

"I also have other concerns about Mitchell," Natasha said. "He likes the male action heroes. Female characters have always been an afterthought for him. And, frankly, he hasn't been that interested in working with me in the past."

"Male action hero movies kill at the box office," Francine said with a smile. "But Mitch can do anything. And he has done other kinds of movies. As to not wanting to work with you, that's definitely not true. Mitchell is very eager to get you on board."

"We'll see," Natasha said, doubt in her eyes. "It's one thing to make lots of money on action heroes, but can Mitchell kill at the box office with a film like *Aces High,* which is more about the subtle ambiguities of human nature?"

"Can I answer that?" a male voice said from behind me.

I was shocked to see Mitchell shuffle over to our table.

"Hello, Natasha." He held out his hand to her.

She took it and gave it a squeeze, surprise running across her beautiful face. "Mitch. It's been a long time."

He sat down next to her. "Too long. You look well."

"You look...better," she replied. "I was sorry to hear about your accident."

"You mean the attempted murder," he said.

I stiffened at his words. He'd implied his accident was not an accident in multiple interviews, but he'd never called it attempted murder.

Natasha sat back in her seat, giving Mitchell a shocked look. "Are you saying someone tried to kill you?"

"Yes," he said flatly. "But they didn't succeed. And I will make sure that there are extensive security precautions on my future sets. No one will hurt me again. Now, I understand you're hesitating about the role of Elena. Why is that?"

"I'm interested in the role, but I'd like to see how the character will be developed," Natasha replied. "Emily told me that the script is being revised."

"Yes. To expand your role. And we'll do additional rewrites when we get your input. This character will be everything you ever wanted in a role, Natasha—challenging, complex, and unforgettable."

As the words flowed from Mitchell's mouth, I was reminded of how good he was at this part of the job. He might be cranky and rude to coworkers, but he understood what actors needed and how to fulfill that need.

I'd tried to sway Natasha with talk about story and character, but I hadn't talked about how she could shine, and now I could see her falling rapidly under Mitchell's spell, and his confidence that he could turn this role into an award winner. My hopes of using her to push Mitchell into the background quickly faded away.

I picked up my menu and perused my options as Mitch and Natasha continued to talk. I wanted to interject, but Mitch barely looked at me or acknowledged I was there, and Francine was all in on facilitating the relationship developing in front of her.

The server stopped by to take our order, and after requesting a salad, I realized my phone was vibrating. I took it out to see a call from Ashton. I wanted to talk to him, but I couldn't leave this table to do that. I needed to know everything Mitchell was saying to Natasha, so I sent the call to voicemail. I got a text a moment later from Ashton apologizing profusely for taking so long to get back to me. He'd lost his phone, and he'd had to pick up a new one.

That was weird—both of us losing our phones the same night. Although, he didn't say he'd been robbed. He added that he hoped I was all right and would try to find me and make sure everything was okay.

I texted him that I was fine and at a work lunch and would call him later.

As I slipped my phone back into my bag, Francine glanced over at me with a frown.

She was probably annoyed that I'd gone quiet, but I was feeling a little defeated at how easily Mitch had gotten Natasha onto his side. Their entire conversation was now about what they were going to do together. So much for Natasha's reservations.

I picked up my drink and took a sip when Natasha suddenly turned to me. "How will you and Mitchell work together?" she asked.

I saw the thunder gather in Mitchell's gaze at her question. Before I could reply, he said, "We'll work exceptionally well together. Just as we did before I got hurt."

"Emily?" Natasha queried.

I appreciated that she wanted an answer from me.

"We're a good team." I had to speak the party line, but I also needed to establish that I was an important and integral part of the team. "Mitchell and I have different strengths. And having two viewpoints can be a good thing."

"Or confusing," Natasha said. "If one of you is giving one direction, and the other has a different idea…"

"There will be one lead," Mitchell assured her. "But Emily's voice will be heard. You can be assured of that. I know what a talent she is."

He really was a good liar. I almost believed he meant that.

"I'm glad to hear that," Natasha said. "You're a brilliant director, Mitchell, but I like a strong female perspective as well. If I come on board, I want both of you, not just one."

"That's what you'll have," Francine said. "That's why we're all here."

"Good," Natasha said, settling back in her chair as two servers delivered our food. "Then let's eat."

As we ate lunch, the conversation turned to typical Hollywood gossip. Natasha ran with a lot of A-list actors, one of whom had gotten married in Paris, which was why she'd been in France the previous week. Mitch had apparently also been invited to that wedding, so was eager to hear who was there and what kind of drama was going on. Francine, too, was familiar with many of the guests, making me feel very much like an outsider. But I'd get there. They all had ten or twenty years on me.

After we'd finished eating, we ordered coffees, and were savoring those when a handsome man approached the table, drawing interested gazes back to our table. It was Cole Weston, a former A-list actor who had won two Oscars and been a Hollywood favorite for three decades. He'd graced the cover of every magazine, his striking blue eyes and dark hair making women of all generations fall in love. Although, their adoration had become a little tarnished when Cole's wife, Faye Weston, who was also a Hollywood star died under mysterious circumstances, leaving many to speculate as to whether Cole might have had something to do with it.

I had met Cole a few times when he'd acted in two of our films, but I'd never really had a personal conversation with him, so I doubted I was one of his favorites. But he'd been close to Mitchell and Francine for years. As I watched him kiss Natasha's cheek, they also seemed to be quite comfortable with each other.

"Are you meeting about *Aces High*?" Cole asked.

"Yes, we're hoping Natasha will sign on," Mitchell said. "The two of you would be spectacular together. Natasha as Elena, you as Jake, her long-lost love from a youthful affair."

"I can see the magazine covers already," Francine said.

"It's definitely intriguing," Cole said. "We'll talk more. I'm on my way to a meeting, but I wanted to stop and say hello."

"Let's get together for a drink soon," Mitchell said.

"Definitely." Cole gave us an all-encompassing smile and then walked over to join a group at another table.

"Cole still looks good, even in his late fifties," Natasha said with a little sigh. "I had a big crush on him for a long time."

"You can use that in this part," Francine said.

Natasha laughed. "You never stop selling, Francine."

"That should tell you how much we want you."

"I didn't realize Cole was a possibility for the part of Jake."

"I've just started talking to him about it," Mitchell said.

Natasha gave him a speculative look. "Are you two friends?"

"Yes," Mitchell replied. "We've been friends for years."

"Then why are you pitching a movie about the death of his wife, Faye? Won't that just put Cole in the hot seat again when the rumors have finally died down?" Natasha asked.

"That film will be about more than Faye's death. And Cole would love to see Faye's life given more focus. Her work was brilliant."

"But you'll still have to deal with the question of whether she died accidentally or if she was murdered," Natasha said.

I was surprised by the turn in conversation. I had heard a little about Mitchell's idea, but not that he was pursuing it with any real energy. But it was certainly an interesting story. The iconic actress, Faye Weston, had drowned after a Malibu beach house party fourteen years ago. It was a story that had drawn a great deal of interest and many conspiracy theories over the years, as to whether she'd accidentally drowned or if one of Hollywood's elite had murdered her.

"Cole and I are still discussing where we might go with the project," Mitch said.

Francine sighed. "I don't know why you want to shake that tree, Mitch. Cole Weston is one of our most bankable stars, and if you proceed with this idea, it cannot be with our company. And it has to be after *Aces High,* or we won't be able to cast Cole. There will be too much attention on him and probably a lot of it won't be good."

"I understand timing, Francine, and I'll do the film on my own if I do it," Mitch snapped. "No one tells me what I can and cannot do."

"I'm just saying it won't be a popular project."

"But it would make a lot of money," Natasha countered. "If you can prove it was either a murder or an accident. No one will want it to end with just speculation."

"Let's table this for now," Francine said, never one to let anyone derail her mission.

"Of course," Mitchell said. He suddenly turned to me. "I saw you run out of the party last night, Emily. You looked upset. Was something wrong?"

"Oh, no," I said, stuttering a little under his sudden attention. "I had a headache. Too much champagne."

"Someone told me they thought you were crying in the restroom," he continued.

"You were crying?" Francine asked in surprise.

"No, I wasn't. I don't know where you heard that." As I saw the small smile play across his lips, I realized he was trying to undermine me, make me seem like an emotional, unreliable woman. I wondered again if he was the one who'd sent me the disturbing note. It made sense, in a sick way. He didn't believe his accident had been an accident at all, and he'd always acted like I'd had something to do with it, but I hadn't been near the set when the explosion occurred. And the incident had been investigated by numerous authorities in Australia as well as by investigators from the US. It had been determined to be completely accidental. But Mitchell couldn't seem to accept that.

"A young woman said she saw you run into a stall, and you looked upset," Mitchell said.

"Like I said, I wasn't feeling well. But I wasn't crying. I felt nauseous. Too much champagne on an empty stomach."

Natasha shook her head, giving me a commiserating look. "It's the way rumors begin, Emily. Get used to it. The better known you are, the more people will be watching you. Every move you make will be scrutinized."

"I don't think I'm that well-known. I'm usually behind the camera, not in front of it."

"You're having your fifteen minutes of fame," Mitchell sneered. "Until that's over, you'll be talked about." He sipped his coffee. "As Natasha said, you'll have to get used to it."

I wanted to run into the bathroom now and get away from this conversation, but instead I put a smile on my face and said, "I doubt I'll get that much interest; I'm pretty boring."

Natasha's phone rang, and she took a quick look at the screen before saying, "I need to take this. Thank you for lunch, for the conversation. I'll discuss the project with my agent, and I'll be in touch."

"Thank you," Francine said, with me and Mitchell echoing her words.

As Natasha left the table, Mitchell's gaze hardened. "Why wasn't I invited to this lunch?" he demanded.

His question surprised me. I assumed Francine had invited him.

"Natasha wanted to meet Emily," Francine said. "She already knew you, so I wanted to accommodate her. How did you hear about it?"

"Kaitlyn mentioned you two were meeting up with Natasha today. I was angry. So, I found out where you were lunching and decided to join you."

I frowned. I needed to speak to Kaitlyn about not discussing business when she was at a party.

"This is unacceptable, Francine," Mitchell continued. "I'm the director, not Emily. She might have made a good substitute based on my setup, but I have years more experience and a hell of a bigger reputation. You need me, and if you don't know that, then I'll move on right now. I guarantee that you won't get Natasha without me."

"I agree," Francine said. "And as I said, Emily is an unknown entity. It made sense that Natasha wanted to get to know her."

Francine's words seemed to ease his anger.

"Just so you know where we stand," he said.

"Mitchell, of course, you're the director. But Emily brings a young female perspective, and I believe you will make a good team. The two of you need to find a way to get past the awkwardness that has developed in the past six months." Francine paused. "Emily didn't steal your movie. You got hurt in an unfortunate accident. Thank God you survived. But it wasn't her fault that you were injured."

I was very grateful to have Francine's support.

His lips tightened. "I still don't know exactly whose fault it was. And that makes everyone who was there a suspect."

"It wasn't my fault," I told him. "The authorities cleared me."

"Yes, well, I'm not satisfied with the investigation. And if you did it, you certainly wouldn't admit to it."

"Mitchell," Francine implored. "This is what I'm talking about. I understand that you're angry about what happened to you, but we need to look forward, and this is the team we have for the next movie. After that, we will re-evaluate. But Emily has done a lot of the preliminary work, and I need you to work your magic with this story."

I had some magic I could work, too, but I clearly had no say in the situation. And if I raised any suggestion of a problem, Mitchell would use it against me and Francine would feel caught in the middle. We needed to find a way to work together, but I didn't see how that would happen anytime soon. Maybe once we got into the work, we could just forget about everything else. It was all I could hope for.

Mitchell shoved back his chair and grabbed his cane that was leaning against the table. "I'll let you pay for lunch. We'll talk again soon."

Francine sighed as we watched him shuffle away. "I know he's going to be a problem, Emily, but he is brilliant at his job. Not that you aren't very good, too."

"I know I haven't proved myself as much as he has, Francine. But he won't listen to me. You know that. And Natasha will know it within five minutes of us having another meeting."

"Do you want to step back from this project?"

I didn't because the movie had so much possibility, and I wanted to work on it. I'd been helping Roy develop the script for weeks. I knew the beats of the story inside and out. I could see the scenes in my head. But I wouldn't be able to direct them; Mitchell would do that. Would I just end up angry and frustrated?

I realized she was waiting for an answer. "I love this movie, but I'm not sure how we'll be able to work together."

"It's important for you to find a way. The two of you working together again after what happened in Australia will give us a lot of pre-release buzz."

And that's what it was really about, I realized. We were a story within a story, and Francine was right; that would create interest in the project. I felt like a pawn on a chessboard, and that was a feeling I'd never wanted to experience again. "It might not be the best press," I said. "Mitchell might try to say I caused his accident so I could get his job. He basically just told you that."

"Any press is good press," Francine said, dismissing my concern. "And it's not like you did it. You have to let his words roll off your back. You're my rising star, Emily. You have so much ahead of you. And you will get another chance to direct on your own. You have lots of time. You're not even thirty yet." She paused. "So, what was going on last night? Were you really just feeling sick? Or was there something else?"

"Just feeling sick. I drank too much because I was nervous. But I wasn't crying in the bathroom."

"I wondered where you'd gone. I saw Ashton talking to Kaitlyn, and you were nowhere in sight. I thought maybe you and Ashton had had a fight. I know you didn't like him sucking up to Mitchell." A knowing gleam entered her eyes.

"Ashton did nothing wrong, and we weren't fighting." I didn’t want to give Francine any more ammunition to dislike Ashton. "I told him to stay and enjoy the party. I just wanted to go home."

"If he'd gone with you, you might not have been robbed."

"Or we both would have been. I can't blame him for what happened to me."

"I suppose not," Francine muttered. "I still don't think Ashton is as good as you think he is, Emily. But I know you won't believe me. You're in love. You're young. And I am old and jaded."

"First of all, I am not in love, and you are not old. But you are jaded. I know you had a rocky relationship with an actor, but Ashton hasn't tried to take advantage of our relationship to get ahead. He's successful in his own right." Even as I defended Ashton, Kaitlyn's words about Ashton being interested in the role of Dominic rang through my head. Was I blind to some secret agenda?

"Just because Ashton has been successful doesn't mean he won't try to use you," Francine said.

"Maybe I'll use him. He has contacts, too. It can work both ways."

"I hope that's true. I need to get going."

"Me, too," I said, as we got to our feet.

As we left the restaurant, I debated what I wanted to do next. I could go back to the office and do some work, or I could head home and work from there. And then I wouldn't have to worry about someone spying on me on my work computer. Although, if someone had hacked into my webcam on my work computer, maybe they'd done the same on my laptop.

Or maybe I was making a problem out of nothing. Sometimes, my imagination got the better of me. On my way home, I called Ashton, but his phone went to voicemail. I left him a message that I was done with lunch and would love to talk to him.

As I turned down my block, I saw Ethan standing next to the door of the jewelry store. He was back at his post. My nervousness about him last night seemed completely unfounded now. The guy had just tried to help me, and I'd treated him like a criminal. I drove into my underground garage and parked in my slot. After getting on the elevator, I chose to get off at the lobby level and walk out front. Maybe Ethan had had a chance to check the jewelry store's security camera.

As I approached Ethan, I couldn't help thinking he was even more attractive than I remembered: rugged, athletic, handsome. He had it all going on, even wearing his security uniform, which consisted of navy slacks and a short-sleeve, navy button-down shirt with an insignia on the left chest pocket that read Stillman Security.

His gaze zeroed in on me as I drew near. He had the kind of penetrating dark eyes that missed nothing, and that made me nervous. Actually, everything about him made me nervous in ways I didn't want to define.

I shouldn't have come out here. I had enough problems in my life. But I felt drawn to him, like he was a buoy in a stormy sea, which was a strange feeling, because he hadn't done anything except help me stand up after my mugging. Anyone could have done that.

But still I kept walking…

CHAPTER FIVE

"HELLO," I said as I stopped in front of Ethan. "Remember me?"

"Emily Hollister. How are you feeling today?"

"Better. I was wondering about the security camera footage. Did you check it?"

"Yes. And I spoke to the police this morning. I gave them the video, but it wasn't helpful. Your assailant came around the corner." Ethan tipped his head to his left side. "When he passed in front of the store, the camera only caught the back of his head…or I should say, his hoodie and cap. He was also moving quickly."

"He was running. I thought he was just a jogger. But it was odd that he was wearing sunglasses at night. I guess that was to disguise himself."

"I'm sorry the camera didn't pick up anything helpful."

"Me, too." I looked around the street at the mix of condos and retail shops. "There must be other cameras that caught him going down the street."

"Possibly. I'm not sure how much time the police will spend knocking on doors."

"I guess I could do it." As he gave me a doubtful look, I frowned. "Why couldn't I do it?"

"You could, and some owners might be helpful. Others might not want to get involved."

"Well, I might as well try. I don't have anything to lose. It's not like the police will do it for me."

"It's your time." He paused as a customer moved past us to enter the store. "I should get back to work."

"How come you're out here and not in the store?" I asked. "Won't shoplifting occur inside? Or are you supposed to catch someone if they try to smash and grab and run out the door?"

"That would be on me," he said.

"Has it ever happened?"

"Not yet."

"So your presence is just a deterrent? What happens at night?"

"A security system takes over for me. Why are you so curious?"

I shrugged, not sure why I was that intrigued by him and his job, except something felt off. "You don't seem like someone who'd want to stand in front of a store all day long with nothing much happening."

"And that opinion is based on what?" His speculative gaze moved across my face.

"Absolutely nothing," I admitted.

"What do you do for work?" he asked.

"I'm a film director."

"That does sound more exciting. Have you directed anything I might have seen?"

"Well, a lot of people saw *The Opal King*."

His brow shot up. "Seriously? That was your movie?"

"Yes."

"That was a great film. Not what I expected when I first heard about it."

"What do you mean?"

"I didn't think there would be much of a story, just action and car chases, but it had everything. It was complex, with unexpected twists."

"Thanks. I'm glad you enjoyed it." The twists he'd appreciated had come from me and not from Mitchell, which made me feel even better.

"So, you're a director, and you like to call the shots. Now I can see why you want to spend the day looking for security footage. Your mugging made you feel vulnerable. You don't like feeling out of control."

"Does anyone?" I asked.

"Some are bothered more than others."

He wasn't wrong about my desire to be in control. "As a director, I like to set the scene and tell people what to do so I get the outcome I want."

"But this isn't a movie set, and people don't have to cooperate."

"I'm aware. I just feel..."

"Helpless?" he suggested.

"I was going to say frustrated and angry, but helpless is part of it. I never thought about what it would feel like to be robbed or attacked. It's much more emotional than I imagined, and I know what happened to me was really nothing. I'm sure that guy didn't give me a second thought. He just wanted cash or a credit card to run up before he got caught. I don't know why it unsettled me so much when I used to live around..." I stopped abruptly, realizing I was about to reveal something very personal to a complete stranger.

"You can't stop there," Ethan told me, his gaze growing more interested.

"I can stop there."

"You're going to leave me on a cliffhanger?" He gave me a disappointed smile. "Come on, Emily."

I felt an odd shiver run down my spine when he said my name in a teasing way, as if we were friends or something, but we weren't.

"You said you used to live around…" he pressed. "Should I finish the sentence—muggers, thieves…"

He was joking, but he was closer to the mark than he realized.

"You're becoming more interesting by the minute, Emily Hollister," he said. "Or is that not your real name? It's starting to feel like we have our own movie going."

If that were true, he would definitely be the sexy, bad boy love interest, but this wasn't a film. "That is my name, and I'm going to leave you now to see what I can find out."

"Come on, Emily, give me something. I'm standing out here on the sidewalk all day long. It's the least you can do."

"You're the one who picked this job."

"I had my reasons."

"Now, you're the one who sounds like he has another story to tell."

"We all have another story to tell. Give me a piece of yours."

I sighed, then relented. "When I was young, I lived in a rougher neighborhood than this one. I guess I'm surprised at how different it feels to be a mark, a target. I never thought I'd be a person who someone else would want to rob."

"But you are. You're a successful director."

"I'm still getting used to that idea. Anyway, that's all I'm going to say. I'll see you around."

"Good luck, Emily."

I was about to leave, then I paused, a thought occurring to me. "I know you gave the video to the police, but could I see it?"

"There's nothing on there I didn't tell you."

"I believe you. I just keep replaying it in my head, wondering if I missed a clue. I want to see what the attack looked like, even if it's from the back."

He hesitated. "I could show it to you, but not until later today, after the store closes."

"Do you want me to come back at closing time?"

"No. I'll come to you. The owner doesn't want anyone near

the security system or inside the store after closing." He checked his watch. "It's almost four. We close at five today. I can bring it by after that."

"That would be great."

"I'll see you later then. Happy hunting."

His words followed me across the street. I wasn't happy, but I was in hunting mode. And it wasn't because of what I'd lost. I could replace my ID and the credit card, but it felt like the mugging could be part of something else, and I couldn't just let it go without trying to see who had attacked me.

A few minutes later, I entered the juice bar across the street. I didn't just want information but also one of their healthy and satisfying smoothies. I came in so often, I'd become friendly with the assistant manager, Larissa, who was working today, and I hoped she'd be open to me looking at her security footage.

Larissa was in her mid-thirties with curly blonde hair, a friendly smile, and a killer body that she worked out twice a day. She was dressed as usual in workout leggings and a crop top that always made me want to order the healthiest drink on the menu, but today I went for a fruit smoothie instead of one heavy on the kale.

The juice bar wasn't crowded, so after getting my drink, I lingered by the counter, waiting for Larissa to finish filling one other order. When she was done, I said, "I have a favor to ask."

"What's that?" Larissa asked. "Oh, and I actually need a favor from you, too."

"What's your favor?" I asked in surprise.

"My niece is turning fourteen, and her celebrity crush is the hot guy you brought in last weekend. I was wondering if you could get her an autograph from Ashton."

"Oh, sure, that's easy. What's her name?"

"Shannon."

"I'm sure I can get that for you."

"Great. What can I do for you?" Larissa asked.

"I was mugged last night in front of my building."

Her gaze widened. "Seriously, Emily? I'm sorry. Are you all right?"

"Fine. But I'm trying to figure out what happened. I noticed you have a security camera out front. I was wondering if you could look at it and tell me if it picked up what happened to me."

"When did it happen?"

"Last night—around nine."

"Okay. We close at eight, and I haven't looked at anything from last night. I usually don't unless I get an alert. Why don't you come in the back?" Larissa turned to the teenager who was also working the counter. "Call me if you get a crowd."

I followed Larissa into the office. She sat down in front of her computer and opened a program. I saw frames from two different cameras. She backed them up to the night before. "So, nine, you said?"

"Yes." I watched the replay on the screen, until I saw Ethan help me up from the ground. "It was right before that."

"Okay." Larissa rewound the video a few more frames, pausing when the man came running down the street. "Is this him?"

"That's him." I stared hard at the blurry, dark figure, who was impossible to recognize. "Damn, it's difficult to see anything."

"These cameras aren't the best, especially at this distance." Larissa played the footage again, and I watched as the man grabbed my arm, then the bag, and shoved me to the ground. "I'm so glad you weren't hurt, Emily. This looks terrifying."

"You don't recognize him, do you? You haven't seen anyone around here that looks like that?"

"I've seen a lot of men who look like that. Track pants and hoodies are very popular."

"I know," I said, feeling discouraged.

"It's too bad Ethan was inside the store when it happened," Larissa commented.

"Yes. Five minutes earlier, he would have been right there." I thought about how easily she'd said his name. "Do you know Ethan?"

"He's been in here the last three days. He got my attention, because he's totally hot."

I smiled. "He is that."

"But he's very guarded. Doesn't say much. At least not to me, which is weird because most people are pretty friendly once we start talking. Anyway, I still like seeing him out there. Although, I guess him being nearby didn't stop someone from attacking you."

"I was lucky. The guy just wanted my bag."

"Hopefully your attacker doesn't make a habit of staking out this neighborhood. I'm going to tell my employees to be careful. I'm sorry I couldn't help you more, Emily."

"It's fine. Thanks for showing me the video. I'll ask Ashton to autograph something for your niece. When's her birthday?"

"I'm going to see her next Friday night, so if you get it before then..."

"I'll do my best," I said, as I followed her into the café.

"Ashton is so handsome," Larissa said. "He doesn't have a brother, does he?"

"Only child," I said with a smile.

"Lucky girl."

"I'll see you later." As I left the juice bar, my phone buzzed, and Ashton's name flashed across the screen.

"Hello?" I asked, moving under a nearby awning to take his call.

"Emily? Are you all right?" he asked.

"I'm okay now, but what happened to your phone? I was worried when I didn't hear from you last night."

"I'm sorry. I don't know what happened to my phone. I had to get a new one today. I feel terrible I wasn't there for you. Something weird happened to me last night, Emily. I think I might have been drugged."

"What are you talking about?" I asked, shocked by his words.

"After the party, I went to Harry's with a bunch of people. And I think we went to another club after that, but it's hazy in my mind. I don't remember anything else until I woke up in a motel room around noon."

"A motel room?" I echoed. "Where? Were you alone?"

"It was a run-down place in Hollywood, nowhere I would choose to go. I woke up alone, but I don't know how I got there. I asked the manager who I came in with, but he said he didn't remember, and there aren't any cameras anywhere."

"That's crazy. Were you robbed?"

"That's the thing—no. I have my wallet, which has about three hundred in cash and my credit cards, but my phone was gone. I tried the app to find my phone, but I guess it was off. I don't know what happened. I don't get that wasted, Emily. You know that."

Did I know that? We'd only been dating for six weeks. In that time, I'd never seen him overly drunk or out of control, although he did like to party.

"Emily?" he said sharply.

"Maybe someone you were with saw you leave the bar. Kaitlyn said she was with you at Harry's. Have you talked to her?"

"No. I don't want this to get out until I know what's going on. I've been trying to reach Liam. If anyone saw me leave, it would have been him. He's usually with me until the end, but he hasn't gotten back to me yet, which is strange, too." Ashton took a breath. "I'm sorry I let this happen, Emily. I need you to believe me when I say that I don't do this kind of thing, especially when I'm dating someone I care about."

I appreciated his words, but I didn't know what to think.

"Tell me about you," Ashton continued. "Are you okay after what happened last night?"

"I'm fine." Although, I felt even less than fine after hearing his story. Were the two events just coincidental or was something else going on?

"I wish we could get together and talk this out," Ashton continued. "But I have to fly out tonight. And I have a bunch of stuff to do to get ready."

"I understand." It disappointed me I wouldn't get to see him before he left.

"I'm hoping that whatever happened last night doesn't come out in some kind of public way," he said, a worried note in his voice.

"Like?"

"Photos. Something tied to blackmail."

My legs felt suddenly shaky. "You think that's what this is about? It wasn't just a drugged hookup?"

"I don't want it to be that, either, but at this point, that would be better than the alternative."

"I guess."

"There's one more thing I wanted to talk about, Emily. It's not the best timing, but I need to let you know."

"Let me know what?" I asked warily, unsure what other shoe was about to drop.

"Before I lost my mind last night, I had a conversation with Mitchell Gray at Harry's."

"Mitchell was at Harry's Bar, too?" I asked with surprise.

"Yes. He and his wife, Tara, showed up."

"So, you were able to talk to him after all."

"I was. He was telling me about *Aces High*, and he thinks I'd be good for the role of Dominic."

My gut tightened once more. "Aren't you tied up with other projects?"

"None that I can't rearrange for something like this. What do you think, Emily? I don't want to mess up things with us, but I read some of the script when I was at your place last week, and I think I would make a great Dominic. The character really speaks to me. Dominic is serious but ironically funny and so damaged. It would be challenging to play that role, and I would love to tackle it."

"Why didn't you talk to me after you read the script?" I asked, interrupting his passionate declaration. "Why tell Mitchell you want a role in my movie without telling me first?"

"I got the feeling you would like to keep some distance between business and your personal life."

"I do. And this movie will be complicated enough with me and Mitchell trying to work things out."

"I could be a buffer between you and Mitchell, someone on your side. Wouldn't that be good?"

I could use an ally, but I preferred to keep our business projects separate. And Ashton's actions seemed shady. "Dominic won't get as much air time as Jake," I told him. "Not if Cole Weston signs on to the movie. Cole and Natasha will be leads. You know that, right?"

"Mitchell told me the character of Dominic will play an integral role in the story. Anyway, there's nothing to decide now," he continued, as if sensing I wasn't thrilled by the idea. "We'll discuss it when I get back from New York. Take care of yourself."

"You, too." I hung up the phone, my mind racing in a dozen different directions. I didn't know what to think about Ashton's drugged night or his request to be in my film. They were both bad. And I wasn't sure which one bothered me more.

CHAPTER SIX

I LOOKED around as I slipped my phone back into my bag. I could continue to canvass the street, but was there any point? It seemed doubtful I'd get any better footage from stores that were farther away from my attack.

I made my way back across the street. Ethan was at his post and gave me a questioning look. "Any luck at the juice bar?" he asked.

"Larissa showed me her security footage. It was grainy and hard to see anything."

"Too bad."

"I should give up on finding who did this to me and move on with my life. I'm probably wasting my time, and you don't need to bother showing me your video."

"I'm happy to share." Glancing at his watch, he added, "I'm off in five minutes. Why don't I grab it now and go up with you? The owner is locking up tonight, so I don't need to stick around."

It was no doubt a waste of time, but since Ethan was willing to show me the video, I might as well take a look. "All right."

As Ethan went back into the store, I looked around the street. I'd always felt safe walking on this block, but now I felt on edge, hoping I wouldn't see some guy sprinting around the corner again.

But it didn't make sense for my mugger to return. I needed to think logically and not emotionally. That said, I still started when the door to my building opened, and Monica came through the front door. She had on white denim shorts and a tank top today, accented by sparkly jewelry and a colorful print bag.

"Hi, Emily," she said. "How are you feeling today? I was thinking about you all night. You haven't had any more problems, have you?"

"No. It's been a normal day. Thank goodness."

"That's good to hear. I haven't seen anyone in the building who doesn't belong there." She paused. "I told Tyler what happened. I saw him earlier today. He said he'd keep an eye out, too."

Tyler was the twenty-something building manager who seemed more interested in surfing and skateboarding than managing the building that was owned by his family, but more awareness on his part couldn't hurt.

"Tyler asked me to have drinks with him," Monica continued. "I wasn't sure if I should say yes or no. What's your take on him?"

"Nice guy, little ambition, but appears to be very happy with his life. He does seem to date a lot. I've seen more than one girl coming out of his unit."

Monica smiled. "I figured he was a player. But he seems fun. What are you doing now?"

"Oh, nothing really. I got a juice across the street, and I was just about to go in," I replied, not wanting to explain further. I moved to the door of our building. "I'll see you later."

"Later," Monica echoed as she headed down the street.

I inserted my key in the lock and opened the door, leaving it slightly ajar as I went into the lobby to check my mailbox.

As I retrieved my mail, I felt the door open wider, bringing a hot breeze with it, and I whirled around, thinking I shouldn't have just left it open so anyone could walk in. But it was only Ethan coming through the door, and he shut it behind him.

I closed my mailbox, and we headed into the elevator.

It felt strange to go upstairs with him. There were tingling feelings running throughout my body, a mix of fear and an odd sense of excitement. But that was ridiculous. I had a boyfriend, and I shouldn't be intrigued by anyone else.

"You okay?" Ethan asked. "You seem tense."

"I'm a tense person."

He gave me a knowing smile. "You're still on edge from last night and wondering if you should have asked a complete stranger up to your apartment."

"You're right on both counts. Where is the footage?" I asked, suddenly realizing his hands were empty.

"I downloaded it to my phone."

"Then you could have just showed it to me outside," I said as we got off the elevator.

He shrugged. "I thought it was better to do it here."

"All right." I opened my door and ushered him inside.

He paused to look around. "Nice," he murmured.

It wasn't the nicest place I'd ever lived in, but it was the first home that was completely mine, that had my name on the deed, and that was an amazing accomplishment that I was incredibly proud of. The one-bedroom unit was small but airy in design. The entry opened onto a combined living room, dining room, and kitchen area. A short hallway to the left led to a guest bathroom and then the master suite with attached bath.

As we walked into the living room, I felt a breeze, and I realized the sliding door leading onto my deck was slightly ajar. That was odd. I thought I'd closed it when I'd left earlier. No wonder my place felt unusually warm. The air conditioning wouldn't go on if the door was open.

I moved across the room to shut the door, and almost immediately, the air conditioning clicked on.

"Okay, show me the video," I said as Ethan pulled out his phone.

He opened an app and then handed me his phone. I watched in silence, noting that the camera was mostly on me. I paused to grab my keys out of my bag. No one was around me. And then there was a rush of motion in front of the camera. A guy grabbed my bag, shoved me to the ground, and ran away. It looked exactly as I'd remembered and matched what I'd seen on the footage from Larissa's juice bar. There was no way to identify the man from the back of his hoodie and dark athletic wear. There was nothing identifiable about him.

I handed him back the phone. "Thanks. You were right. There's nothing there. I'm not going to figure out who he is."

"Maybe it's better that way," Ethan suggested.

"How could it be better?"

"You might find out things you don't want to know."

"Like…"

"Like things I don't want to put in your head. Be happy all he got was your purse, and all you got were skinned knees."

"I am grateful that's all that happened, but I still feel like I lost something. And I'm not talking about my ID, my money, or my credit card."

He gave me an understanding nod. "I know. It was a violation. You lost some innocence last night."

"I didn't think I had any innocence left to lose, but that is what it feels like."

My words drew a questioning gleam to his dark eyes. "You don't look like someone who should be that cynical, Emily."

"People often don't look like who they are."

"Well, I can't argue with that." He tugged at the collar of his polo shirt. "It's hot in here."

"I guess I left the deck door open this morning. The air conditioning just went on. Do you want something cold to drink?"

"Sure. What do you have?"

I walked into the kitchen to check the refrigerator. Ashton

had stocked my fridge with beer, and I had a selection of sparkling waters. "I have beer or flavored sparkling water."

"I'll take a beer."

I took out two cans and walked back to the table, handing him one, and then opening one for myself.

The cool slide of beer down my throat felt incredibly good.

"This is good," Ethan said.

"It is. And much better than the expensive champagne I drank last night."

"You did look fancy. Where were you coming from?"

"A party for the Top 30 Under 30 people in LA. I made the list for my direction of *The Opal King*."

His eyebrow shot up. "That sounds impressive."

"It was a fun event, and it was nice to be honored. But I care more about moving forward with my career, getting the next job, doing even better work if I can than I care about an award or a list."

"You must have producers knocking down your door after your success with that movie."

"You would think it would work that way," I said slowly, his words making me wonder what opportunities I was giving up to be loyal to my production company while they were being loyal to Mitchell.

"It's not working that way?" Ethan asked curiously.

"It's complicated with the director who got hurt. My company is about to shoot a new film, and I thought I would be directing, but they're bringing Mitchell Gray, the other director, back in to do this new movie. I will be his assistant."

"It doesn't sound like you're happy about that." Ethan leaned against the kitchen counter as he sipped his beer.

"I'm not. It's a step back, and Mitchell hates me. He thinks I had something to do with his freak accident, which I did not. But he keeps trying to tear me down because he can't stand that I'm getting the credit for what he thought was his movie."

"That's rough. How will you work with him if he thinks you tried to hurt him?"

"No idea."

"What exactly happened?" he asked curiously.

"We were in a remote part of the Australian Outback, and it was really hot, like over 115 degrees. Someone moved propane tanks into an area with no cover, and I guess the heat was so high, they exploded. Mitch was the one closest to the explosion. I was actually still at the hotel that day. I hadn't gotten to the set yet."

"Who moved the tanks?"

"I don't know. No one admitted to moving them, and there was no proof of anyone doing it. In the end, it was written down as an accident."

"Huh," he said, taking another swig of beer.

"What's the *huh* for?"

"I can see why Mitchell would think it was a deliberate act if no one admitted to even touching the tanks. They didn't magically get there."

"There were a lot of people moving a lot of things, not just our crew but also locals we had hired to work on the project. But no one had a motive to hurt Mitchell."

"Except maybe you, because you're the one who benefited."

I frowned, not liking his reasoning. "I didn't do it, and I don't appreciate you suggesting I did."

"I wasn't suggesting that. I just think it's likely someone didn't tell the truth about moving the tanks."

"Possibly, but it was eight months ago, and no one's story has changed. I understand why Mitch is upset about what happened. He almost lost his life. But I'm not to blame, and I saved the movie for my company. We had a tight timeline, and it was me or no one."

"And you did a great job."

"I did." I took another sip. "I know Mitchell is a good director, or he used to be, but I don't see how we can work together in the future. I also don’t see a way out of it."

"You could quit."

"I don't want to quit. I love my job. I've been there for eight years, and my boss, Francine, is great. I've learned so much and she's given me opportunities."

"But she's not giving you this film."

"She promises that it will just be this one movie. I have to suck it up and do what needs to be done and hope that she means what she says."

"Or you could look around, see what your options are, and use those options to leverage your position where you are."

I raised a brow. "That's pretty strategic thinking for a guy who stands on the sidewalk outside a door all day long."

He smiled. "Which gives me a lot of time to think. And who are you to judge my job choice?"

I suddenly felt guilty for being so snarky. "You're right. I shouldn't have said that. I know your position is important. You're protecting someone's property and maybe the customers in the store as well. You're putting your life on the line. That's all very admirable."

"Are you done trying to back yourself out of the corner you just got into?"

"I think so." I suddenly realized he hadn't been offended by my words. "You enjoyed that, didn't you?"

He finished his beer and set it down on the counter. "A little. You judged me the first minute you saw me, but that's okay. That is what I do all day long. I look at who comes into the store, and I assess whether they're a security risk. But I could be wrong, because appearance isn't everything." He paused. "Seeing you in that sexy short dress last night made me think you were an actress or a model, not a film director."

"I don't usually dress that way."

"You looked good," he said, a gleam in his eyes that I did understand. He thought I was attractive, and I liked that he thought that. But I shouldn't like it. I was seeing someone else. Turning away from his sexy smile, my gaze caught on the plant by the fireplace, the one Francine had given me as a housewarming present. It was on its side, dirt spilling onto the floor.

My heart jumped in my chest. "That's weird." I walked over to the fireplace and put the plant upright.

"What's weird?" Ethan asked, following me into the living room.

"The deck door was open, and this plant was knocked over, but it wasn't like that this morning when I left." I tried to make sense of what I was seeing without going to the worst-case scenario, but my brain was already halfway there.

"Maybe the wind from the open door knocked it over," Ethan suggested.

"It's pretty heavy," I said, meeting his gaze.

He stared back at me. "Let's take a walk around."

I nodded, feeling fear creeping up my spine. Everything in the living room and dining room seemed the same, except for the door and the plant. My computer on the dining room table was in plain view. If someone had broken in to steal something, wouldn't they have taken my laptop?

I forced myself to walk down the hall to my bedroom. I always made my bed, and the only other furniture in the room was a dresser. Both were undisturbed. I looked in the closet, which also seemed normal.

While I was doing that, Ethan moved into the bathroom. Then he said, "Emily. You better come in here."

I was suddenly afraid to go into the bathroom. He had to have found something, but what?

"Do I want to see it?" I asked.

He stuck his head out of the bathroom, his expression somber. "It's probably going to upset you, but it's not that bad. It's just a note on the mirror."

"Another note?" I murmured, feeling my throat tighten so much I could barely get the words out.

"Another?" he queried.

I didn't answer his question, but I did force myself to move into the bathroom. And there, on the mirror, was a heart drawn in red lipstick. In the middle of that heart was a yellow sticky note that had the same five words on it: *YOU KNOW WHAT YOU DID.*

My breath left my chest so fast, I thought I was going to pass out. Someone had been in my home. They'd opened the door to the deck. They'd knocked over the plant. They'd come into my bedroom, my bathroom. How could that be? How could they have gotten in when I had my keys with me the whole time?

"Emily?" Ethan questioned, drawing my gaze to him. "What did you do?"

CHAPTER SEVEN

ETHAN'S QUESTION sent a mix of emotions running through me, from guilt to fear to frustration. "I'm not sure."

He gave me a doubtful look. "Whoever broke in here thinks you know what you did."

"Someone is messing with me."

"Clearly. Why?"

"I don't know. And I've had my keys on me the whole time. They weren't in the bag that was stolen last night." I shook my head in confusion. "I don't know how anyone could get in here."

"No one else has a key?"

"I live alone."

"What about a building manager?"

I shook my head. "I own this condo. Tyler doesn't have access. He has to notify me if he needs to come in."

"What about a neighbor?"

I started at his question. "I gave Delores a key when I moved in. She owns the unit across the hall, but she's been in a convalescent center for the last three months. Although her granddaughter moved in a few weeks ago."

"That's a place to start."

Did I want to start anything?

My first instinct was to run. Pack a bag, and then bolt. I'd learned how to do that when I was a kid. And it wasn't like I had a lot to pack up. This was another reason why I never had too much stuff. I needed to be able to move if I had to go quickly. But those days were supposed to be behind me. And I couldn't run now. I had a job, a career, a life.

"Emily? What are you thinking?"

"I don't know. I guess I could talk to Monica, the woman who moved in across the hall. But she's not home. I saw her leave when I was waiting for you. I can't imagine she'd have come in here though, or that she would even know where her grandmother had stashed my key. I was in Delores's unit before she fell and her place was filled to the rafters with everything she'd collected throughout her life. I wouldn't even know where she'd put my key."

"But this woman is the only one you know of who might have access to a key."

At his words, I realized that wasn't true. "I keep my keys in my bag, and my bag is often sitting on my desk when I'm at work or on a movie set or really anywhere."

"That definitely expands the suspect pool. Let's get back to the message on the mirror." He waved his hand toward the sticky note. "You really have no idea what this note is referring to?"

"I could venture a guess, but I'm not sure."

"Because you've done more than one thing?" he queried.

I let out a sigh and then nodded, feeling an old burning shame that had never really gone away. "I have done some things in my life that someone might have had a problem with."

Surprise ran through his gaze at my honest response. "Okay. Maybe we can narrow it down. You said something about another note."

"I got one at the party last night, a server delivered it to me. It said exactly the same thing." My gaze traveled to the note once more. "Is there a way to get a fingerprint off that?"

"I'm sure whoever came in here was careful not to leave any prints behind. Let's go into the other room and talk."

I didn't want to talk, because I was sure he was going to ask questions I didn't want to answer. But I was eager to get away from the disturbing message.

We moved back to the living room. I sat down on the couch and crossed my arms, feeling suddenly chilled by the air conditioning. Ethan sat in the chair across from me.

For a long minute, he just looked at me.

"What are you thinking?" I asked, repeating the same question he'd asked me.

He didn't answer right away. Then he said, "I'm thinking I should go."

I frowned. "Really? Because I was hoping you might help me figure this out."

"It sounds complicated," he muttered, conflict going on in his eyes. "And personal."

"It feels personal," I agreed. "I wish I had asked the server last night who had given her the note, but I didn't think it would be anything scary until she was gone, and then I couldn't find her again."

He pressed his fingers together as he rested his arms on his legs. "So, two threatening notes, a mugging, and a break-in, all within twenty-four hours."

"I don't see how the mugging is connected."

"They wanted your purse. which included your ID and your phone."

"I was hoping it was just a random and bad coincidence."

He gave me a direct look. "I don't believe it was."

"You're scaring me."

"I'm just telling you the truth, and I think you should be concerned. You should definitely get your locks changed."

"What about the police? Will they be more interested in finding my mugger if I tell them about everything else?"

"Possibly. But you might want to hire a private investigator, someone who can dig into your life and figure out who has a motive to mess with you."

The idea of unraveling my life to a private investigator was horribly unappealing, but I was going to need some help. "You work in security. Do you have any experience with cases like this?"

"I stand on the sidewalk and look for shoplifters or smash-and-grab thieves," he said. "You need an investigator. However, I can probably help you get your locks changed. I have a friend who's a locksmith. He might be willing to come over and help you out."

"That would be great. It might be difficult to get someone on a Saturday night, and I don't think I can stay here, knowing someone has a key."

"I don't know if he's free, but I'll call him."

"Thanks." I would love to get one problem solved.

Ethan pulled out his phone and a moment later said, "Tom, it's Ethan. I need a favor. A woman needs her lock changed immediately for security reasons. It's just one door, so it shouldn't take too long." He paused. "That would be great." He smiled to himself. "Yeah, yeah, put it on my tab." Ethan rattled off my address, then said, "See you soon."

"Sounds like it's a go," I said as he ended the call.

"Tom can do it, but he can't get here until seven."

I checked my watch. That was about ninety minutes from now. I hated the idea of waiting even that long to feel more secure, but it was better than I could have hoped for. "That's great."

He gave me a knowing look. "I can wait with you, Emily."

"Really? I hate to ask."

"You didn't ask, I offered."

"I can pay you for your time."

"How about you buy me dinner? I'm starving. We could order something in. There's a great Thai place about a block from here."

"If you're talking about Ruby's, I love that place."

"Then we'll order food, and while we're waiting for Tom, we can talk about who might be threatening you."

After we ordered dinner, Ethan said, "So, let's talk about people who don't like you, Emily. Who's at the top of the list?"

"Mitchell Gray," I said, the director's name popping into my mind immediately.

"Because he thinks you tried to kill him. He would be at the top of my list, too."

"He was also at the party last night. And he has a devious, creative mind. I can see him getting off on making me afraid."

"Is there a but?" Ethan challenged.

"Mitch is in his fifties and he's much more established than me, despite my one-off success, which was based on some of his choices. He has also been spending a lot of his time rehabbing and trying to get his physical condition back to a hundred percent. Would he really waste time sending me threatening notes, especially when he's already been put in charge of the next film?"

"It's a good question. What about someone close to him? Is he married? Does he have children?"

"He's married. Tara is his second wife. He has one college-aged daughter, Rachel, who lives with his first wife, Noelle Page."

"I recognize both those names. They're well-known actresses."

"Yes. Mitchell likes actresses," I said. "I've never met Noelle, but Tara was in Australia when he was injured. We spoke a few times. We had no issues between us. She never implied it was anything but an accident. I didn't even realize Mitchell was angry with me until a couple of months ago. But he was severely injured, so maybe it just took him a while to get up enough energy to hate me."

"Or he realized how much attention you were getting and didn't like it."

"Or that," I agreed.

"Who else would be jealous of you?"

"I don't know."

"How about someone in your office?"

"I'm sure there are at least a few people who are envious of the lucky break I got. It's Hollywood. Everyone is jealous of someone."

"True. What about a personal relationship? Are you seeing anyone? Have you broken up with anyone recently who might be angry about that?"

"I've been dating Ashton Hunter the past six weeks. Before that, I hadn't really been seeing anyone for a long time. I was busy with work."

"So, you like actors."

"Actually, I've tried to stay away from actors and others who might want to date me purely because of my job or my connections, but in this area, it's difficult to find someone who isn't tied to the film industry."

"You need to expand your circle."

"At any rate..." I said, not needing to discuss my dating life, "something strange happened to Ashton last night, too. We were at the party together, but I left early because I wasn't feeling well after I got that disturbing note. Ashton stayed behind. After the party, he went to a bar with friends. At some point, he lost track of where he was. He thinks he was drugged. He woke up in a sleazy motel around noon today, but the only thing missing was his phone, not his money or his credit cards."

"That's quite a story."

"He thinks someone may have taken some photos, possibly setting him up for blackmail."

"No one saw him leave with anyone?"

"He said he hasn't wanted to tell anyone what happened, but he has been trying to reach his closest friend who was at the bar with him. He hasn't gotten a call back."

"Ashton is a well-known actor. Someone had to have seen something."

"I hope so. He's very upset about it."

"Where is he right now? Why aren't you two together? Why isn't he making sure you're safe?"

His questions put me on the defensive. "Ashton is flying to New York tonight. He has business there. He couldn't rearrange his schedule." I paused. "It's hard to believe that what happened to him has something to do with what's going on with me. But the timing is strange."

"Does he have a key to your condo?"

"No. I haven't given him one. We haven't been going out that long."

"All right. We've covered coworkers and boyfriends. What about girlfriends?"

"There was someone at the party last night that I hadn't seen in ten years—Cassie Byrne. We went to high school together. She works for *VIP Magazine*. They published the Top 30 Under 30 List, and she planned the event, so it wasn't odd that she was there, just surprising because I'd lost track of her, and I had no idea she worked for them."

"Did you have a happy reunion?"

"It wasn't unhappy, but Cassie has always been a little snarky. We were really just friends because we had a mutual friend in common—Alina Price."

"How was she snarky last night?"

"Cassie made a comment about how I always seem to get lucky at someone else's expense. Our senior year in high school, we were all in the drama club together, and at a party right before our big spring show, the star of the play, Kimmy Taylor tripped down some stairs at a party, and she broke her leg and couldn't perform. I stepped into her role."

His eyebrow shot up. "Interesting. Did you push her down the stairs?"

"Of course not," I said sharply. "But I was at the party where it happened, and I might have handed her a drink, but it was on her how drunk she got. And I was nowhere near the stairs." I paused. "And don't say, 'was it just like you were nowhere near the propane tanks on the set in Australia?'"

"Is that where your mind went?"

"I'm sure it's where yours went," I returned.

He shrugged. "It crossed my mind. So, this woman at the party—Cassie—you haven't seen her in ten years?"

"Not since high school graduation. She also made some comment about how she'd suggested I'd be a good candidate for the list, as if she had something to do with the award. But I think she just wanted me to think she had influence and had helped me out."

"It sounds to me like Cassie has a problem with you."

"I don't know. That's just the way Cassie talks. She's sarcastic and likes to needle people."

"She was at your party, which gave her the ability to send you a note."

"That's true."

Ethan thought for a moment. "Who else did you tell about the note you got at the party?"

"No one," I replied. "Just you."

"Why?" he asked, surprise running through his eyes. "What about your boyfriend? What about a coworker or someone else at the party?"

I shook my head. "I didn't have time to tell Ashton. He was caught up in his own problems, so we didn't go that deep into mine." My phone buzzed with a text that the restaurant delivery was downstairs, and I was relieved to say, "Our food is here."

"I'll get it."

"Thanks." As Ethan headed out the door, I let out a breath. It was a little exhausting to be grilled by Ethan. As nice as it was to not be alone in my apartment right now, answering questions about my life and trying to imagine who would want to hurt me was taking me down a dark road, and we hadn't even gotten to the darkest part of that road yet.

My phone buzzed again—a number I didn't recognize. I opened the message and saw a photo. It had been taken in my living room—a picture of the pot turned on its side. The text said: *Oops. Sorry I didn't have time to clean that up. Next time I'll be more careful.*

CHAPTER EIGHT

I WAS PACING around the living room when Ethan returned with the food, the text message running around in my head.

Ethan took one look at me and said, "What's happened now?"

I handed him my phone.

His lips tightened as he looked at the photo and read the message. Then he gazed back at me, a grim expression on his face. "They wanted to make sure you'd seen that they were in here."

"How could I miss the note or the overturned plant? Do you think we could trace the phone number?"

"You watch a lot of crime shows, don't you?"

"Why would you ask that?"

"Because your expectations are unrealistic. Whoever is doing this has a carefully orchestrated plan. They're not going to make a mistake by using a traceable number."

"So I do nothing?" I asked in frustration.

"I don't know. Why don't we eat while we think about it?"

I didn't think I could stomach any food, but I followed Ethan to the dining room table and sat down. I directed him as to where plates and silverware were, too emotionally exhausted to find the energy to be a good host. My brain was spinning. And

Ethan's reminder that someone was executing some carefully choreographed plan hadn't made me feel better.

"What do you think is next?" I asked, as he spooned noodles onto a plate and then passed it to me.

He shook his head. "I don't know."

"If you had to guess?"

He didn't answer as he filled his plate with food. Then he said, "Someone wants to scare you, make you nervous and uneasy, but I would doubt that is the end game."

"They're working up to something," I said. "But what?"

"Could be anything. It's probably better to focus on the why and not the what. There's a personal motivation behind the notes, the break-in, maybe even the mugging. You have to figure out who has the most to gain by tearing you down. Is it just for personal satisfaction, revenge, a way to get even for something? Or do they want to drive you crazy, get you second-guessing yourself and so anxious you can't think straight, can't do your job?"

"It could be a combination of both scenarios. It could also be something else."

He gave me a thoughtful look as he ate. Swallowing, he said, "Like what?"

"I don't know," I said quickly, sorry I'd even suggested there was anything else.

Frowning, he washed down his next bite with a sip of a bottled water he'd gotten from the fridge. "You're holding something back, aren't you, Emily?"

"I've told you a lot."

"A lot doesn't mean everything. And I think what you haven't told me is why you haven't told anyone else about the note you got last night. Because it doesn't make sense to me you wouldn't have told your boyfriend, and I don't believe it was just a matter of time. Something else held you back. Maybe it's something embarrassing, shameful, possibly criminal."

I sucked in a breath as his words were too close for comfort. "You're reading too much into me not talking to Ashton."

"I don't think so, but it's your life. You're entitled to your secrets," he said with a shrug.

I watched him eat for another minute, debating if I wanted to share any of my secrets. I never talked about my past, not with anyone, but he was a stranger, and there was some comfort in that. He wasn't a friend or a boyfriend I wanted to impress. He wasn't even someone I would necessarily see again.

"Okay," I said, breaking the lengthening silence. "I didn't tell Ashton about the note because I wasn't sure if it referred to a time in my life that I've never talked about."

He studied me with an even gaze. "Do you want to talk about it with me?"

"No. But I feel like I should because maybe it would help us figure out what's going on."

"It's up to you."

I drew in a breath. "I told you I grew up in a rough neighborhood. That was only part of it. When I was ten, my mom died, and I ended up living with her boyfriend, a man named Jimmy Smithers. At least, that's the name he was using at the time. I honestly don't even know what his real name is. Jimmy claimed that he and my mom were married when she died. He had a marriage certificate to prove it, although my mom never told me she'd married him. But that made him my stepfather, and he ended up with her life insurance and me."

"I'm getting the sense this Jimmy isn't a good guy."

"He's a complicated person. He was charming and charismatic, and he didn't mistreat me, but he did use me in his cons. That's basically what he did for a living. He conned people, and I became his shill. I didn't realize that's what I was for a long time. I just knew that he wanted me to help him, and I needed someone to take care of me, so we were a team. Jimmy taught me how to lie, cheat and steal, but at the same time he made me feel like everything was a game. Sometimes, it felt like we were in a movie. I had to pretend to be deaf once when he wanted to seduce a woman he met at a fundraiser for deaf children."

Ethan didn't comment, and I couldn't really tell what he was thinking, but the shame of my upbringing was turning my stomach into knots.

"In the beginning," I continued, "I didn't know anyone was getting hurt. But as I got older, I realized he was preying on people at their most vulnerable moments. He was very good at seducing women who had just been widowed or divorced. And they never saw through him. They fell head over heels for his charm every single time. Some women who weren't widowed or divorced left their husbands for Jimmy. They gave him access to their bank accounts. They wrote big checks to cover whatever grand plan he was selling them. He used to say that people just liked to help him, help us. But as girlfriends came and went, as we moved from city to city, sometimes in the middle of the night, I knew we were leaving a trail of heartache behind us."

I took a breath, then continued. "Jimmy was all the family I had. I couldn't go against him, and he was mostly good to me. We had some wild adventures. Sometimes, we lived like royalty, in mansions with huge swimming pools. We went to parties on yachts and spent time at exotic resorts. Of course, those were the good times. They never lasted long. Then we were staying in sleazy motels until he found our next mark. When I eventually became of less value to Jimmy, he bailed on me."

"How old were you then?"

"Fourteen. He dumped me off with a cousin of his. He told Rhea he'd be back soon and never showed up again. I was not so cute anymore. I had braces on my teeth, and I was awkward. Worst of all, I aged Jimmy. Having a teenage daughter didn't work as well with his plans as when I was ten. Luckily, I was old enough to be of use to Jimmy's cousin. Rhea ran a delivery service, and I helped her with packing after school. In return, she let me stay with her. She lived in El Segundo, near the airport. That's where I went to high school and where I made up a new story about my past. I'd spent the past five years learning at the feet of the master how to tell people what they wanted to hear, how to ingratiate myself into a group, and how to be who they needed me to be. And that's it. That's the story." I paused and let out a breath. "I can't believe I just said all that. I've never told anyone."

"Why did you tell me?" he asked curiously.

I thought for a moment. "Because I need help, Ethan. I realize that it's crazy to ask you for that help. We don't know each other. We aren't friends. You have no reason to care what happens to me, but I don't know what to do next, and I have to do something, because I don't think this is over."

"I don't believe it is, either." He thought for a moment, and then said, "I can offer some advice, maybe help a little, but you should hire an investigator. You have a lot of parts of your life that you need to dig into."

I was disappointed by his answer and more than a little sorry I'd told him so much when he now didn't appear interested in helping me. But why should he? He had a job, and he probably thought I was a nutcase by now…or worse, someone who might deserve whatever was happening to her. "Okay, I understand. Thanks for listening."

He frowned. "I'm not judging you, Emily. It sounds like you had a terrible childhood. And you were a kid, so whatever Jimmy was forcing you to do wasn't your fault."

"Some might argue that by fourteen I was old enough to make better choices."

"Is that what you think?" he challenged. "Do you feel guilty?"

"Yes—sometimes. I saw a lot of people get hurt, and I could have probably stopped some of it from happening."

"At a personal cost. Jimmy was the only one taking care of you."

"That's what I told myself. But maybe that was just an excuse."

"Where is Jimmy now?" Ethan asked.

"I don't know. I haven't seen him in years."

"You might want to try to find him. Maybe he's the one who's gaslighting you."

"Gaslighting," I echoed, seizing on the word. "That's exactly how I feel. Like someone is trying to drive me crazy. And it's working." I paused. "But it's not Jimmy. I have nothing he would want."

"Don't you? You live in a nice place. I'm assuming you have some cash."

"Not the kind of cash that Jimmy goes after. He moves in much richer circles."

"Still? He hasn't been found out yet? No one has caught on to his games?"

"I don't know for sure, but I've never heard anything to the contrary. Jimmy is smart, and he moves around a lot. I'm not sure he can be caught."

"Everyone can be caught."

"You've never met Jimmy. He's like a shadow or a ghost. One minute he's there, and then he's gone, and it's like he didn't even exist."

"But he's not a ghost. He's a human, a criminal, who will one day make a mistake."

"Maybe so. But I don't think he's behind my gaslighting. It has to be someone else, possibly someone who was hurt by Jimmy. And perhaps I was involved." I paused. "There's something else I didn't tell you, Ethan. When I went into the office today, my video light on my computer was on. That can't be a coincidence either, right?"

"Now that might be something you could get checked. If someone hacked into your computer camera, there could be a trail."

"Who would I find to do that?"

"An IT person at your work?" he suggested.

"I can't bring this to work, not until I know what's going on. I can't give them a reason to cut me from the upcoming movie."

He frowned. "Well, I have a friend who might be able to look at your computer."

"Really? Do you think your friend could come to my office tomorrow? It's Sunday, and the office should be empty. It would be the perfect time to look at the computer."

"You don't ask much, do you?" he said dryly.

"I know. I'm asking for a lot of help. I'm just feeling a little desperate to get some control over what's going on in my life."

"I can make a call. But then, I need to be done, Emily. I'm sorry. I just don't have the time to dig into this, and you'd be better off hiring someone. You need help."

"I understand, and I appreciate all that you're doing for me." I paused. "You're a good guy."

He smiled. "I try to be."

"How long have you been a security guard?"

"Awhile," he said vaguely.

"Did you do something else before?"

"I was in the Marine Corps. I did my stint and when I got out, I decided to do something else."

"Like become a security guard."

"Yes."

"How long have you been working at the jewelry store? I thought I saw an older guy out in front last week. Or do you only work part-time?"

"That was Stan. He had to take some time off, so I'm filling in."

"Then it's a temporary job?"

"Probably. I'm not making a lot of plans these days. I go with the flow."

"I can't imagine what that feels like. I start every day with a plan. Which is why all these unpredictable events are maddening."

"Having heard how you grew up, I can understand why you need control over your life. But control is a funny thing, isn't it?"

"What do you mean?" I asked curiously.

"It's mostly illusion. Even when you think you have it, you don't. There's always something unexpected that could happen. You can't plan for everything."

I reflected on his somewhat dark words, on what little he'd told me about his life. "Did you see combat, Ethan?"

"Yes. I was deployed several times."

"Did you like being a Marine?" I asked curiously.

"It was a growing experience," he said. "I probably should have thought longer about enlisting than I did, which was about a minute."

"Really? It wasn't a lifelong ambition to be in the Marine Corps?"

"God, no!" He shook his head. "I enlisted when I was eighteen because I wanted to get out of the house, out of our neighborhood, and there was no money to go anywhere else."

"Where did you grow up?"

"I think we've shared enough personal information."

I was disappointed at the abrupt cutoff. "Hey, I told you my life story."

"But I didn't ask," he said pointedly. Then he glanced down at his phone. "We also don't have time. Tom is here. I'll let him in."

While I was relieved that the locksmith had arrived, I was a little sorry our conversation had been interrupted. I would have liked to know more about him. Not that it mattered. Ethan had made it clear that he couldn't wait to be done with my problems, and I couldn't blame him. I couldn't wait to be done with them, too.

CHAPTER NINE

As he went downstairs to let the locksmith in, I cleared the table. Ethan had finished eating, and I still wasn't hungry. Maybe later, I'd heat it up.

When the men entered my unit, Ethan introduced me to Tom, a stocky guy with a big frame and a big voice. He gave my hand a hard, almost painful shake and then got to work.

While Tom and Ethan were focused on changing my lock, I sat down at my computer and did what I always did when things got too muddled in my mind: I made a list. And this list was comprised of possible suspects. I started with Mitchell Gray, adding his wife, Tara, next to his name. I thought about who else had been with us in Australia, and added three more names from that trip, only because they hadn't been particularly welcoming to me when I'd taken over for Mitchell.

Then I moved on to my company, starting with the top. Francine was my mentor. She wouldn't tear me down. David Valenti and Curtis Nolan barely had anything to do with me, and my stock had gone up with both of them after I'd proved my value on *The Opal King*.

I looked at the next level of coworkers. Jonah was my peer but also one of my best friends. The other associate producers were all fairly new hires, no one who would have reason to dislike me. It wasn't like I'd jumped over any of them. But I wrote down all their names. And then I got to my assistant, Kaitlyn.

I'd hired her three months ago, and while I thought her work was all over the place, she had a lot of enthusiasm, and we got along well. But it bothered me she'd had private conversations with Ashton that I hadn't known about, and that she had partied with him and his friend Liam last night. She had also spoken to Mitchell and told him about the lunch with Natasha. In addition, Kaitlyn had access to my computer, my phone, my purse, and my keys...

My pulse sped up at the idea that Kaitlyn could be involved. She could have made a copy of my key. On the other hand, what would Kaitlyn have to gain by messing with me? I was giving her opportunities. It wasn't like I was keeping her down.

Unless Mitchell had put her up to it? Maybe he was using her to get to me.

I was still thinking about that when I realized Tom and Ethan were testing out my lock. I got to my feet and joined them.

"All done?" I asked.

"Yep," Tom said, giving me a smile. "You're good to go."

"Thank you so much. I really appreciate you coming out on a Saturday night."

"My wife was happy to get me out of the house for a few hours," Tom joked. "She likes to catch up on her reality TV shows on the weekends and doesn't enjoy my doubleheader baseball games."

"Is Kirsten still working in the ER?" Ethan asked.

"Yes, and she loves it," Tom replied. "Speaking of jobs, what are you doing these days, Ethan? I ran into Landon a few weeks ago, and he said you were working as a bouncer somewhere."

"That was a few weeks ago," Ethan said with a shrug.

"And before that, you were working at a surf shop? When are

you going to settle into something?" Tom quizzed, a somewhat worried gleam in his eyes.

"Who knows? I enjoy mixing it up," Ethan said lightly.

"You didn't used to," Tom said.

"Well, I do now," Ethan replied, making it clear that he wanted Tom to drop it.

"Okay, then, but if you decide you want some longer-term work, my brother-in-law's construction firm is getting busy. He could use some labor."

"I'll keep it in mind. What do I owe you for tonight?"

"Actually, I'll pay," I interrupted. "My door, my lock, my problem."

Tom gave me a curious look, as if he wasn't sure what my relationship was to Ethan. Then he said, "Okay. How about twenty bucks?"

"That's all?" I asked in surprise.

"You get the friends and family discount."

I should have told him that Ethan and I were not friends or family, but that would only necessitate explanations, which I didn't want to make. Since Ethan hadn't corrected Tom, I just said, "All right. If you're sure."

"I am."

I paused, suddenly realizing I had no cash. "I only have a credit card, or I could pay you on an app if you have one. My wallet was stolen last night, and I haven't been to the bank yet."

"I've got this," Ethan said, pulling a twenty-dollar bill out of his wallet. "You can pay me back later," he added as I gave him an apologetic look.

"I will pay you back, Ethan. And thanks again, Tom."

"No problem. It sounded like you needed this done right away, so stay safe." He handed me two new keys.

"I'm going to try," I said.

"Ethan—don't be a stranger," Tom said. "Let's get a beer soon."

"We will," Ethan promised.

As Tom left, Ethan closed and locked the door behind him. "Do you feel better now?"

"Much better, and I will not let either of these keys out of my sight."

"Good idea."

"So you were working as a bouncer before the security guard job?"

"Yes."

"Why did you stop?"

He shrugged. "I got bored."

"What will you do when the other guard comes back to the jewelry store?"

"Don't know. Like I said earlier, I'm enjoying living my life without having a plan. I don't live to work. I work to live."

"But what if there isn't enough work to pay for living the way you want to? I've been in that position. I didn't like it at all. I swore I would never end up with an empty bank account and not knowing where my next paycheck was coming from."

"Your life is different than mine. And that's okay. I should get going. How are you feeling about being here alone tonight?"

I was feeling worried and edgy, but I couldn't ask Ethan to babysit me. "I'll be okay," I said, trying to mean it. "No one has actually hurt me, not physically anyway…not even the guy who robbed me last night. They're just trying to mess with my mind. Right?"

"Right," he said, but there wasn't a lot of certainty in his voice. "I'm not working tomorrow. The store is closed, so I'll give my computer expert a call and see if we can check out your computer while your office is empty."

"That would be great. I promise not to ask for more."

He smiled. "I don't think you should make that promise."

"I know you want to be done with me, Ethan."

"It's not personal. I like my life to be simple, and yours is very complicated."

"I can't argue with that. Let's exchange numbers," he said. "I'll call you tomorrow and let you know what I find out."

"Great."

I gave him my number.

He sent me a quick text, then said, "Good night, Emily."

"Good night."

He stepped into the hall, and I locked the door behind him, feeling a cold and somewhat familiar chill as he departed. I'd thought I'd left this feeling of dread and uncertainty in my childhood, that I'd taken control of my life. But Ethan was right. My control had just been an illusion.

Shaking my head, I moved back to the computer, determined to get some control back. I needed to do something proactive, but I didn't know exactly what.

As my fingers hovered above the keyboard, I found myself typing in Ethan's name.

Nothing popped up, or at least nothing that had to do with the man I knew. There were lots of Ethan Burkes with active social media profiles, but not him. I probably shouldn't be surprised. He didn't seem like someone who would post photos of his life.

When I added the word *marine* to my search, I got a hit on an article in the *San Diego Journal* about a shooting at a bar where a marine was killed, a man named Steven Harbison. A second marine, Ethan Burke, was injured. I gasped at that piece of information, then read on, feeling a sense of dread. The shooters had escaped and had not been identified. Anyone in the vicinity was encouraged to call in with any information. The article was five years old.

I searched for additional updates on that shooting, but I couldn't find anything. Obviously, Ethan had recovered. But I wondered what had happened and how that incident had affected him.

Maybe that's why he'd gotten a dark look in his eyes when he'd told me that control was just an illusion, that when you thought you had everything right where you wanted it, something unexpected could happen.

Finding nothing more on the shooting, I went further back in time, eventually stumbling upon a photo of the two men taken when they were teenagers. They'd gone to high school together, played on the same baseball team, and apparently had ended up in the Marine Corps. Ethan looked young and carefree in the picture, but that had been before he'd seen war, before he'd lost his friend. He must have been devastated.

I sat back in my chair, feeling guilty for spying on him. Ethan had helped me because he was a good guy, and here I was, digging into his life. My excuse was that I needed to know who he was because I'd told him so much about myself, but that wasn't completely true. I was just intrigued by Ethan and his story. But I needed to let him tell me the rest of it himself. Not that that would probably happen. He'd agreed to get his computer expert to look at my computer, but that was it. I was on my own after that, and I needed to be okay with that. He'd already done more for me than anyone else.

I shook my head, annoyed with myself for getting caught up in Ethan when I should have spent the last hour looking into the other people in my life.

My phone buzzed, drawing my attention to an incoming text from Cassie. *Damn!* She was persistent. I hadn't heard from her in ten years, and she'd texted me twice since the party.

Alina said she can do lunch Tuesday. We're thinking Silverman's on the Sunset Strip. Can you join us at noon? We really want to see you. Please say you'll make it.

I stared at the text for a long minute, not sure what to say. I had fond memories of Alina, and I wouldn't mind seeing her again. But I didn't trust Cassie, and I didn't like that they were suddenly back in my life again at the exact same time someone was working really hard to scare me.

Cassie texted again: *We won't take no for an answer, Emily.*

The more she pushed, the more I wanted to say she would

have to take a *no*. But if she was the one trying to get back at me for something, wouldn't it be better if I played along?

Jimmy had always told me to keep my enemies close. I didn't know if either of them was an enemy or just an unwelcome reminder of my past, but either way, I might as well play it out.

I picked up my phone and texted: *I'd love to do lunch. See you then.*

My reply was met by a smiley face. The emoji should have made me feel better, that this was just a normal interaction between old high school friends, but it didn't feel normal. Nothing in my life did.

I went to my office at four o'clock on Sunday afternoon to meet Ethan and his computer expert. I'd tried to distract myself during the day with work, reading through two scripts that Kaitlyn had pulled out of the slush pile for my attention. What I really wanted to work on was the new draft of *Aces High*, but Roy wouldn't get that to me until tomorrow.

When I arrived, I was surprised to see Jonah back in the conference room. I stopped in the doorway. "I thought you were going to Newport today."

Jonah sighed, his usual smile missing. "Palmer and I had a disagreement. He decided today was not the day to introduce me to his parents."

"Sorry." I gave him a sympathetic smile.

He shrugged. "I'm thinking Palmer will always find an excuse."

"Have you asked him why he's reluctant?"

"He says his parents can be difficult, and he wants to find the right time for all of us to gather. But I'm good with parents. I don't know what he's worried about. It's like he doesn't trust me to use the right fork or something."

"I'm sure that's not it." I didn't enjoy seeing Jonah down. He was usually the happiest person in the office, and the one individual I could count on to cheer me up.

"We'll see," he said. "What are you doing here?"

I hesitated, realizing I was going to need a reason for my Sunday afternoon meeting. "A friend of mine wants me to hear a pitch from a friend of his."

"The old friend of a friend deal," he said, a knowing gleam in his eyes. "I thought you had a policy against mixing business and friendship."

"I owe him a favor, so I said I'd hear his friend out. I thought it would be easier to do it today when I'm not busy with other things. Roy is supposed to get his revised script back to me tomorrow. And if it's all good, we'll be able to get going on preproduction and casting."

Jonah leaned back in his chair. "I hear Ashton wants a role."

My gaze narrowed. "Let me guess—Kaitlyn told you that. I'm beginning to realize she has a very big mouth."

"She talks too much," Jonah agreed. "But she's excited about her job. Don't you remember how overly energized we were when we first started working here? We were constantly thrilled by every star who came into the office."

"That's true," I admitted.

"What are you going to do about Ashton? Will you let him audition?"

"It won't be up to me. Ashton spoke to Mitchell about the role after the party Friday night. Since Mitchell will direct, he'll have the final say."

"I heard Mitchell is now in charge. It should be your job, Emily."

"Thanks for saying that." I sat down in a chair at the table as I waited for Ethan to text me when he was downstairs. "I wish Francine and David felt that way."

"They're probably conflicted. They know you're good, but Mitchell is a power player."

"I'm aware," I said with a sigh.

"You may not want to hear this, Emily, but you might need to leave this company to get what you deserve. Francine, David, and Curtis consider Mitchell to be their "guy". He has made three films with them that garnered Oscar nominations. He will always be ahead of you."

"Well, he can't direct every movie."

"He'll get the big ones. And you won't get the smaller films, because you'll be assigned to help him look good."

Jonah's words echoed my thoughts. But I'd been with Holly Roads Productions since I'd graduated from college. I'd never worked anywhere else. I was comfortable here. It was almost like a home, a family…albeit a dysfunctional family. But still better than any I'd had. "Francine has assured me I'll get my chance. And I believe her. She has always given me opportunities."

"You are her pet," he agreed.

I frowned. "I'm not her pet."

" Protégée, star pupil...call it what you want. She definitely favors you."

"She mentors me, but she makes sure I work hard for everything, Jonah."

"I never said you didn't work hard."

"Well, I don't like it when people think I've gotten things I didn't earn," I snapped.

His jaw dropped in surprise. "I was just teasing you. Sorry."

Was he just teasing? Jonah had a dry, sharp wit, and sometimes he could be extremely blunt, but I'd never thought of him as malicious.

"Are you okay, Emily?" he asked, concern in his gaze now. "Kaitlyn said you weren't feeling well Friday night, and you look really pale."

"I'm fine. I just have a lot on my mind." A part of me wanted to share what was happening to me. But after the dig Jonah had just given me, I felt less in a sharing mood.

"I'm sorry if I hurt you. I didn't mean anything. You know I have no filter."

"It's okay. I've just gotten a lot of shit from Mitchell about taking over for him, and I'm a little sensitive about it all."

"He's an ass. Kaitlyn said he tried to hit on her at the afterparty."

"It sounds like Kaitlyn was pretty busy at that party…making out with Liam Shelton, fending off Mitchell. She's quite popular, isn't she?"

"Are you jealous?" Jonah teased.

"No. But I am concerned she's not the person I thought she was when I hired her."

"Who would that person be? She's a young woman, who is learning her job. She's going to make mistakes. You were her once."

"I don't think I was ever her."

"She's like a puppy, a little all over the place, but she'll grow into her position. I like her. And Kaitlyn has a good eye. She gave me some thoughts on my documentary that were helpful."

"That's nice to hear. I like her, too. I just want her to be discreet, to act professionally."

"You should talk to her."

"I will." I got to my feet as a text came in from Ethan. "My friend is here."

"I could use your opinion on some editing after you're done with them, if you have the time."

"Sure. I'll come back when we're finished."

"Great. I'll probably be here all night. Oh, and Emily…"

I paused at the door. "Yes?"

"Kaitlyn said you thought someone was watching you through the camera of your computer. Is that true?"

"I thought the green light was on." I was beginning to realize just how much Kaitlyn talked about me. "But then it went off, so I don't know."

"It would be creepy if someone was watching you. Who would do that?"

"I can't imagine. It was probably nothing."

"I hope so. I'd hate to think you picked up a stalker with your new fame."

"I'm not famous."

"Well, be careful. And I'm here for you, if you need me."

"Thanks." As I walked out of the conference room, I really hoped that Ethan's friend could reassure me, because Jonah's words had amped up my anxiety again.

Someone was stalking me, but whether it had anything to do with my newfound fame or not was a big question.

CHAPTER TEN

I WENT DOWNSTAIRS to meet Ethan in the lobby of my office building. He was with a pretty brunette named Sophia. I'd expected his cyber expert friend to look more like his friend, Tom, the locksmith. But Sophia could have been a model, not an IT specialist, and I couldn't help wondering just how good of friends she and Ethan were. Not that that was any of my business.

"Thanks for coming," I said, as I waved them into the elevator. "I really appreciate it."

"Hope I can help," Sophia said.

"Any problems today?" Ethan asked.

"Not so far. I'm hoping that continues."

When we entered the office suite, I took them down a back hallway, avoiding the conference room. Not that Jonah couldn't see them, but I wanted to prevent any conversation that might contradict what I'd told him about a movie pitch.

I ushered them into my office and then shut the door.

Sophia headed straight for my computer. The screen was dark, and the green light was off.

"What's your password?" she asked.

I gave it to her and then said, "I thought at first I'd left a video chat open, but that wasn't the case. And then the light went off a few minutes later." I watched as her fingers flew across the keys. "What are you doing?"

"Trying to find out what happened," she replied, without looking up. "You two can take a break. This might take me a few minutes."

I was relieved she was talking about minutes instead of days or weeks. "Do you want something to drink? Our kitchen is stocked with sparkling waters and sodas."

"I'm good. You two go. I work better alone."

Ethan followed me down a short hallway and into the kitchen. I pulled out a couple of waters and handed him one. "Thanks for getting her here."

He opened his water and took a sip as he leaned back against the counter. "Let's see if she finds anything before you thank me."

"I appreciate the effort either way."

He gave me a smile, and my heart fluttered. I couldn't help thinking how good he looked today in worn jeans and a short-sleeve, light-blue T-shirt. He certainly didn't look like a security guard, or even a marine—more like a guy who'd be comfortable on a hike or walking the beach. Maybe it was the tan that made me think of him as an outdoors guy, although the sun on his face could have come from his days guarding the front door of the jewelry store.

As our gazes clung together for far too long, I saw something shift in his eyes, almost as if he'd decided we were getting a little too friendly. I was probably the one who should worry about that since I was seeing Ashton. Although, come to think of it, I didn't know if Ethan was seeing anyone. He could have a girlfriend.

"How do you know Sophia?" I asked as I opened my water, breaking the eye contact between us.

"She grew up down the street from me."

"Where was that street?"

"San Diego."

"That's a nice city. Did you live by the beach?"

"I wish. We lived farther inland."

"It's funny, but my new neighbor, Monica is also from San Diego."

"It's a big city."

"I know, just another little coincidence."

"What's her name again?"

"Monica Paul?"

"Doesn't ring a bell."

"She's probably seven or eight years younger than you." I licked my lips. "I have a confession to make, Ethan."

He stiffened. "That doesn't sound good."

"I did a computer search on you last night. I didn't find much. But I saw an article about you and another man getting shot at a bar."

His lips tightened. "That's right."

"Were you badly hurt?"

"I survived. I can't say the same for Steven."

"It said you were childhood friends."

"We were. We played baseball together from the time we were ten until we graduated high school. And then we joined the Marine Corps. For years, we dodged bullets and the worst that could happen, only to run into gunfire after we were back home, out of the service, starting our lives over." There was a sad, cynical note in his voice.

"I'm so sorry."

"Me, too." He took a swig of his water.

"Did they ever catch whoever did it?"

"Nope," he said shortly. "Sometimes you don't always get an answer. It's hard to accept that, but it's the truth."

I had a feeling that message wasn't just directed to me but also to himself. I wondered if his friend Steven's senseless death had made Ethan give up a little on his own life. Maybe that's why he was fine with guarding a door. He'd already spent a lot of time trying to save the world. It also made me understand why he only wanted simple now, and not complicated.

"But you're not at that point," Ethan said, bringing my attention back to him. "Of giving up," he added. "And you shouldn't, because the stakes are high."

"I hope Sophia can trace the camera hacker."

"If anyone can, she can."

"By the way, I was talking to my coworker, Jonah, a few minutes ago. He's working in the conference room. If he comes in here, I told him you were a friend of mine bringing a friend of yours in to pitch me a movie idea."

"You didn't want to tell him why we're really here?"

"I need to keep this problem away from work as long as I can."

"It must be difficult to live with so many secrets," he mused, giving me a thoughtful look.

"I thought I was done with secrets when I turned eighteen. I told myself I was going to live an authentic life."

"Can you live an authentic life when you can't tell anyone who you really are?" he challenged.

"Do people need to know everything about me?" I countered. "Why can't I just start from where I am? Why does the past have to matter?"

He gave me a thoughtful look. "That's a good question. I think you can't just start from the middle of your life, because your past is part of what forms you. And maybe people can't really understand you if they don't know where you come from."

"Where you come from isn't who you are. It's how you act every day, how you treat people, and I treat people well. I'm sure that you have a different idea of me now. But once I got out from under Jimmy and became an adult, I vowed I would be a different person going forward, and, for the most part, I've kept that promise."

"But you keep everyone at a distance, because you can't let them past your wall of secrets."

"I'm not saying I would never tell my truth. Obviously, I told you, although now I'm regretting it, because you're becoming a little too insightful for my comfort."

He smiled. "Yes, but you made me want to help you, so you're getting something out of your confession."

"Up to a point. After Sophia, we're still done?" I asked.

"Yes, I think so, Emily. You need more help than I have time to give you."

"Okay, that's fair." I tried not to let the disappointment show. He had already helped me a lot. I couldn't ask for more.

"Have you come up with any more suspects since last night?" he asked.

"I don't know about suspects, but when I was talking to Jonah, he mentioned everyone thinks I'm Francine's favorite. I thought I heard jealousy in his voice. We started at the same time."

"And you're ahead of him?"

"Yes. But he's doing well, too. And he is one of my best friends here. I don't think he'd go out of his way to psych me out. Although, I have to say that he's closer to Kaitlyn than I realized. Kaitlyn has been my assistant for the past three months. She's a very outgoing, energetic twenty-three-year-old who can't wait to make her mark on the industry."

"Are you standing in her way?"

"No. I'm trying to help her learn. She's young. She's green. She needs a lot of experience in a lot of areas. I've always thought we had a good relationship. But she talks a lot, and she says things outside of work that she shouldn't. Jonah thinks she's like an overeager puppy, but he has a high opinion of her, and he rarely thinks that much of people who work here, so I don't know." I gave a helpless shrug. "Honestly, I can't imagine Jonah or Kaitlyn breaking into my condo or sending me threatening notes. But Kaitlyn was at the party. She has had access to my purse where I keep my keys, and she was also at the bar with Ashton after the party when bad things went down with him."

"You definitely need to keep an eye on her. I assume she also had access to your computer."

"Yes," I said with a nod. "She's probably the closest person to me in this office. She knows where I'm going to be every minute of the day. But she has no motivation, Ethan. She's only been here a few months, and she is learning fast. She works hard. I can't see her trying to hurt me."

"Well, whoever is trying to hurt you is probably close to you. You need to prepare yourself for that. Maybe someone else is using her."

"I had that same thought. If someone powerful asked for her help, maybe she'd give it to get ahead." I sighed at that depressing thought. "Anyway, should we check on Sophia?"

"Yes." He tossed his empty water bottle into the recycle bin while I carried mine back to my office. Sophia was working at my computer but looked up when we entered.

"Did you find out anything?" I asked.

"There was malware on your computer. I've erased the hack and built in a safeguard to prevent it from happening again. Even with that, I'd do this." Sophia picked up a sticky note and covered the camera. She gave me a smile. "Sometimes, the most obvious solution is the best solution."

"I like the idea of covering the camera. But can you tell me who hacked into my computer?"

"It looks like you downloaded an attachment that was infected about two weeks ago."

"Two weeks ago?" I echoed. "That's how long someone has been watching me?"

"Possibly," Sophia said.

"I'm so careful about what I download. Can you tell me what email it came from or what the attachment was?"

"I can." She moved through a screen on the computer. "I found the email in your trash bin. The subject line was marketing buzz analytics."

"That's an email I get every month from a marketing firm we use. Can you show me the one that was infected?"

Sophia nodded. "Here you go."

I peered over her shoulder at the email. It looked like every other email I'd gotten from our consultants until Sophia pointed out that the email address had a typo in it. "You probably opened it without realizing it wasn't from the person you thought it was."

"Or my assistant did," I said with a frown.

"It would have been difficult to catch," Sophia said.

I looked over at Ethan as his phone started buzzing.

"Sorry," he said pulling it from his pocket. Frowning, he added, "I need to take this."

I wondered if everything was all right, but Ethan had stepped out of my office before I could get the question out.

"Emily?" Sophia drew my attention back to her.

"Oh, sorry. What did you say?"

"I asked if you have a laptop computer. It might also be compromised."

"I have one at home. I guess if they hacked this one, they might have done the same for my laptop, but I don't know why. If I'm at my computer, I'm just looking at email or websites or reading a draft of someone's screenplay." I paused. "Do they track where I go on the computer?"

"I did not find that capability in this hack, but it might be on your other computer."

I felt sick to my stomach. "It's so creepy, knowing that someone has been watching me. It feels like such a violation, but, thankfully, I don't do anything X-rated in front of the computer. It's not like I'm sitting there naked. You didn't want to ask me that, did you?"

Sophia shrugged. "The camera can capture a distance beyond the computer. If it's set up in your bedroom, it might catch you coming in and out of your bathroom or your closet or wherever you change."

I swallowed back a knot of panic at that thought. "I do sometimes take it into my bedroom."

"Sometimes the hacker will capture a screenshot and use it for blackmail, or there could be any other number of motivations."

"I wish I knew what the motivation was."

Sophia checked her watch. "I wish I could check it now, but I have to go to my sister's house for an early dinner before her new baby goes to sleep. If you want to drop your computer by my office tomorrow, I'm in Santa Monica."

"I could do that."

"Great. I'll text you my address. What's your number?"

I gave her my number, and she sent me a text. Then she began to pack up her things. I wondered where Ethan was and why it was taking him so long to come back.

"Ethan said you two grew up in the same neighborhood," I said.

"We did," she said, adding nothing more.

"You must know him pretty well then."

"I'm not sure I'd say that. Ethan isn't one to open up, especially the last few years."

"Is that because his friend was killed?"

"He told you about that?" she asked in surprise. "Ethan never talks about that night. It really did a number on his head. I was worried about him for a long time." She paused. "Look, I can see you have questions, and I get that, because Ethan is a great guy who can also be annoyingly silent. But whatever you want to know about him, you should ask him."

I felt bad that I'd tried to press her for information. Ethan's life was none of my business. Thankfully, Ethan returned, breaking the now awkward tension between Sophia and me.

"Are you done?" he asked.

"Yes," I replied. "I need to get Sophia my laptop computer tomorrow so she can check that one. I didn't even think about bringing it with me."

"I should have thought of that, too."

"If you use your computer tonight, cover the camera," Sophia said, as she swung her large tote bag over her shoulder. "And it might be a good idea not to access any banking or financial sites until I can check everything."

"I won't. Thanks again."

"Are you leaving now, Emily? Do you want to walk out with us?" Ethan asked.

"Actually, I promised Jonah I'd look at his film after we were done."

"Okay. Be careful," he said.

"I will. Thanks again for coming over here on a Sunday."

"No problem," Sophia said.

As they left, I sat down at my desk and stared at my computer. Sophia had told me it was safe to use it, but it didn't feel like anything in my life was safe. That someone had gone to great lengths to put malware on my computer added a new level of concern. It made everything feel premeditated, and, of course, it had to be.

The note could have been a spur-of-the-moment thing, but not the attack, the break-in at my home, or the malware. Someone was executing a plan, a carefully conceived plan.

That took my thoughts back to Jimmy. He'd always had a plan. He never went into a con without one. He did his research. He knew what he wanted to get before he went after it. We'd sometimes spend hours rehearsing the approach to the mark, the exact words, the choreography of actions, what was his part, what was mine. Even when I'd get tired, he'd make me do it again, saying it had to be practiced enough so that it sounded natural, which had always seemed like a contrary idea to me. But he was right. By the time I was ready to play my part, I was so well prepared there was no possibility I could mess it up.

Was Jimmy the one playing a game on me now?

Should I try to find him?

Or should I stay away from the person who had ruined a sizeable chunk of my life and concentrate on the present?

It was more than likely that whatever was happening to me now was based on more recent events.

The fact that someone had gotten into my condo and into my work computer made me feel like it was someone I knew well, which took me back to Kaitlyn. Was she just an overexcitable puppy-like assistant who ran her mouth too much, or was she much smarter and more conniving than I thought? She could also be the go-between, someone Mitchell could use to help him get revenge on me. But if he was out for revenge, he was going after the wrong person, because I didn't move the propane tanks that had exploded, and I didn't order anyone else to do it.

Frustrated by the circular whirl of questions going around in my head, I got up and went back to the conference room to find Jonah. I might as well help him get something done. But Jonah wasn't in the conference room. The monitor was dark, and his notepad was gone. I walked down an adjacent hall to his office. It was empty as well. That was strange. He'd said he'd be working all night.

As I moved around the suite, the silence tightened my nerves. There was no point in me staying here on my own. In fact, now I wished I'd left with Ethan and Sophia.

I ran back to my office, grabbed my bag, and then jogged down the hall and through the reception area. I locked the doors to the suite behind me and then pressed the button for the elevator. It seemed to take forever to arrive, and every nerve in my body was tingling with the arrival of my latest panic attack. I needed to go somewhere crowded, where there were people, where I could get help if I needed it.

Finally, the elevator doors opened. I got on, pressing the button for the garage twice in quick succession as the doors closed. When they opened, I ran out of the elevator and into the lot. There were at least a dozen cars in the garage. Obviously, there were other tenants in the building who were working today. I needed to relax and get a grip.

But I'd only taken a few steps when the lights in the garage suddenly went out, and my heart jumped against my chest as I froze in place. I couldn't see anything but dark shapes. I reached into my bag, searching for my phone. As I grabbed it, I could hear footsteps, but I didn't know where they were coming from or who they belonged to.

I fumbled with my phone, wondering if I should call 9-1-1. But what was my emergency? The lights in my garage had gone out?

Forcing myself to breathe, I turned on the flashlight on my phone, relieved to see no one around me. The sound of steps had stopped, too. Then I heard the closing of a car door. It was just someone else getting into their car, I told myself.

I moved forward. My car was about twenty-five yards away, parked in the slots assigned to my company.

And then the footsteps came back. They sounded like they were behind me now. I stopped, whirling around, aiming the light behind me. The footsteps stopped. I thought I saw a shadow move behind a car.

God! Was someone following me?

I turned toward my vehicle. I just had to get into my car and lock the door. I ran, then stumbled over a patch of uneven ground. There was so much terror racing through my blood, I couldn't hear anything but my heartbeat.

I could feel someone behind me. It felt like they were getting closer. At any moment, I expected to feel a hand on my shoulders, someone grabbing me from behind.

And then an enormous shaft of light lit up the space around me as a car entered the garage, headlights blazing, speeding straight toward me, blinding me. I flung up my hand as the car came to a screaming halt in front of me and a man jumped out.

CHAPTER ELEVEN

"EMILY?"

It took me a second to realize it was Ethan. I didn't know what the hell he was doing here, but I was more than happy to see him. I ran forward, throwing my arms around his neck.

"You're okay," he said, giving me a tight hug. "Why are the lights out?"

"I don't know. They went off when I got into the garage. There's someone else around. I could hear their footsteps." I took a breath as I forced myself to step out of his embrace.

His gaze swept the area, as did mine, but even with the beams from his headlights illuminating the area, nothing seemed out of place. Maybe whoever had been following me had ducked out of sight when Ethan's car had come into the garage.

"Let's get you out of here," he said. "Where's your car?"

"Right there," I said, pointing to the white SUV parked about ten feet away.

He walked me to my vehicle. It was locked, and there was no sign that anyone had tampered with the car. I opened the doors, and he motioned for me to wait as he checked out the interior. Then he dropped to his knees and flashed the light from his phone on the undercarriage of the car.

That did nothing to ease my fears.

"What are you looking for?" I asked.

"Problems," he said vaguely. "I think you're okay. But why don't we switch cars? I'll drive yours out of the lot. You follow in mine."

I stared at him in surprise. "I can't let you do that."

"You can," he returned.

"But what if there is something wrong?"

"There's not. I just want you to feel more comfortable."

"I can drive my car," I said, steeling myself to slide behind the wheel.

"I'll follow you," Ethan said. "But let's not go to your place. Why don't we get a drink, maybe some food?"

I liked the idea of going somewhere besides home where I had no idea what else was waiting for me.

"Maverick's Burger Joint is about a mile from here," he said.

"I know it."

He gave me a reassuring look. "It's going to be fine, Emily."

I didn't think that was true, but I appreciated his attempt to make me feel better. "I hope so," I muttered.

He waited until I'd locked the door and then returned to his car. He pulled to the side so I could back out, then followed me up the ramp to the exit. When I got there, I realized both the entrance and exit doors were open, which was unusual. It was also probably how Ethan had gotten in without a security code and maybe how whoever had been in the garage with me had come in.

Although, I still had no idea if the lights going out had been deliberate. It wasn't like anyone had grabbed me. And they had had the opportunity to do that. I'd heard footsteps, but no one had gotten close enough for me to see them.

But wasn't that the whole point of this reign of terror I was living under? Someone wanted to scare the hell out of me, and they were succeeding more and more each day. Now I would be constantly on edge, always looking over my shoulder, suspecting the worst from any unforeseen situation, like the lights going out.

Despite trying to tell myself that it could have been a coincidence, I knew it wasn't. Someone had cut the lights when I'd entered the garage. They'd been waiting for me.

Who?

The word screamed at me as it ran around my head in unrelenting repetition. Someone from my office? Was it Jonah? Was the guy I thought was my friend secretly trying to drive me crazy? He'd known I was in the office. He'd asked me to help him after my friends left. Had he known that request would make me stay alone on my own in the office?

I stopped at a light and ran a hand through my hair, then turned up the air conditioning, because I was sweating through my shirt. Looking in the rearview mirror, I saw Ethan behind me.

That brought forth another question. Ethan had left with Sophia. Why had he come back at just the right time?

Could I trust him?

My gut twisted into another knot.

Everyone was looking like a suspect. But it wasn't everyone; it was just one person, and I couldn't imagine Ethan having any kind of motive. He was the only one in my life who couldn't possibly think I had wronged him.

Coworkers might be jealous of my success, angry about my alleged favoritism from Francine, my good luck at getting to step in for Mitchell. And if I looked outside my work life, there wasn't really anyone to think about, except those people further back in my past, my high school friends, maybe Cassie who thought I'd pushed Kimmy Taylor down the stairs and had done the same to Mitchell. Hell, maybe it was Kimmy herself, although I hadn't seen her in a decade. And then there were the people I'd known when Jimmy and I had pulled off his cons. There were too many of those to count.

With a sigh, I hit the gas, thrilled to turn in to the restaurant parking lot a few minutes later. It was almost six, but it was a

Sunday night, so hopefully we'd be able to get a table at the popular restaurant. I hadn't eaten all day. And I was hungry. But first, I just wanted a glass of wine and a chance to feel safe enough to take a full breath.

Ethan met me by my car, and we made our way into the restaurant. After a momentary wait, we were ushered to a table by the back wall, which was quieter than those near the bar and kitchen. I sat down and let out a breath. Ethan rested his arms on the table as he gave me a thoughtful look.

Then he said, "Want to tell me exactly what happened?"

"First, I have a question for you. Why did you come back? How did you know I was in trouble?"

"I didn't know, but I had a bad feeling. When I left your building, I was parked out front, on the street. After Sophia and I got in the car, I saw someone come speeding out of the garage. It looked like the guy I'd seen in your conference room earlier."

"Wait? How did you see Jonah?"

"When I took my call, I walked by the conference room. You mentioned you were sticking around to work with him, and I wondered why he'd left. I couldn't get it out of my head. Luckily, Sophia's apartment was just a few miles away. I dropped her off so she could get her car, and I headed back. When I saw the garage door open, my bad feeling got worse."

"I'm so glad you came back. I didn't know Jonah had left until I went looking for him. I was thinking about what Sophia said, so it took me a few minutes to pull myself together and seek him out. I was shocked when he wasn't in the conference room. When I realized I was alone in the suite, I left immediately. As soon as I hit the garage, the lights went out.

I turned on the flashlight on my phone, but I couldn't see much, and I started to panic. I could hear footsteps behind me, but I couldn't see anyone. I thought I heard a car door open and close. I felt someone's presence closing in, and then you came roaring into the garage. That terrified me, too, until I realized it was you." I paused. "You seem to show up when I need you the most."

"Why do you think Jonah left without telling you?"

"I don't know. Maybe he thought I was tied up with you and Sophia. I should ask him." I took out my phone, then paused as the server took our order. When that was done, I sent Jonah a text, asking him why he'd left without telling me. He answered immediately with a sad face emoji and *SORRY* in all caps, adding Palmer had gotten a flat tire, and he needed to help him get home.

"Does he have an explanation?" Ethan asked.

"His partner got a flat tire, and he had to leave. He apologized."

"Do you believe him?"

"A couple of days ago, I wouldn't have thought twice about Jonah disappearing, but everyone I thought was a friend is looking like an enemy."

"That's what your enemy wants. Their goal is to make you feel rattled and paranoid."

"They're doing a very good job," I said, happy to see my wine arrive. I picked up the chilled glass of chardonnay and took a bigger gulp than normal. "Thanks for suggesting this. Being in a busy restaurant feels like the safest place to be right now."

He took a swig of his beer. "Did you actually see anyone in the garage?"

"No. I just heard footsteps. And before you ask, I've never seen the lights go out in the garage like that. It's never bright down there, but it's always lit. There are a dozen other companies in the building that use that garage. You saw how many cars were in there, even on a Sunday. I never think twice about parking there. And I've never seen the gates open like they were."

"I think the garage doors were deliberately left open, or they opened when the lights went out in case it was an emergency.

With the power off, the gates might not open, which would trap vehicles inside the garage."

"That makes sense. This is good. I need your objectivity. I was feeling panicked even before I entered the garage, so maybe things weren't as dire as I thought."

"I'm not saying you imagined anything, Emily."

"I wish you could say that. I'd rather think I was just being paranoid than that there was something to be scared about."

"You're not being paranoid. Something is going on. And I suspect the lights were part of it. But we can't solve the problem right this second, so what are you going to eat?"

His pragmatic question eased my tension and gave me something else to think about. I picked up the menu. The burger choices were so vast and varied, I couldn't focus. Luckily, I'd been to Maverick's before. "The Surfrider," I said, putting down the menu.

"That looks good," Ethan said. "I'll join you. With sweet potato fries."

"Me, too. That's funny. Most of my friends opt for regular or truffle fries."

"Nothing better than the sweet potato fry."

I smiled. "I have to agree, and I'm a connoisseur when it comes to burgers and fries."

"Really? How did you get to be so experienced?" he asked.

"A steady diet of fast food as a kid. I have a fondness for the burger over tacos, chicken tenders, or pizza, because whenever I was sad, my mom would always take me out for a burger. Burgers and a trip to the beach solved all problems. She probably should have been taking me for salad or vegetables, so I would have started a love affair with a healthier option, but it was always a burger. There's a place called Tommy's. Do you know it?"

"I know it," he said with a nod. "Late-night chili burgers at Tommy's. Nothing better."

"Slightly better if you add the chili fries with onions."

"Good point."

"So, tell me a little about yourself, Ethan. I don't know much about you. Did you grow up with two parents? Any siblings?"

"Yes. I grew up with two parents, who were probably too young to have me. My mom got pregnant when she was nineteen and my dad was twenty. He was a surfer, and she was a student. They did whatever jobs they could get to keep us afloat. My dad worked at a fish and bait shop on the wharf and taught surfing. My mom was either working in retail or restaurants. They were always trying to make ends meet, sometimes not so successfully. But they were good parents. And when I was eight, my younger brother was born. I quickly realized that he would be my responsibility as well as theirs, but that was okay with me, because I loved him the second he was born."

I leaned forward, fascinated by the emotion I heard in his voice, making me realize how distant Ethan had been until now. "What did your parents think of you joining the Marines?" I asked.

"My mother was terrified I was going to die. My father distrusted institutions of any flavor, so he wasn't a fan of me signing up. But there was no money for college, so that wasn't an option. And I couldn't see myself working for next to no money like my parents had done their whole lives, always barely scraping by. When Steven started talking about joining up, I decided why not? I liked adventure."

"That's really how you thought about joining the Marine Corps?" I asked in surprise "That it would just be an adventure? You weren't worried about being killed?"

"Did I mention I was a stupid nineteen-year-old who didn't give it a lot of thought?"

"It must have been a shock when you found it was more than an adventure."

"I wanted to quit at least six times in the first week, but there was something about it I liked. I found a structure I'd longed for. My parents had had no rules. They were too busy working or enjoying the little free time they had to worry about what I was doing, and I was going down a dangerous road. With some distance, I could see that. When I joined the military, I grew up fast. I realized that there was a much bigger world out there, and I wanted to see it. I found a patriotism I hadn't really known I had. It felt good to protect my country, to feel like I was doing something that mattered. And while I missed my little brother, I was part of a very close team."

"It still must have been terrifying at times."

"It was, but I survived."

Hearing the passion in his voice as he described the military, I wondered where all that drive had gone, because he didn't seem to have it anymore. Even Tom had wondered why he was just drifting from job to job. "Why did you leave?" I asked.

"It was time," he said. "Coming home didn't turn out the way I had hoped, but it was still the best decision."

"Because Steven died."

"Yes," he said flatly.

"Do you miss being in the military?"

"I miss my unit, my friends, but I don't miss the action." He paused as the waiter delivered our food. "This looks good."

It did look good, but I was a little sorry the arrival of the food had interrupted our conversation. But Ethan was already digging in, so I did the same.

For a few moments, we just ate in comfortable silence. As we finished up, Ethan said, "Let's get back to you, Emily."

I sighed. "Do we need to?"

He smiled. "Tell me when you decided to be a director."

That was the easiest question he had ever asked me. "In high school when I joined the drama club," I answered. "I didn't know if I could actually do it. I didn't have an education. In fact, most of my school records were faked at one point or another. But I always loved the movies, escaping into a story that would take me far away from my life. I wanted to be a part of that world. I thought about acting, too. But that felt too close to the life I wanted to leave behind. I also thought about writing, but while I'm good at seeing the big picture, I get impatient writing down details. I see them in my head. I want to make them come to life through action and dialogue. So when I was in college, I focused on classes in directing, thinking that was my path. Only there aren't many female film directors, so I knew it would be an uphill battle."

I popped a sweet potato fry into my mouth and let out a sigh of pleasure.

Ethan smiled. "You look happier now."

"I feel better. Eating was a good idea. And this hits the spot."

"I agree," he said. "You mentioned college. Where did you go to film school?"

"USC."

He raised an eyebrow. "Hold on. You came from nothing, had no parents to speak of, no money, and you got into the University of Southern California? There's a story there."

"I got a scholarship," I said, feeling a little uncomfortable. "I was acting in high school and doing community theater, which gave me a chance to audition for the program, and I got in."

"How did you pay for it? Or did the scholarship cover everything? I know that school costs a ton of money."

"Uh..." I drew in a breath and let it out, knowing I was about to cross a line that I wouldn't be able to cross back. "Does it matter?"

"You decide."

I wiped my face with my napkin, happy I'd already demolished most of my meal, because my stomach was churning again. I'd never told anyone that story, either, but I'd already told him so much. What did one more truth matter? Plus, I was tired of keeping so many secrets. They were eating me up inside.

"Emily?" Ethan queried.

I took a breath and met his gaze. "I blackmailed Jimmy."

CHAPTER TWELVE

ETHAN'S BROW shot up at my words. "Do you want to explain that? I thought Jimmy dropped you off at his cousin's house, never to be seen again."

"I saw him one time after that, when I was eighteen. I had a partial scholarship, but I needed more money to make it all work. Rhea, Jimmy's cousin, couldn't help me. She suggested I see if Jimmy would help. That's when I realized she had an idea where he was. Apparently, he had given her some money to take care of me, which I didn't know. Although, she said it was only a minimal amount to cover food, which bothered her, because he was once again living in a luxury high-rise condo in Beverly Hills with some woman named Tina. From that information, I was able to find him."

I paused, thinking about when I had confronted him outside his building. "He was shocked to see me again. And when I told him what I needed, he said no, he didn't have any extra cash. I looked at the luxury building we were standing in front of, and anger ran through me. He was lying, and he owed me. I wasn't going to take no for an answer. I told him if he didn't help me out, I would go to the authorities and blow up his life."

Ethan gazed at me with a gleam of admiration. "That took some guts, especially doing it face-to-face."

"I was shaking on the inside. I'd never gone against him before. I'd always known that if I did, I'd lose what little security I had. But I had to take my shot."

"He just handed you the money?"

"No. At first, he argued with me, told me he could take me down, too. That my dream of graduating from USC would never happen. That terrified me. But I couldn't let him see that. Emotion was what Jimmy played off of. I lied and said I had evidence from the years we lived together and that if he didn't pay, it would be worth it to me to skip school in order to take him down."

"What did he do?" Ethan asked.

"He just looked at me. Silent, assessing, his bright-blue eyes piercing through me. I felt like a year passed in those few moments, a million things running through my mind, wondering if I'd blown it. But then he told me he would think about it. He asked me for my bank account number, and I gave it to him. After I left, I went to work at my part-time job at a grocery store, and about an hour later, it occurred to me he was probably going to drain my bank account, not make a deposit."

"I was wondering about that," Ethan said.

"I went online as soon as I got the chance, which was about two hours later. I was afraid that I'd see nothing but zeroes in my account. It wasn't like I had a lot of money, just a few thousand dollars from my various jobs, but it was all I had that was mine. But Jimmy hadn't drained the account. He had wired enough money into my account to pay for the first two years of school."

I blew out a breath and then continued, "I never heard from him again after that. And I figured out how to pay for the rest of my time there by working multiple jobs and applying for grants." I paused again. "I don't feel guilty for blackmailing him, but I do feel guilty for using money that he probably ripped off from someone else. Jimmy made no money by actually working, so it wasn't his money. I don't know whose it was. I made a promise to myself that I would never ask him for more. I would never lie or steal or blackmail anyone. I would start fresh, and I have kept that promise, although you might think I'm lying now." When he didn't answer right away, I said, "Do you think I'm lying?"

"No. I don't believe you're as good a liar as you think you are. You show a lot of emotions in your eyes, Emily. Most liars don't. They shut down emotion, because it gets in the way of a lie."

"That's true. That's how Jimmy was. He could be inscrutable. And if he showed emotion, it was deliberate." I ran my tongue over my dry lips, feeling parched from telling Ethan the rest of my story. "That's it. You know everything now."

"I doubt that."

"Well, maybe not all the little details of all the things we did, but that's the big stuff."

"Do you feel lighter now? Getting that heavy secret off your chest?"

"Surprisingly, I do. But I have to admit I'm wondering what you're thinking about me now."

"It doesn't matter what I think. It only matters what you think, Emily. Do you regret what you did?"

"No, I don't. I thought Jimmy owed me. And I was desperate to build a life for myself. I wanted to take control and live like a normal person inside the law. I needed money and an education to do that. I couldn't have a fake life anymore. I had to make something about myself true. I had to have an actual degree, not a pretend one. I needed to learn, not pretend to know things I didn't. And I made the most of school. I studied like crazy. I did internships. I worked part-time to cover everything else that I needed. All I did was work and study, and it paid off. It got me here. So, I don't regret it, but I wish it hadn't had to be that way."

"You were born into a life that no one would choose. As a

child, you had no choice but to do what Jimmy wanted you to do. You had to survive. You had to grow up," Ethan said. "And I understand how desperation can drive decisions. You used your desperation to go in a positive way, to change your life for the better."

"But it started with blackmail."

"Maybe that's what the note was referring to—the one on your mirror that said they knew what you did. Maybe Jimmy wants to pay you back for what you did to him."

I shook my head. "I can see why you'd think that, but it's not Jimmy's style."

"Isn't it? It sounds like he enjoys playing games, tormenting people, teasing out their fears, using that against them."

Frowning, I considered his suggestion. "That is true, but why would he wait ten years?"

"You're successful now. Maybe he wants his money back."

"I suppose it's not impossible."

"I have a question," Ethan said.

"Only one?" I asked lightly. "I thought you might have a thousand by now, or that you'd be finding a way to make a quick exit."

"Not a chance. You're one of the most interesting people I've ever met, Emily."

"I wish I was interesting for other reasons. What's your question?"

"What was the basis of your blackmail? Was it one event? Or just an accumulation of everything?"

"It was a vague, sweeping threat. I mentioned a few of the women he'd conned, like the last one I'd known about, Vanessa Chambers. She had left her husband for Jimmy, and in the almost two years she lived with us, he drained her dry, took everything she had, because she was head over heels for him. If he said jump, she asked how high. There were some other names I threw out, too, but it was all mostly just implied stuff. Jimmy had taught me the basics of blackmail before I was twelve. Evidence wasn't required, I just needed to threaten exposure, so that's what I did. I pretended I had been collecting proof of his crimes the last few years we were together in case I had to save myself. I used what he had taught me on him."

Ethan sat back in his chair as he thought about that. "I'm surprised he paid you off based on no hardcore evidence."

"He probably thought paying me off was cheaper than losing whatever sweet role he was playing out at the moment. And like I said before, it wasn't his money, so I didn't really take anything that was his."

"True." He gave me a smile. "I have to say, I'd like to meet Jimmy."

"Why?"

"Because he sounds like a character in a movie."

"Our life together felt like a movie. But I would have written the ending differently."

"Would you have?" he challenged. "I know he dumped you, but maybe that's what saved you in the end."

"I have wondered if that saved me, because it got me out of his world, out of his crimes." Pausing, I added, "So, what now?"

"Do you want dessert?"

"Absolutely."

He grinned at my enthusiastic response. "Hot fudge sundae, whipped cream, nuts, cherry on top?"

"No nuts. I'm allergic. But I'll take everything else."

Ethan looked around for our server and then waved him over.

After our table was cleared and the sundaes were on their way, I opened my bag and took out a piece of paper that I'd printed from my computer last night.

"What's that?' Ethan asked.

"I made a list of everyone who might hate me or want to punish me for something."

"Wow, you made an actual list," he said as I handed him the

paper. "And it's organized by time period and alphabetical. Impressive."

"I can't help it. I'm an organized list maker. It started when I was a little girl. When things got muddled, I made lists. A psychologist would probably say that was another way I thought I could control my life."

"You have a lot of people on here, Emily."

"Yeah, I'm pretty popular, huh?"

He smiled. "I'm sure all these people don't hate you." He glanced back at the list. "I see the high school group has expanded."

"I started thinking about Cassie mentioning Kimmy's fall down the stairs and how I was nearby when she fell, so maybe someone thought I pushed her."

"Maybe Kimmy thought you pushed her," he suggested. "Have you seen her again?"

"Not since high school. And she never acted like she believed I was responsible for her fall." I took a breath. "My class has its ten-year reunion this Saturday, though, so I could go and see these people."

"Wait. You have a class reunion coming up?"

I nodded, surprised by the interested gleam in his eyes. "Yes. Why does that intrigue you?"

"The timing. The reunion is about to happen, and someone shows up in your life, threatening to tell the world what you did. If the threat is tied to your past, then it might be coming from someone who's back in town for the reunion. In my experience, a lot of people return for their ten-year reunion. Not too much time has passed to make those relationships irrelevant, and some people want to show that they are nothing like they were in high school."

"That's true. But I wasn't going to go because I'd prefer not to think about any of my past that happened before I got to USC."

"Understandable," he muttered. "But you might need to dig into this group of girls a little more deeply."

That was the last thing I wanted to do, but he was probably right. I looked up as the waiter set down an enormous sundae in front of me. "Wow. I forgot these were huge."

"Somehow, I think we'll get through it," Ethan said, eagerly picking up his spoon.

I smiled and did the same, wanting to scoop up the fudge while it was still hot. Of course I had to get through a mound of whipped cream first, but I found a way. I only made it halfway through the sundae before I had to surrender, though. It was just too much. "I'm done," I said, sitting back in my chair.

Ethan finished the last spoonful of his dessert. "You still have some to go."

"Do you want the rest?"

"No, I'm good." He picked up the list once more, scanning through it again. "Your past is more than a little interesting, and while I see possible suspects from earlier in your life, I keep coming back to your current situation with Mitchell, the freak accident that he alleges you set up and the jealousy from your coworkers. That note could definitely have been referring to the propane tank explosion."

"I agree. And that happened within the last year, not ten years ago. I just hate the thought of this being someone I work with. My office is my second home."

"A home you found incredibly scary earlier tonight," he reminded me.

"True. And I'm more scared because I don't know what's coming next. Alfred Hitchcock had a famous quote: 'There is no terror in the bang, only in the anticipation of it.' That's what's filling me with fear. I have no idea where the danger is coming from or how bad it will get. Is this just about scaring me or about hurting me? Will it be an emotional hurt, a public shaming, or physical violence?"

Ethan's gaze turned serious. "It could be all three."

"That isn't reassuring."

"I don't think a lie will help you." He paused for a moment, then said, "I noticed you didn't put Ashton on your list."

"Why would I do that?" I asked in confusion. "Ashton doesn't know about my past. He wasn't in Australia. He has no motive to want to hurt me. And he was victimized, too."

"Well, that's what he said, but you don't know what really happened Friday night."

His words puzzled me. "It sounds like you have a theory. What is it?"

"I wouldn't call it a theory, but I have questions. Was he really drugged, or did he make a terrible decision and someone is going to blackmail him for it, so he's trying to prep an excuse for what he did?"

"Even if that's true, it happened after I got the note and was mugged, so how does he tie into what's happening to me?"

Ethan thought for a moment. "What if there's someone else who's in love with Ashton? She wants him. He wants you. You're in a love triangle you don't know anything about."

That was an idea I hadn't considered.

"Do you know anything about his past relationships?" Ethan asked.

"I know he's dated quite a few women, and his relationships have often been documented online. He never mentioned having a bad breakup, but to be honest, we haven't talked about other people. We've only been going out six weeks. It's just been fun stuff…no heavy, emotional talks."

"Well, you should have whatever investigator you hire look into his past, too."

I frowned. "Are you sure you can't just help me, Ethan? You have good instincts, and you seem to have friends who might be able to help, like Sophia."

"I can't protect you, Emily. And I don't have time to dedicate myself to your problem, which is what you need."

His answer was disappointing, even though I understood where he was coming from. "I get it. I just hate the idea of having to tell someone else everything I've told you. I'm not even sure I can do it all again."

"Maybe it gets easier the next time around. I know an investigator. I'll call him tomorrow and see if he can help you out."

"I would appreciate that. Otherwise, I'll just be picking someone out of the blue, and they might be totally worthless."

"Hopefully he can help you."

As the waiter stopped by the table to drop off our check, I quickly reached for it. "I've got this."

"We can split it."

"No. It's the least I can do."

"All right. Thank you."

A few minutes later, with the check paid, we headed out the door.

"I can follow you home and make sure you get in okay," Ethan said as we walked out to the parking lot.

"I'm not going to say no to that."

His car was nearby, and as we got closer to it, Ethan suddenly tensed.

"What the hell?" he muttered, as he strode forward.

I followed him to his car, seeing long scratches in the black paint. "It looks like someone wrote a word," I said, my gaze narrowing as the reality of that word became clear. "Oh, my God!"

"Emily," he said. And he wasn't talking to me—he was pointing to the name scratched on the car.

My heart pounded against my chest. Someone had followed us here to the restaurant, maybe the same someone who had been in the parking garage.

Ethan turned to scan the lot. There was a male teenager standing outside the restaurant, looking at his phone and smoking a cigarette. Ethan headed straight for him. "Hey," he said.

The kid looked up. "What?"

"Did you see anyone by the black SUV over there?"

"Uh, yeah," the teen said. "There was a girl. She looked like she was wiping something off."

"A girl," I echoed, my pulse leaping at the thought of suddenly getting some good information. "What did she look like?"

The kid gazed at me. "Well, she kind of looked like you."

CHAPTER THIRTEEN

"Me?" I asked, more shock running through me. "It wasn't me. I was in the restaurant."

"She had jeans on, and a white cropped sweater, just like what you're wearing," the kid said. "And her hair was the same —brown, long, loose. But I didn't see her face. Just the back of her." He straightened as he got a text. "I gotta go. My girlfriend is getting pissed that I'm still out here." He tossed his cigarette butt on the ground and then headed into the restaurant.

I met Ethan's gaze. "Someone followed us here from my office."

"Yeah," he said with annoyance. "I looked for a tail, but I didn't see anyone." He moved back to his car to examine the damage once more.

"I'm sorry," I said, as I joined him. "This is a warning for you to stay away from me."

"I got that."

"I'll pay for this to be repaired."

"I'm not worried about that."

"I guess we know it's a woman," I said.

"Does anyone on your list look like you?"

"Probably. I'm not that unique. Cassie has brown hair. Kaitlyn does, too. From the back, we might look alike. But that could be true of lots of other women."

"It's also possible this woman is part of a bigger crew."

"There seems to be a lot going on for one person. But a bigger crew doesn't feel right either because this is really personal."

"I agree. But a crew could just be one person and a friend."

As a breeze lifted my hair, I shivered despite the warm evening air. "I'm sorry about your car, Ethan. You want your life to be simple, and I keep complicating it."

"This isn't your fault. Let's get you home."

I wasn't thrilled to go home, but I also didn't like standing in the middle of a parking lot, where anyone could be watching, where something else could be about to happen.

"All right. When we get to my building, I'm going to pull into my garage. If you want to come in behind me, the code is 34657. There are three guest spots by the elevator. But if you don't want to come in, that's fine, too. I know I'm taking up a lot of your time."

"I'll go into the garage and walk you upstairs."

"Thanks. I feel a little nervous about entering another garage."

"Understandable."

Ethan walked me to my car, which was untouched, something that brought another irritated frown to his face, but he didn't comment on my perfect paint job, just waited until I had locked the door and then returned to his car.

As we left the lot, I wondered about the restaurant cameras. Maybe they had caught the person scratching Ethan's car. I was going to need someone to help me investigate because I had to go to work tomorrow, and I couldn't spend more time trying to chase down security footage that probably wouldn't reveal anything, anyway. Perhaps my car hadn't been touched because it was in view of the cameras and Ethan's was not. Or they'd just wanted to scare him away from helping me.

But he hadn't been scared; he'd been pissed. He was now

more invested in my problems, not less, and I secretly liked that. Because I felt like I needed him. When I'd run into his arms in the garage, I'd felt safe for the first time in a long time. I'd also felt comforted, which was another unusual experience. I'd been self-comforting myself since I was ten, but having someone put his arms around me and hold me in a moment of panic and terror had felt unbelievably good.

Not that I hadn't had a man hug me before, but this had been different. This hadn't been about passion or lust or sex. It was like I finally had someone I could count on, and that was a weird thought because I barely knew Ethan.

But we were getting to know each other better. Since Friday night, he'd been a constant and increasing presence in my life, coming at a time when everyone else's presence was suspect, when my current relationship seemed to be falling apart and I wasn't even sure why.

Ashton was like a ghost now. I'd barely thought about him today, and that was telling. I hadn't rushed to call him, and he hadn't rushed to call me. What did that say about us?

We definitely needed to have a conversation, but it would have to be tomorrow. It was almost eight here, nearly eleven in New York. Maybe Monday would bring some clarity to my life. Or maybe it would bring the opposite: more chaos, more fear, and whatever intangible something that someone was dragging me toward. That's what I really worried about—where all this was going. But I had no answers and there probably weren't any more coming tonight. I'd regroup tomorrow.

Ten minutes later, I pulled into the underground garage at my building, and Ethan followed me inside and grabbed one of the guest parking spots.

As I got out of my car, I saw my neighbor Monica putting something in the trunk of her vehicle, which was parked one spot away from mine. Monica had on denim shorts and a gauzy top, bright, dangling earrings hanging from her ears.

"Hi, Emily," Monica said, as she shut her trunk. "How's it going?"

"Good," I lied. "How about you?"

"I had a great day. Went to the Santa Monica Pier with a woman I met in my yoga class. It was nice to have someone to hang around with."

Ethan gave me a questioning look as he joined us, his gaze encompassing both of us. I realized in that moment that Monica also had brown hair about my length, but her eyes were more gold than brown.

"Hello," he said, giving Monica a nod.

"Uh, hi," Monica replied. "You look familiar."

"I work security for the jewelry store next door."

"Oh, of course. That's where I've seen you. I'm Monica Paul, Emily's neighbor."

"Ethan Burke."

"Ethan has been trying to help me figure out who mugged me Friday night," I said, feeling like I needed to give Monica some explanation for why I was with Ethan when she knew I was dating Ashton. Although, why I felt I had to explain anything was beyond me. But since I'd been living my authentic life, I seemed to care more about what people thought of me, maybe because I was putting the real me on display.

"Any luck?" Monica asked.

"Not yet."

"I really wish the police could catch the guy. I think twice every time I go out the front door now," she added as we walked toward the garage lobby.

"So do I," I said. "How's your grandmother feeling?"

"Improved," Monica said, as we got on the elevator. "She's bounced back a little. She still needs care, and I don't think she'll be getting out of rehab any time soon, but I'm hopeful one day she'll be back in her own bedroom. I'll be sad to leave then but happy to know she's home."

"Give her my best, will you?" I asked as we walked down the hall, and Monica paused in front of her door.

"I will. She asks about you, too, Emily. She says you're a sweet girl, and she keeps hoping you'll find the right guy." Monica gave me a mischievous look. "Seems like I should tell her you're doing just fine."

"I am doing fine," I replied, ignoring the innuendo in her comment. Clearly, she thought I was messing around with both Ethan and Ashton.

"Have a good night," Monica said, as she entered her unit.

As I unlocked my door and pushed it open, I silently prayed that there would be no unwelcome surprises waiting for me inside. I had changed the locks, but I wasn't sure a lock could stop my stalker. They seemed able to get into all aspects of my life with no problem. On the other hand, I had the only keys to this lock in my tight possession the last twenty-four hours, so I should be good.

My condo was quiet, and nothing appeared out of place. There were no open doors, nothing overturned, and I let out a breath of relief as I turned on all the lights and drove the darkness away. I wished it was that easy to do in the rest of my life.

Ethan walked through my apartment and came back with a smile. "Everything looks good to me."

"Me, too. Thank goodness."

"The woman across the hall. How long have you known her?" he asked.

"About three weeks. Her grandmother, Delores, fell and has been in rehab for a few months. Monica moved in so she could be closer to her grandmother." I paused. "Are you asking about Monica because she has brown hair? Because half the women in LA do."

"Maybe a quarter," he said with a small smile. "A lot of blondes around here. But I get what you're saying. You mentioned her grandmother had a key to your place."

"I don't think Monica would know that. I certainly never told her."

"Perhaps her grandmother did."

"I doubt it. And Monica would have nothing against me. We barely know each other." I paused as I heard my phone buzz with an incoming text. I took it from my bag to see a text from an unknown number. As I clicked on the text, photos appeared, and I gasped.

"What's wrong?" Ethan asked.

I stared at the first image in horror, and that horror only deepened when I saw the next two photographs.

Ethan moved closer to me, looking over my shoulder.

"Is that you?" he asked.

"No, it's not me," I snapped. "It's Ashton and some woman having sex. This has to be from Friday night."

"Her hair looks about the same length as yours," he mused as he gave me a long look.

"Well, like I said, it's not me."

"But they want people to think it's you."

"I don't know if that's true."

"Oh, I think it is." He took the phone out of my hand and enlarged the pictures. "This isn't just about sex; it's also about drugs. Look at the nightstand."

"Ashton doesn't do drugs."

"Maybe it's part of the setup." He handed me back the phone.

I didn't want to look at the photos again, but I knew I had to. I couldn't run away from this. I couldn't miss a clue. But I felt sick to my stomach as I saw the look on Ashton's face as the woman straddled him, her brown hair falling down her back, exactly the same length as mine.

"Maybe this is about blackmail. But does that make sense?" I looked back at Ethan. "These photos will hurt Ashton more than me, because this isn't me."

"They're going to imply it is you. That's why you were sent the photos."

"Okay." I tried to think how that would work. "Let's say it was me, and I was having sex with my boyfriend—how is that so damning?"

"The drugs on the nightstand."

"That's true. That's not good. But I work in Hollywood, Ethan. Sex and drugs don't take people down. It's not like Ashton is a politician or a married man."

"I think it's just a piece of the puzzle," he said. "You need to figure out what the puzzle is going to look like when it's done, because if you don't get ahead of this soon…"

His voice trailed away, and I could easily finish the sentence. "It's going to be too late to stop them."

He met my gaze. "Yes."

CHAPTER FOURTEEN

MY PHONE BUZZED AGAIN, this time with an incoming call. I looked at the name flashing across the screen. "It's Ashton," I said.

"You should take that. Do you want me to leave?" Ethan asked.

"Could you wait? He might have more information."

"Sure. I'll give you some privacy."

I answered the call as Ethan opened the doors to the deck and stepped outside. "Ashton?"

"God, Emily! My life is so fucked up," Ashton said.

"I know. Someone just sent me photos of you and a woman in bed together," I said, a little irritated that his first sentence had only been about himself. But I tried to give him a little leeway for that. He was the target in this latest incident. It was understandable that he was upset. I also realized he didn't know what else had happened to me. That was my fault, not his.

"I don't remember anything from that night," he said. "I know someone drugged me. It's the only explanation."

"Have you gotten a request for money to not publish the photos?"

"Not yet. Just a text message saying there are lots more, as well as a video. I can't believe this is happening to me. Just when I have a chance to get taken more seriously as an actor."

"What do you mean?" I asked, confused by his words.

"I had another chat today with Mitchell about the role of Dominic. I know everyone thinks I can only do comedy, but I like the darkness of Dominic's soul, hidden by his dry humor. I can bring that character to life, Emily."

"I don't understand how you even know that much about the character if you just glanced at the script in my apartment one night. And that draft is being rewritten."

"Mitchell sent me a copy of the script."

"When did he do that? You just talked to him Friday night."

"He sent it yesterday. Do we have a problem, Emily?"

I heard the terse note in his voice. "We have a lot of problems, Ashton, and the biggest one isn't the role of Dominic. The woman that you're with in the photos—do you think she looks like me?"

"What? No. Of course not. I mean, it wasn't you." He paused. "It wasn't you, was it?"

"Absolutely not," I said, astounded by his question. "I was at home that night after getting mugged, remember?"

"Hey, you brought it up. Why would you even say she looks like you? I can't see her face in the photos I saw."

"And nothing about the photos rings a bell in your mind as to her identity?"

"Zero. I don't know if I had sex with her or if it was just made to look that way."

"What about the drugs? Did you have drugs on you?"

"No," he snapped. "I don't do that shit. Do you even know me at all?"

"How could I? We've only been going out for six weeks."

"I'm sorry." He let out a breath. "I'm pissed. And I'm taking it out on you. It's late here. I need to go to bed, but I don't think I can sleep. I hope these photos don't derail my career. I need you on my side for the part of Dominic, Emily."

"Do you?" I asked wearily. "Mitchell will have final say, not me. And it sounds like he wants you."

"I want you to be happy about it."

"Right now, I'm having trouble being happy about anything."

"I know you're upset about the photos. But I didn't knowingly cheat on you, Emily, if that's even what happened. Anyway, I'm burned out. We'll talk tomorrow."

Before I could tell him there were a lot more things we needed to talk about tonight, he was gone.

"Dammit," I muttered, angry with him, myself, and the whole situation.

I walked out to the balcony, feeling the need for some fresh air. Ethan was leaning against the railing, looking out at the city, his brown hair mussed from the wind. He turned to me. "Are you all right?"

At his simple question, I realized that's what I'd wanted Ashton to say, but the man I'd been seeing hadn't asked me anything about myself, my situation. Maybe he didn't know it all because I hadn't filled him in, but he knew I'd been robbed. He knew I'd gotten the same disturbing photos he had, but his first thoughts—and maybe all his thoughts—had been for himself, his situation, what was going to happen to him.

But Ethan was here for me. He'd gone above and beyond to help me, and now he had a damaged vehicle because of it. But he was still here. And I felt both gratitude and something else I didn't really want to define as our gazes clung together.

"Emily?" he questioned, as if reading something on my face. "What's going on?"

I pushed aside the odd feelings running through my body. I had too much to think about. I couldn't put Ethan in the mix. "Ashton got the same photos—or, actually, I don't know if they were the same, but he got a text with the threat of more photos and a video."

"Is he supposed to pay them off?"

"That's the thing. There wasn't a demand attached to it, which is confusing."

"It's probably coming. Whoever is running this play we're a part of enjoys making people sweat."

I felt sweaty right now and was grateful when a light breeze lifted my hair off the back of my neck. "It's like they get an evil pleasure out of watching me squirm." I looked down at the street. "Maybe they're watching me now, hidden in some car or a doorway."

"Do you want to go inside?"

"I think so," I said, heading into the living room. As we sat down on the couch, I said, "Ashton is terrified that the photos will hurt his reputation as a serious actor. I didn't realize he was so worried about his image. I thought he was happy being known as a television comedic actor. Apparently, he wants more dramatic film roles."

Ethan's gaze narrowed. "Is that what you were talking about?"

"Yes. He wants a part in the movie I'll be co-directing with Mitchell, and I guess they're talking about it, and now he's afraid of what these photos or video will mean for him."

"Like you said, it's Hollywood. Is it really going to hurt him?" Ethan asked dryly.

"I don't know. Maybe if he has to come up with a lot of cash to get rid of them, that will hurt." I tucked my hair behind my ears. "I didn't have time to tell him anything about what's going on with me. He said he was exhausted, and he was going to bed. It is late there. I understand that he's upset. He was drugged and used. That's terrible."

"You're making a lot of excuses for him, Emily."

"I'm just trying to see things from his point of view," I said defensively.

"Or you don't want to see him for who he is."

"You don't know who he is, Ethan."

"Do you?" he challenged.

I wanted to say I did, but I wasn't sure anymore. "I don't know," I admitted.

"Even if Ashton didn't know all the shit that has been going on with you, he should have been worried about what you would think of the photos. Staged or not, you're looking at your boyfriend having sex with another woman."

"But he didn't know what he was doing. I don't think his eyes were open. Were they?" My hand tightened around my phone. "I really don't want to look at the photos again."

"Then don't."

"It feels like this situation has to do with me, too. But I don't understand the connection, the motivation to screw with Ashton like that. Maybe your love triangle idea is more on the mark than I thought."

"It would make sense now that we've seen the photos. A lot of planning went into that setup, too. It wasn't like sending you a note with a couple of words on it."

"I agree."

"You said your assistant was with him after your event. Why don't you ask her if she knows where he went after the first bar and who he went with?"

"I guess I could do that tomorrow."

"It's not that late."

I frowned. "I've never called Kaitlyn at home. It seems unprofessional."

"It's more unprofessional to have a conversation about your boyfriend at work," he countered.

"Good point. I'll call her."

"Put it on speaker, if you don't mind."

"All right." Opening my phone, I punched in her number.

"Hello? Emily?" Kaitlyn asked, surprise in her voice. "Is something wrong?"

I had no idea how to answer that question. Kaitlyn talked a lot. I needed to be careful. "Ashton lost his phone on Friday night. He's desperate to find it. He said he went somewhere after Harry's, but his memories are a little off."

"Ashton doesn't remember where he went?" Kaitlyn asked, eager interest in her voice. "Was he that drunk? He didn't seem that drunk. Unless—was he doing other stuff? He and Liam disappeared for a while."

I ignored her stomach-churning question. "Do you know where Ashton went after he left Harry's? Did you see him leave with someone?"

"Like another woman?"

I sighed. This phone call was a bad idea. "With anyone who might know where he went after leaving Harry's."

"He might have left with Tara, Mitchell's wife. Or maybe both of them. Tara and Mitchell joined us at Harry's after the party." Kaitlyn paused. "I'm pretty sure it was Tara that I saw him talking to by the door. She has brown hair, and I remember seeing him with a brunette. Mitchell was probably with them."

I was beginning to wonder about the sudden connection between Ashton and Mitchell. I was also wondering when Ashton's interest in the movie had begun. Had he sought me out because of my connection to the movie? I thought it had all been happenstance.

"Do you have any idea where they went?" I asked again.

"Well, there was some talk about them going to Ravenswood, that new bar in Beverly Hills. I don't know if that's where they ended up. Sorry."

"It's fine."

"Did Ashton ask you to talk to me?" Kaitlyn asked.

"No, and I'd prefer if you didn't say anything to anyone. He's just trying to find his phone."

"He should be worried about losing his phone. He's a star. If the wrong person gets into his phone, that could be bad. Maybe check with Mitchell or Liam."

Mitchell was the last person I was going to call. "Thanks. I'll let Ashton contact them. I'll see you tomorrow."

"Sure. Hey, Emily, before you go... I've been meaning to talk to you. I know I've only been on the job for three months, but I also know you'll be hiring a crew for *Aces High,* and I'd love to work on set. What can I do to make that happen? I will do anything. I want to watch you work. You're one of the top rising directors. It would be amazing to see you in action. I know I could learn a lot."

"I'll think about it. Those decisions won't be made for a few weeks. And Mitchell will be directing."

"I know. He's good, too, of course. Anyway, I just wanted to put myself out there. I love working for you, Emily. I'm excited to learn as much as I can."

"I understand. We'll keep talking about it."

"Okay. Good night."

As the call disconnected, I turned to Ethan. "That wasn't very helpful."

"I thought it was interesting," Ethan replied.

"You did? Kaitlyn didn't know much of anything."

"Maybe Ashton and Mitchell are working together. And if Tara has brown hair…"

I sighed. "I have to remind you again that many people look like me. I'm not very special. Brown hair, brown eyes, girl next door. There are millions like me."

He smiled. "You're underrating yourself, Emily. You are not as common as you think."

I gave him a doubtful look. "I have a mirror."

"I don't think you see yourself for who you are when you look at that mirror. In fact, I'm not sure you know who you really are."

"I did know who I was," I contradicted. "I was a hard-working film producer and director who was making movies and moving her way up in the industry, and I was doing it all without lying or scamming or faking it."

"But that's not the girl you see in the mirror, is it?"

His provocative words gave me pause. "Maybe not."

"You've been running away from her for ten years."

"That might be true. But she's catching up fast. And since when did you become a psychoanalyst?"

He shrugged. "Just telling you what I see."

"Is that what you do in front of the jewelry store? Try to predict who might want to lift a thousand-dollar necklace?"

"More like a fifty-thousand-dollar necklace," he corrected. "And, yes, it's part of it."

"Well, instead of analyzing me, I'd rather hear your thoughts about Kaitlyn."

"She wants your job."

"Every assistant I've ever hired has wanted my job, and when I was an assistant, I wanted my boss's job."

"That's fair. But she seems a little over-the-top."

"She isn't afraid to ask for what she wants," I agreed. "I'm going to keep an eye on her. But she's not worrying me as much as Ashton is. I wonder if he has been using me the entire time we've been together. I thought we met by chance at the gym. I dropped my wallet, and he picked it up, and we started talking. I couldn't believe how nice and down-to-earth he was, as well as charming and funny. I was headed to the café for a juice, and he came with me, and then he asked for my number. It felt so much better than swiping on someone's photo online. And he was a celebrity, a TV star. He wasn't like the struggling writers or actors I usually ran into. Nor was he boring or in a job I didn't understand. We had a lot in common. It was easy." My voice trailed away as I realized how foolish I'd been. "It could have been a setup. I saw Jimmy set women up like that a million times. Why didn't I question his sudden interest in me?" I shook my head in annoyance. "I guess I was rusty. I wasn't living on the edge anymore. I didn't have my guard walls up. I was an easy mark."

"Don't be so hard on yourself, Emily. Obviously, Ashton is a good actor. And maybe it's not so cut-and-dried. He could have learned about the movie after you got together and was afraid to show you how much he wanted it because he didn't want it to get in the way of your relationship."

"Now you're a relationship counselor?"

He grinned. "Definitely not that. Forget everything I just said. I have no idea if he used you or not. I was just trying to make you feel better."

"Then tell me what you really think."

"He sounds like a self-absorbed actor. Whether he was using you from the beginning or not, who knows? But I think it's strange he's been very out of touch since you got mugged, and also odd that you don't seem to feel the need to tell him what's going on."

"I didn't have a chance," I said again.

"Maybe on this last phone call. But you weren't eager to tell him about your problems before this."

"I told you why—I didn't want to get into my past with him. Our relationship was too new, and I didn't want to complicate the situation."

"Then maybe you're both to blame."

"That's not what I wanted to hear."

He laughed again. "Well, I rarely tell anyone what they want to hear."

"You just like to speak the truth."

"That usually keeps my life simpler." He got to his feet. "I'm going to take off. Lock the door after me. Call me if you have any more problems."

I stood up, feeling a little panicked at the idea of being alone, but I couldn't ask Ethan to stay. I'd already asked far too much of him already. "When—when will I talk to you again?" I asked, hating the needy note in my voice, but I couldn't hide it.

"Well, I'll be on the sidewalk tomorrow, so I won't be hard to find," he drawled.

"That's true."

"Oh, wait. Sophia wanted to look at your laptop computer.

Can you give it to me now? I can drop it off to her tomorrow morning. Or do you need it tonight?"

"Um..." I hesitated. I had work to do, but was I really going to do it? I felt suddenly exhausted. "I guess I don't need it. I'll get it for you." I walked over to the dining room table and unplugged it, then brought it back to Ethan. "How long do you think she'll need it?"

"No longer than a day. I'll make sure you get it back tomorrow night. So I guess I'll see you then."

"Good," I said, liking the fact that we now had a plan. "Thank you, Ethan, for everything you've done for me. And if you have a name of a private investigator, I will reach out tomorrow."

"I'll check with him in the morning and text you." He paused. "I wish I could help you more."

"You've done a lot already, and none of this is your problem. Well, maybe the car is your problem. I'll pay to get those scratches painted over."

"We'll worry about that later."

He opened the door, then paused. "You can always call me, Emily. Even if you just wake up in the middle of the night and hear a noise and start spinning out. I'm reachable."

He was starting to know me a little too well, and I felt incredibly touched by his offer. "Why are you being so nice to me?" I asked, genuinely curious. "I've caused you nothing but trouble."

He gave a helpless shrug. "When I figure it out, I'll let you know."

CHAPTER FIFTEEN

Somehow, I managed to sleep on Sunday night, which seemed like a miracle considering how many things were running through my mind. I woke up Monday morning feeling better than I had the day before. One thing I knew was that I had to go on the attack. I couldn't keep waiting for the other shoe to drop. I had my list of suspects. At the very least, I needed to check some of them off the list.

I got my first chance when I arrived at work. Kaitlyn brought me a coffee and joined me for our standard Monday morning meeting where we planned out the week.

As we sat down in my office together, I noticed more similarities between us than I had before. We didn't look alike, but we matched up in the things someone might notice: The color of our hair and the length of it. We were about the same height. I was probably a few pounds heavier than her, but not noticeably. However, Kaitlyn had blue eyes and mine were brown. You couldn't miss that. However, from a distance and from the back, no one would know that.

"Are you all right, Emily?" Kaitlyn asked, as I sipped my coffee and stared at her from the other side of my desk. "It seems like something is bothering you. Is it that I asked you for too much last night on the phone? I hung up thinking you were annoyed with me. I was pushing too hard. I can do that sometimes. But I can also back off. I just really want to do well on this job."

There was no mistaking the earnest light in her eyes. I believed she wanted to do well, and she wanted to get ahead. I just didn't know how far she would go to get there. But instead of wondering, maybe it was time to ask her. "Could you close the door?" I asked.

She gave me a surprised look and then got up to shut the door. When she sat back down, there was worry in her eyes. "Now you're making me nervous."

"Did you leave Harry's Bar with Ashton on Friday night?"

"What? No," she said quickly. "I told you he left with another woman, a dark-haired woman…probably Tara, Mitchell's wife."

"Someone else told me he was with a brunette who looked a bit like me."

Kaitlyn stared back at me, a question in her eyes. "Are you saying you think we look alike?"

"From a distance, someone could make that assumption."

"I didn't hook up with Ashton, Emily, if that's what you're asking. I wouldn't do that to you. You're my boss. You're my friend. How could you think that?"

"Well, you've been talking to Ashton more than I knew. You spoke to him about the movie that is under wraps."

"Ashton brought it up to me. He knew everything about the story, and the character he was interested in. I thought you'd spoken to him about it. I didn't know I was telling him a secret. He said you let him read the script."

"I didn't. If he read it in my apartment, it was without my knowledge."

"That's not what he made it sound like. I'm sorry, Emily. I thought you'd talked about it with him. He just wanted to know if I'd read the script and whether I thought he might be good for the role of Dominic. I told him I was a big fan of his and thought he could bring some interesting undertones to that character, because Dominic is darkly funny, and we know Ashton can be funny. I liked the guest appearance he did on that legal show, *Courtside*, a couple of years ago, where he showed a more serious side." Kaitlyn paused. "How can I make this right?"

"First of all, you need to stop talking so much."

"I can do that."

"And not just to Ashton. You told Mitchell about my lunch with Natasha Rodrigo and Francine, and he showed up to it."

A frown crossed her face. "That was kind of the same thing, Emily. Mitchell said he was supposed to go to lunch with you, but he forgot the name of the restaurant and the time. He wanted to know where to go. That's why I told him. You never said he wasn't invited. He is going to direct the movie, and he's way above my pay grade, so when he asked a question, I felt I had to answer. I didn't want him to miss a meeting."

"You could have told me that he'd asked you for the information."

"It was Friday night. You had already gone home, and, frankly, I forgot about it. I didn't know it was a big deal."

Kaitlyn seemed to have an answer for everything, and I had to admit her reasoning made sense to me. It would have been easy to assume I'd told Ashton about the part and that Mitchell had been invited to lunch. Maybe I was being too hard on her. "Okay," I said. "Let's chalk all this up to a learning curve. But in the future, please don't discuss my meetings with anyone else, even if they're above your pay grade."

"Not even Francine, David, or Curtis?" she queried.

"If they ask you, then say you'll need to speak to me first."

She gave me a doubtful look. "All right. If that's what you want."

"And no more discussions with Ashton about business."

"You're angry with him, aren't you?" Kaitlyn asked. "He said he thought you might not want him to be in the movie because of your personal relationship."

"My relationship with Ashton is not your business," I snapped. "This is exactly what I'm talking about. We have to have boundaries, and my personal life is off-limits."

"I'm sorry. I understand. I won't discuss movie stuff with Ashton. But can I just say one more thing? I told Ashton I didn't know what you would think about him wanting to be in your movie and that he should ask you. And it feels like you should be talking to him right now. He played me for information. It wasn't the other way around."

Kaitlyn had a point. Maybe I was blaming her for Ashton's actions. "I will talk to him. I just want us to be on the same page. We're a team, right?"

"Yes, we are," Kaitlyn assured me. "I want to be the best assistant you've ever had, Emily. I know I sometimes gossip too much. I will watch it."

"Okay. Then let's go over the schedule for this week."

Kaitlyn was eager to turn to business, and so was I. While I hadn't gotten much information out of her, at least I'd let her know I was aware of her loose talk, and hopefully she'd be more discreet in the future. Whether or not she was involved in trying to ruin my life, I couldn't see the motivation, but I also couldn't check her off the list. Just because she was eager and ambitious didn't mean she was trying to stab me in the back. Although it also didn't mean that she wasn't.

That was a dark thought, and when we'd finished talking about the calendar, I was happy to wave her on her way. I didn't want to distrust the people I worked with, but I couldn't seem to help it, and I felt more alone than I ever had.

Thankfully, Roy's revised script appeared in my inbox, and I settled in to read for the next few hours.

After a quick lunch at my desk, I'd realized three things. The revised script was great. Ashton would probably be good for the role of Dominic, but his backhanded way of going after the role still grated. And, lastly, Mitchell and Roy had had a conversation without me because there were two new scenes listed per Mitchell's request. Not that Mitchell had no right to jump in. He was directing, so he was ultimately in charge. But it just emphasized my new role going forward as basically his assistant, even though I'd been working with Roy since the beginning. Now Roy was answering to Mitchell and not to me. That was a reality I could not ignore.

As I finished putting my notes on the script, Ashton called.

"It's getting worse," he said, barely getting out a hello before he launched into a rant. "They sent me a video, and they want five hundred thousand dollars by tonight, or the photos and video go up online."

"What? That's a lot of money." Ashton was a TV star, so maybe not too much for him to pay, but it seemed ridiculously high to me, especially for photos or a sex tape that might or might not hurt his career.

"They also texted me that you're going to be named as the woman in the video," he added.

"But it's not me, and my face isn't shown, so how could anyone know for sure?"

"The way it's shot, it could have been you."

"But I wasn't there, Ashton. Whoever you had sex with was not me."

"I can't believe I was in any condition to have sex with someone. This only happened because I was drugged."

"Did you get a hold of Liam? Does he know who you left the bar with?"

"He said he didn't see me leave."

"Someone must have seen you. Maybe you should go to Harry's Bar and talk to the people who work there."

"Oh, sure, that won't draw any more attention," he said with an angry, sarcastic snap in his voice.

"Well, I don't see how you're going to find out who did this without talking to someone. I asked Kaitlyn if she saw you leave Harry's, and she mentioned you were talking to Tara, Mitchell's wife. She thought you left with her. That you were all talking about going to Ravenswood."

"I vaguely remember that. I was talking to Mitchell and Tara for a while, but I'm sure I saw them leave the bar before me. I don't know what to do, Emily. Do I pay the blackmailer off?"

"Can you afford to do that? And even if you paid them, how do you know they wouldn't put the video up, anyway? I think you have to ride this out."

"That's easy for you to say. It's not your career on the line. If you'd stayed at the party Friday night, this never would have happened."

His petulant tone annoyed the hell out of me. "And if I'd never met you, maybe it wouldn't have happened, either," I said, feeling an icy chill down deep in my bones. "Was our meeting at the gym a setup, Ashton?"

"What are you talking about? You dropped your wallet. Why would you even say that, Emily?"

"Because I'm beginning to think our entire relationship was about you getting the part of Dominic in *Aces High*."

"That's insane. I can't believe you would think that."

"Well, you read the script without telling me, spoke to Kaitlyn about it, got me to introduce you to Mitchell, and then you went to a bar with him and his wife and apparently struck up a quick friendship. It feels like I was just a stepping stone for you to become a serious film actor."

"You don't think I could get there without you?" he challenged.

"Actually, I think you could do anything without me. That's what I liked about you, Ashton—that you were successful in your own right, that you didn't need me, and that I didn't have to worry about you using me. But you know how I feel right now? Used." I hadn't really meant to say all that, but it had just come pouring out. "You went behind my back. I didn't leave that script on my table. You had to have gone through my bag to find it and read it."

"I didn't. It was on the table. You left it out one night, and I was up early the next morning. I started reading it, and I couldn't stop. I never used you. But we can talk more about this later. I can't do it now. I'm in the middle of a disaster."

"I'm in the middle of something, too," I said, not sure I would get the words in before he hung up.

"What are you talking about? Work? Mitchell?" he asked impatiently.

"No, it's something else, something more insidious, more dangerous and terrifying. My mugging on Friday night was part of it. Someone broke into my apartment after that. I've gotten threatening notes, and I found out that there was spyware put on my computer. Someone has been watching me through the camera on my desktop."

"Are you serious? Why didn't you tell me all this before?"

"Because you haven't been available. I was going to tell you last night, but you were flipping out about the photos and then you hung up on me. You didn't even ask me how I was doing." I sounded like a whiny girlfriend, and I hated being that girl, but I also didn't want to be the woman who let her boyfriend walk all over her. "Anyway, I don't know if what happened to you is related to what is happening to me, but there's a possibility that it is, especially since they claim they're going to state that the woman in the photos is me."

"This is about you?" he mused. "Well, that's a unique spin, isn't it? Maybe they figure I'll pay to protect you."

"Maybe. But I don't want you to pay. I don't need you to do that for me. They can't prove it was me because it wasn't."

"It looks like you were doing drugs and having sex with me. It could hurt you, Emily, just like it could hurt me. Have you spoken to Francine about all this?"

"Not yet, but I was thinking about it," I admitted.

"You should. I just got off the phone with Mitchell and explained what's going on. Of course, I didn't know how you might be involved in it, except that they were going to claim the woman in the video was you. Based on what I told him, he advised me not to pay, just to let it go. He didn't think it would hurt me that much. He thought it might hurt you more."

"Why would it hurt me more?"

"Because you want to be seen as a serious director, and you look like a party girl with a sex and drug addiction."

"Did you show him the photos and video? How would he know what I look like?"

"I sent him everything. I wanted to get his opinion, and I told him you can confirm that this was all a setup. You can do that, can't you? Because I really want the role of Dominic, and I can't let this tape get in the way of that."

"Sure," I said wearily. "But then we're done, Ashton."

"We're not done. We've just hit a bump. We'll get through it."

My hand tightened on the phone. "We won't get through it. And it's not because of the photos. It's because I can see who you are now."

"I'm who I've always been," he protested. "You're just worked up about everything else and blaming me for it."

"I'm not blaming you for any of it. But I don't like that you keep going around me to get to Mitchell."

"He's in charge, Emily. I know you're not happy about it, but it's the way it is."

"That part is more important to you than our relationship."

"It shouldn't have to be one or the other. You should want the best for me, just as I want the best for you. I told you I'd be a good buffer between you and Mitchell, and I will be."

I sighed, seeing Francine out in the hall. I needed to talk to her more than I needed to speak to Ashton. "I have to go."

"We're not deciding anything right now," he said hastily. "We'll work everything out when I get back to LA."

"Goodbye, Ashton." I ended the call, feeling a little shaky. He probably hadn't thought it was our last goodbye, but it felt that way to me. No matter what he said, I couldn't trust him anymore.

I got to my feet as Francine appeared in my doorway, a serious expression on her face. "Emily, we need to talk."

"I was thinking the same thing. Do you want to come in?"

"No. We're going to have a meeting in the conference room in ten minutes. David, Curtis, and Mitchell will join us."

My heart sank. "You know about the pictures, the sex tape," I said, seeing the truth in her concerned eyes.

"Yes. I wish you'd given me a heads-up before Ashton talked to Mitchell and got him all worked up. Mitchell wants you off the movie, and David and Curtis don't know what to think. I felt like an idiot being the last one to find out, Emily. Why didn't you tell me?"

"I'm sorry. Everything has happened really fast. Can we speak now before everyone else gets to the conference room?"

Francine shook her head. "I'm afraid I can't. We'll all hash this out together in ten minutes."

I nodded as Francine moved down the hall to her office. This conference would not go well for me. I could feel it. Maybe Mitchell was behind my problems because it looked like he might get his wish to remove me from his movie. I needed to convince the others that would be a huge mistake. I just didn't know how I would do that.

CHAPTER SIXTEEN

As I left my office to go to the conference room, I ran into Tara Gray, Mitchell's wife. She was standing next to Kaitlyn's desk, and they were chatting like they were old friends. What the hell was going on? When did Kaitlyn become so chummy with Tara? It had to have happened Friday night. I really should not have left that party early.

Tara looked attractive in a mid-length sleeveless dress and wedge heels, her brown hair falling around her shoulders, much like mine was today. I frowned at that thought. But we weren't close to the same age. Tara was forty-six years old. Although, she probably could pass for someone in their thirties. I didn't know if she'd been blessed with good genes or a generous cosmetic surgery budget, but something was working for her.

"Hello, Tara," I said, putting a polite smile on my face. "It's nice to see you again."

"Emily," she said, an odd glint in her eyes, as if she knew something I didn't, which she probably did. "I'm sorry about all the trouble."

"If you're referring to the sex tape that Ashton is in, it's his problem not mine. I wasn't the woman in the pictures or the video."

"Really?" Tara asked doubtfully. "The woman in the photos I saw looked just like you. And Ashton said they're claiming it's you."

"It wasn't Emily," Kaitlyn cut in. "Emily went home early Friday night." She gave me an earnest look. "I know it wasn't you."

"Does everyone here know about the pictures and the video?" I asked.

"I don't know about everyone," Kaitlyn hedged. "But Tara just mentioned it to me, and after what you said about Ashton losing his phone, I put two and two together."

"Well, you're right. I was home Friday night. It wasn't me in the video or the still photos."

"So it was your boyfriend with someone else?" Tara asked. "That can't feel good, either."

"It doesn't. But Ashton was set up."

"That's what he told Mitchell," Tara said with a nod. "I can see how that could happen. Celebrities like Ashton will always be a target. Hollywood is a rough business. Someone is waiting for you to turn around so they can stab you in the back."

"Do you know who Ashton left the bar with Friday night?" I asked. "He said he spoke to you at Harry's."

"Yes. We talked for a bit, but I don't know where he went after that. Clearly, somewhere, he shouldn't have gone." Tara paused. "At first, Mitchell was upset about the video, because he's very interested in using Ashton in the upcoming film. I reminded him that any press can be good press. Ashton is a sexy guy. Girls will be dying to see that video and the guys will just think Ashton is doing okay for himself," she said, with a cynical note in her voice. "Men never really suffer from leaked videos. Women sometimes do."

I wondered if she was trying to warn me. Not that she'd care about giving me a warning. While we'd had a relatively pleasant relationship in Australia before Mitchell's accident, after that she'd clearly been persuaded to see me as an enemy.

"Emily," Kaitlyn said hesitantly. "I see Francine motioning to you."

"Right." I could also see Francine waving to me from the door to the conference room. The last thing I needed was to be late for this meeting.

Or maybe it was going to be my execution, I thought wearily, as I moved down the hall.

When I entered the conference room, that thought only got stronger. Francine, Curtis, and David were on one side of the table, while Mitchell sat in a chair at the head of the table. I took a seat across from my bosses, feeling like I was facing a firing squad, and Mitchell was there to witness my demise. There was a somewhat gleeful expression lurking around the corners of his mouth.

"You know what this is about, Emily," Francine said. "Ashton sent Curtis the video and we've all taken a look at it."

"I haven't actually seen the video," I said. "Only the still shots. But I understand that the woman with Ashton looks like me from the back and that Ashton's blackmailer is insinuating that it is me, that Ashton and I were having torrid sex fueled by a bunch of party drugs. Is that where we're at?"

"Yes," Francine said.

"Can you prove it wasn't you?" David asked, his dark gaze boring into mine.

"I was at home asleep when it happened. But I was alone, so I don't have anyone to corroborate that, except for Ashton. He knows I wasn't there."

"He said he didn't know *who* was there," Mitchell interjected.

"This is very disturbing, Emily," Curtis said. "It's one thing if Ashton was the only one involved, but this video could hurt your reputation."

"It's not me," I repeated. "Ashton will tell people that. I will tell people that. And that's all we can do." I paused. "But we don't know what else might come and/or if this video will even be released online. Right now, it's just a threat."

"You must be upset by what happened," Francine said. "If it wasn't you in bed with him, then it was someone else."

"Ashton said he was drugged. I believe him."

Francine nodded, but I could see the doubt in her eyes. "Mitchell is very interested in signing Ashton for the role of Dominic. What do you think about that?"

"It's not up to her," Mitchell interrupted. "It's my movie. I have final say on casting."

"But Emily knows Ashton well, and she also knows the script inside and out," Francine said. "I'd like to get her opinion."

I was pleased that she was speaking up on my behalf, but I had a feeling we were outnumbered. I considered my options and decided to stick with the truth. "Ashton has never played a character like Dominic, but he's talented, and he wants to stretch himself as an actor. I believe he'll put his heart into it, and he should be able to do the character justice. But there are other contenders, and Ashton should audition."

"His need to stretch isn't what I care about," Curtis said.

I understood that. Curtis only ever cared about the money. But his focus on the cash kept us in business and gave me a job, so I couldn't complain.

"Will Ashton help the film by signing on, or will these allegations create a distraction we don't want?" Curtis continued.

"He's a popular actor," David said, answering before I could reply. "His fans will be of value."

"I agree," Francine said. "And I appreciate your honest assessment, Emily. I know you don't like to mix business and personal."

"I don't," I admitted. "But I want what's best for the movie."

"And I want Ashton," Mitchell said. "I know exactly how to direct him into giving the performance of his life."

"Okay. Let's move forward," Curtis said.

"Is that it?" I asked.

"No," Mitchell said forcefully. "We need to discuss Emily's role. With all this going on, I think she should step back from the movie starting today. At our dinner meeting on Wednesday with Cole and Natasha, we can tell them that someone else will step in for Emily."

"That can't happen," I said passionately. "I've been working on the project for months. You just got involved a few weeks ago."

"Because you tried to kill me," he said.

Francine gasped. "Mitchell, stop. That is not true."

"Is that what you really think, Mitchell?" David asked, surprise in his gaze.

"I haven't made it a secret," Mitchell replied. "Emily benefited tremendously from my accident."

"There's no proof she had anything to do with moving the propane tanks," Curtis said, shaking his head, a grim look on his face. "You need to stop with the allegations, Mitch."

"There's no proof she didn't. And I don't know how you all think we're going to work together."

"Natasha wants to work with both of you," Francine said. "If we pull Emily, she might drop out, and we need her."

"She won't drop out. I can convince her to stay," Mitchell said with his usual arrogance. "It comes down to this—do you want me, or do you want Emily?"

A tense silence followed his ultimatum. I wasn't going down without a fight. "I'd like to work on the film," I said. "I had nothing to do with Mitchell's accident, and I've been developing this project for a long time. I know it better than anyone."

I saw Francine, David, and Curtis exchange looks, and I sensed that I'd lost before I'd even entered the room.

"We need to discuss this matter further," Francine said, surprising me with her words.

Mitch spluttered with anger. "Then perhaps you've already made your choice."

"Calm down," Curtis told Mitch. "We need to think about this entire situation, and we will get back to both of you with an answer in the next day or two."

"If Emily is on the film, I'm not," Mitch said as he got to his feet. "You have until tomorrow morning to decide. That's it. I will not risk my life again by working with her." He shot me a dark look and then shuffled out of the conference room.

"He's out of his mind," I said heatedly. "I never did anything to hurt him."

"Emily, why don't you go back to work?" Francine said.

"I need to stay on the movie," I reiterated. "I need to be at the dinner on Wednesday. Please don't make a hasty decision."

"We'll talk later." She gave me a pointed glance that told me I should back down now.

"Okay." I wished I could say something brilliant, something that would swing this situation in my favor, but I was beginning to wonder what exactly I was fighting for. Even if they kept me on the film with Mitchell, I wouldn't be in charge, and the experience would be awful. Did I really want to put myself through all that?

I was still thinking about that when I left the conference room and walked down the hall to my office. Kaitlyn was sitting at her desk, her gaze on her phone. There was no sign of Tara. She'd probably left with Mitchell.

"Kaitlyn?" I questioned. "Aren't you supposed to be reading a script right now?"

She lifted her gaze to mine. "I just got an alert on my phone about you and a sex video. It's already going viral, Emily. I'm sorry."

My stomach turned over. I'd expected the video to go live. I'd even told Ashton not to pay the blackmail demand. But the reality of being caught up in this nightmare still hit me hard. And the video had gone online fast. I'd thought I had a little time to get ready, but time was up.

Kaitlyn's office phone rang. She looked at me with concern. "I have a feeling that questions are coming."

"I'm not taking calls. Just say no comment."

"That won't work for long. If you want my advice—"

"I don't," I said, cutting her off. "I really don't." And with that, I walked into my office and shut the door. I leaned against it for a long minute. Then I sat down at my desk and tried to work. Even with the door closed, I could hear the constant ring of Kaitlyn's phone, not to mention the incessant buzzing on my cell, which I eventually turned off, not wanting to read the texts or hear any voice messages. I needed to be alone. Grabbing my bag, I headed out the door.

"I'm leaving," I told Kaitlyn. "I'm going to work from home for the rest of the day."

"Is there anything I can do, Emily? I feel so bad for you."

"There's nothing you can do. Just continue to say no comment, okay?"

"Of course."

I saw more than a few curious glances as I walked out of the office, but my stony expression kept the questions away, and I made my way down to the parking garage. This time, the lights in the garage stayed on, and I got into my vehicle with no problems.

Maybe it was over, I thought hopefully. Maybe the video was what it had all been leading up to, and now it was done.

But, somehow, I didn't think so.

Instead of going home, I drove to the beach next to the Santa Monica Pier. I avoided the amusement park area where a roller coaster was roaring and a Ferris wheel was spinning. I couldn't imagine wanting to feel more unsettled than I did now. I opted for the sand, walking across a vast expanse of beach to settle into an empty spot about thirty feet from the water.

The sand was warm, and I let out a breath of relief as the crashing waves, the ocean breeze, and the bright sunshine washed over me. For a moment, I closed my eyes and tried to get every disturbing thought out of my head.

It was surprisingly easy, because in my mind I could suddenly see my mother's laughing face. She'd looked like me, with brown hair and eyes, but she'd been much more outgoing, more of a free spirit, and an optimist. I could hear her familiar words in my head, as I remembered the last time we'd come to the beach. I'd tried out for the elementary school talent show, but they'd had too many acts, so they didn't need my clumsy dancing rendition of a Spice Girls song, and I was crushed.

"When things look down, you gotta look up, baby," my mother said.

I gave her a doubtful glance. "What good will that do? I still won't be in the show."

"That means you'll have time to do something else."

"Like what?"

"Whatever you want, Emily. That's what I mean by looking up and also outward." She pointed to the horizon. "There's a whole world out there. There's so much for you to learn, to explore, to achieve. The sky is the limit."

"Do you think I can be in a show one day?"

"You can do anything you want," she said, putting her arm around me. "You, my baby girl, are destined for greatness. I know it. You just have to believe it, too."

"How do you know it? It's not like anything great has happened so far."

A shadow passed across my mother's face. "Good luck skips generations. Whatever bad luck I've had will be good luck for you."

"But I want good luck for you, too," I said, hearing a sad note in her voice.

"You're my good luck."

"Really?"

"Yes. I love you more than I've ever loved anyone in my life. And I want you to feel that love every single day." Her gaze turned serious as she looked at me. "Even when you're a grown-up. Even when we don't live together anymore."

"That's a long time away, Mom."

"It will go faster than you think, Emily. Whenever you get down or sad, come here to the beach and remember this moment when we're together, and how much better things will be if you keep looking up,

taking action. That's how you stay in control of your life. You don't wait for things to come to you. Go get them. Even if you make a mistake, you'll still be better off because you'll learn from that mistake, and you'll know what to do the next time."

I didn't really understand what she meant, but I could see how much she wanted me to hear what she was saying. "I'll try."

She stroked my head. "You'll be okay. You're smart and strong, and if someone knocks you down, you'll get back up because that's what we do. We bounce back. Right, baby?"

"Right," I said. "Maybe I'll just make the signs for the talent show."

"And they'll be the best signs in the world. You just have to be you, Emily, and that will be enough."

I smiled back at her. "Can we get ice cream now?"

My eyes fluttered open, and I wiped the back of my hand across my teary cheeks. I hadn't known that would be the last time we went to the beach, the last time we had a conversation like that because my mother, who valued control over her life more than anything else, had died a few weeks later from an incurable cancer that she'd been unwilling to postpone with painful chemo treatments. Instead, she'd gotten Jimmy to drive her across the state line so she could end her life the way she wanted.

As I thought about her last words of wisdom to me, I knew exactly why I'd come here; I'd needed to be reminded of who I was.

Ethan had suggested that I didn't know who I was because I'd been different people in my life, but this was the real me, this girl on the beach. And I thought I'd done a good job of taking over my life when I turned eighteen, when I started down my career path. But now someone was trying to take that life away, and I had to stop them. I might have been knocked down, but I was getting back up.

I turned on my phone and was instantly overwhelmed by the flood of messages, but I forced myself to read through the texts from concerned coworkers and friends. The last two were from Ethan.

Saw the video and heard your interview. Are you all right? Call me.

He'd heard my interview? What the hell was that about? I hadn't given an interview. My stomach flipped over once more. I suspected things were about to get worse.

I ran back to my car and called Ethan. It was after five, so hopefully he was off work, but my call went to voicemail. I left him a message and then sped home. I needed to find out what interview I'd allegedly given and what I'd allegedly said.

When I turned down my street, I saw that the jewelry store was closed, and there was no sign of Ethan. That was disappointing. I should have come straight home instead of going to the beach and taking a daydream into the past. My mom couldn't help me now. I had to help myself, which was what she'd told me to do.

I parked in my garage and carefully exited the vehicle, keeping a watchful eye on my surroundings. As I entered the parking garage lobby to get on the elevator, someone came out from behind the large plant in the corner, and I froze in fear.

Was I about to come face-to-face with my tormentor?

CHAPTER SEVENTEEN

THE MAN SAUNTERED FORWARD, a tall man with silver-white hair, bright-blue eyes and a still youthful, energetic, and charming smile. "Hello, Emily."

"Jimmy?" I whispered in shock. "What are you doing here?"

He opened his arms. "A hug for old time's sake?"

"I don't think so." I put up a hand, as he took another step. "Stop right there. You didn't answer my question. What are you doing here?"

"I came to see you, Emily. I saw you all over the internet today, and I was worried about you."

"I don't believe that for a second."

"You've gotten yourself into quite a mess. The sex tape was not a good choice, but the interview was even worse. You shouldn't have mentioned me, Emily. We had a deal, remember?"

"Of course I remember our deal. But I haven't talked about you to anyone. Nor was I in that video. I wasn't even there."

He gave me a speculative look. "Why don't we have this conversation in your condo?"

"We don't need to have a conversation at all."

"Oh, we do. We definitely do."

"How did you even get in here?"

"A very helpful young woman buzzed me into the building when I couldn't juggle my groceries and my key."

His words took me back. "The groceries, no key trick," I said, remembering one of his favorite ways to get into a security building.

"It works every time. Who would try to break in somewhere with two bags of perishables?"

"Where are they now?"

"In the dumpster. I couldn't, however, get into your condo. So I decided to come down and wait for you. I figured you'd have to come home at some point."

As the elevator dinged, I started. Someone else was coming.

"I want to talk to you, Emily," he said sharply. "If you don't want me to make a scene with whoever is about to step off that elevator, invite me up."

I didn't trust him, but I wasn't afraid of him. Jimmy had had years in which he could have hurt me, and he had never raised a hand to me. He might have taught me to lie and steal and used me in his cons, but he'd never been my enemy. Of course, that was before I'd blackmailed him.

The elevator doors opened, and Monica stepped out. She stared at us in surprise. "Oh, hi, Emily," she said. "And Mr. ..."

"Conway," Jimmy supplied. "Thanks again for letting me in."

"No problem." She turned to me, her gaze softening. "I saw the video online, Emily. I'm so sorry. You must feel incredibly violated to have your personal life on display like that."

"It wasn't me in the sex tape," I said flatly.

"Oh." Monica appeared taken aback. "I'm sorry. I thought I saw your name."

"Someone is making it look like it's me, but it's not."

"But it is Ashton, right? And he is your boyfriend?"

"Not anymore. I don't want to talk about it. I have to get upstairs."

"I understand," Monica replied. "If you need someone to have a drink with you, you have my number or just knock on my door. I have to run a couple of errands, but I'll be back around eight."

"Thanks, but I have some work to do tonight."

"The offer is open—anytime."

"Sounds good," I said shortly. I moved past her and pushed the button for the elevator. The doors opened immediately, and I stepped inside, with Jimmy quickly following.

When the doors closed again, he said, "I might be able to help you, Emily."

"I don't believe you came here to help me, so why don't you tell me why we're talking again after ten years of silence?"

He didn't answer until the elevator doors opened on my floor. "Did you expect us to talk after you blackmailed me?" he asked curiously.

"No, I didn't. So, why are you here?"

"Invite me in, and I'll tell you."

I didn't think there was any way I could shake him, and I didn't need him sitting outside my door when Monica got back. Nor did I want him talking to any other neighbors. "Fine. But I have someone coming over in fifteen minutes," I said. "This will have to be quick."

I knew Ethan was coming over at some point. At least, I hoped he was. So it wasn't a total lie. Ethan was supposed to bring back my computer.

"Nice place," Jimmy commented, as I ushered him inside. "You're a homeowner now."

"Yes. A real homeowner. Not a fake one. There's an actual deed with my name on it—my real name."

"I get it," he said with a small smile. "But you could do some decorating. Or do you still think it's unlucky to hang pictures on the wall?"

"There's a picture," I said, pointing to the one over the fireplace.

"Only one."

"I've been busy. Decorating is at the bottom of the list."

"I know you've been busy. I've been following your career since it took off. What a break you caught, with Mitchell Gray getting hurt, and you taking his spot. Amazing good fortune."

"Not for Mitchell," I said dryly, not liking the gleam in Jimmy's gaze. "Did you come here for payback? Now that I'm doing well, you want your money back?"

"I never say no to money, but that's not why I came."

"Then spit it out." I ran an impatient hand through my hair.

"I think you're in trouble, Emily."

"I told you. I wasn't the one in the tape."

"Are you going to tell me you also didn't do the interview with the *Hollywood Daily*?"

My stomach tightened. Ethan had mentioned something about an interview, too. "I haven't done interviews with anyone. What did it say?"

"That you're furious someone intruded into your personal life, revealing your most private moments."

"Well, that doesn't sound too bad, except that this person is pretending to be me. I didn't give that interview."

"She sounded like you, Emily."

"Sounded like me?" I asked in shock. "I thought you were talking about a written interview."

"There was audio. I hadn't heard your voice in a long time, so I wasn't sure it was you or not, but now that we're talking again, I can say it was definitely your voice."

"But it wasn't me. Someone is pretending to be me."

"How could they take over your voice?"

"I have no idea. Maybe artificial intelligence or something. But the past few days, someone has been trying to ruin my life. This is just part of that."

"What are you talking about? How is someone taking over your life?"

He sounded like he didn't know, but Jimmy had always been a great actor. That he'd shown up now also made me suspicious. But I might as well see how he reacted to the rest of my story.

"They've sent me threatening notes, broken into my home, put spyware on my computer so they could watch me, and scratched my name onto the car of a friend of mine. They also made the sex tape with drugs, making me look like a wild party girl. Now they're apparently giving interviews using my voice."

His eyebrow raised as he gave me a questioning look. "Why would someone do all that to you?"

"The notes all said the same thing: I know what you did."

"What you did," he echoed. "And what is that?"

"You tell me. The fact that you're here right now means this has to be about something you and I did together."

"I'm sure you've done plenty of other things without me. In fact, this sounds like it has something to do with the accident that took Mitchell Gray out of the movie you ended up directing."

"Could be," I admitted. "But if that were the case, why would you suddenly come over here? We have had nothing to do with each other in years."

"I came to find you because the video made you look out of control and that bothered me. I hated to see you going down a dark road after having gotten so much success."

His fake sincerity made my blood boil. "Stop lying to me. I'm not a little girl anymore. You can't make shit up, so I'll think you're someone you're not." I felt suddenly overwhelmed by emotion. It would have been nice if I could have believed him, if I could have thought he came to help me, that he'd been worried about me. But I'd been on my own a long time, and he'd never once shown up to see if I needed something. "You've never cared about me. You only kept me after my mother died because you wanted the insurance money and then you decided I made a good shill for your games. Let's not pretend it was anything else."

He waved my words away with a dismissive hand. "That small amount of insurance was barely enough to feed you. And you weren't a great shill as you got older. You felt too guilty. You didn't want to go along, play the game."

"Because we were hurting people, real people. It wasn't a game. It was their lives. I just wish I could say it was my choice to quit, to leave you, but that's not the way it happened, is it? You dumped me at your cousin's house because I was too old to be of use to you."

He shook his head. "That wasn't the entire story. I cared about you. And I took care of you for four years because your mother asked me to look out for you. I wanted to keep my promise to her."

"I don't believe you. In fact, sometimes I wonder if you didn't drive her to Oregon because you wanted the insurance money."

Anger entered his blue eyes at my words. "She asked me to take her there. She begged me. I wanted her to get treatment, but I couldn't convince her it would work. The odds were against her. She knew it, and she persuaded me to believe it, too." He cleared his throat. "I loved your mother, Emily. She might have been the only woman I really loved."

There was plenty of emotion in his voice, but I knew what a good actor he was. "I don't believe you. The only person you've ever loved is yourself. You need to go."

"No. This is worse than I thought," he murmured.

"Worse than you thought? What does that mean?"

"I thought you were partying too hard and saying things that could get you hurt, so I came here to tell you to stop before it's too late. But clearly there's more going on, and that changes things. You're not just talking nonsense. Someone is putting words in your mouth."

"What exactly did this person in the interview say?"

"She said she wasn't who the world thought she was, that she'd made the video because it was the first step in revealing her true self. She just wished she'd had the opportunity to release the video at a time of her choosing, but since someone stole that from her, she wants everyone to know that the rest of her story will come out as she desires."

"What does that mean? The rest of her story?"

"She's writing a book. She'll release the chapters one at a time. She'll be talking about how she grew up with a con man, how she pulled off scams with him and partied with Hollywood's elite. How they lived like the rich and famous and how she knows a lot of dirt about a lot of powerful people." Jimmy paused. "She specifically said she knows who murdered Faye Weston, and that the world will be shocked when they hear the truth."

My jaw dropped in shock. "That's crazy. I'm not writing a book, and I sure as hell would never tell the world about my past with you. I also have no idea who murdered Faye Weston. How could I? I was fourteen years old when that happened." I paused. "But this is about you. You were at the house party at Faye's house. That must be how she's planning to back up that statement. She must think you know something, or maybe you told her you did. What is going on, Jimmy? Are you setting me up?"

"I was going to ask you the same question," he returned, his gaze meeting mine. "I told you when you blackmailed me that taking me down would also take yourself down."

"But you didn't totally believe that, because you paid me."

"I paid you because I wanted you to go to school. It was what you needed. I could see the desperation in your eyes, and I heard your mother's voice in my head reminding me I was supposed to take care of you."

I rolled my eyes and shook my head. "You are laying it on way too thick."

"The part about your mother might have been too much," he agreed. "But it actually was true. I found myself in an unusual position. I wanted to help someone other than myself, so I gave you the money. And I was pleased that you used it to better your life, to make yourself happy. But now you're throwing it away."

"I'm not throwing anything away. Someone is trying to take my life apart." I paused. "And based on what the woman said about Faye's murder and my life with a con man, I'm guessing your life is about to be shredded as well."

He folded his arms across his chest, giving me a speculative look. "Let's say I believe you."

I let out a cynical laugh. "Sure, let's say that, because I'm the one you can't believe."

"Let's say I believe you," he repeated, ignoring my comment. "This woman knows a lot about you, about us."

"No kidding. It didn't used to take you this long to catch up."

"The interview only came out a few hours ago. I think I caught up remarkably fast."

He had a point. "How did you find me?"

"It wasn't difficult, Emily. You haven't been in hiding. I knew where you were living before today. I've been keeping track of you."

That gave me a chill. "Why would you do that?"

"I wanted to know that you were okay."

"As if you would have tried to help me if I wasn't." I sighed, feeling exhausted by Jimmy, which reminded me of how often I'd felt that way when I was living with him. His schemes had always been so complicated, so tiring, and while I'd gotten some benefits of the payoff, he'd always been the real winner.

"This woman has to be someone you hurt," Jimmy said.

"Or we hurt," I countered.

"It's not about money," he mused. "It's about revenge."

"It's someone we hurt together," I said. "Because the person who hates me the most is Mitchell Gray, and he wouldn't know anything about us." An odd gleam flittered through Jimmy's gaze. "Wait, would Mitchell know something about us?" I asked. "Do you know him?"

"Mitchell was at Faye's house party," Jimmy admitted. "So was his wife, Tara. Vanessa and I talked to both of them at the party."

"My boss, Francine, was there, too. And Curtis, as well, I think," I murmured, suddenly realizing that that party connected Jimmy and me to more people in my current life. "Do you know them as well?"

"I've met most of the people you work with at one time or another, Emily, but I didn't know any of them well," he said. "And I doubt they would have put us together. You weren't there that night, and I didn't talk about the fourteen-year-old kid I'd left at home."

"That I believe," I said with a sigh. The last few months we'd been together, I had played a lesser role in Jimmy's schemes.

"I heard that Mitchell wants to make a film about Faye's life and her tragic death," Jimmy added. "Perhaps that's what this is about."

My stomach rolled with that reminder. "That's true. Maybe Mitchell is creating buzz to generate investment. I know my company isn't interested. Francine told Mitchell that she didn't see the point. He has no good ending to the film, and we use Cole Weston in many of our movies, so why would we want to put Cole on the hot seat again?"

"But if Mitchell gets the world talking about Faye's murder again," Jimmy said, "that could make the project more inviting to another investor."

"Who did he know you as?" I asked. "At the party. Who were you then?"

"I was Jimmy Smithers, agent extraordinaire," he said, a gleam in his eyes. "I took several of my clients there that night, up-and-coming young actors who I was representing. I got one of them a job at that party."

"Was Vanessa with you?"

"Yes, of course. She was quite an asset. The beautiful Vanessa with the impeccable Hollywood credentials, was essential to my business."

"You mean your fraud," I said dryly. "Maybe Vanessa is the one who's after us now."

"Vanessa was a sweet, trusting woman. She wouldn't have the guts to frame someone with a sex tape or boast about knowing a murderer. After we broke up, she just wanted to disappear. She moved to Newport Beach. She got out of the Hollywood scene."

"What about Rhea? Your cousin knows who you are and how you dumped me on her. I know she hasn't been thrilled with me lately. She thinks I've gotten too high on my horse after my success because I couldn't make a lunch with her a few months back." As I told that story, a surge of adrenaline ran through me. "Maybe it is Rhea. She could be behind this."

Jimmy started shaking his head before I'd even stopped talking. "No, Rhea would not tell anyone anything."

"How can you be so sure?"

"Because I paid off her house, and she knows that if she ever wants my help again, she needs to stay on my good side."

I let out a sigh. "Then I don't know. Maybe it is Mitchell. He knows you. He hates me. I just don't get why I'm the target and you're just collateral damage. Shouldn't it be the other way around if someone wants revenge on both of us?"

"Well, I didn't blow up any propane tanks."

"Neither did I."

"It doesn't matter. You're in real trouble, Emily. This woman is using your name, taking over your life, stealing your voice, and she's not stopping there. We need to find this other Emily."

"Don't call her by my name. And I want to find her, but I don't have any leads. There are a few people I suspect, but I don't have proof."

"Then I'll help you find some."

"I don't want you in the middle of this."

"I'm already in the middle of it."

I thought about that, seeing genuine worry in his eyes, and I didn't think it was all for me. "You're afraid this woman will say you killed Faye, aren't you?"

Before he could answer, my doorbell rang, and I jumped. I

drew in a quick breath, but I knew trouble wasn't going to ring my bell. It had to be Ethan. "That will be my friend," I said. "I'm going to let him in."

"No, send him away. We need to keep talking."

"You'll have to talk in front of him, Jimmy."

"I'm not going to do that."

The doorbell rang again, and I went over to the intercom. "Hello?"

"It's Ethan. I have your computer, and I'm worried about you, Emily."

"Come on up." I hit the buzzer to open the downstairs door.

"We're not done," Jimmy said, as he moved toward me. "We'll talk tomorrow."

I stepped in front of the door, blocking his exit. "We're going to talk now. And just so you know, I told Ethan about you, about our life together."

He raised a brow in surprise. "I thought you said you never talk about me."

"I made an exception when all this began."

"Who is this guy to you? I thought you were dating the actor in the sex tape."

"I am—was—dating Ashton. Ethan works as a security guard at the jewelry store next to this building. He was there when I got mugged, and he was here when I realized my home had been broken into. He's helping me figure out what's going on. And I think he should hear what you have to say."

"I don't talk to strangers, and I thought I taught you better than that."

"He's not a stranger. He's my friend, and right now, he's the only one I can trust, and I'm including you in the group of people I can't trust."

"Why does he have your laptop?" Jimmy asked, surprising me with the question.

"His friend was checking it to see if there was spyware on it, like there was at my work. I told you someone was watching me through the camera on my computer."

"Maybe not just watching you. They could have been recording your voice, too."

That suggestion sent a chill through me. "You're right."

A knock came at my door. I looked through the peephole, then opened the door. Ethan gazed back at me with concern in his dark-brown eyes. He wasn't in his security uniform, but dressed down in jeans and a polo shirt, his brown hair damp as if he'd recently taken a shower. A tingle ran down my spine that had nothing to do with gratitude for him bringing back my laptop.

"Are you all right, Emily?" he asked immediately. "I've been texting you all afternoon."

"I'm not all right, and I'm not alone. Jimmy just showed up."

"Jimmy, the con artist?" he asked in surprise, as I waved him into the entry.

"I prefer just Jimmy," my stepfather said.

I watched as the two men sized each other up. They were both tall, confident, with a commanding presence, and neither one seemed to know what to make of the other.

If I were being honest with myself, I wasn't sure what to make of them, either. They were both a mystery to me. But I was going to have to trust someone, and it couldn't be Jimmy. It had to be Ethan.

"What's going on?" Ethan asked, his gaze shifting from Jimmy to me.

"Too much," I replied. "Let's sit down in the living room. Maybe you can help figure it all out."

CHAPTER EIGHTEEN

"I SHOULD GO," Jimmy said.

"Maybe you should stay," Ethan countered. "I'd like to hear what you have to say."

"I don't know who you are."

"I'm Emily's friend."

"I'm not sure Emily has any real friends."

Jimmy's words stung because they also felt very true.

"Let's sit down in the living room and talk for a few minutes," I said. "I think we're all on the same side." I wish I could have said I was sure we were on the same side, but I wasn't.

Jimmy reluctantly moved into the living room with me and Ethan. The men took the opposing chairs across from me, while I sat in the middle of the couch.

Ethan looked the most comfortable of all of us. Jimmy kept casting glances toward the door as if weighing his opportunity for escape, and my stomach was twisting in knots from what I'd already learned and from what else Jimmy might have to say.

"I heard the interview you gave, Emily. It was disturbing. There were a lot of dangerous claims made," Ethan said, the first one to break the silence. "Is that what brought this guy to your door?"

"Yes. But obviously I didn't give that interview. I'm not writing a book about my life as a con artist, and I don't know who killed Faye Weston."

"This other woman faked your voice?" Ethan asked, a frown crossing his lips. "That's sophisticated."

"She seems to have excellent technical skills," I agreed.

Silence followed my words.

"So, were you involved in Faye Weston's death?" Ethan asked Jimmy.

Jimmy bristled under the direct question and immediately stood up. "No, and I'm leaving."

I jumped up. "Hold on. Just wait. Please," I added. "You said you came here to help me, so help us figure this out. Tell us about the party and how Faye Weston might have been killed. Because that seems to be important. It's the one specific thing this other woman said in the interview, right?" As I asked the question, I knew I needed to listen to the interview, but first I had to find out what Jimmy knew.

"We can talk tomorrow, Emily," Jimmy said. "I don't trust this guy."

"I don't trust you, either," Ethan returned, as he stood up. "Emily told me you're a con man. Are you conning her now?"

"No." Jimmy took a few seconds, then added, "I can tell you this much. I was at Faye's house the night of the party. My wife, Vanessa, and I stayed in one of the eight guest bedrooms at the estate. There were probably seventy-five people at the party, and another twelve or so who spent the night."

"Ethan, Mitchell Gray was also at the party," I interjected, feeling like he needed to know that. "He and his wife, Tara. As well as Francine from my office and maybe some others from my production company."

"Interesting," Ethan commented. "Go on."

"Faye was drinking a great deal that night," Jimmy said. "There was tension between her and her husband, Cole."

"Cole was a suspect, wasn't he?" Ethan asked.

"The primary suspect," Jimmy agreed. "And Cole might have killed her, but no one knows."

"You keep saying she was killed," Ethan said. "How do you know that if the official police report found it was an accident?"

"I overheard an argument," Jimmy replied. "It was between Faye and someone else, but I couldn't hear the other voice clearly. I'm not even sure if it was a man or a woman, but I could hear Faye. She had a shrill voice, and she was upset. I distinctly heard her say, 'You have to leave me alone. I need to be done.'" He paused. "Those were the last words I ever heard her say."

"Did you tell the police that?" Ethan asked.

"I did not," Jimmy replied, without a trace of remorse in his voice.

"Why not?" Ethan challenged.

I didn't need Jimmy to answer that question to know why not. He would have never talked to the police about anything. That might have exposed his game or whatever else he was doing in the house that night. "Wait a second," I said, not that I'd needed to ask Jimmy to wait, because he clearly had no intention of answering Ethan. "Faye Weston's diamond necklace also went missing that night. That's why there was speculation that someone had stolen it and killed her. Were you stealing her necklace when you overheard this conversation, Jimmy?"

"Of course not," he said.

I probably knew Jimmy better than most, but I had still never acquired the ability to know if he was lying or not.

"But the necklace isn't important," Jimmy continued. "You—or your alter ego—made a claim to know who killed Faye. That was a stupid and dangerous statement to make, because whoever killed Faye will not let their identity be revealed without trying to do something about it."

"You think they might come after me?" I asked, feeling sick again.

"Yes. That's why I came here to tell you to shut the hell up. I thought it was you trying to be dramatic, sell some books, make a name for yourself, but clearly, there's more going on than I thought. You should be very careful, Emily. Don't trust anyone." His gaze moved pointedly to Ethan.

"She can trust me," Ethan vowed, his voice hard and firm.

"I hope that's true, but Emily likes to see the good in people, at her own peril. And you've known each other for what? Four days?" Jimmy moved toward the door, then looked back at me. "Just remember, I tried to warn you, Emily. I tried to save you."

His foreboding words only shot another wave of worry through me. "I'm warned, but that doesn't really help me. An actual name or some kind of proof would be more valuable. This person who's gaslighting me works just like you did, which still makes me wonder if it is you."

"Don't let your hatred of me blind you to someone else. Because that's probably what they want." He opened the door and stepped into the hall, shutting the door firmly behind him.

I blew out a ragged breath.

Ethan moved to the door and turned the deadbolt, then faced me. "So, that was Jimmy."

"That was Jimmy," I echoed, feeling shaky. I walked back to the couch to sit down.

Ethan sat next to me. "He's a real prize."

"That's probably the nicest thing anyone has ever said about him."

"You can't trust him, Emily."

"I don't trust him."

"Do you still trust me?" Ethan asked, his brown eyes questioning. "Or did he get in your head? He's right. We haven't known each other very long."

"We haven't. And there are things about you that don't always seem to add up. I sense there's a mystery in your past, too."

"Don't you have enough mystery in your life to worry about?"

"That's not a denial."

He gave me a smile. "You know what I've learned over the years? Trust your gut. What does your gut say?"

I thought for a moment. "My gut says you're helping me. My mind questions why?"

"I haven't gone that far out of my way. In fact, I have the name of a private investigator who said he will try to help you. His name is Peter Edgehill. I'll give you his number. You can call him tomorrow. He's good. He'll dig into every single person in your life, which is what you need to do, Emily."

"I agree. I keep jumping from one person to another, because something happens, or someone says something that makes me go in a different direction."

"What else did Jimmy say? I'm surprised you let him in."

"I didn't let him in. He conned his way into the building using his old guy carrying two grocery bags of perishables routine. My neighbor, Monica, fell for it and let him in, thinking he lived in the building. He couldn't get in my apartment, so he waited for me in the parking garage. I almost jumped out of my skin when I saw him. Parking garages are not my favorite places these days."

"I can see why."

"Anyway, he insisted on speaking to me, and I didn't want to have the conversation in the hall, so I let him inside. I'm not afraid of him, not physically. Mentally and emotionally, he could probably destroy me. But I had to find out what he knew."

"There is a chance he killed that actress, Faye Weston. His story about overhearing a threat but not knowing who was talking has a lot of holes in it."

"I don't think he killed her, but he might know more than he said about who did," I agreed. "I'm more inclined to believe he was slinking around that house, trying to steal her necklace, or someone else's. Part of his cons involved lifting jewels and other valuables at fancy parties. Sadly, I helped him a few times." I paused. "But once, I actually put something back. He'd taken an emerald ring from the bedroom of someone's teenage daughter, and I saw it in his bag, and I knew how much she loved that ring. It was her grandmother's, and the woman had just died and left it to her. When Jimmy wasn't looking, I put it back. I felt too sorry for her."

"I'm guessing Jimmy did not like that."

"He was furious, but I didn't care. And he didn't hurt me or punish me in any way. I think he just became more careful about how he hid his stolen items. He knew I had too much empathy for his victims. I sometimes think that's why he got rid of me."

"I'm sure it was part of it," Ethan said.

"You must think I'm a terrible person."

He stared back at me. "I think you're a survivor. And you're trying to make something good out of your life. Some people would have just followed Jimmy down his path, going for the easy pickings. But not you, Emily. You wanted to make your own way in the world."

"I haven't gotten too far."

"Are you kidding? You're only a target now because of how far you've gotten."

"I appreciate you saying that."

"It's the truth."

I drew in a breath. "I also really appreciate you being here, Ethan. I know I dragged you into this one-sided friendship, or whatever you want to call it, but I'm more than a little happy I met you, that you were outside the jewelry store on Friday night."

His eyes filled with shadows. "I wish I could have prevented you from getting robbed."

"You might have prevented something worse in the parking garage yesterday." I licked my lips. "There's a lot going on, and I know I need to move on to your investigator, but I just want to say that..." My voice drifted away as I wasn't really sure what I wanted to say, except I didn't want to stop talking to him, stop seeing him. There was a pull between us...attraction, connection.

I couldn't define it, but it was there, and it was getting stronger all the time.

"You don't have to say anything," he told me. "I want you to be safe, Emily. I want you to get your life back. And I'm happy to help you. I understand where you're coming from more than you might think."

His words were a tiny hint to the mystery of Ethan, but I didn't want to ruin the moment by pointing that out. Instead, I said something I probably shouldn't have said, but I couldn't seem to stop myself. "I like you, Ethan, and I trust you. I don't think I'm making a mistake, but if I am, I am. I'm going with my gut."

His lips tightened as if he were uncomfortable with my admission, which really hadn't gone that deep.

"Anyway," I said quickly. "We don't need to keep talking about you and me."

"I like you, too, Emily. I just wish we'd met at a different time."

"My timing has never been great."

"Mine, either," he admitted, a small smile now playing around his sexy, full lips that I found myself wanting to taste.

He must have read something in my expression. His smile disappeared, and his eyes suddenly sparked with the same interest that was overwhelming me.

"Bad idea," he muttered.

"Are you talking to me or yourself?" I asked, leaning toward him.

He answered by putting a hand behind my head and pulling me in for the kiss I wanted. His lips were hot and grew more demanding as our kiss went from light and exploring to hungry and passionate, as if we'd both been waiting for this moment for far longer than the time that we'd known each other.

We finally broke apart, our gazes still clinging together. My heart was beating fast. My body tingled, wanting more. It was crazy to feel something so strong for a guy I barely knew, but I couldn't deny the feelings running through me. I felt almost feeling dizzy with longing. I blinked a few times, my eyes watering.

That wasn't from desire. That was from...

"Gas," Ethan said suddenly. "It smells like gas."

My throat was suddenly burning, and I coughed in response.

Ethan jumped to his feet. "Something is on fire."

"There's nothing on in here," I said, but as I stood up, I saw smoke seeping in through the edges of my door. "It must be coming from the hall or another unit. We should get out."

As I started toward the door, Ethan grabbed my hand and yanked me back. "No. Let's go on the deck. We'll call the fire depart—"

A horrendous blast of fire and heat cut off his words, as the door to my apartment flew open, throwing us into the air in an explosion of fire.

CHAPTER NINETEEN

PAIN SHOT through my body as I landed hard on the floor. I instinctively threw up my arms as a fiery rain of wood, plaster, and pieces of furniture fell around me. Something crashed down on my head, and I fought back a wave of pain and blackness. I couldn't pass out. I couldn't give in. I had to get away from the fire. But there was a thunderous, painful noise in my ears that made me wince.

However, that pain reminded me I was alive, and I needed to stay that way. As I rolled over, knocking off pieces of plaster, I saw Ethan several feet away, and my heart stopped. He wasn't moving.

"Ethan!" I shouted. Or maybe I whispered his name. I couldn't hear much over the noise in my head, the roar of the fire eating up my home. I crawled across the floor to him. There was blood on his face, and his eyes were closed. He was too still.

Putting my hands on his face, I said his name again, anxiety ripping through me. He could not be dead. Not now. Not because of me. Not when we were just beginning to know each other.

Tears streamed from my eyes, and I lowered my head to his,

relieved to feel a whisper of breath against my cheek. I kissed his lips—a kiss of breath, of life, maybe the last kiss...

But finally, thankfully, he stirred.

I lifted my head as his eyes fluttered open, and he blinked a few times as a groan came through his parted lips.

"You're alive," I said, so grateful to see his beautiful brown eyes again.

"Emily," he said hoarsely, ending my name on a cough.

"We have to get out of here," I said, as the smoke choked my voice. "Can you move?"

"I think so."

"I don't want you to injure yourself."

"I'm okay," he said forcefully.

Relief ran through me. "Good, because the fire is getting worse."

I helped him up. Then we turned toward the doorway. The smoke was so thick I couldn't even see the hall. I also couldn't hear anything. Where were the sirens? Surely, someone had already called 911.

"Why isn't anyone coming?" I asked.

"They might not be able to get up the stairs."

His answer terrified me. We were on the fourth floor, and the only fire escape was by the stairwell, at the other end of the hall.

"Should we go out on the deck, wait for help?" I asked, but even as I said the words, I could see that the fire was already blocking that doorway. In fact, it was worse there than by the main door to the hall. "I have to call 911."

I looked around for my bag and saw it had tumbled onto the floor by the dining room table. I raced toward it and took my phone out of the front pocket.

"There's no time to wait for the fire department," Ethan said. He grabbed two dishtowels from the kitchen and soaked them in water. "Put this around your head."

I wanted to tell him that there was no way a wet dish towel

was going to get us through the doorway, but he was already wrapping it around my head.

I stuffed my phone back into my bag and put it over my shoulder as Ethan covered his head with the second towel.

"We're not going to make it," I said. "The fire is too intense."

"We will make it," he said fiercely. "Trust me, Emily."

There was no one else to trust, and I wanted to believe him, so I took his hand.

"We have to commit," he said. "No stopping until we get to the stairs."

"What about Monica? I saw her go out earlier, but I don't know if she came back. She could be trapped in her unit."

"I'll get you out first. Then I'll go back for her."

I didn't like that plan, but there was no time to argue. Ethan squeezed my fingers, gave me a determined look, and then we ran toward the door, through the leaping flames and the thick black smoke that made it almost impossible to see. Luckily, there wasn't anything to trip over. We just had to get to the end of the hallway, and I prayed the stairwell would be clear.

The smoke clogged my throat, and the heat burned my face. I batted away sparks as we raced toward what would hopefully be an escape route. Finally, we made it. As we pushed through the door to the stairs, we found the area filled with smoke, but no fire yet.

There were sparks clinging to Ethan's shirt, and he patted them out with his hand.

I tried to help him, but he pushed my fingers away.

"It's okay, I'm okay," he told me. "Go. I'll check on Monica."

"You can't go back there," I said, grabbing his arm. "You can't, Ethan."

"I have to try," he said, meeting my gaze. "I have to, Emily. I can't leave someone behind. Go downstairs. I'll meet you outside."

And with that, he disappeared into the smoke and the fire. I couldn't believe he was gone, that he was risking his life to save a stranger. Monica might not even be home. She'd been on her way out when I'd seen her in the garage. This could all be for nothing.

I knew I should go, but I couldn't move. I couldn't leave Ethan here alone. It didn't seem right.

I heard a sudden clatter of footsteps coming up the stairs, and sirens growing louder. Help was coming—finally!

As I turned toward the stairs, I saw Tyler, the manager, taking the steps two at a time, his face dripping with sweat, fear in his eyes. I'd never seen him look so serious or so determined.

"Emily. Thank God you're alive. What the hell happened up here?" he asked.

"I don't know. I smelled gas, and then there was an explosion in the hallway. My door blew into my unit. My friend went to check on Monica."

"Come on. Let's get out of here."

"I can't leave without my friend."

"The fire is getting worse," Tyler said. "You could die here, Emily."

"I'll be down as soon as Ethan comes back," I said stubbornly.

Tyler shook his head. "Fuck it. I'm leaving. It's on you if you stay."

I didn't bother to answer as he disappeared down the stairs. Instead, I peeked through the door. The smoke was getting thicker and more fear ran through me. If Ethan didn't make it back, it would be because of me. And because he had to be a damned hero. How had I ever doubted him? This guy was literally willing to risk his life to save someone. I had never met anyone like that before. Most of the men in my life had put themselves first. But not Ethan. Maybe it came from his military training. Or maybe it was just who he was, someone who couldn't stand by or run away when there was a life to save.

My anxiety ramped up to a fever pitch, and when he finally reappeared, I couldn't even speak. I was overwhelmed with emotion. I threw my arms around his neck and hugged him tight. Then we kissed again, as if we both needed the reassurance that we were still breathing.

"I'm okay," he said when we broke apart. "Monica wasn't in the unit. Let's get out of here."

I was more than ready to leave, and we ran down the stairs together, meeting a crew of firefighters on their way up. One of them escorted us all the way down and out of the building while the others went up to fight the fire.

When we got to the street, I could see a crowd of people had gathered. Many of them I recognized from the building, but there were plenty of other people drawn to the spectacle.

Two EMTs took us over to a waiting ambulance, giving us oxygen and water, checking us for injuries or burns and cleaning up the cuts we'd gotten from flying debris. Thankfully, they were all superficial. It could have been so much worse.

A uniformed female police officer came over to speak to us, and I spent the next ten minutes telling her what little I knew. As I was talking to her, Ethan moved away to speak to a man who also had a badge at his hip but was not in uniform. Maybe he was a detective.

"Do you have somewhere to stay tonight?" the officer asked me.

I turned my attention back to her. "Uh, I guess I'll find somewhere." I was still clinging to my purse so at least I had some money and my phone. I could find a hotel room. I was sure my unit had been completely destroyed.

As the police officer moved away to speak to the detective, Ethan returned to me.

"Who were you talking to?" I asked.

"He said his name was Detective Caldwell. I told him that there was gasoline in the hallway, and there was probably an incendiary device that set off the explosion."

I'd known that the explosion had not been accidental but hearing Ethan talk about an incendiary device brought the truth home. "Someone set off a bomb in front of my door," I said dully, hardly able to comprehend that thought.

"Yes. And I wonder if it wasn't Jimmy."

My eyes widened. "Jimmy?"

"He was in your building before you got home. And he did not like the way our conversation was going when he left. He was angry that you'd told me anything about him. And he was worried about that interview."

"Which I didn't give," I reminded him.

"That might not matter. You or someone impersonating you could still be a problem for him. And I would be an additional complication."

He made a strong point, but it just didn't feel like something he would do. "Jimmy doesn't blow things up. He talks people out of their life savings. He cons them."

"Maybe he does more than that. He was at a party where a woman ended up dead, and someone is threatening to reveal who killed that woman. You do the math."

"I know it adds up, Ethan. But it doesn't ring true."

"All right."

I could tell he wasn't thrilled by my defense. "I could be wrong."

"Well, right or wrong, we should get out of here."

"Can we just go?"

"We've talked to the police. I don't see any reason to stay. Come on. My car is parked down the street."

"Mine is in my garage. Do you think it will survive the fire?"

"Hopefully they'll put the fire out before it takes out the other floors."

"Or the building next door," I said, glancing toward the jewelry store. "You might be out of a job."

"I'll worry about that tomorrow." He took my hand again, and we hurried through the crowd of onlookers to his vehicle. It was parked at the end of the block and away from the fire engines and police cars crowding the rest of the street.

I got into the car with a breath of relief, feeling better as soon as Ethan started the car and pulled away from the scene.

"Where are we going?" I asked a moment later. "Your house?"

"Not yet. We'll stop at a hotel. The Beverly Hilton is a few blocks from here."

"I don't need to stay at that nice of a hotel. A motel will do."

"That's good. Because we're not staying there." He sent me a brief smile. "We're going to leave my car there, go inside, check in, and then leave through another door. We'll find a taxi from there."

My brows drew together. "That's quite a detailed plan. Where do we go after we get the taxi?"

"My house to start. I want to pick up a few things, and then we'll decide where we're going to stay."

"Why wouldn't we just stay there?"

"I've been seen with you. It might be too easy to find my home. That's why I want someone to think we're staying in a hotel."

"You're going to a lot of trouble to hide where we are," I said.

He flung me a quick look. "Yes. Because someone just tried to kill us."

"They were aiming for me. I'm so sorry, Ethan. If something had happened to you, it would be on me."

"I made a choice to be in your apartment tonight. Nothing is on you, Emily."

"You're being way too nice. All you've done is try to help me, and you might have lost your life because of that generosity. You should start putting your life ahead of others, especially mine. In fact, you should drop me at the hotel and get as far away from me as you can."

"That wouldn't matter. Like I said before, we're connected now. Whatever you know, they'll assume I know. For the time being, we're staying close."

I couldn't say that I didn't like that idea, because being on my own sounded terrifying. "Okay," I said. Then I reached into my bag and pulled out my phone. "I'm going to call Monica. She gave me her number when she moved in, just in case we needed to grab each other's packages or something. I need to tell her what happened. The police might not know how to find her, since it's her grandmother's place."

"Hang on," Ethan said.

"Why?"

"Someone could track your phone. Monica will get filled in by the police or the fire department when she gets back. I'm sure they'll be there all night. You need to turn off your phone."

"Okay," I said, following his instruction. "What about yours?"

He stopped at the next light and turned off his phone as well. And then we drove in silence to the Hilton. We chose to self-park and then walked into the hotel together. Ethan asked for a room and put down a credit card. I didn't like the idea of him putting out several hundred dollars for a room we weren't going to stay in.

"Let me get this," I said. "This is my problem."

"Don't worry about it."

There was no point in arguing, so I let it go, but I would pay him back once we got through this situation. The clerk gave us a funny look, which made me realize our clothes were covered in smoke, and we had cuts on our arms and faces.

"Fire," I said at her unspoken question. "At our home. That's why we need a place to stay."

"I'm so sorry," the woman said. "That's terrible." She handed us our keycard and ran over some instructions that weren't going to matter. Then she handed us an emergency pack of personal hygiene items, which might come in handy.

When we were done with the check-in, we headed toward the elevators, then backtracked through a crowd of tourists in the lobby and left through a side door. We walked two blocks and then hailed a cab. Ethan gave the driver his address, and we were on our way to our next stop—Culver City, which was a working-class town about five miles from the beach.

He had the cab let us off a block away, and then we walked down the street to his building. Ethan seemed to think of everything. Maybe that was part of his military training, or perhaps he'd undergone more training when he'd become a security guard. I certainly never would have taken so many circuitous steps.

His apartment was on the sixth floor, and it felt strange to be walking into another building, which was not really similar to mine, except that it was a multi-unit building, and I'd barely gotten out of the last one alive.

When he let me into his home, I was immediately struck by how different it was from my ultra-modern, sparsely decorated unit. There was a mix of furniture in the living room that looked like it had been chosen for comfort, not style. The couches were big, with lots of pillows. The coffee table was piled high with books, which surprised me. Apparently, Ethan was a reader of fiction novels.

There was a bike in one corner of the room, along with a golf bag and a loose basketball. There was a big fruit bowl on the kitchen counter that was overflowing with apples, oranges, and bananas. And I suddenly realized I was hungry.

"Do you want something to eat?" Ethan asked, following my gaze.

"Maybe I could grab a banana before we go."

"We can do better than that. How about a frozen pizza?"

"Do we have time? Shouldn't we leave right away?"

He opened the freezer and pulled out a box. "We've got at least thirty minutes."

"It seems risky. What if someone is headed here now? We might not make it out of another fire alive."

"It will take them time to find us."

As he turned on the oven and opened the box, I grabbed a banana and slid onto a stool at the counter to eat it. I felt almost immediately better once I had something in my stomach. And that feeling only increased when Ethan filled a glass with ice water and handed it to me.

"Your throat must be as dry as mine," he said.

"Still stinging from the smoke but it's nothing compared to what we might be feeling if we'd gotten burned."

"I can't disagree." He drained one glass and then went back to refill it from a pitcher in his fridge. He returned with a bowl of sliced fruit and a cheese tray.

"This looks good," I said in surprise.

He shrugged. "I'm on the go a lot. I like to have stuff I can eat without having to cook."

As I eyed the fruit, I said, "Just the cheese and crackers for me. It looks like there might be kiwi in there, and I'm allergic."

"Nuts and kiwi, huh?"

"And shrimp. I know, I'm high maintenance," I said dryly.

"It's not your fault. How bad are the allergies?"

"Some worse than others. I haven't had an attack in a while, but I carry an Epi-Pen just in case." I slid my bag off my shoulder and set it on the floor, putting some distance between the smoke-filled leather bag and myself.

"I'm glad you brought your purse with you."

"I wish I'd grabbed my computer, although you never told me if Sophia found anything on it."

"She found the same spyware that was on your office computer."

"Great." I shuddered to think of what I might have done in front of that camera. Although, I usually kept it on my dining room table and not in my bedroom.

I took a couple of slices of cheese from the tray and popped them in my mouth. As I chewed, my mind went over the trauma we'd just been through. "I can't believe someone put a bomb outside my apartment. Wouldn't that take some planning? Everything seems like it's happening so fast. The video and the audio interview were only released today. How is someone reacting so quickly?"

"It might not have been that sophisticated. It could have been gasoline, some rags, and a match," he said, as he peeled an orange and bit into it.

"I guess. It was a big bang."

"They might have mixed in a firecracker."

"I don't know how we survived. When I woke up and you were unconscious, I thought the worst. I thought you were dead, Ethan. And it would have been my fault if you were."

He set down his orange, wiped his hands on a dishcloth, then came around the counter and put his hands on my shoulders. "I'm not dead," he said, gazing into my eyes. "And nothing is your fault. It's the fault of the person who set the fire."

"They set it because of me."

He shrugged. "The act is still on them. And the worst didn't happen." He paused as a light entered his eyes. "In fact, I got something pretty good out of it."

"What?" I asked in amazement.

"Another kiss," he said. "You kissed me when I was out, didn't you?"

"I was trying to make sure you were breathing," I said, feeling a little embarrassed that he'd woken up to me kissing him.

"Well, you woke me up, and that's what allowed us to get out. So you saved my life, before I saved yours." He rubbed my tight shoulders. "I'd say that makes us even."

"I'd say your idea of even is very skewed," I said, feeling a wave of emotion at his sweet words.

He grinned. "Okay, if we're not even, then you owe me another kiss."

"Are you sure you want one? Back in my apartment, before everything happened, you said it was a bad idea."

"Well, that's probably still true. But I don't care." He paused, giving me a questioning look. "Unless you care?"

I shook my head. "I don't care about anything but right now." I clasped his head with my hands and brought his lips down to meet mine.

Ethan tasted like the juicy orange he'd just eaten, which made the kisses between us even sweeter. And those kisses were filled with emotion, too: desire, gratitude, joy at being alive. It all mixed together, and the connection that had been building between us strengthened even more.

As Ethan lifted his head, he said, "You pack a punch, Emily Hollister."

"I think that's you. Or it's us—together."

He nodded and took a step back, and I felt as if my words had brought down some curtain between us. The closeness I'd felt was suddenly further away.

"What's wrong?" I asked.

"Nothing."

"It's something."

"There's a lot going on. We should put a pin in this," he said.

Disappointment ran through me, but I couldn't argue his point. There was a lot going on, and maybe I was moving too fast toward what might just be another bad ending. I'd barely broken up with Ashton. In fact, Ashton probably didn't even know we were broken up.

"For now," Ethan added, making me feel better. He moved around the counter, looking relieved to have a solid buffer between us.

For a few minutes, we both munched on cheese and crackers, and while I would have preferred to savor the afterglow of kissing Ethan, my mind started spinning back to the earlier events. So much had happened, I couldn't grasp it all. It made me want to run back to the beach and lose myself in the past, but I couldn't do that again. I had to keep pushing forward.

"My tormentor had a busy day today," I said finally. "They put out a video, faked my voice in an interview, and blew up my apartment."

"That might have been someone else," Ethan suggested. "Someone who thought your interview was a threat to their secret."

"But again, they would have had to act really quickly. Is that likely?"

"Jimmy found you fast."

I sighed. "Back to Jimmy again."

"Just saying. That interview was enough to make him come out of hiding. Maybe it triggered someone else."

"Before I do anything else, I need to hear the interview. I have to know exactly what she said." I reached for my phone, then stopped myself. "But you said I shouldn't use my phone."

"You can use my computer," he said, leaving the kitchen. He came back a moment later with his laptop. He set it in front of me and logged in, then left me to search.

I put in my name, wincing at all the shocking headlines that came up in less than ten seconds. "Wow, I am really popular today."

He gave me a commiserating smile. "What do they say in your business? Any press is good press?"

"I've told people that, but I don't know that it's true. I had a meeting with my bosses earlier today before the video was released online. Mitchell was there, too. Ashton had called Mitchell and sent him the video, so he could preemptively excuse himself for what happened. Mitchell was ecstatically happy to fill my bosses in and told them he wants me pulled from the next movie. He doesn't want to work with someone who tried to kill him, and he thinks I'm bad for business."

"I'm sorry, Emily. That sucks. And it's not fair."

"Totally unfair. Francine got David and Curtis to hold off on a decision, but I suspect this interview, and whatever is coming next, will seal the deal for me being removed."

"There's no way to get rid of Mitchell?"

"I don't think so, unless I can blame him for any of this, but I'd need proof, and I don't have it."

"It is interesting that he was at the party where that actress died."

"It is, and it isn't. A lot of people were there. It was an industry party."

"How did Jimmy get in there? What was his play?"

"He was pretending to be an agent. He even got clients through Vanessa's family ties."

"Who is Vanessa again?"

"She was his wife for a couple of years, another one of the women he bled dry. Her father had run a Hollywood agency, and she had connections there that got Jimmy his job."

"Jimmy knows how to get ahead. I'll give him that," Ethan said.

I looked back at the computer, searching for the audio clip. "Here's the interview with someone named Sienna Kline." I put on the sound and hit play, listening in stunned amazement to what sounded like my voice answering the interviewer's questions about the sex tape. The woman pretending to be me came across proud and confident, and it felt incredibly strange to hear someone who sounded exactly like me.

"My boyfriend and I have sex like every other couple," the other Emily said. "It's disturbing that a private video was made public, and Ashton and I are determined to find out who hacked into our phones to get this tape."

I paused the recording. "Unbelievable," I muttered. "She's suggesting that Ashton and I videotaped ourselves, and someone stole the video."

"Yes," Ethan agreed. "And people will believe it."

I pushed play again, as the interviewer's voice came across the recording. *"Are you concerned about this hurting your career?" Sienna asked.*

"No. I'm not ashamed of my life. In fact, I've been thinking for a while that I want to come completely clean, tell everyone who I really am. There's a lot of interest in my life since The Opal King *came out, and I'm tired of others suggesting what kind of person I am, where I came from, what I know or don't know."*

"That sounds intriguing, Emily. What are you going to come clean about?"

"How I grew up. My stepfather was a con artist, and when I was a child, I was his partner. We had a lot of illegal adventures. I know many things about many people. I know where they hide all their dirty laundry."

"Tell me more," Sienna urged.

"Well, you'll have to read my book."

"Oh, you're writing a book?"

"Yes, and I'm going to be releasing the first chapter soon, where I'll be teasing some of the dirt I have to spill. I've been working in Hollywood for a long time. I know where the skeletons are buried. I know who created some of those skeletons."

"I don't think I can wait, Emily," Sienna said. "Give me something now. The viewers are dying. My phone is lighting up right now with incoming calls. Are you going to be talking about the accident that put Mitchell Gray in the hospital, the one he suggests you might have had a hand in?"

"Of course. But that's not all. I'll also be discussing Faye Weston's tragic death…or should I say murder?"

"Are you serious? You know something about that? Was it Faye's husband, Cole?" Sienna asked.

"I can't tell you that."

"It's been a mystery for a long time. How do you know so much when you had to have been a teenager when it happened?"

"I was a teenager, but you don't know who I was living with or what we were doing. I'm not going to tell you more now but stay tuned."

"Wait, don't go, Emily," Sienna said.

Her protest was met with silence.

"I guess we'll have to leave it at that," Sienna said. "But don't worry, I'll be getting Emily Hollister back on the line as soon as I can."

I blew out a breath as the recording ended. "That was worse than I imagined."

"She has definitely upped the ante," Ethan said.

"I just wish I knew who I was playing against. She has skills: hacking, voice-altering, and she knows how to tease out a good story. No wonder Jimmy came running to my door. He thought I was about to blow his life apart."

"Have you heard from Ashton about any of this?" Ethan asked.

"I haven't spoken to him in hours. He might have called. I turned off my phone earlier. I didn't want to see or talk to anyone, especially after I realized he'd gone to Mitchell, which has had a serious impact on my career."

"It seems like he threw you under the bus."

"It does. I wonder why this other Emily brought Ashton into it at all. Why go to the trouble of setting him up like that? She could have done the radio interview without the tape."

"It wouldn't have been as interesting."

"I suppose."

"There was probably another motive as well. She wanted to break you and Ashton up. Rip your relationship apart. Isolate you. Make people look at you differently. That's what everything seems to be about. She wants to take away everything that you have: your job, your boyfriend, your home, your sense of safety. She's going to strip you bare, Emily."

His words sent a chill through me. "And then send the vultures to feast on me."

"Well, that was more graphic than I was going for," he said, trying to ease the tension with a small smile.

"But it's the truth. I must have hurt her."

"Or the person she's working with. Like I said before, this could be more than one individual."

"I know," I said with a sigh. "I wish I could go back to the beach. The few hours I spent on the sand this afternoon were a nice break. That's where I went when all the news broke. I had to get out of my office, and the beach has always been my happy place. It's where my mom and I went whenever things got hard."

"It must have sucked to lose your mother at such a young age."

"It was awful. This afternoon, I remembered the last time we went to the beach together. I didn't know she was already sick then. I didn't know she was sick until the very end."

"I'm sure she didn't want you to know."

"She didn't. She acted like nothing was wrong, that she just had some doctor appointments to go to, that there was nothing to worry about. And then one day she told me she and Jimmy were going to take a trip. I wanted to go with them, but she said she didn't want me to miss school, so I was going to stay with a friend from school. She gave me a long, tight hug, so hard I felt like my ribs were going to break. She said she loved me and that I need to be a big girl and be strong. I realized later that was goodbye."

"Where did she go? The hospital?"

"No. She had Jimmy drive her to Oregon, where she took some medication, and she died."

Ethan sucked in a breath. "I was not expecting you to say that. That's rough, Emily."

"Jimmy came home alone and told me she was in heaven, and he was going to take care of me. That's what my mom wanted. I guess she did want that, because she must have known that's who I'd end up with. There wasn't anyone else."

"So, they were a couple?"

"Yes. I think it was real because my mom wasn't rich. She had nothing for him to steal. She told me once that he made her laugh, and she knew who he was and that made her comfortable. She didn't have to figure him out. I don't know if that meant she knew he was a con artist, or if she was conned into thinking he was a good guy. Either way, she was gone, and I was with him."

"Damn." Ethan shook his head. "I'm really sorry. That's even worse than what you said before. Didn't social services check on you to make sure you were with someone? They weren't married, were they?"

"Jimmy said they were married. There was a certificate at some point. Later in my life, I thought he probably faked that whole thing to get her insurance money, but maybe she wouldn't have cared if he got the money, since she knew he'd be taking care of me. I try to take solace in the fact that she went out the way she wanted to. She was very big about taking control of her life. She'd want me to take control of mine now. In fact, sometimes I think she would have been really disappointed in me."

"How could you think that? Look what you've lived through, how you've gotten past the huge obstacles in your life."

His words were like a soothing salve. "Thanks for saying that, but I've done bad things. I've lied. I've stolen from people. I've kept secrets. I've pretended to be someone I wasn't. Maybe everything that's happening to me now is karma."

"It's not karma; it's revenge," he said flatly. "And what you did as a kid, you had to do to survive. How you've been living your life since you turned eighteen is admirable."

"Even though I blackmailed Jimmy?"

"He deserved that."

I was glad not to see judgment in Ethan's eyes, but maybe that's because he'd gotten an up-close and personal view of Jimmy. "I have to do better. I can't go into hiding like I did this afternoon. I can't keep pretending that there's a way to hang on to my secrets. They're going to come out, every single one of them, and even if I can't stop that from happening, I have to control the narrative."

"Maybe you should give your own interview."

"It's a thought. I need to consider all my options, but I'm going to fight. If I'm going down, I'm going down swinging."

"That's the only way to go down."

"This woman who's pretending to be me has already destroyed most of my life. What's left?"

"I think you know," he said quietly.

"She wants to completely erase me," I said.

"Which she isn't going to do."

"She seems to be succeeding so far."

"Well, your turn at bat isn't up yet," he said lightly.

"I opened myself up to the baseball metaphor, didn't I?"

"Yes, you did," he said, as the oven timer went off.

He pulled the pizza out of the oven, and my mind was immediately focused on the hot, bubbling cheese, and the smell of spicy pepperoni and garlic. Ethan only gave it a minute to cool before he started slicing it up. And I was eager to join him in eating it.

When we'd finished, I cleaned up while Ethan went into his bedroom to get some things.

I wasn't sure what those things were, but he returned a moment later, with a duffel bag in one hand, having changed into clean jeans and a T-shirt. His face was still bruised, with a tape over one cut that had been put there by the EMTs, but he looked fresher than I felt.

"I grabbed you a T-shirt and some sweats to sleep in," he said. "They'll probably be huge on you. We can get you some clothes tomorrow."

"That's fine. Thanks for thinking about it. You took a shower. I'm jealous."

"I'd offer you one now, but I think we should go. You can shower at the hotel." He grabbed his laptop and put it in the duffel bag.

"All right. Are we taking a taxi?"

"No. A friend of mine has an extra car. He lives down the street. We're going to borrow it. Are you ready to go?"

I'd followed Ethan through fire. I might as well follow him to a friend's house and wherever he wanted to go next. "I'm ready."

CHAPTER TWENTY

A HALF HOUR LATER, just before ten o'clock at night, we checked into a beachfront, high-rise hotel in Santa Monica, and Ethan requested a high floor with an ocean view. He constantly surprised me. I thought we'd be checking into some third-rate motel, but this hotel was very nice, and we had a one-bedroom suite with a kitchenette and a deluxe bathroom.

"Okay, I'm definitely paying for this," I said as I picked up one of the two truffle boxes that were sitting by the pillows on the king-size bed. "And we each get one of these."

"You can have both. It seems like a two-chocolate kind of day."

"I can't argue with that. I didn't think you'd pick a hotel like this."

"It has decent security, and tomorrow you'll wake up to a view of the ocean. Maybe it will perk you up like when your mom took you to the beach."

I was touched by his thoughtfulness. Ethan was certainly someone who paid attention to details. I hadn't been around that many men who listened closely to my stories. Although, to be fair, I wasn't one to share personal details, so if they didn't know me that well, it probably wasn't completely their fault.

"Thanks," I said, knowing the word didn't begin to encompass my gratitude, but I also knew that Ethan didn't want to hear more. He wasn't someone who wanted acknowledgment. In fact, he often seemed uncomfortable with appreciation.

"The couch in the living room is also a pullout, so you can have this bed to yourself," he added.

I flushed, thinking I wouldn't mind sharing the bed with him, but he'd backed off after our kiss in his kitchen, so I needed to do the same. And the last thing I should be thinking about right now was sex. Although, it would be really nice to lose myself in his arms for a while and not think about anything. But that wasn't going to happen.

Clearing my throat, I said, "I can take the couch."

"No. Not only do you deserve the bed, I would like to be the one closest to the door."

"You're acting like my personal bodyguard. I should pay you."

"Why are you so obsessed with paying me?" he asked curiously.

"Our relationship feels very one-sided."

"If I'm not concerned, you shouldn't be, either." He returned to the living room, and I followed, taking one of the chocolates with me. As Ethan sat down on the couch, he pulled his laptop out of his duffel bag and set it on the coffee table. I joined him on the sofa.

"I'm glad you brought that," I said. "I feel very disconnected without my phone, and I need to see what else is being said about me online."

"Do you need to see more? It's been a long day."

"The more I know, the less opportunity this other woman will have to blindside me."

"Good point."

"If I text my boss from your computer, will someone be able to find us?" I asked Ethan.

"No, I have the computer set up to block my ISP address. She also won't know the text is coming from you, since it won't be your number. She may delete it or not read it."

"Maybe I'll just send her an email then." I wrote Francine a note, keeping it brief, saying there had been a fire in my building, and I needed a day off to regroup, but I'd be back in the office on Wednesday, and I was planning to attend the dinner Wednesday night at Mitchell's house. I hoped she wouldn't make a decision about taking me off the movie until then. As I hit Send, I knew that the decision about the movie had probably already been made, but I had to try to change it.

When that was done, I suddenly felt exhausted. I should go through the rest of my inbox and look online for stories about me, but I didn't have the energy. I closed the laptop, feeling immensely relieved after doing so, as if I'd completely shut out the rest of the world.

"Done already?" he asked.

"You were right. I need a break from knowing more. Whatever is happening will have to happen without me. I should probably go to bed, but I feel tired and wired at the same time."

"How about some cards?" he asked, reaching back into his duffel bag.

"You brought playing cards? What else is in that bag?"

He grinned. "A few things."

"Why cards?"

"They were in the bag from a camping trip I went on."

"I haven't played cards in years, not since I used to play poker with Jimmy. He tried to teach me how to bluff, but I was terrible at it. I gave way too much away."

Ethan smiled. "I can see that. You have very expressive eyes."

"I'll bet you're good at bluffing, because I have a hard time figuring out what you're thinking."

"Good. I like to be mysterious," he joked.

"I could use a little less mystery in my life."

He shuffled the cards on the table. "How about some blackjack? No bluffing required."

"I like that idea. It will feel less like one of Jimmy's poker games when he used to use me to figure out what cards the other men were holding."

"He took you to adult male poker games when you were what—ten?"

"Yes. No one pays attention to a kid in the corner, looking at videos on her stepfather's phone."

Ethan shook his head. "I like this guy less and less the more I hear about him."

"To be fair, Jimmy could be fun. When we were riding high, we were living in mansions in Beverly Hills with pools and tennis courts, and I was going to birthday parties with rich kids whose party favor bags probably cost at least a hundred dollars each."

"And when you were riding low?"

"Skanky motels that smelled like beer and sweat, broken-down TV's that barely got cartoons, and eating food that came out of a vending machine." I paused. "There wasn't a lot in between those experiences. It was one or the other."

"How could Jimmy get so rich that you could live in a mansion?"

"It wasn't about being rich…it was the illusion of money. We'd leave as soon as the illusion faded or someone arrived to evict us."

"Jimmy must have changed his name a lot. What about you? Were you always Emily?"

"Always Emily, but I had different last names when I was with him."

"Would the people who knew you in high school know you as Emily Hollister or someone else?"

"Hollister." I suddenly frowned as a disturbing thought occurred to me. "Dammit. I forgot I'm supposed to have lunch tomorrow with Cassie and Alina, my two high school friends."

"The woman from Friday night's party?"

"Yes. I really don't want to meet them tomorrow. They're

going to ask a million questions about the video and the interview, and they'll know I lied to them about my past, and that will bring more questions." I shuddered at the thought.

"What did you tell them about your past?"

"I made up a big story about how I grew up with parents who worked for the Peace Corps. We traveled the world, helping people, until one day they were caught in an earthquake when they were delivering water to a poor village in Mexico. I wasn't with them at the time, so I survived. I painted them as incredible people, amazing heroic individuals. My father was a doctor. My mother was a nurse. It was all a lie, a beautiful story to tell about my parents, and a way to explain where I'd been all my life. Part of the lie came from Jimmy. He'd gotten me school records from a school in Mexico City, so I built on that." I smiled to myself. "I told it so often I almost believed it."

"You haven't told me anything about your real father."

"I have nothing to tell. My mom said it was a one-night stand, someone she met in a bar. She didn't even know his last name. It was a bar she'd gone into on vacation, so it was hours away from where we lived. She never tried to find him, and since I only know his name was Kyle, I haven't ever looked for him. To be honest, I'm not even sure that wasn't just a story, too. Maybe that's why I like to direct now. I can take the story where I want it to go."

"And you can make it true for your characters."

"Yes, I can do that. Anyway, that's what Cassie and Alina know about my past. They thought Jimmy's cousin was just a relative who took me in after my parents died, and Rhea went along with it. She didn't care to explain anything, either. They'll be pretty shocked to learn I grew up with a con man." I shook my head. "I need to get out of lunch."

"I think you should go. They're from your past. And they might have information you can use."

"That's true, but it will be so awkward and uncomfortable. They'll want to talk about Ashton and the sex tape and everything else. Do I tell them the truth or pretend that the interview is a lie?" Groaning, I added, "I thought I was done pretending."

"That's the problem with secrets. They always come back to bite you. Let's play some blackjack. You can think about lunch and decide tomorrow."

"Good idea. And while we're playing, you can tell me more about your life."

"I already told you."

"Barely anything," I scoffed.

"I told you about my parents, my little brother, the Marine Corps. And you already know about Steven."

"What about personal relationships? Have you ever been married? Lived with anyone? Been in love?"

"That's four questions," he complained.

"And that's not an answer to any of them," I said pointedly, as he dealt me two cards.

"Never been married. Never officially lived with anyone, although there have been a couple of women who seemed to end up with a lot of shit at my apartment for a few months."

"And none of those were serious relationships?"

"When I was in the service, I was deployed for months at a time. I wasn't around long enough to have a serious relationship."

"What about after you left the Marine Corps?"

He shrugged. "Nope. What do you want to do with your cards?"

I looked at my cards—sixteen. "I'll stay."

He played out his hand—a king, a two, and nine. "Twenty-one," he said.

"The hard way—twenty-one without an ace."

Ethan gave me a sexy grin. "Story of my life. Every time I go for simple, I end up in a complicated mess. The hard way describes my life."

"Mine, too." Pausing, I added. "You could leave, Ethan. Not that I want you to go, but I'm probably safe here on my own."

He met my gaze. "I'm not going anywhere, Emily. I'm not someone who walks away from people who are in trouble."

"I know. It's kind of an amazing trait."

"You haven't met enough good people."

"You're right, I haven't. And despite everything that brought us together, I'm really glad I met you." I felt a knot of emotion grow in my throat, and I needed to get rid of it, because I was afraid if I gave in to all my feelings right now, there would be a flood of tears, and that wasn't going to be good for anyone. "Deal me another hand," I said.

"You got it."

As we continued to play, I steered the conversation away from the personal, and Ethan was eager to join me in random small talk. We talked about movies and books, and I was surprised how some of his favorite books were also my favorites.

As the hours passed by, we talked about other things we enjoyed. Ethan liked to bike and surf. I told him about my work with a local community theater group and how I liked to mentor budding film students and give them opportunities to come on set. What we didn't talk about was Ethan's job or his career plans. It seemed to be an area he wanted to stay away from, and I respected that.

When the clock passed midnight, and I'd lost three hands in a row, I couldn't stop the yawns from coming. I stumbled off to bed, feeling safe with Ethan watching over me and filled with hope that tomorrow would be a better day.

But the way things were going, that was probably an overly optimistic thought.

CHAPTER TWENTY-ONE

TUESDAY MORNING CAME TOO FAST. I was tempted to close my eyes again and snuggle back under the covers, but then my gaze caught on the bedside clock, and I realized it was almost nine. I never slept in until nine. But then, I hadn't gone to bed until after midnight.

Rolling onto my back, I stared up at the ceiling, wondering if Ethan was awake. It was very quiet in the hotel suite. Although, I could hear the muffled sound of the ocean. That got me out of bed.

I walked over to the window, wearing nothing but one of Ethan's T-shirts that hung down to my thighs. I opened the curtains and blinked at the bright sunshine.

It was such a pretty day. It seemed at odds with the darkness in my life. Maybe it was over, I told myself optimistically. What more could they do to me? They'd almost blown me up and burned me out of my house.

Unfortunately, I couldn't believe that was the end, because they hadn't succeeded in getting rid of me. I was still alive. And if they thought I knew something, I was still a threat.

Blowing out a breath, I turned away from the window and

headed into the bathroom. I showered and then put on my still smoky clothes before making my way into the living room.

Ethan was sitting on the couch, gazing at his computer, looking deliciously rumpled, with a shadow of beard on his cheeks and his brown hair tousled. A surge of desire ran through me, and I clenched my fists to stop myself from running across the room and throwing myself into his arms. Which was a good idea, because I suddenly realized he was talking to someone on his computer.

He motioned me forward. "She's awake," he said aloud, facing the screen. Then he turned to me. "I want you to meet Peter Edgehill, your new private investigator."

He patted the couch next to him, and I awkwardly sat down, glad I'd at least showered before this surprise appearance. Not that Peter Edgehill was overdressed. Peter had longish blond, curly hair, a short brown beard, and light-blue eyes. He wore a red T-shirt with a girl riding a surfboard on the front. He was drinking a coffee, with a bowl of cereal in front of him.

"Hi," I said. "I'm Emily Hollister."

"I've been learning a lot about you," Peter replied.

"Do you think you can help me?"

"Absolutely. I was just telling Ethan that I have to go to court this morning, but as soon as I get back, I'll get started on your case."

Relief ran through me. "That would be great. Thank you."

"Don't thank me yet. I haven't done anything. I hate to cut this short, but I have to change before I see the judge. We'll talk later, Emily."

"Thanks," I said, sitting back on the couch as Peter's face disappeared and Ethan shut down the program.

Ethan turned to me. "This is the right move. Peter can help you more than I can."

"I'm not going to turn down help."

"Good. How did you sleep?"

"Surprisingly well. How about you? Was the couch comfortable?"

He gave a careless shrug. "It was fine."

"It smells like coffee in here."

"I just made some." He tipped his head to the coffeemaker on the counter in the small kitchenette.

"Thank God." I got up and moved quickly to the counter and poured myself a cup. The first sip was delicious. "It's good."

"I also ordered food. It should be here in a few minutes. I wasn't sure what you liked, so I got eggs, pancakes, and French toast. I also ordered some bacon and some fruit, with a specific note that no nuts, kiwi, or shrimp be anywhere near the preparation of our meal."

"Good memory. Thank you." I sat down in the chair next to the couch. "What are you working on?"

"A little research on Faye Weston's mysterious death. You were right. There were a lot of stars there that night."

I sipped my coffee, then said, "Most of the speculation centered on Faye's husband, Cole."

"I saw that. Have you ever met him?"

"Several times. He has been in a few of our films over the years. I haven't had a lot to do with him, but he's quite close to Francine. She was friends with both Cole and Faye. That's partly why she's against producing a movie about Faye's death. She also thinks it would be disrespectful and only fuel more negative rumors about Cole."

Ethan sat back against the couch. "It sounds like she's protective of Cole."

"She can be very protective of her friends. I thought at one time I fit into that category, but I'm not sure anymore. Everything that is going on now is putting a strain on our relationship. I'm not sure what she thinks, except that I'm complicating all of our lives." Ethan gave me a thoughtful look, and I could see the wheels turning. "What are you thinking?" I asked.

"You won't like it."

"What else is new? Just tell me."

"I'm wondering if Francine could have another reason for not wanting Mitchell to make a movie about Faye. A reason that goes beyond her friendship with Cole."

I knew what reason he was talking about. "She couldn't have killed Faye. They were friends, too."

"People kill their friends all the time. Haven't you heard that love and hate are two sides of the same coin?"

"I've never heard Francine say anything but good things about Faye. And she's crazy about Cole."

"Maybe there was a love triangle going on between the three of them."

"You really like love triangles, don't you? First, you thought I was involved in a love triangle I knew nothing about. Now you think Francine, Cole, and Faye might have been in one."

He grinned. "Hey, it's a solid theory."

"I'm thinking you have as big of an imagination as I do." I paused. "And I can't stand the idea of Francine trying to hurt me. She's been like a second mother to me, or at least a big sister."

"Well, it's probably not her, although she would have access to your computer, your bag, your keys..."

I sighed. "You have a point. But I can't see how messing up my life would help her. Although, it is possible that Francine knows Cole did something to Faye, and she's trying to protect him."

"Or Cole might think Francine did something to Faye, and he's the one coming after you."

"Or maybe Mitchell did it, and by making a movie, he can put the blame on someone else and make sure that no one suspects it was him," I countered. "We could spin this a lot of different ways."

Ethan smiled at me. "Maybe we should write a story together."

I smiled back at him. "Maybe we should."

A knock came at the door, and I jumped, relaxing only when I heard the words, "Room service".

"I'll get it," he said. As Ethan got up, he grabbed something out of his bag, and I was shocked to realize it was a gun.

"You have a gun?" I asked.

He looked back at me. "Yes. Sometimes I need one on the job."

"I haven't seen you wearing a gun at the store."

"That job doesn't require me to do so," he said evenly. He glanced through the peephole and said, "It's room service. But just to be sure, why don't you wait in the other room?"

I gave him a worried look, then got up and went into the bedroom. I closed the door and pushed the lock, feeling suddenly nervous again. Was it room service? Or had someone found us and was about to shoot their way into the suite? Even with a weapon, Ethan might not be able to take down more than one person.

My heart raced with every passing second, but all I heard was muffled voices, and then Ethan called out.

"All clear, Emily."

I blew out a breath of relief and returned to the living room to find breakfast set up on the small table by the kitchenette. I joined Ethan, who was already settling into what looked like a feast. I normally wasn't a big breakfast eater, but this looked too good to pass up. Plus, I doubted I'd have much appetite for lunch when I met up with Cassie and Alina.

"So," Ethan said, as he worked his way through the pancakes. "I need to go to work after this. I'm sorry to run out on you."

"I understand. You have a job to do."

"I wish I could leave you the car," he said with a frown. "But I'm going to need it."

"It's fine. I'll get a taxi to the restaurant to meet Cassie and Alina. That's not until twelve thirty. There are plenty of shops within walking distance, so I'll pick up some clothes before that."

He nodded, his gaze somewhat distracted.

"I'll be fine," I reassured him, sensing he was worrying about leaving me alone.

"I know. That sounds like a good plan. I can get off at two o'clock today, so I can probably pick you up after lunch."

"Are you sure?"

"Yeah. Maybe we can meet up with Peter after that. I'll check with him later to see what time will work." He took one last bite of his pancakes, then pushed back his chair. "I'm going to take a quick shower."

"Thanks for ordering breakfast."

"No problem."

While Ethan was showering, I finished eating and then wandered back to the computer he had set up on the coffee table. I checked my email first. Francine's name popped up right away, and I clicked on her message.

I'm worried about you, Emily. Why aren't you answering your phone? I've called you a dozen times. I just went by your building on my way into work this morning and was shocked to see the extent of the fire damage. There was a guy out front, who told me that there was an explosion on your floor. I didn't realize a bomb had gone off. What the hell is going on? Please call me or email me. I want to help you. I need to know that you're okay. Everyone here is very concerned. As far as tomorrow night's dinner goes, I need to talk to you about that, so let's chat soon.

I was touched by her concern. It was nice that Francine had gone by my building to try to find me, which reminded me she had always been a friend to me as well as a boss. There was no way she was trying to kill me. However, her last sentence had implied that I probably wasn't going to get to stay on *Aces High*.

I wrote her back, choosing my words carefully, because while I really didn't think she had it in for me, she was tightly connected to Mitchell and Cole, and I didn't know if either of them was involved. I told her I was all right. I was staying with friends, but I needed to take the day off to figure out where I was going to live for the foreseeable future. I would call her as soon as I could.

After sending that, I opened one of Kaitlyn's emails that had come in a few minutes before Francine's.

Emily, OMG!!! What is going on? The media are calling nonstop. Ashton says he's been calling and texting you since yesterday afternoon, but you haven't gotten back to him. He said he needs to respond to the press today about your relationship, and he'd like to talk to you first. I told him I haven't heard from you. I'm really concerned, and Francine and Jonah are feeling the same way.

I want to help. What can I do? Is there any work I can take care of while you're dealing with these personal issues? I hope you know you can count on me. I've already rescheduled your meetings for today. The one at eleven this morning I couldn't switch. The author and her agent are only in town for the day, so I'll take it with Jonah. I hope that's okay. I keep thinking that you'll want me to keep working and make sure nothing falls through the cracks, so that's what I'll do. Call me as soon as you can. Kaitlyn.

Of course Kaitlyn would take over for me. She was probably thrilled to have the chance. I was out of the action, and she was the heroine for stepping up to keep my projects running smoothly.

Frowning, I realized how difficult it must have been for Mitchell to lie in that hospital bed in pain, knowing that his movie was being directed by someone else. Like Kaitlyn, I'd embraced the idea that I was saving the day and didn't really think much about the person I was saving the day for.

But as I thought more about Kaitlyn taking over my job, I wondered if this was the plan all along: to drive me out of my job, so people like Kaitlyn, and probably Jonah, could take over for me. They were both taking part in a meeting that they wouldn't have otherwise been invited to. And it wouldn't stop with this meeting. The longer I stayed out of work, the more access they would gain to my projects.

I looked up as Ethan returned, looking even more attractive

after a shower, although his uniform still felt odd to me, like he was in the wrong clothes, the wrong job. But it was his business, and I needed to let it go.

"Everything okay?" he asked.

"Kaitlyn and Jonah are taking over my meetings today."

"At your request?"

"No. They're taking the initiative to help me," I said, unable to hide the sarcasm in my voice. "I wonder if it's a mistake not to go to work. But at the same time, I know I need to pull myself together first."

"It's just a day, Emily. They can't take your job that fast."

"You're right. It's just a day. I'll check in later this afternoon. Francine also sent me an email saying that she went by my place this morning and talked to some guy out front, probably Tyler, the building manager. He told her there was an explosion on my floor, and she wants to know what's going on."

"Don't we all," he said dryly. "Did you write her back?"

"Yes. I said I'd explain later. I didn't want to get into details, because of all the various scenarios we went through earlier that involve people at my office."

"That was smart."

"I hope so. But I do need to talk to her. I want to turn on my phone."

"It's best to keep it off for now."

"Unless I get a prepaid phone?"

"That's an option," he agreed. "We can get you one later. At any rate, I'll be in the parking lot of the restaurant by two fifteen. If you're done earlier, wait inside. I'll come find you when I get there. But I won't talk to you until you're away from your friends."

"It's fine. You don't have to avoid them."

"I'm sure it would be easier not to have to explain who I am, considering the other questions that you'll have to answer during lunch."

"Good point. So you're off?"

"In one second." He surprised me by walking across the room and leaning down to give me a kiss. He smiled. "Had to do that first."

My lips tingled from the brief kiss. "I thought we weren't doing that anymore."

"That was yesterday. I didn't say anything about today."

I smiled. I liked this teasing, playful side of Ethan. It almost made me feel like my world was not about to end.

"I'll see you later, Emily. If you have any trouble, turn on your phone and call me, or call the police. Just make sure you're safe."

"I've been taking care of myself for a long time."

"I know, but just saying."

"Thanks," I said, meeting his gaze. "For everything."

"I'll see you this afternoon."

After Ethan left, I got to my feet and moved to the window, taking a minute to look out at the ocean. I could hear my mom's words in my head again. *You get knocked down. You get back up.* Well, I was up. And I would bounce back. But first I needed to get some clothes.

I grabbed my purse and hotel key and left the room. It felt strange to be by myself, and as soon as I left the hotel, I felt even more vulnerable. Fortunately, it was only three blocks to the Third Street Promenade, where there were lots of people on the street and in the stores.

It was unlikely that anyone had followed us to the hotel, so I needed to stop being paranoid. An hour later, I'd found an outfit for today, some clothes for tomorrow, as well as shoes and other necessities. It wasn't a lot, but it was more than I'd had before. I also picked up a tote bag I could use to pack my extra clothes when I had to move again. It was a little like the old days when I'd lived with Jimmy, and he'd insisted I have a "go bag" just in case we had to leave somewhere quickly, which happened quite a bit. But that wasn't going to become my new norm. I just needed to get through the mess I was in and start over again.

By the time I returned to the hotel, it was after eleven. I

quickly changed clothes and got ready to meet Alina and Cassie. I was looking forward to seeing Alina again. But the fact that she was with Cassie, and Cassie had made such strange remarks about me always being ready to step in when someone got hurt, I couldn't trust that this lunch wouldn't be an ambush. I hoped not. I hoped it would just be about catching up with two old friends.

I arrived at the restaurant on time but saw Cassie and Alina already seated at a table by the window. Cassie was facing the door, saw me, and gave a wave. As I moved toward them, Alina turned around and gave me a happy smile. And in that moment, I was reminded of something I'd forgotten—that Alina's brown hair and eyes were very much like mine, that we'd often been mistaken for sisters.

My stomach suddenly turned over. I hadn't seen Alina in at least eight years. There was no reason she'd suddenly reappear in my life to torment me in such a cruel way. She was the closest person I'd ever had to a best friend.

But was that even true? Wouldn't best friends have kept in touch during college and after college? Alina and I had drifted apart very quickly.

That was because of me. I'd wanted to put some distance between the present and the past and Alina and Cassie and my high school friends had been part of the past. So I'd moved forward. Until now.

And I had a feeling that going back in time would turn out to be a terrible idea.

CHAPTER TWENTY-TWO

WHEN I GOT to the table, both Cassie and Alina stood up, and we exchanged quick hugs and flattering comments about how good we all looked and how long it had been.

As we sat down, Cassie said, "We weren't sure you were going to come, Emily. I've been calling you since yesterday. I even tried your office today and spoke to your assistant, Kaitlyn. She told me you were taking the day off, and she had no idea if you were coming to lunch or not."

"I'm sorry. There's been a lot going on."

"We know," Alina interjected, giving me a compassionate smile. "I'm sorry, Emily. It seems like you're going through a lot right now, but I'm so glad you came. I've been following your career for the last few years, and I am so happy for your success. And when you started dating Ashton Hunter, I could hardly believe it was the same girl who lamented that she would never have a boyfriend."

I smiled at her words. "We both did a lot of lamenting."

"Hey, I was there, too," Cassie put in, never wanting to be the one who was left out.

"But you had more boyfriends than we did," Alina said.

"Well, that's true," Cassie said with a smug smile. But when she looked at me, her expression changed. It seemed to be a mix of empathy and also a little glee. "Tell us what happened with Ashton. Is he speaking the truth? Did you leak the tape to ruin his career because he wanted to break up?"

"What?" I asked, shocked by her words.

"Cassie," Alina protested. "She doesn't have to talk about that. We're here to catch up."

"How can we not talk about it?" Cassie asked. "It's all over the news. People in here are staring at us."

Was she right? I looked around. One server was eyeing our table, but the other customers didn't seem to be that interested in our conversation.

"You don't have to answer," Alina assured me. "We can talk about whatever you want."

"Just tell us if what Ashton said was true," Cassie pleaded. "Then we'll talk about whatever you want."

"Wait a second," I said, confused again. "Did you talk to Ashton? Did he tell you I leaked the tape?"

"No, I didn't talk to him," Cassie replied. "I read his post online. He said the sex video and the drugs were your idea. That you set him up because he wanted to break up with you. He hadn't realized you were that kind of person. He took a little responsibility for getting too drunk to be aware of what you were doing, but he hoped you would get some help and understand that not all relationships go the distance."

I stared at her with astonishment. "What the hell are you talking about? None of that is true. Ashton said that?"

"He posted it on his social media," Cassie said. "You haven't seen it? It went up this morning, a few hours ago."

"It's bad, Emily," Alina put in. "If he's lying, that's a really shitty thing to do."

"Ashton is lying. He got drunk or drugged on the night that video was taken. I wasn't even there."

Cassie gave me a disbelieving look. "You were in the video."

"It wasn't me. The girl's face is never shown. It's just someone with brown hair. And it happened after the party Friday night. I went home early because I wasn't feeling well."

"It looked like you, Emily," Cassie said doubtfully. "And Ashton said it was you."

"Well, it wasn't," I snapped.

"Hey, it's okay," Alina interrupted. "If you say it wasn't you, then I believe you. *We* believe you," she added, looking pointedly at Cassie.

"I did notice you left the party early," Cassie admitted. "But why would Ashton say it was you?"

"Because he's trying to save himself." It was sinking in that Ashton had just thrown me completely under the bus in order to protect his career. Maybe Mitchell had encouraged him to do that so he would be able to put him in the movie. But where did that leave me? I really needed to go to work. But first, I had to get through this damn lunch.

"Well, then Ashton sucks," Alina said, giving me a sympathetic smile. "You're having a rough week, aren't you?"

This was the friend I remembered, the one I'd been able to lean on when I'd run into problems, which had been often since I'd had to start a new high school midway through my freshman year and most of the kids had known each other since kindergarten. "Thanks," I said. "Let's talk about both of you. I know Cassie has a cool job, planning exciting parties. What about you, Alina?"

"I'm still teaching," Alina replied. "But I moved from middle school to high school, and I'm in charge of the drama club this year. Can you believe that?"

"I can. That's exciting. And Drew?"

"He's still waiting for his big break," she said, a somewhat tense note in her voice as I mentioned her longtime boyfriend.

Alina and Drew had gotten together after high school. I'd only known them as bickering friends in the drama club, but they'd gone to college together, and apparently had fallen in love. I knew that much from social media, although I'd stopped following them years ago. It felt a little strange, knowing Alina and Drew were together now, because Drew had been a big crush for me in high school. We'd gone out for a couple of weeks before I found him kissing someone else—which come to think of it had been Cassie.

"Drew is such a good actor," Cassie said. "I don't know if you caught his guest appearance on *Legal 101*, Emily, but he was so good."

"I didn't see that. I'll have to check it out." I was starting to feel a little uncomfortable and wondered if we'd gotten to the hidden agenda part of this lunch.

"You might want to consider him for one of your projects," Cassie continued. "He's incredibly talented."

We had definitely gotten to the hidden agenda. "Well, sure," I said. "I would be happy to consider him if the right role presents itself."

"Stop," Alina said, shaking her head as she sent Cassie another pointed look. Then she turned back to me. "This lunch is not about you helping Drew. I told Cassie not to bring it up."

"Hey, we all started out together," Cassie said. "Why shouldn't we help each other if we can? I helped Emily get on the *Top 30 Under 30* list."

I wondered if that was true. Maybe it was. Maybe Cassie thought she'd have something over me if she did that.

"Emily deserved to be on that list. I saw *The Opal King*," Alina said. "It was brilliant. I saw it twice in fact. I could see you in some of those scenes, especially at the end…the confrontation between the father and the daughter. There was so much emotion, conflict, and moral ambiguity. You loved playing in those gray areas where people aren't all good or all bad."

"I do find the complexities of human nature extremely interesting," I agreed. "Although, based on what I've been going through the past few days, I'm starting to wonder if everyone really does have a good side, or if some people are just plain bad all the way through."

"I'm sorry things are difficult for you right now," Alina said. "You've been through a lot in your life, losing your parents the way you did."

Cassie cleared her throat. "Or maybe your life isn't what you told us."

I drew in a breath. "I know you're referring to an interview that I allegedly gave, but it wasn't me. Someone is pretending to be me. They've stolen my voice and my identity. It's all tied up with that damn video, too."

"So you didn't live with a con artist?" Cassie challenged. "Because all I remember hearing about were your loving and kind parents who served the world in the Peace Corps."

Alina sighed. "Stop, Cassie. This isn't an interrogation."

"It's a simple question," Cassie said.

I looked at them, wondering what I should do, and then I knew. There wasn't an option to lie. Even if I tried, they wouldn't believe me, because I barely believed me. "The story I told you when I met you was a lie," I said. "My mother died from cancer when I was ten. I never knew my father. And I lived for a few years with my stepfather, who did some shady things. Fortunately, he dropped me off at his cousin's house, and Rhea took me in. She gave me the most normal version of a life I'd had in a very long time."

"Why did you lie to us?" Alina asked.

"I wanted a fresh start. I didn't know either of you when I told the lie, and then it was too late to take it back."

"I wish you could have trusted us at some point," Alina continued. "I told you everything, Emily. We were best friends."

"I know. But you didn't have dark things to tell, and I did." I drew in a breath, feeling lighter for having spoken the truth. "That said, I am not the person who gave the interview today. I am not writing a book. I don't know where the skeletons are buried. All that is a lie. Someone is trying to destroy my life, and I don't know who it is."

"It's a crazy story," Alina said.

"How can we know you're not lying now?" Cassie challenged.

"I guess you don't. This lunch was a mistake. I should go."

"No," Alina said immediately, her sharp word keeping me in my seat. "Please don't leave," she added with a plea in her voice. "I've been looking forward to seeing you. I'm a little hurt you lied to us about your past, but I also understand. You were a new kid in high school, and you didn't want to look bad."

"I just wanted to be normal, and I wanted my parents to be normal." I shrugged. "I can't take it back, but I am sorry."

"Thanks for saying that," Alina said. "Can we start over? Because I know we have good things to talk about, too. Your career is going well, right?"

"It has been very good," I admitted. "I love being a director."

"You always had a huge talent," Alina said. "Let's look at the menu and decide what we want to eat, and then we can catch up some more."

I was happy to look at the menu, but I was still full from breakfast, and being attacked by both Cassie and Alina had definitely put a dent in my appetite. So I ordered a salad and an iced tea, as did Alina and Cassie.

As the waiter brought us our drinks, Alina said, "I heard you're working on a new movie."

"Possibly. Things are a little up in the air now. But there are lots of projects coming up, so I'll be staying busy doing something." As I said the words, I realized they were true. Maybe I should let *Aces High* go. I loved the story and I felt attached to it, but I could find another story to love that wouldn't involve Mitchell.

"I bet you've met a lot of celebrities," Alina said.

"I've met a few. I'm sure Cassie has, too."

"Definitely," Cassie said. "It's a huge part of my job, and the bigger the stars, the bigger the party. And the magazine just increased our budget for next year, so we may be going to Cannes and throwing an incredible party at the film festival."

"That sounds amazing," I said, adding a quiet thank-you to the server who placed my salad in front of me.

"Have you been to Cannes?" Alina asked.

"No. I've been to Sundance, though. That's a fun festival, too."

"I've been there as well," Cassie said. "I'm surprised I didn't see you, Emily. It's not that big of a town."

"Maybe we went different years."

"Probably."

"So, you're serious with your boyfriend?" I asked Cassie, searching for topics that did not involve me and my past.

"Expecting a ring any time now," Cassie said. "But I know he wants to ask me in some elaborate and incredible way. He's big on romantic gestures."

"Lucky you."

"I am lucky. Jonathan is the best boyfriend. And his family is awesome, too. They have a house in Aspen that's like a castle."

"You two are really living the glamorous life," Alina said, a little edge to her voice. "Film festivals, big romantic gestures, a castle in the mountains. I don't think either of you would have predicted you'd end up where you are when we were in high school."

"I know I wouldn't have," I said, as I munched on my salad. "But moviemaking isn't that glamorous. There's hours of tedious planning and egotistical actors to deal with. It's not all parties and film festivals."

"Same for event planning," Cassie said. "I still have to stress over logistical problems like how many shrimp to serve and whether or not we'll go over our bar budget."

For the first time, I actually felt like Cassie was being a real person, and it was refreshing.

"Don't do that," Alina said. "Don't downplay your exciting jobs because mine is not. I like what I do. And it's right for me."

I gave her a smile. "I bet you're great with the kids."

"I do love my students. I'm excited to work at the high school level. That will be different." She paused. "I like my life, but sometimes I worry a little that Drew isn't as happy with it as I am."

"Really? Why not?" I asked.

"He has big ambitions, and he's had some success, but not what he thinks he should have. It's just a tough business. And he's been at it awhile now."

"Being an actor can be rough," I agreed. "For every success story, there are thousands of actors who quit every year."

"Drew just needs a break," Cassie put in. "Or someone to break a leg, so he can take over."

My tension returned with her snarky words. I set down my fork. "Okay, that's enough, Cassie. I know that's a dig at me."

"We're talking about Drew, not you," Cassie protested.

"You said something similar to me Friday night, that I got lucky when Mitchell was hurt, just like I got lucky when Kimmy Taylor fell down the stairs, and I had to take over her part in high school."

"Well, you have to admit, you got a good break off their bad breaks."

"Which doesn't make me happy. I don't wish anyone misfortune." I paused. "I've been honest with both of you today. It's time for you to be honest with me. Did you want to meet for lunch, because you want me to give Drew an audition, a part? Is that why we're really here? If it is, just say so."

"It's part of it," Cassie admitted.

"No, it's not," Alina said, shooting Cassie a dark look. Then she turned to me. "I really wanted to see you, Emily. I regret that we lost touch, and when Cassie ran into you, it seemed like a good time to catch up. I didn't come here to ask you to pull strings for Drew, and I told Cassie not to ask you for any favors."

"And I told Alina she was being silly; that's how Hollywood works," Cassie said, without a trace of remorse in her gaze. "Connections get you jobs, and Drew is really good, Emily. He just needs a connection. You were once his friend. Actually, you were more than his friend."

"Until you kissed him," I reminded her.

She dismissed that comment with a wave of her hand. "I was a drunk high school girl. I kissed everyone. It didn't mean anything."

"Not to you."

"Well, sorry if I hurt you."

I almost laughed at her response. "You're not sorry, but okay."

"It wasn't a big deal. And you and Drew were breaking up anyway."

"It's fine. I don't need to talk about that." It felt even more awkward to discuss Drew cheating on me when he was with Alina now. I turned back to her. "I don't know that there's a part for Drew in *Aces High*, but we have a couple of other projects in the works with roles that might be good for him. I'll send you some information. If he's interested in any of them, I'll make sure he gets an audition."

"That's very generous," Alina said. "Are you sure? I don't want you to feel like you have to."

"It's fine. But I'm curious. Did Drew want you to ask me?"

"He didn't say that exactly," Alina replied. "But he was excited that we were reconnecting. Not just because you might find him some work, but he's a big fan of yours, Emily. He thinks you're brilliant."

"Well, thanks."

"Speaking of brilliant," Cassie interrupted. "This restaurant has the most amazing crème brulée. Let's get dessert." She waved the server over. "We'd love three crème brulées," she said.

"Uh, I don't need my own dessert," I said hastily.

"Okay, make it two," Cassie said. "But we need three spoons. You have to try a little."

"Can I get anyone coffee or tea?" the server asked.

"I'll take a coffee," Alina said. "What about you, Emily?"

I really wanted lunch to be over, but I still had fifteen minutes before Ethan would pick me up. "I'll have a coffee as well," I said.

Cassie got to her feet. "I'm going to use the restroom."

As she left, the server cleared the table and brought our coffees.

"I know Cassie gets on your nerves," Alina said with a soft smile. "But she's not as tough and sophisticated as she makes herself out to be. She's just insecure, and she balances that out with a cockiness that can be unattractive. But she has been a good friend to me over the years, and she was excited to see you again."

"Cassie and I were really only friends because we both liked you. I don't have anything against her, but I do wonder if she has something against me."

"She doesn't have anything against you."

I sipped my coffee, letting that comment go. "I have missed you, Alina. I'm glad you're doing well."

"Thanks. I didn't want to say this in front of Cassie, but Drew and I haven't been doing that great, lately. It feels like he's outgrowing me. We used to talk about marriage but now he drops out of any conversation that goes in that direction. I think he blames me for him not being more successful."

"How could you be responsible?"

"I made him live in the valley because I had a good job there, but he felt like he would have made more connections if he was living right in the heart of Studio City. And when we get invited to parties, he always seems like he's embarrassed by me. I'm not some six-foot-tall, blonde model/actress, and he doesn't care to tell people I'm a high school drama teacher. I take him down."

"There is no way you take him down. And while I understand the importance of networking, I think it's just difficult to get good jobs. There's a lot of competition."

"I tell him that, too. But Drew has always been good at everything he has ever done, and he's struggling with the fact that he's not the best yet. He's not at Ashton Hunter's level, that's for sure."

"Ashton is not a good guy," I said flatly, thinking about what he'd said about me.

"I'm beginning to realize that." Alina paused. "I have to admit that Drew has been raving about you so much lately that I was starting to feel jealous. Since you directed *The Opal King,* he's been obsessed with your work. He talks about you a lot."

My discomfort returned with her words. "I appreciate his interest in my work, but there's no reason for you to feel jealous. I haven't spoken to him since high school."

"I know that. But I bet he sometimes wishes he'd ended up with someone like you rather than someone like me."

"I'm sure that's not true. Have you spoken to him about any of this?"

"A little." Her brows drew together. "I probably shouldn't have said any of that. Now you won't want to bring him in for an audition, and I don't want him to have another reason to blame me for missing out on something."

"It's all good," I assured her. "We're just talking like we used to."

"I do miss our talks. Let's stay in touch. Let's not wait another ten years to have lunch."

"I agree."

Cassie returned to the table and gave us a questioning look. "What did I miss?"

"Nothing much," I said, as the waiter set down dessert.

"Just saying that I'd like to do this again," Alina put in.

"I would like that, too," Cassie said. "And I'm sorry for being bitchy, Emily. I know you're going through a rough time, and I shouldn't have piled on. Can we start over?"

"Sure." I didn't trust her, but I didn't need any more enemies at the moment.

Alina handed me one of the desserts.

"I'm good," I said.

"Don't be silly. A few bites. Cassie is right. This is a fantastic dessert. Trust me."

"Okay, maybe I'll have a little," I said, as I spooned some of the crème brulée onto my plate. I took a bite, and as they'd both avowed, it was incredibly good. The crunch on top was perfect, and the crème was smooth and flavorful. I tasted vanilla, but something else, too.

"Isn't this amazing?" Cassie asked. "It's the reason I picked this restaurant. I love this dessert. I can't get enough."

"It's wonderful," I agreed, taking another bite. "Is there something in here besides vanilla?"

"I think there's some fruit," Cassie said. "But just a hint. It's not chunky or anything. It's very smooth."

As I swallowed, my throat started to burn, and a horrifying thought ran through my mind. "What kind of fruit?" I asked, setting down my spoon.

"I'm not sure," Cassie said. "Why? You don't look good, Emily."

"Kiwi?" I bit out, as my throat began to close.

"I don't think so," Cassie said.

"Did you do this on purpose?" I gasped.

"Do what?" Cassie asked.

Alina gave me a look of concern. "Emily, are you all right?"

I shook my head, my throat too tight for words. I wanted to tell them to get my Epi-Pen from my purse, but I couldn't get the words out. As I tried to reach my bag, I fell out of my chair, landing hard on the floor. I could feel my skin burning, my throat closing. I hadn't had a reaction like this in years.

A waiter and manager ran over. Someone called 911 as I put my hand on my throat, looking in panic at Alina and Cassie.

"Help is coming," Alina reassured me.

"Hang in there," Cassie told me.

As their faces swam through my blurred vision, I couldn't help wondering if they were trying to help me or if they were just going to watch me die.

CHAPTER TWENTY-THREE

SUDDENLY, Ethan's face came into view, blocking out Cassie and Alina. He took one look at me, grabbed my purse off the back of my chair, rifling through it until he found what I needed. He grabbed my Epi-Pen and stuck it into my thigh, exactly where it needed to go.

At first, I thought it might be too late, but then the tightness in my throat began to ease.

"Emily?" Ethan said, leaning over me, his beautiful dark eyes piercing through me, making me feel like he was literally bringing me back to life.

I sucked in my first gasp of real air, and it was a blessed relief. I'd felt like I was suffocating.

"She's coming back," Alina said, relief in her voice.

"Thank God," Cassie proclaimed.

As my vision cleared, I wasn't sure what to think of either of them. Cassie had ordered the dessert. Alina had encouraged me to eat it. At some point in our relationship, they'd known I was allergic to a variety of foods. Cassie had even teased me once about being a princess when I worried a cookie had come into contact with some peanut butter at a slumber party.

Although, I still didn't know what was in the crème brulée. It hadn't tasted like nuts or kiwi, and definitely not shrimp, but something in there had sent my body into anaphylactic shock.

The crowd around me stepped back as the EMTs arrived. I told them I was feeling better, but no one took heed of me. Apparently, they were required to take me to the hospital for further evaluation in case the one injection wasn't enough. Ethan told me he'd meet me there, and within minutes, I was in the back of an ambulance, speeding across town.

While I felt much better with an oxygen mask providing welcome air, the aftermath of a near-death experience made me feel very emotional, and it was all I could do not to burst into tears and freak out the EMT who was by my side.

I didn't want to believe my two old friends had tried to kill me with dessert, but it was weird that neither had suspected I was having an allergic reaction. Neither of them had looked in my bag for my Epi-Pen, and at least Alina should have remembered I always had one with me. Maybe they'd just forgotten. Or it had happened too fast.

Or they hadn't wanted to save me.

If I hadn't made it, who would have blamed them? I'd have died of an allergic reaction. Although, if the kiwi had been planted in just my dessert, that might make a difference. There would be scrutiny over who could have changed the recipe for the dessert and if it was just for the order that came to my table.

I went over the sequence of events in my mind. Cassie had ordered the dessert, then gone to the restroom. Or had she gone into the kitchen?

Alina had never left the table, but our conversation had gone back and forth between sweet and caring and twinges of jealousy. Alina had clearly been bothered by Drew's apparent fascination with me.

Were they both just jealous of me? Cassie clearly thought my career success wasn't warranted. And Alina was envious of her boyfriend's admiration of her one-time best friend. Alina had said she thought Drew was outgrowing her, that he wanted someone who had more going on—someone like me.

But even if they both felt that way, killing me seemed like a huge and unthinkable reaction.

Although, the first threatening note had come at the party that Cassie had planned.

"Breathe normally," the EMT said, interrupting my thoughts. "Try to relax. Your blood pressure is rising."

I did as he ordered, but I could feel my blood racing through my veins with each disturbing thought. What I needed to do was stop thinking. Stop reading into every comment, every moment. But every day, my paranoia grew. I didn't know who was real anymore. I was caught up in an insanity-inducing gaslighting game.

Had I just had lunch with the other Emily?

It turned my stomach to think that might have been the case.

"Breathe," the EMT told me again.

I pulled the oxygen mask down. "I think someone might have just tried to kill me," I told him. And then my freaked-out brain wondered if he was even an EMT, if the ambulance was real, if I wasn't going to make it to the hospital.

"I'm going to give you something to help you relax," he said.

"No," I practically screamed as he started to prepare an injection. "I don't want anything. Don't," I begged.

He put down the needle and placed a calming hand on my arm. "Okay. No one is going to hurt you. Whatever happened before, you're safe now. We'll be at the hospital in a few minutes. But you need to breathe. We'll do it together. Slow inhale, slow exhale. Clear your mind. Only good thoughts. Here we go."

As he counted the breath with me, I forced myself to do what he said, and I was finally starting to calm down when we arrived at the ER. They'd brought me to the hospital. The EMT wasn't trying to hurt me. Everything was going to be all right. I just wished Ethan was with me because he was quickly becoming the only buoy in my stormy sea. Hopefully, he would arrive soon.

I was taken into an exam room where a nurse checked my vitals again and hooked me up to more oxygen. A doctor came in several minutes later and told me they were going to give me an IV with a bronchodilator to increase the flow of air and that they would keep me there for several hours to ensure that I didn't have another reaction when the epinephrine injection wore off.

The last thing I wanted to do was lie in a hospital bed for four hours, where I would be a sitting duck. On the other hand, maybe this was the safest place I could be right now.

As I came to terms with the fact that I wasn't going anywhere anytime soon, I started to relax, and the exhaustion of the attack caught up to me. I felt so tired. Maybe I would just close my eyes for a bit and hope that when I woke up, everything would be normal again. That was a silly thought, but I clung to it because it was all I had.

I was discharged just before seven o'clock Tuesday night. As I walked out of the ER department, I found Ethan waiting for me in the lobby. I couldn't believe he'd hung out there all afternoon. "Hi," I said feeling a rush of emotion, just looking at his handsome face. I was quickly becoming addicted to seeing him.

He put his arms around me, and I rested my head on his broad chest and closed my eyes, savoring his warmth and his strength. I felt safe for the first time in hours.

"You're okay," he murmured.

I lifted my head. "I don't think I really believed that until just now."

His sharp gaze swept across my face. "You still look pale. Are you sure you should be leaving?"

"Yes, and I want to get out of here. They just told me to take it easy the rest of the night. I hope I can make that happen."

"We will make that happen," he assured me.

I stepped out of his embrace, but when he took my hand, I didn't pull it away. I needed him, and I didn't have the energy to pretend that I didn't. "Have you been here all afternoon?"

"I left for a while when they told me they'd be keeping you for several hours. I asked the police to investigate the restaurant, to find out whether anything was added to your food."

"And?"

He shook his head. "According to everyone in the kitchen, it was dessert as usual, and I believe them, because the crème brulée has a blend of fruits in it, including kiwi."

I nodded and blew out a breath. "So, Alina and Cassie didn't try to kill me."

"Well, I can't say that for sure. Not if they knew you were allergic to kiwi and that it was in the dessert."

"Kiwi isn't usually in crème brulée, so I didn't think anything about taking a bite. I usually do ask about ingredients if I'm uncertain, but to be honest, I just wanted to be done with lunch and get out of there. That was a mistake I won't make again. Can we go? I also want to be done with this place."

"Of course." He walked me out to the car he'd borrowed from his friend last night and put me into the passenger seat like I was a fragile package.

It felt wonderful and somewhat strange to have someone caring for me. I'd been taking care of myself most of my life. It was almost difficult to believe it was actually happening.

We didn't talk on the way back to the hotel. Ethan had his gaze on the LA traffic, which was in the thick of rush hour, and judging by the way his gaze continued to check the mirror, I thought he was probably also looking for a tail. I should be doing that, too, but I was too tired. Almost dying had taken a lot out of me.

When we arrived at the hotel, Ethan showed me the same

concern as we made our way up to our suite. I was relieved to step inside and see that everything looked exactly as we'd left it, except housecleaning had clearly been in the room to tidy things up. There were fresh towels in the bathroom, and the bed was made.

"Maybe you should lay down," Ethan suggested.

"I'd rather sit in the living room," I said, settling in on the couch. "I've been laying down for hours." I propped my feet up on the coffee table and let out a breath of relief.

Ethan went into the kitchen and brought back two cold waters from the fridge.

I drank half of my bottle in a couple of very thirsty gulps.

Ethan sat down in the chair, his gaze fixed on me, as if he was still debating whether I was really okay or not.

"I'm fine," I told him. "It was just an allergy attack."

He nodded, his expression taut, as if he still couldn't accept that fact.

"It's true," I added.

"I know. I'm just thinking about everything that's happened. I talked to your friends after you went to the hospital."

I straightened at that comment. "What did they say?"

"Alina, the girl with brown hair and brown eyes," he said pointedly. "She was very upset. She said she should have grabbed the Epi-Pen before I got there. She was shocked by how fast you went to the floor that she just froze. She did admit to me that she knew you were allergic to certain foods, although she couldn't remember which ones. She was very apologetic, rambled on with a lot of words of apology."

"And Cassie?"

"She seemed stunned and was much quieter. She didn't seem to know what to say about your attack. Although, she had a lot of questions about who I was to you and why I was there."

"What did you say?"

"I told her I was a friend. That only made her more curious. She wanted to know if I was a friend with the same benefits as

Ashton. As soon as she said that, Alina told her to shut up. And she immediately apologized, saying she was rattled by what had just happened and she didn't mean anything by it."

"Cassie always blurts things out and then pretends she didn't mean them when they are almost always very personal, targeted comments."

"I wasn't impressed with either one of them. I can see why you haven't seen them in ten years."

"I was close to Alina at one time. She was my best friend in high school."

"But you didn't keep in touch after that. Why not?"

"Because I wanted to put the past behind me. I wanted to start over at USC with a clean slate—no more fake backstory, no more lies—and I did that. The friends I made in college didn't hear my Peace Corps heroic parents' tale. I didn't tell them everything, but I did admit that I had a single mother who died when I was ten and that I was raised by my stepfather and then one of his relatives. It wasn't the whole truth, but it was closer to it."

"Did you tell Alina and Cassie the truth today?"

"Every last bit of it. I could tell Alina felt betrayed by my lies. Cassie just wanted to dig at me a little more. I think she liked the scandal of it all more than anything. They were both also very interested in my relationship with Ashton." I let out a breath. "It was bad, but then it got better. We agreed to move forward and talk about the rest of our lives. By dessert, I was feeling better about both of them. But then Cassie went to the restroom, and Alina made a weird comment about her boyfriend and how he admired me so much and wanted to work with me. Did I mention that part of the reason they wanted to get together was so they could remind me that Alina's boyfriend, Drew, who I also went to school with, is an actor who could use a break?"

"Got it," he said with a nod. "That must have sucked for you."

"I should be used to it by now. It wasn't so much the ask that bothered me, it was the way Alina kept looking at me like she was jealous of what her boyfriend thought about me."

"You said you went to school with him. Did you two have something?"

"For like two weeks. It was high school. We kissed, made out, groped a little, but it didn't go farther than that, and we broke up when I caught Drew kissing Cassie at the prom. Alina and Drew weren't together then. She never said she liked him. In fact, I thought they disliked each other. But a few years later, they reconnected and fell in love. Now, it doesn't seem that their relationship is very good. She's a high school drama teacher, and he thinks he's outgrowing her, or she thinks that and assumes he does, too. It could all be in her imagination."

"Or not."

"Or not. But I also know that fear makes you see things that might not really be there. When I was in the ambulance, I started flipping out. I had this crazy idea that the ambulance was all a setup, that they were taking me somewhere to kill me. The EMT got so worried he wanted to give me an injection to calm me down, but then that made me freak out even more."

"I'm sorry, Emily. I should have gone with you."

"No. I'm glad you stayed to ask questions, to call the police, to look into everything. I appreciate that. It was just my imagination on overdrive."

"Well, you had some extra adrenaline running through your system, too."

"It's a good excuse for today, but it's happening a lot." I licked my lips. "I feel like I'm seeing evil in every person I speak to, everyone who walks by me, gives me a glance. And it's worse with women, especially women who look like me. And, yes, I did notice Alina's hair and eye color, and it did cross my mind that she was the other Emily." I shook my head. "I guess she still could be. I don't know. I feel overwhelmed and helpless, and I don't want to live like this. I don't want to distrust everyone, to see the dark side of life everywhere I look."

"We'll figure out who this other Emily is," he assured me.

"We missed our meeting with Peter."

"I talked to him while you were being treated and told him about the latest attack on you. It might have just come from some errant kiwi, but we need to find out. I also talked to him about Jimmy. I didn't get into everything, just asked him to look into a man who had gone by the name of Jimmy Smithers and was a Hollywood agent fourteen years ago. I also asked him to get more details on the Faye Weston investigation. Peter is a former cop, so he can get one of his friends to pull the investigative records. We need to find out what the police know, not just what the public thinks."

"Thank you so much," I said, relieved that he'd pushed forward without me. And suddenly all the emotion of the day bubbled up inside me. I tried to tamp it down, to maintain control, but I was losing it fast.

"Emily?" Ethan questioned.

"I—I think there's a storm coming. I should go in the other room."

I started to get up, but he was suddenly on the couch next to me, pulling me into his arms. "It's okay. I can handle a storm," he told me.

I bit down on my lip. "I'm just so tired, Ethan. And it's not just about this other Emily. I've been pretending and holding things in since my mother died. I've faked so many emotions, so many accomplishments, so many backgrounds, sometimes I can't remember who I really am. I thought I was coming into my own with my work, but I was still holding all these secrets in, and now, this other woman is ripping all the layers of my life away, and as terrified as I am of how I'm going to look at the end of this, maybe it will be a relief. Maybe then I'll be free. I want to be free." My eyes filled with tears, and I quickly wiped away the first drops that slid down my cheeks.

"You can cry, Emily," Ethan said quietly. "You can let it out."

"Crying makes you weak."

"Or it does the opposite. The release makes you stronger in the end."

His words brought forth a sob that I couldn't hold back, and as I'd predicted, once the dam opened, there was no stopping the flood of tears.

Ethan held me tighter, and I soaked his shirt with my tears, crying it all out until I was completely spent.

When I finally sat back, sniffling and probably looking like a red-faced, slobbering idiot, I gave him a teary, grateful, and embarrassed look.

He got up, walked into the bathroom and brought me a box of tissues and a towel. I blew my nose, wiped my face, and then said, "Well, that was bad."

He smiled. "I've seen worse."

"You're a very sweet guy."

"Uh, no thanks. No guy likes to be called sweet."

And now I smiled. "How about a very attractive, ruggedly handsome, and also sweet guy?"

"Marginally better."

I blew my nose again and said, "I bet I look pretty sexy right now. I'm sorry I cried all over you."

"You look like someone who's had a tough day. Do you feel a little better?"

"I think I do. That storm was a long time coming."

"I know. To be honest, I'm surprised you didn't snap before this."

"Maybe I'll go wash my face. Although, I'm almost afraid to look in the mirror." I started to get up, but he put a hand on my leg.

"Don't judge yourself too harshly, Emily. You've been through a lot in your life, and you've held it together until now. In five minutes, you'll have it back together. Crying doesn't make you weak."

"Have you ever cried?"

"Like a baby," he said.

I gave him a doubtful look. "I can't see that. You're very confident, self-assured."

"I've had some bad moments, too."

"Like when your friend died?"

He stiffened, then slowly nodded. "Yeah, that was one of the lowest points of my life. That night at the bar is one I'll always regret."

"Can you tell me what happened?"

"We'd been together all night, hitting up different spots. Steven was getting drunker by the minute, and I wanted to take him home. He'd been having a rough time since we'd left the corps. I tried to cut him some slack. But when he went into the bathroom and came back high, I got pissed. I said I was done with him, and I walked away. I went outside and was looking for a taxi and realized I couldn't leave him in there. So, I went back in, but he wasn't in the bar. Someone told me he'd gone out the back. I did the same and found him in the alley making a drug buy."

As he paused, I found myself holding my breath. "What happened next?"

"A car came down the alley and two guys started shooting. Steven was hit immediately. His dealer took off, and the next bullet hit me. I woke up in the hospital hours later and found out Steven was dead."

"Oh, Ethan." I put a hand on his arm. "I'm so sorry."

His lips tightened. "I sobbed like a baby."

I found myself wanting to cry again, but this time for him. "It wasn't your fault."

"It was," he snapped. "And no matter how many times people tell me that, it still won't be true. If I hadn't left the bar for those few minutes, he never would have been in that alley. I took my gaze off of him, and he died."

"He died because he was in the wrong place at the wrong time," I argued. "And because he had a drug problem."

"I still should have been there, Emily. I'm a marine. I don't leave people behind, especially not my brother."

I knew there was nothing I could say that would change his mind. Clearly, others had tried, probably people who were closer to him than I was. "Well, sometimes you can't stop the bad things from happening. I think you said that to me a few days ago."

"Yeah," he said, running a hand through his wavy brown hair.

"What was Steven like?" I asked.

"He was the life of the party. Never met a stranger he couldn't turn into a friend. Told terrible jokes. Was always the loudest one in the room. But he was a bright light in my life." Ethan smiled sadly. "He got me into some trouble, I can't deny that. But he was also there for me. I wish I had been there for him." He cleared his throat and drank his water, then said, "Man, there must be something in this water. We're both spilling our guts tonight."

"Thanks for telling me about him. I know you like to keep things close to the chest. You have a lot of walls up. I only know that because you do what I do, which is keep people at a distance. You only tell them what they need to know, not what they might want to know."

"That's true. You know what I need to know right now?"

"What's that?" I asked warily.

"Whether or not you think you might want to eat again tonight, because I'm hungry."

"Oh. That was an easier question than I was expecting."

"I think we're both ready for easy."

"I could eat something," I said slowly. "I actually didn't eat much at lunch. Do you want to do room service? Because I don't think I can go out."

"Room service is perfect." He grabbed the menu off the side table and handed it to me. "Why don't you take a look?"

I gave the menu a quick glance and opted for comfort food. "I'll go for the roasted chicken and mashed potatoes, no dessert, no fruit."

He smiled. "Got it. I'll make sure they know about your allergies."

"Thank you. I know I'm a lot of trouble."

"You're a lot more than that," he commented. "A lot more."

I felt another tug of attraction at his words, at the look in his eyes, but there was too much going on to ask him exactly what he meant. I headed into the restroom to freshen up while he ordered dinner.

CHAPTER TWENTY-FOUR

THE ROOM SERVICE arrived after I'd taken a shower and pulled myself together. My nose was still red, but I looked a lot better than I had when I sat down at the table with Ethan.

As we ate dinner, my energy also started to return. The crying release followed by the shower and food had put me in a better headspace.

"So, how was your day?" I asked him as we finished eating.

He smiled. "Shouldn't you put the word *honey* before that question?"

"So, honey, how was your day?" I asked again, smiling back at him. "You know, before you had to save my life again. Was there anything going on at my building?"

"I saw a few tenants taking things out of the building. But I heard they limited access to residents on the first two floors. The garage is still locked off, so I don't know about your car. There were some crime scene investigators that went in and out, but they didn't speak to me."

"I wonder if they found anything helpful."

"I don't know. Hopefully. I did talk to Monica. She stopped by to speak to me. She was very upset by what had happened and also worried about you."

"What was the damage like at her place?"

"She said she hasn't been allowed inside but was told that the condo is ruined. What wasn't burned was destroyed by smoke and water. She hasn't told her grandmother yet. She's not sure there's any point in upsetting her. Apparently, her grandmother may never be well enough to come home, so it might be better for her to think that her things are all still in her home."

I nodded in understanding, feeling guilty about that sweet old lady losing all her belongings. "Delores, her grandmother, was very nice to me when I moved in. She made me cookies. I was blown away. No one had ever done something like that for me. We had a couple of good talks before she fell and had to go into the hospital for surgery. After that, things went downhill fast."

"That's too bad. I have to say, Emily, you have a low bar when it comes to people in your life if a plate of cookies got you excited."

"I do have a low bar, so when people do something unexpectedly kind, I almost can't believe they don't want something. But Delores just wanted to be friendly." I paused. "What did you tell Monica about me, about how the fire might have started?"

"I didn't say anything about the explosion. She had already spoken to the police, so she knew the fire was arson. She assumed it had something to do with your mugging and what she'd seen online about the sex video. I didn't disagree. I said you were staying with friends, that you were shaken up, and if I heard from you, I'd let you know that she was thinking about you. She said one of her coworkers is letting her stay in her apartment for a few days until she figures out what to do."

"I should probably text her at some point."

"The fewer people you talk to right now, the better."

"That's true. But there is one person I want to see if I can track down tomorrow—Vanessa Chambers."

He raised a brow at my words. "That's the woman Jimmy was married to when he went to Faye Weston's party?"

"Yes. And I'm thinking she would know better than anyone what Jimmy did that night. He told me she had moved to Newport Beach. I don't know if she's still there, but perhaps Peter could find her."

"We'll add her to the list. Do you think she'd be honest with you about what she knows?"

"I have no idea. Vanessa and I never had any problems. She was very kind to me. Most of the women in Jimmy's life ignored me, but Vanessa would sometimes come and talk to me when Jimmy was out. I liked her. And the more I liked her, the worse I felt about what Jimmy was doing to her bank account. But when I tried to say anything to her about him, she would immediately brush me off. She was madly in love with him. She told me he'd changed her life completely. I don't think she knew then just how much he would change her life."

"What happened with them?"

"I don't know the details, but he broke up with her the day before he dropped me at his cousin's house."

"Interesting timing. How long was that after Faye Weston died?"

"About a week, I think." I narrowed my gaze at the expression on his face. "Is there a connection?"

"I don't know." He paused at the sound of a phone buzzing. He pulled a phone out of his pocket to check a text.

"I thought we weren't using our phones," I said in surprise.

"It's a prepaid phone. I picked it up earlier. It's not traceable. I need to be able to get in touch with my work."

"I understand. But I need one, too. I wish you would have picked one up for me."

He gave me an apologetic look. "Sorry, I forgot." He frowned as he glanced back at his phone. "I need to go in to work."

"Now?" I asked in surprise. "It's after nine. Isn't the jewelry store closed?"

"There's been a problem."

"A break-in?"

"I'm not sure what's happened, but they need me to come down there. Sorry, but I have to do this."

"I understand."

He got to his feet, a concerned gleam in his eyes. "You'll be okay here?"

"I think so."

"I don't know when I'll be back, so deadbolt the door when I leave."

"If I fall asleep, you won't be able to get in."

"I have a feeling this could take awhile. If it's after midnight when I'm done, I'll just go home."

"I thought home wasn't safe. I don't want anything to happen to you, Ethan. They went after Ashton…they could go after you, too." I felt suddenly intensely concerned about his unexpected departure.

"I'll be fine," he said. "Don't worry. I'll talk to you in the morning. I'll send you an email so you can keep your phone off. What's your address?"

I gave it to him. I wasn't excited about him leaving and not returning until tomorrow, but I was being ridiculous. The man had a job, and he was needed to do more than babysit me.

"You'll be okay," he murmured.

It almost felt like he was talking to himself, but I still answered. "I will be. Don't give me another thought, Ethan."

"I don't think that will be possible." His gaze met mine, and he shook his head as if he had more to say, but no time to say it.

And then he was gone. I walked over to the door and locked it behind him. But I didn't feel safer because of the bolt. I was beginning to realize that I only felt safe when Ethan was with me. But he was gone, with a sudden work emergency. That seemed weird, too. Even if there had been a break-in, why would they need Ethan to stay all night? He guarded the front door. There wouldn't be anyone coming in and out now.

Something didn't ring true. But Ethan wouldn't lie to me, would he?

My stomach rolled with that thought. I told myself to calm down, to not let the paranoia take over. Ethan hadn't left me to set me up for something. He was the only one trying to help me. He'd saved my life twice already. I couldn't start doubting him now.

I didn't fall asleep for a very long time, watching old sitcoms when the late-night talk shows were over. The noise helped distract me from every little creak or noise coming from outside in the hall or in the rooms on either side of me. The last time I looked at the clock, it was after four. I must have drifted off at some point because it was after ten o'clock on Wednesday morning when I opened my eyes again.

I jerked out of bed and ran to the computer to check for an email from Ethan.

There was nothing. Had he gone home and then just gone back to work without checking on me? That seemed unlikely. I couldn't shake the feeling that there was more about his absence that I didn't know.

Was I trusting the wrong person again?

Had our chance meeting last Friday night been a setup?

Pacing around the living room, I told myself not to go down that road, not to look at every moment between us and turn it into a lie. I had to focus on the facts. Ethan had been with me when an explosion could have killed both of us. He couldn't be part of anything nefarious going on against me. He could have easily died along with me.

Ironically, that made me feel better.

I sat back down in front of the computer and ran through my emails. The first was from Ashton.

I know you've turned off your phone, Emily. I've left a lot of messages for you. I don't understand why you set me up, why you didn't tell me you're writing a book or that you have all this dirt on people. Your interview didn't make sense. You didn't sound like yourself.

"Because it wasn't me!" I shouted at the screen.

Blowing out a breath, I read on, wondering when he would take responsibility for what he'd done.

This whole situation is disgusting and awful. I know you lost faith in me, Emily, but I've also lost faith in you. Mitchell told me that you're off the movie, and I'm sorry about that. I know you had a lot invested in that project. But it seems like you have some mental health issues that you need to deal with, and you should concentrate on that. Your well-being is the most important thing, and you are not yourself these days. I care about you, and I hope someday we can be friends again.

"Not a chance," I said aloud, shaking my head at how he was spinning the whole situation.

The world was going to think I was either a sex addict, drug addict, liar, in the middle of a nervous breakdown, or all of the above. The other Emily had done a really good job of destroying my life. And Ashton had helped.

Or maybe the other Emily was Ashton…

Look what he had gained through all this. He'd gotten the part he wanted. He'd gotten me off the movie. Hell, maybe he and Mitchell had been partners all along. They could have planned this whole thing together to pay me back, because as far as I could see, the people who had benefited the most from my destruction were Mitchell and Ashton.

They could have hired a woman to be in the video. Ashton might not have been drugged at all. The more I thought about it, the more sense it made.

But, of course, I didn't have any proof.

I closed Ashton's email and moved on. There were two messages from Kaitlyn, one about the business meeting that I'd missed the day before, and one reiterating her support for me and asking me to call her because she was worried about me.

Francine's email was even more disturbing. They had made a

decision to move forward with Mitchell on *Aces High*. Jonah would be taking my place as assistant director. She knew I would be disappointed, but she already had some other projects in mind for me, and we should talk as soon as I felt able to do that. She finished by saying she had my back, even if she couldn't give me this movie. She would make sure I had other opportunities.

I appreciated that, but I still hated that she'd let Mitchell win.

Jonah's email came next. His message was filled with shock and anger toward Ashton for throwing me under the bus. He also asked me if I was upset about losing *Aces High* and told me that he felt uncomfortable taking my place, so he wanted to talk to me about it.

I didn't know what to think about that. Jonah was going to benefit from my demise, too.

There were other emails from other coworkers, offering support. Their notes made me feel a little less alone, but I wondered if I could trust any of them or take their words at face value.

As I sat back on the couch with a weary sigh, I knew I needed to do more than wonder. I wanted to talk to the PI but realized that Ethan had never actually given me Peter's number or his email. Although maybe it was on the computer. I checked the video call app and found the last number. There was no name, but I punched it in anyway. It rang several times, and then went to Peter's voicemail, so I ended the call.

I was on my own—again.

I'd been here before when I was ten and I found out my mother was dead. That I was going to live with a man who wasn't family, who wasn't anyone I even knew that well. I'd had the same feeling of isolation at fourteen when Jimmy had dumped me at Rhea's house. With his disappearance, the one last link to my mother was gone, too. And at eighteen, walking across the stage at graduation with no one in the audience, because the only person who might have come was Rhea, and she'd had to work that day, I'd once again been reminded of just how alone I was.

I definitely knew how to take care of myself.

Getting up, I walked back to the window, looking out at the horizon. I was down but I wasn't out. I wasn't dead. Which meant I could still fight. I'd do it on my own, just like I always had.

I just needed to figure out where to start.

And suddenly, I knew where I had to go—my office. A lot of the people I didn't trust were there. I needed to be there, too. I had to let them see I wasn't going anywhere.

Jumping up, I went into the bedroom, getting dressed as quickly as I could. Then I grabbed my bag and hotel key.

For a split second, I hesitated, wondering if it was wise to leave my safety zone. But I couldn't sit here all day and do nothing. Hiding might keep me safe for now, but not forever. And I couldn't keep playing defense.

It was almost noon when I went downstairs and caught a cab in front of the hotel. I started to give the driver my office address, then made a quick change and gave him my home address. I wanted to talk to Ethan, to let him know where I was going and to find out why he hadn't contacted me.

While a part of me was angry that he hadn't gotten in touch, another part of me knew it was completely out of character for the man I'd grown to know and to like. Which made me wonder if he'd been set up, or pulled away from me so that I would be alone. I had to find out what was going on with him before I went to the office.

When the taxi driver pulled up across the street from my building and the jewelry store, I was surprised to see crime scene tape in front of the store and a bunch of cops at the entrance. I jumped out of the taxi and ran across the street, shocked to see that the windows of the store had been shattered. There was glass all over the sidewalk.

My heart jumped into my throat, dark thoughts running through my mind.

As I got closer to the entrance, a female officer stopped me, putting up a hand. "You can't go inside," she said.

"What's happened? Where's Ethan?"

"Who's Ethan?"

"He's a security guard here. He was called to come in last night. He said there was a problem. What happened? Was there a robbery?" I tried to look past her, desperate to get a glimpse of Ethan.

"I can't talk about it," she said. "It's an ongoing investigation."

"Please, can you just ask someone if they know if the security guard, Ethan Burke, is all right?"

She hesitated. "Wait over there."

She pointed toward the front of my building where there was more cautionary tape. I took a few steps back as she went to confer with a man in plain clothes. He gave me a look and then walked over to me.

"I'm Detective Marsh. Can I help you?" he asked.

"I hope so. I'm looking for the security guard who works here. His name is Ethan Burke."

"The security guard's name is Stan Robinson."

"No. That was the other guy, the older guy," I said. "Ethan started working last week. He's young, with brown hair, brown eyes. He works for Stillman Security."

"I don't know who you're talking about, but maybe you should call the security company and ask. I need to get back in there."

"Wait," I said as I saw the coroner's van pull up. "Is someone dead?"

"I can't give you that information."

My heart jumped into my throat. "You're sure the person who's dead isn't named Ethan Burke?"

"That I am completely sure about," he said, and then he walked away.

I wanted to believe him. But I was completely confused. *How could he not know who Ethan was? What the hell was going on?*

I looked across the street. My taxi was long gone. And I didn't see any other cabs. I glanced at the door to my building, but it was boarded up with a warning sign not to enter. I had no idea if my car had survived the fire, but I wasn't going to find out now. I took my phone out of my bag and turned it on, then called for a rideshare.

While I was waiting, I glanced through the emails again, but there was nothing from Ethan there or in my text messages. It was as if he was a ghost. He'd completely vanished from my life.

That got my heart pumping again. *Where on earth was Ethan? And why didn't the police know his name?*

Thankfully, a car pulled up a moment later, and I got into the back seat. As we drove away from the place where I had thought to make my life, I realized again that nothing is forever, absolutely nothing.

CHAPTER TWENTY-FIVE

I'D HOPED that the trip to my office would be quick so I wouldn't have time to change my mind about going in, but only a mile from my home, we ran into a huge traffic jam, caught in the middle of roadwork and an accident. While the driver muttered that there was no way to get out of it, I thought about what I needed to do next.

When I got to the office, I'd talk to Francine about the movie. I knew the decision was made, but I needed to know where I could go from here. I also wanted to speak to her about Faye Weston, the night she died, and all the people who had been at the party. Maybe I'd even tell her about Jimmy, about who he was to me, and how he thought someone had killed Faye.

Thinking about Jimmy reminded me that I also wanted to find Vanessa. She might be able to give me information about the party, about where Jimmy had been that night, because there was a chance he had killed Faye. Maybe it had been an accident and not an intentional act. Or I might just be making excuses for him.

I had to focus on the facts. Jimmy had broken up with Vanessa right after that party and then dropped me at Rhea's and disappeared from my life. He'd said he'd wanted me out of harm's way. Was that because he was afraid he might be charged with murder? Or that the murderer might come after him?

I looked back at my phone and put Vanessa's name into the search engine along with Newport Beach. Five minutes later, I found a photo of her online. It had been posted five years ago. Vanessa was cutting a ribbon in front of her new clothing boutique in Newport Beach.

I stared at her face for a long minute, a little shocked that I'd found her. She was still beautiful and blonde. She hadn't aged at all. As my gaze moved across the photo, I saw two other women, standing next to her, Sally Davenport and Mila Chambers.

Mila was Vanessa's daughter. I'd met her once when I was thirteen and Mila was eight. She'd been a cute little kid who probably hadn't realized when we were at the park that day that a few weeks later, her mom was going to run off with someone other than her father. Vanessa hadn't just left her marriage... she'd left her kid. And as I studied Mila's now adult face, my heart began to pound.

I knew Mila. But I knew her by another name.

God! How could I have been so blind?

Mila was the other Emily. *Was she working alone? Or did she have help?*

Maybe Vanessa was helping her. That might make sense, although I'd never thought of Vanessa as my enemy, but clearly her daughter was.

There was only one way to find out. And I didn't need to talk to Vanessa anymore. I would go straight to the source. But I wouldn't give anything away yet.

I clicked out of search and hit a contact on my phone. When the woman answered, I said, "Hi, it's Emily. I need your help. I'm in trouble. Can we meet somewhere and talk?" At her confirmation, I licked my lips, then said, "How about two o'clock at Calypso Coffee on Sunset?" I waited for her reply, relieved when she agreed to meet me. "Great, I'll see you then."

As I ended the call, I let out a breath, hoping I wasn't making a mistake, but I wanted to control our meeting. I wanted it to be somewhere loud and public. Somewhere I could be safe but also in charge. The destruction of my life was about to stop.

My phone buzzed, and I hoped she wasn't calling back to cancel, but it was Ethan.

"Hello?" I asked warily.

"Emily, where are you? Why did you turn on your phone?"

"Because I'm done hiding. Where have you been, Ethan?"

"Working."

"That can't possibly be true. I just went to the jewelry store. There's a crime scene investigation going on, but the detective assured me that you were not a part of it. In fact, he's never heard of Ethan Burke. So maybe you should tell me who you are."

"I am Ethan Burke."

"Then why didn't he know you?"

"Because I was working at the store under another name."

My stomach clenched. "Why?"

"I need to tell you everything, but that will take some time, and we need to do it face-to-face. Where are you?"

I didn't like that he hadn't answered my question, that his only concern was finding me. "It doesn't matter. I'm going to handle the rest of my situation on my own."

"What does that mean? Did you find out something?"

"Yes, no thanks to you. Were you playing me, Ethan? Are you a part of this? Was our meeting last Friday a setup?"

"God, no!" he exclaimed. "You're twisting everything. I can explain, believe me. Tell me where you are, and I'll come to you."

"I don't think so. You lied to me. I can't trust you."

"I did lie to you but only about my job, Emily. I was working as a security guard, but that was my undercover job. I'm a police officer. Last night, we busted a ring of drug dealers and money launderers who have been working out of the jewelry store. I've been tied up since then. I didn't mean to leave you alone, and I wanted to tell you who I was, but I couldn't. I knew we were close to catching these guys, and I've been after them for over a year."

His explanation only confused me more. "I don't understand. Why couldn't you tell me that?"

"I couldn't tell anyone, especially not someone who lived in the neighborhood, who was a regular at the juice bar."

"The juice bar?" I echoed. "Was Larissa involved in your operation?"

"Unfortunately, yes. Now, tell me where you are."

"I'm on my way to Calypso Coffee," I said, my mind still reeling from what he'd just told me. "I know who the other Emily is. I'm going to meet her now."

"You can't do that on your own. Who is she?"

I wanted to tell him, but alarm bells were still ringing, and a voice inside my head suggested that I shouldn't trust him, that he might warn the other Emily. The story he'd just told me could be a total lie. But it did feel like it had truth to it. Ethan seemed much more like a man who would be an undercover police officer than a security guard. I'd always thought that job felt off.

I wanted to trust him, but I was hurt, angry, and exhausted, and from here on out, I really should only be trusting myself.

"Emily," he said, a plea in his voice. "I want to help you. I'm worried about you confronting this person. It's possible they weren't acting alone. You could be walking into a trap."

"They don't know I know who they are. They think I want them to help me."

"Are you certain of that?"

I wasn't. "I have to go. I have to take control of this my way. Maybe you're telling the truth. Maybe you're not. I can't tell the difference anymore."

"Em—"

I ended the call because I didn't want to weaken. I'd seen too many other women trust the wrong man. If I was going up in flames, it would be on me and no one else.

The traffic finally cleared, and we were on our way. I changed my destination in the rideshare app to Calypso Coffee, and only then realized I had given Ethan the location of our meeting. Damn! If he knew who the other Emily was, he could be warning her right now.

Well, it was too late to change my plan.

I was going to meet her, and if she didn't show up, then I'd find another way to get to her.

I arrived at Calypso Coffee at five minutes before two. The coffee shop was located in a crowded tourist area, which was exactly what I wanted—lots of people around. I moved into the café and looked around, but she wasn't there, so I went back outside.

A moment later, a car pulled up, and she hopped out of the back seat. She came toward me with a worried smile, a look of concern, and I couldn't help thinking how pretty evil could be, because what she'd done to me had been evil, cruel, and premeditated. She'd set up Ashton with a sex tape. She'd spied on me through my computer, written me threatening notes, and almost killed me.

The anger that rose within me blew away whatever fear I'd had of confronting her because now that I knew who she was, she no longer had the upper hand. She was no longer haunting me. She was right in front of me.

"Emily, I've been so worried about you," she said. "You've been completely out of touch. I was afraid you were spiraling somewhere all by yourself. Ashton told me he thought you were having a nervous breakdown."

"That's what you wanted, isn't it, Kaitlyn? Or do you want me to call you Emily?"

Kaitlyn's eyes widened with shocked innocence. Maybe she was surprised I'd figured it out, but she definitely wasn't innocent.

"What on earth are you talking about?" she asked. "Why would you call me Emily?"

"Because you've been impersonating me. The sex tape, the audio interview, and God knows what else."

"You're losing it, Emily. I haven't been doing any of that. Don't try to blame me for your problems."

"Problems you created. When did you come up with the plan? It must have been before you started working for me. What were you going to do if I didn't hire you? How were you going to get to me then?"

"I don't know what you're talking about. You need to see a doctor. I don't know if it's the drugs you've been taking or you're just falling apart, but you're not yourself. Everyone is worried about you. I spoke to Francine and Mitchell right before I came here. They wanted me to tell you to take some time off. Jonah will work on *Aces High,* and I'll take over your other projects. Only until you're better, of course. It's not like they want to fire you, but you've gone off the deep end."

I shook my head at her nerve. "You are smarter than I gave you credit for. Has Jonah been helping you? Was he in on it?"

"In on what? You're talking nonsense. Can I call someone for you, maybe a friend? I guess I can't call Ashton anymore, since he broke up with you."

"Is that what you wanted when you set him up? Or did you set him up? Is Ashton your partner?"

"You and Ashton were terrible together. I'm not surprised it ended."

"You know what surprises me is your level of hatred. I know who you are. Your name isn't Kaitlyn. It's Mila. Your mother, Vanessa, was married to my stepfather, Jimmy. We met a long time ago at a park. I was thirteen, and you were eight. But I didn't do anything to you. That was Jimmy. That was your mother. So why come after me?"

Finally, the mask fell from her eyes. "You were part of it. You and that horrible man took my mother away from me. You ruined my life. You took all my mother's money. You broke up my family."

"I didn't do anything. I was a kid under Jimmy's control. Why didn't you go after him?"

"Because I couldn't find him," she admitted. "But I could find you. And I thought you could bring him out of the shadows."

Another piece of the puzzle clicked into place. "That's why you gave the interview, threatening to tell all his secrets. He knows it wasn't me, by the way. He came to see me. I told him the truth, that someone faked my voice."

"I know he was at your place," she said. "I know everything. I've known what you were doing every second of the day for the last three months, Emily. I had spyware placed on your computers so I could see you at work and at home. I had a copy of your key made so I could go into your condo when you weren't there. I hired someone to steal your purse, to make you feel unsafe. I took a crop top and jeans one day, but you didn't even notice so the next time I went in, I turned over your plant and left you a little love note. I wanted you to know that I could get into your life any time I wanted to."

A shiver ran through me at her creepy words. "If you had so much control over my life, why didn't you set off your explosion when Jimmy was in my home, instead of after he left?" I challenged.

"I didn't set that explosion," she said, frowning. "When Francine told me about the fire, I was shocked. I figured it was just a weird coincidence. Someone else doesn't like you. In fact, I thought maybe it was Mitchell. He hates you. And you tried to kill him, so why wouldn't he try to kill you?"

"I never tried to kill Mitchell. That's ridiculous. And, of course, you set the fire. Why lie? You've admitted to your plan, why back off on it now? Why not take credit for everything?"

"Because I didn't set off an explosion in your building."

"What about poisoning my dessert at Silverman's?"

"You are nuts. I don't know what you're talking about. And if you try to say I did any of those things, I'll reveal more of how you and Jimmy conned people out of their life savings."

"You didn't exactly end up in the poorhouse. Your father had money."

"My father was a cold, angry, bitter man who couldn't stand that the only thing he had left of his marriage was me. He wanted nothing to do with me after my mother left. I grew up alone."

I heard the pain in her voice, but I steeled myself against her words. It didn't matter if she'd been hurt. That didn't excuse anything.

"But you weren't alone. You had my mother," Kaitlyn added. "You had my life."

I shook my head in disbelief. "You think the life I had with your mother was so great? It wasn't. It was shit. She and Jimmy were in their own little love world."

"That's not true. She told me that she helped you with your homework, that you were the only good thing about her marriage to him."

"Why don't you hate your mother then?" I challenged. "She's the one who left you, and you know where she is, because I saw you in a photo with her. In fact, she can't be that broke if she opened a boutique."

"She got an inheritance from an aunt," Kaitlyn muttered, awareness entering her gaze. "I forgot about that photo. I cleaned every other picture off my social media, but it was in the paper. Dammit."

"Yes, you made a mistake," I said. "A lot of them. And for what? How will taking me down change anything? Your mother is living her life and so is Jimmy. Where's the payoff in destroying me?"

"I'm going to take Jimmy down, too. But I need you to do it with me."

I looked at her in astonishment. "You think I'll be your partner? Who's insane now?"

"You won't have a choice, Emily. That's what all this is about. Stripping you down to nothing so your only way out is to help me lure Jimmy into a trap. That's how you save yourself, by helping me take him down."

"Take him down how?"

"I'm not going to kill him," she snapped. "I'm going to reveal who he is and send him to jail so he'll have plenty of time to rot there while he thinks about what he did to me and my mother. She's not blameless, but he brainwashed her."

"I won't help you. I won't participate in any of this. I don't care what else you say about me, because I'm going to start talking for myself, and you are the one who will end up in the hot seat."

"I don't think so," she said, a glint of steel in her eyes. "I've learned a lot about you in the past three months and all you care about is your career. You won't have one if you don't help me. That's the only way you get out of this with minimal damage."

"Minimal damage?" I echoed.

"It can get worse," she warned. "I can completely destroy your career. And I didn't do this alone, so if you think you can hurt me and get away with it, you can't. My partner will make sure of that."

"Who is your partner?"

Before Kaitlyn could answer, a van pulled up on the sidewalk in front of us and the side door flew open. I froze as two masked men jumped out. One grabbed me and the other grabbed Kaitlyn, throwing us both into the van before we could scream or fight back.

My head bounced off the side wall as the vehicle took off. Kaitlyn screamed in fear, wrestling with her captor.

I struggled to sit up, to get up, but the man who grabbed me was right in front of me, holding me down as he stabbed me in the arm. I thought it might be a knife but realized a second later it was an injection.

And I couldn't stop the black curtain that fell over my eyes.

CHAPTER TWENTY-SIX

THE FIRST THING I noticed was that my throat was so dry I could barely swallow. The second thing I felt was the cold, the wet on my bare legs, the wind on my face. I struggled to open my eyes. My lids felt so heavy, but finally, I squinted one eye open, then the other. What I saw shocked the hell out of me.

It was dusk, and I was laying on my side on a strip of sand, facing the ocean. The tide was coming in, covering my feet with salty sea water. I tried to get up, but then realized my ankle was zip-tied to a heavy barbell. That shocking fact drove the cobwebs out of my brain. I suddenly realized the danger I was in.

I sat up, searching for clues as to where I was. There was a deck over my head. To the right, there appeared to be a larger sandy area, almost a small beach, as well as a rock wall, a path above it, more rocks and in the distance, what appeared to be the back of a house.

I was at someone's house—probably someone's beach house.

I turned to the left, eager to find more clues, and saw Kaitlyn. She was on her back, her dress pushed up to her thighs, her foot tied to the same kind of weight.

Confusion ran through me. Kaitlyn was my enemy. She was the other Emily, the one who was tormenting me. She'd admitted it. But she'd been grabbed and shoved in the van, too. And she was tied up, just as I was.

Someone else was doing this. *Maybe her partner?* Had that person turned on her?

A gust of wind made me shiver, and I also became aware of the lengthening shadows. I'd met Kaitlyn at two o'clock. It had to be after six now.

I suddenly remembered the jab in my arm. I'd been injected with something and hours had passed.

Looking beyond Kaitlyn, I couldn't see much. The property we were on seemed isolated from any other homes. I turned my head, noting that the deck above me went ten feet behind us. The ground was sloped so that the space beneath the sand and the deck at its lowest point was about two or three feet high.

As my gaze traveled across the wooden support pillars, I realized how weathered and wet they were. Jimmy and I had stayed in a house in Malibu once where the ocean came right up under the deck, crashing against the foundation of our home.

Jimmy had liked the sound of the waves pounding the sand as he went to sleep, but I'd been scared at times, feeling like we could get washed away. Looking out the window at night, all I could see was dark water, and that sight was not the joyful beach view that I'd enjoyed with my mom. That was the dark side of the ocean, the dark side of my life, the side that had begun when Jimmy came into it.

And that sea was in front of me now, getting blacker by the minute.

The area we were in would soon be flooded with water. There would be no more beach, no chance to escape. We wouldn't be able to swim away, weighted down as we were. We'd drown in the ocean. Our bodies would be found, just like Faye Weston's body had been found.

Or would we be found? Faye's body hadn't been attached to a weight.

Maybe that's what the killer wanted to avoid. He or she

didn't want our bodies to resurface. We would sink to the bottom, be swept out to sea. Who knew if we would ever be found?

The morbid thoughts overwhelmed me and sent panic rushing through every vein in my body.

I was going to die.

I didn't want to die.

The words screamed inside my head. I had to find a way out.

"Kaitlyn," I shouted. "Wake up." I wasn't as interested in saving her as I was in getting help to figure things out. We might be mortal enemies, but right now we were in the same dire situation.

She rolled over and her eyes opened. She gave me a bewildered look. Then she sat up and gasped as the water splashed over her legs "What the fuck?" she cried out, looking back at me in horror and fear. "Where are we?"

"I'm guessing we're in Malibu, at one of those houses where the water comes right up to the house during high tide."

She stared at me in confusion, and then I saw the gleam of understanding enter her eyes, followed by sheer terror. "We have to get out of here."

We both tried to move, to scramble toward the house, but the weights on our legs were heavy, the ocean current was strong, and despite our best efforts, neither of us moved more than a few inches.

"Oh, God!" Kaitlyn cried. "We're going to die. Jimmy is going to kill us."

"This can't be Jimmy."

"Who else would do this?"

I had to think about that. I'd thought my enemy was her—the other Emily. But now, there was clearly someone else involved. "Who have you been working with to hurt me?"

She stared back at me without answering.

"You might as well tell me, Kaitlyn. We're going to die if we don't figure this out."

"We're probably going to die anyway. This wasn't supposed to happen. I was supposed to hurt Jimmy, not the other way around."

"Who were you working with?" I repeated.

"Jonah," she bit out. "Your best friend at work, Jonah." A smug smile followed her words. "He hates you, by the way."

I gasped. I'd really wanted to believe Jonah was a true friend. "Why? Why would he hate me?"

"You leapfrogged over him. You got every chance he didn't. He told me all about it one night when we got drunk together. He said he wanted to destroy you so he could get what he deserved. That's when I told him I had a plan. He was eager to go along. His friend helped with the spyware and the fake audio. Jonah said you'd been the favorite for too long. That you'd kissed Francine's butt so much, your lips were practically planted there."

"I worked hard for Francine. That's why I got opportunities."

"Yeah, yeah, tell it to someone who might believe you."

Her flippant response barely touched me, my brain focused on Jonah. I remembered how he'd defended Kaitlyn, how he'd told me she was just an eager puppy who wanted to get ahead and how I should help her out more. Of course, he'd said that. He wouldn't have wanted me to fire his partner in crime. They probably hadn't been working on his movie at all when I'd seen them in the office over the weekend. They'd been plotting to destroy me.

"It sucks when someone you love betrays you, doesn't it?" Kaitlyn asked, her voice dripping with dislike and also pain.

Ignoring her question, I said, "What about Ashton? Was he in on this, too?"

"No. He was just a part of the plan to discredit you." She smiled. "By the way, even drugged, he was really good in bed. But you already knew that."

"You're disgusting, Kaitlyn."

"Oh, please, like Ashton would care that a hot girl had sex

with him while he was a little out of it." She paused, cocking her head to the side. "However, I must say I didn't expect him to disavow you so quickly. He made my plan even better. I just wanted to break you up, make you feel the sting of being alone and in danger, but Ashton didn't just want to take a pause on your relationship—he decided to take you down so he could save himself. He was willing to throw you away to get the part of Dominic. You picked a winner there, Emily."

"I made a lot of bad choices, including hiring you."

"I was a good assistant. I worked hard for you. You just didn't appreciate anything; you were so caught up in yourself. It only made me want to take you down even more."

"Well, you did your worst, but look what happened—you're down in the dirt with me, literally," I added, cringing as the cold water ran up to my waist.

"I don't know who would want to hurt me," she said, bewilderment in her voice.

"You thought you were so clever, but you were incredibly dumb, Kaitlyn. You took it too far when you gave that interview. You told the world you knew who killed Faye Weston. What did you think was going to happen? Didn't it occur to you that the murderer would want to shut you up?"

"I thought they'd want to shut you up," she returned. "You were the one talking. It was your voice. The murderer should want to silence you, not me. I shouldn't be here."

I shook my head at the irony of her words. "You wanted to be me, Kaitlyn. We're the same person now, aren't we? You're the other Emily. What I know, you know. And we're going to die together."

"I can't die. I'm too young," she whined.

I'd thought the exact same thing, but she could die, and so could I.

If that was going to happen, I wanted to find out the rest of the story. "Did you know I was on to you when I called you to meet me earlier today?"

"I thought there was a chance," she said with a shrug. "But I didn't know for sure, and I wanted to hear what you had to say."

"You wanted to see me squirm right in front of you, didn't you? Your ego put you in a dangerous position."

"I wasn't afraid of you."

"Clearly. I wasn't afraid of you, either. That's why I came to meet you on my own." I paused. "You could have had a great career without taking me down. You weren't bad at your job, except when you talked too much, but I realize now that was part of your plan. You may have ruined my life, but you ruined yours, too. And it didn't have to be this way. You should have talked to me, Kaitlyn. I could have told you what went on between Jimmy and your mother. I could have made you realize that we were all victims. Jimmy was running the show back then. It wasn't your mother, and it wasn't me; it was him. But he's not here, is he? And once again, innocent people pay."

"You're not innocent," she scoffed. "My mother told me you worked right alongside Jimmy. You were in on every con. You were old enough to know what was going on. I'm not going to feel sorry for you, Emily."

"Well, believe it or not, I did feel sorry for you when your mother left you. I wasn't shocked that she left her husband, because I'd seen lots of other women do that, but she left her little girl. I couldn't understand that."

Kaitlyn's gaze narrowed. "Don't lie. You didn't give me a second thought."

I watched her try to move again, only to collapse on the sand with more frustration as the ocean rose higher. I could try to do the same thing, but it wouldn't work.

I felt a wave of anger at myself for not having told Ethan who the other Emily was. Or waiting for him before confronting her. I wouldn't be in this position if I hadn't stopped trusting him. But that was his fault. He'd lied to me. And I'd thought he was the one person who wouldn't do that.

But Ethan had had a good reason, if what he'd told me was

true...if he was an undercover cop and that his lie had only been told to protect his job.

It made sense. I wished I'd asked him more questions, but I'd been too caught up in anxiety and fear and a feeling of betrayal. But he hadn't betrayed me. This wasn't on him.

I wanted to tell him that. I wanted to see him again. I desperately hoped he could pull off another miracle rescue, that he would suddenly appear in the twilight, wrap his arms around me and carry me to safety. But that was fantastical thinking. He wouldn't know where I was.

Although, I had told him about Calypso Coffee. Maybe he'd gone there. If he had, someone had surely seen what happened. But he'd still have to figure out where the van had taken us, and that could be anywhere.

As that thought ran around in my head, a new idea entered my mind. "I bet I know where we are," I said. "We're probably at Cole Weston's house. This is where the party was held fourteen years ago. This is probably the beach where Faye's body washed up."

"Why would Jimmy try to kill us at the exact same spot?"

"It wasn't Jimmy," I told her again. "Just open up your brain, Kaitlyn."

"You're blinded by him. I'm not."

"I know him. You don't," I countered. "It's not Jimmy, but it's someone tied to Faye's death, tied to the party. Because that's why they came after both of us. They don't know what we know about the murder."

"Are you saying Cole is behind this?" Kaitlyn asked. "If we're at his house, then he must know we're here."

"Or to get on the property, someone would have to know Cole or how to get access to this area," I murmured, my brain spinning fast. It landed on the person I disliked the most. "Mitchell knows Cole. He lives less than a mile away. He was at the party that night. And he wants to make a movie about Faye's life and death. He's been trying to convince Cole to support that goal."

"You think Mitchell had someone kidnap us?" Kaitlyn asked.

"Yes."

"Well, he does hate you. I can see why he'd want to kill you."

"I don't think I'm here on this beach because he thinks I caused his accident," I said slowly, my plot line not ringing as true as I wanted it to. "Maybe it's not Mitchell. It could be Cole."

"Killing someone on your own property seems stupid," Kaitlyn said.

"Exactly. So it's not Cole but someone who wants to set him up as Faye's killer." I met her gaze. "It has to be Mitchell. He needs a villain for his movie. He needs an ending that makes sense. He's setting up Cole."

Kaitlyn didn't look happy with my analysis, probably because I'd come up with it, but she was smart enough to know I was right. But my momentary feeling of victory immediately faded as I realized the truth was going to die along with us. The next wave crashed over my head, making me gasp for breath.

Kaitlyn was crying now. It was getting darker. In a half hour, we probably wouldn't be able to see each other anymore. We probably wouldn't be under this deck anymore, either.

"I shouldn't have started this," Kaitlyn sobbed.

"You shouldn't have," I agreed. "Your need for revenge will end up killing you."

"You don't know what it's like to see your mother walk away and join someone else's family. She had a new man, a new daughter. And I was nothing. I was just left behind."

I felt a wave of sympathy toward her. "I'm sorry that you lost your mom. I lost my mother when I was ten. Yours didn't die, but she left you, and I know what that feels like. But you went after the wrong person."

"I couldn't stop myself. The more successful you got, the angrier I became. My mother followed your career, and she was always happy to tell me how well you were doing. So, I decided to go to film school. I wanted to show her I could be just as good as you. In fact, I could beat you."

"So this plan has been going on for a long time," I said in shock, realizing the depth and complexity of Kaitlyn's pain and misguided anger.

"It wasn't a specific plan, but it was a goal. I thought I would feel better if I could pass you, take you down, and step into your shoes. I'd get back what I lost."

"If only you'd realized that my shoes weren't that great, that I had my own problems and a life that wasn't much better than yours, Kaitlyn."

She didn't reply, as we were once again choking in water.

This time, the current moved me down the beach. I tried to dig my fingers into the sand but just ended up making a big groove that didn't impede me from sliding into knee-deep water.

Kaitlyn yelled for help. I screamed, too, but I didn't think anyone would hear us. The beach was deserted. The house was probably empty. Even the guys who had taken us were no doubt long gone.

But screaming was all I could do, so I joined Kaitlyn, yelling until my throat was raw and I was floundering in the water, no longer feeling the ground beneath me, knowing that only minutes were left until I went under completely.

I prayed it would be quick, that it would feel like going to sleep, that I'd see my mother again.

And there she was in my head, her face lined with worry, yelling at me to fight, to kick, to pull.

I tried to do what she said, but I was getting tired, and sinking deeper.

Her voice was drowned out by the crashing of the waves, the sound of my own heartbeat, and then a voice that had to have come out of my imagination, because there was no possible way he could be here.

"Emily," he shouted.

I felt someone grab my arm. I looked at Ethan in shock as he tried to pull me backward, but he was fighting the ocean, and he wasn't winning.

"Kick," he yelled.

I tried as hard as I could to kick with my free leg, but the ocean was pulling me away.

Miraculously, Ethan held onto me, practically ripping off my arm as he did so. But that pain only motivated me to fight harder, and with the next wave coming in, he was able to pull me toward the beach.

The sand was my sole focus, and somehow, we made it out of the water and onto that strip of beach. I gasped for breath, wanting to just rest, but Ethan was dragging me toward the rocks and away from the incoming tide.

"Kaitlyn," I said suddenly. "She's out there, too."

"I know. Peter has her."

"Peter?" I turned my head to see the private investigator pulling Kaitlyn out of the water.

"Peter helped me find you," Ethan said as he knelt in front of me. "God, Emily! I've never been so scared in my life." He put his mouth on mine, and the heat between us was searing. The kiss warmed me from the inside out, driving away the icy shivers racking my body.

Then I heard a blast. Something whizzed past my ear.

Ethan swore, covering me with his body as another shot rang out.

And then there was a long, blood-curdling scream.

I didn't know who it came from until I saw the body falling into the ocean from the high, rocky ledge to the side of us.

"Who the hell was that?" I asked in shock.

Ethan pushed me toward the rocks and pulled out his gun. Jumping to his feet, he pointed his weapon at the man standing above us.

"Don't shoot me. Thank me," I heard a voice say.

I knew that voice. Looking up, I was shocked to see Jimmy on the rocks about fifteen feet away from us, looking like an avenging angel in white pants and a white shirt, his white hair glittering in the twilight.

"I just saved your lives," Jimmy added. "Are you all right, Emily?"

"Don't move," Ethan ordered.

"Who did you push into the water?" I asked.

"The man who was trying to kill you," Jimmy replied. "Sorry I got here a little late, but I see your friend Ethan was right where you needed him to be."

"Yes, he was," I said.

"You did this, Jimmy!" Kaitlyn yelled, interrupting our conversation. "This is your fault. You're the reason we almost died."

Turning, I saw Kaitlyn and Peter now sitting on the beach only a few feet away from us.

"Mila," Jimmy said, shaking his head. "I couldn't believe it was you who was behind all this until I spoke to your mother this afternoon. I heard all about how you had gone to film school and were working at a production company. But Vanessa didn't know you were working for Emily, did she?"

I wanted to know the answer to that question, too.

"No," Kaitlyn bit out. "I didn't want her to know that I was going to take down the girl she so admired for making something of herself."

"Who is Mila?" Ethan interrupted.

"Vanessa's daughter," I told him. "She left her daughter for Jimmy. And for two years she mothered me, something Mila AKA Kaitlyn, blamed me for."

"It didn't have to be like this, Mila," Jimmy said.

"It did. I just wish you hadn't won—again," Kaitlyn said bitterly. "Can someone get this damn weight off of me?"

"Emily first," Ethan said.

Peter came over and cut the zip tie on my ankle with a knife. I felt a blessed relief to be free of that weight. I immediately rubbed my skin that had been burned by the tie and stung from the mix of blood and saltwater.

Peter moved back to Kaitlyn, giving her a wary look. "I'll wait to free you until the police get here," he said. "I don't feel like chasing you down the beach. And I have a feeling you're a runner."

As Peter finished speaking, I heard the distant sound of sirens.

Ethan helped me up, putting his arm around me, all the while keeping his gun pointed on Jimmy.

"He's not going to hurt us," I told Ethan.

"No, but he's going to jail," Ethan vowed.

"I came here to save you," Jimmy said. "And this is how you thank me?"

"He's telling the truth," I said. Looking back at Jimmy above me, I added, "It was Mitchell who killed Faye, wasn't it?"

"I honestly never knew who killed her," Jimmy replied. "But I thought the killer might have seen me in the shadows. After the party, I decided to leave Hollywood, to put some distance between us and everyone who knew me."

"Please don't use the word *honestly* ever," I said wearily. "It doesn't fit you." But his words did make sense. He'd run because he was afraid someone would try to take him down for what he knew.

"After your interview on Monday," Jimmy continued, "I put out some feelers to sources I have on the dark web, and I caught wind of a job for hire, a kidnapping, the target a young woman in her twenties. The details provided suggested you might be the target. An hour ago, I got a call from one of my sources that the job was done and that you were at this address. As soon as I realized it was Cole's house, there was no doubt in my mind that you would be here. That's when I figured out it was Cole who killed Faye, who was now afraid you were going to reveal his secret."

I couldn't believe I'd been a job for hire on the dark web. I turned to Ethan. "Did you find me through that posting, too?"

"No, Peter and I traced the van through security cameras and caught two of your kidnappers in a supermarket parking lot. One of them had this address in his phone," Ethan said. "He told us what he'd been hired to do. He didn't know the name of his employer. But Peter's assistant is trying to trace the payment link."

"Why would Cole kill me on his property?" I asked in confusion. "It would be too easy to track back to him." I paused as Peter walked over to join us, his phone now at his ear.

Peter ended his call, then said, "That was my assistant. We traced the payment to someone online using the name of Raven431. We're still trying to figure out who that is, but we'll get there."

"You don't have to track Raven431 down," Jimmy said. "I know who that is. And I know where he is."

CHAPTER TWENTY-SEVEN

I GAVE JIMMY A WARY LOOK, never sure I could trust him. "Who is Raven431?"

"Mitchell Gray. He uses that moniker on a video game," Jimmy replied. "I was wrong; Cole didn't kill Faye. Mitchell did."

"You're right," I said. "I played that game with him in Australia. He made me set up an account so I could play against him. He was obsessed with it." I turned to Ethan. "It makes sense that Mitchell is behind this and not Cole. Mitchell needed a killer for his movie, a satisfying ending, and a way to make sure he could never be punished for killing Faye. Instead, he could deliver the real killer—Faye's husband, Cole. Think about it. It would be a stunning statement. And if Cole could be tied to my death, to Kaitlyn's death, there would be enough evidence to convict him for that, never mind having to come up with proof about Faye." Pausing, I said, "I hate to admit it's a good plot."

"It's also complex. When did he decide to do all this?" Ethan asked. "The other Emily only announced that she knew the murderer on Monday. It's Wednesday."

"True. But he still had two days, and that interview must have forced him to act. He knew he had to get me out of the way.

When the explosion didn't kill me, he must have decided to kidnap me."

"Kaitlyn could have been behind the explosion."

"I wasn't," Kaitlyn snapped.

"It had to be Mitchell," I said.

"Okay, let's go with that. But you didn't figure out the other Emily was Kaitlyn until earlier today. How did Mitchell know where you were going to be?" Ethan asked.

"Kaitlyn told him she was going to meet me." I turned to Kaitlyn. "What exactly did you tell him?"

"I said you were making crazy statements to me about revealing Faye's killer and other Hollywood secrets. Mitchell was meeting with Francine and Curtis. They all looked very worried. I assured them I'd tried to get you to come in so they could talk to you."

"You must have scared the hell out of Mitchell," I said.

"The point is, he knew where you were going to be," Kaitlyn snapped. "I just don't know why he took me, too."

"Because you made yourself into me," I reiterated.

"And the kidnappers probably didn't know which of you was Emily," Ethan added. "We need to find Mitchell." He turned toward the rocks. "Dammit. Where did Jimmy go?"

"I didn't even see him move," Peter said in amazement. "I thought I was watching him."

"No one ever sees him leave," I said. "But we don't need Jimmy. I know where Mitchell is. He's at his house, hosting a dinner for my bosses and my replacement on the movie, my good friend Jonah who was in on all this with Kaitlyn, by the way. Kaitlyn wanted to use me to smoke Jimmy out and take us both down for ruining her life by stealing her mother and her family's money. And Jonah helped her because he's jealous of my success."

Ethan's eyebrows shot up as he shook his head in bemusement. "Unbelievable."

"Emily deserved it," Kaitlyn interjected. "She knew what

Jimmy was doing. She was helping him. She's a terrible person."

"Shut up," Ethan said so harshly that Kaitlyn actually did what she was told. "Get her out of here," he told Peter.

"Gladly," Peter said. "I'll meet you out front."

"Will Kaitlyn be arrested?" I asked. "Will we have enough to charge her with anything?"

"Judging by what I just heard, Kaitlyn will talk, and she'll probably convict herself. But we'll figure it out."

"We will, and that can wait," I said, meeting his gaze. "We need to get Mitchell before he realizes his plan didn't work."

When we reached the street, I saw Kaitlyn in the back of a squad car. Ethan and I got into Peter's vehicle and drove a mile down the road to Mitchell's house. I'd been there before we'd gone to Australia, when I was still honored to be working with him. I'd had no idea who he really was. I guess I wasn't the only one who'd been wearing a mask.

A squad car followed us to the property with two uniformed officers inside. Ethan asked them to wait with Peter and make sure no one left the property. Then we headed to the front door.

As we did so, I realized the group was gathered on the deck, and there was access to that deck through the side yard. I motioned for Ethan to follow, and we walked purposefully toward the party.

I was freezing cold in soggy clothes, my hair a tangled mess, but I didn't care one bit about what I looked like. Because this was the real me. And I was on fire now.

Adrenaline pumped through me. I wasn't afraid to face Mitchell. In fact, I couldn't wait.

There were lit tiki torches on the deck and the sound of light conversation filled with laughter. They had no idea what was coming.

We moved up the steps to the deck where the group was

sitting at a large square table, sipping wine, and enjoying their fancy dinner under a starry sky and candlelight. Francine and Cole were on one side of the table, David and Jonah next to them, Mitchell and Tara on the opposite side, and Ashton and Natasha filling out the group. I was surprised to see Natasha, but apparently she'd signed on to the movie.

"Emily," Francine said in shock, as she caught the first glimpse of me.

"Surprised to see me?" I asked. "There was a time when I was invited to this dinner."

"You look terrible," Francine said. "Let's go and talk somewhere."

"Sit down," I ordered as she started to get up.

She stared at me in shock. "Emily—"

"You need to leave my house now," Mitchell interrupted. "Or I will call the police and have you removed."

"I'm not the one who's going to be leaving in a police car, Mitchell," I said, as he got to his feet.

"You're insane," Mitchell declared. "Ashton was right. You are unstable."

"Emily, don't do whatever you've come here to do," Ashton pleaded. "We're all worried about you. You've had a breakdown. We want to help you."

"I'm perfectly sane, and I'm not broken, Ashton." My gaze moved to Jonah. "Your plan didn't work, Jonah. Kaitlyn is on her way to the police station, and you'll soon be following."

The color drained from his usually cheerful face. "I don't know what she told you—" Jonah began.

I put up a hand. "There will be time for you to make excuses later. Kaitlyn already confessed to impersonating me in that interview and on the sex tape where she set up Ashton. She spied on me through my computer, and she broke into my house. You helped her because you were jealous of me."

"It was all her idea," Jonah said defensively. "I didn't do much of anything."

"I don't know what this is about," Francine said in confusion. "But this is not the place, Emily. I have always had your best interests at heart."

"Maybe. Maybe not." I was no longer sure of Francine, either. But I turned my attention to Mitchell. "You got nervous when Kaitlyn gave that interview as me and said I knew who killed Faye. But I didn't know and neither did Kaitlyn, until tonight." My gaze moved to Cole. "Mitchell was going to frame you for Faye's murder so he'd have a good ending to his movie."

Cole's jaw dropped. "That's ludicrous."

"Is it? Well, later tonight, you'll find out that Mitchell hired three men to kidnap me and Kaitlyn, who was pretending to be me. He had us tied to weights under your deck so when the tide came in, we would be dragged out to sea, never to be seen again. Or if our bodies did come to the surface, our murders would be tied to you, the man who killed his wife in the same location."

Cole jumped to his feet, his face reddening. "That's impossible."

"Sit down," Ethan ordered.

"Who are you?" Cole demanded.

"I'm a police officer," he said. "And I'm here to arrest Mitchell Gray for the attempted murders of Emily and Kaitlyn."

"No way," Mitchell said, shaking his head. "I didn't have anyone kidnapped. Emily is trying to frame me now, just like she tried to kill me in Australia. She'll do anything to get rid of me."

"You're being arrested," Ethan said calmly. "Because we traced the money you sent to the hired kidnappers to your web account Raven431." As Ethan moved toward Mitchell, Tara rose.

"I can't believe you tried to kill them, Mitchell. I don't even know who you are," she said dramatically. "But I can't stand here and listen to this. You killed our friend Faye? That's unbelievable."

"Tara, no," Mitchell cried. "You can't believe them."

As Tara tried to leave the table, Francine jumped up in front of her and grabbed her by the arm.

"You aren't going anywhere," Francine said. "Mitchell isn't Raven431. He's 432. Tara is 431. I've played enough video games with them to know that."

I sucked in a breath at her shocking words.

Tara struggled to get away, but Francine held on to her with an iron grip.

"You did this, Tara?" Mitchell asked in shock.

"No. They're all lying," Tara said desperately.

"You killed Faye?" Cole asked, disbelief in his gaze. "Why?"

"You know why," Tara spat out.

"You killed her because I chose her over you, Tara?"

I was stunned again by Cole's words. Tara and Cole had had an affair?

"How could you do that?" Cole continued. "Faye was your friend."

"She was your wife, and you still slept with me," Tara said, not a trace of remorse in her voice, only bitter pain. "And then you threw me away, and she lorded it over me. She couldn't wait to tell me that I was worth nothing to you."

"So you killed her?" Cole asked. "How?"

"She was drunk. We were outside. She fell and hit her head. I tried to revive her, but she was dead. The tide was coming in. She was already halfway in the water, so I just let the ocean take her away. I didn't think her body would wash back up. But I didn't kill her. She just fell. It was an accident."

"You should have told me," Mitchell interrupted, drawing his wife's gaze back to him. "You should have said something, Tara."

"I told you to leave Faye's death alone. I told you not to make a movie about her life. I knew you were going to ruin everything by creating all this doubt about her death and investigations would be reopened." Tara shook her head as words flowed out of her mouth. "That's why I had to try to stop you."

"Oh my God," I said as I realized another truth. "It was you who set up that explosion in Australia. You tried to kill Mitchell so he wouldn't make the movie."

"You did that, too?" Mitchell asked, anger blazing out of him.

As Mitchell moved toward his wife, Ashton jumped up and held him back.

"You bitch," Mitchell screamed. "You fucking tried to kill me?"

"It was your own fault. You wouldn't listen," Tara said. "And then Emily was shooting off her mouth about Jimmy and the night Faye was killed, and I was afraid Jimmy had told her that I did it. I'm pretty sure he saw me arguing with Faye."

"Jimmy didn't tell me anything," I said. "I didn't know it was you until just now."

As I finished speaking, Ethan waved to Peter, and the officers came onto the deck. At Ethan's direction, they cuffed Tara and Jonah and took them both away.

"Emily, I'm sorry," Jonah said, giving me a pleading look. "It was just a game. I didn't think Kaitlyn was going to go as far as she did. I thought she was just going to mess with you a little."

I didn't bother to reply.

Mitchell sank back down to his chair, holding his head in his hands. Cole walked to the edge of the deck, staring out at the sea, probably thinking about his wife's death.

The rest of the group was silent, too, varying degrees of shock on their faces. Ashton gave me an imploring look, as if he wanted to say he was sorry, but I wasn't going to listen to anything he had to say.

Finally, Natasha spoke for the first time. "Well, that was quite a scene," she said. "I hope one day we work together, Emily. Since I'm not involved in any of this, I'm going to leave."

As Natasha left the table, Francine said, "I'm sorry, Emily. I had no idea about any of this."

I wanted to believe her, and maybe I did. In the end, she'd been the one to call Tara out as the real killer. But I couldn't talk to her now. I needed time before I heard any more explanations or excuses .

"I have to go," I said. I turned my back on Francine and everyone else. I was done.

Ethan and I walked out to the car together. I felt absolutely drained. I slid into the back seat while Peter drove, and Ethan sat next to him. The men exchanged a few words, but I barely listened. My brain was still replaying that last scene. I couldn't have directed it any better, one surprising twist after another. I just wished it had been a movie and not real life.

Peter dropped us off at our hotel, and I made my way wearily into the lobby. "You can go home now, Ethan," I said. "There's no reason for you to stay here anymore. I'm no longer in danger."

"I will go home if you want me to, Emily. But I'll walk you up first."

"Okay." I didn't have the energy to argue.

As we got into the elevator, I saw more than a few curious glances thrown our way. I probably looked like a drowned rat, but I didn't care.

I was thankful when we finally reached our floor and got into our suite. It felt like a million years since I'd been there. So much had happened. I felt numb and cold, and I couldn't stop shivering.

"I need to take a shower," I said.

"Sure. Or try out the big tub. Take as long as you need. I'm not going anywhere until you tell me to leave."

I saw the determination in his eyes and just gave him a nod.

A bath would have been nice, but I couldn't wait for the tub to fill up, so I hopped in a steamy hot shower and let the water pour over my head until my teeth stopped chattering.

I'd experienced so many emotions in one day, that I wasn't surprised when a few tears mixed with the shower spray.

But they weren't tears of pain or grief or unhappiness. They were tears of gratitude and joy. I was alive. I'd survived one woman's attempt to destroy my life and another woman's attempt to take my life. I had to call that a good day.

CHAPTER TWENTY-EIGHT

WHEN I STEPPED out of the shower twenty minutes later, I finally felt warm. My hair smelled like flowers, and my skin no longer felt dry and salty. After drying my hair, so I wouldn't get another chill, I wrapped myself in a fluffy, terry cloth robe that the hotel had provided and returned to the living room.

Ethan was sitting on the couch, his phone at his ear. He motioned for me to come over.

I sat down next to him as he said, "Good. I'll be in as soon as I can."

"You have to go?" I asked when he ended the call.

"Not just yet. That was the detective who'll be interviewing Tara and Kaitlyn. As predicted, Kaitlyn is already talking, but Tara has asked for her lawyer, who won't be able to get down to the station for a couple of hours. I'd like to be there when Tara is questioned. I wish I could take you with me, but—"

"I don't need to be there," I interrupted. "I know everything now."

He nodded. "You made a hell of a speech on that deck, Emily. You were in command of that group. I don't know where you were in the hierarchy of that company, but you're at the top now."

I gave him a dry smile. "At the top? I'm probably going to be fired."

"They won't want to fire you after all this. It would look bad."

"Maybe that's true." I paused. "I have to say, I was shocked it was Tara who killed Faye. Even more stunned that it was Tara who caused Mitchell's injuries. I really did think the propane tanks were put there by accident. But Mitchell was right this whole time. Someone did try to kill him. It just wasn't me. It was his wife."

"He never saw that coming."

"No, he didn't. He also had no idea Tara killed Faye. When he kept pushing to make the movie about Faye and talking about needing to find the murderer, Tara must have been afraid that her crime would be discovered after all these years. She probably should have just confided in Mitchell. Maybe he would have dropped it to protect her."

"She didn't want to take the chance that he wouldn't," Ethan said.

"It sounded like Tara and Cole had something going on, too," I added. "But Cole chose Faye, and Tara got so angry she fought with Faye and whether or not it was an accident, Faye ended up dying."

"I don't think it was an accident. It was probably a crime of passion. And the fact that she was willing to send you and Kaitlyn out to sea in the cruelest way possible only reinforces my belief that Tara was capable of killing Faye."

"That's true. She could have just gotten one of those guys to shoot us in the head, instead of slowly forcing us to drown." I shivered at the memory.

"Don't think about it, Emily."

"I'm trying not to, but it's not easy. I guess Tara didn't want anything messy at the house. The weights were supposed to take us down to the bottom of the ocean. There would be no blood spatter, no evidence left at Cole's property. If there was something that didn't get washed away, if somehow her plan didn't work, then she would frame Cole for killing us like he'd killed his wife. It might have worked. At least in the court of public opinion. Cole couldn't survive two more unexplained deaths at his house." I took a breath. "I guess whatever feelings Tara had for Cole vanished awhile back."

"Self-preservation trumps everything. Plus, he didn't choose her. She didn't like that."

"No, she didn't."

He gave me a warm smile. "You look a lot better now than you did. The color is back in your face."

"I feel good—exhausted, but good. I'm finally free. Free from Mitchell's accusations and speculation, free from Kaitlyn's evil gaslighting plan, and free from my own secrets. I feel twenty pounds lighter."

"What do you think will happen now with Mitchell and the movie you were going to make together?" Ethan asked.

"I'm not sure. I need to speak to Francine about it, but after everything that has happened, I don't know if I will keep working there. I thought Jonah was my friend, but he was helping Kaitlyn. God knows how many other people there secretly don't like me. I know for sure that I won't work with Mitchell again. Even if his anger toward me was displaced, I still can't stand him. And Ashton wouldn't be on my list to work with, either. Maybe I'll move on. I'm not sure anyone will hire me after all the press I've gotten recently, but that's a problem for tomorrow."

"You're very good at what you do, and now you'll have a chance to tell your side of the story the way you want to tell it. Hell, it might even make a good movie. I know I'd watch it."

"That's a thought," I said, meeting his smile. "I owe you another big thank-you for saving my life. It's getting to be a habit."

"I had to save you, Emily. I couldn't stand the thought of losing you. And I was afraid that that might happen because I didn't tell you the truth about my job. I hurt you, and that's why you wouldn't tell me who the other Emily was."

"I didn't know what to think," I agreed.

"I was just lucky that you mentioned the coffee shop. I arrived a few minutes after you were kidnapped, but someone witnessed what happened and called the police. I got Peter and half the police department on your case, and we were able to track the van."

"Finally, a security camera provided something of value," I said dryly.

"But it took us over four hours to get to you. It was the longest four hours of my life. When I saw you struggling in the water and then realized you had a weight on your leg..." He drew in a breath and shook his head. "That was a bad moment. The current was strong, and I was afraid I wouldn't be able to pull you in."

"But you did. You got me out, and Peter saved Kaitlyn."

"Are you sorry Peter saved her?" he asked curiously.

"Not at all. She hurt me a lot, and I want her to pay for everything she did, but she didn't deserve to die."

"You're being generous. She tried to kill you, Emily."

I shook my head. "No, that wasn't the plan. She just wanted to torment me and strip me of everything I had and then force me to help her smoke Jimmy out of hiding so she could hurt him, too. She didn't set the fire in my building. I believe that was Tara. But we need to find out for sure."

"We'll get all the answers." Pausing, he added, "I should have known that third guy was on the property. When Peter and I found the other two kidnappers, we knew there was someone still on the loose. They claimed they didn't know where he was. I assumed he was at the house, but when we arrived, I didn't see him and then I heard screams." He shook his head, his lips drawing into a tight line. "I knew I had to find you fast."

"And you did."

"But he could have killed us after I pulled you out of the water."

I saw the guilt and stress in his eyes. "That didn't happen, Ethan."

"No thanks to me."

"Well, you were a little busy saving me. Luckily, Jimmy was in the right place at the right time."

Ethan frowned. "Yes. I kind of hate that."

"I kind of like it. You wouldn't understand my complicated relationship with Jimmy, but it was nice to know that he was trying to help me. I didn't think he would ever help anyone but himself."

"He was helpful until he disappeared," Ethan said dryly. "I should have seen that coming, too."

"Jimmy is very good at disappearing. But he doesn't matter anymore." I took a breath. "Do you think there will be enough proof to convict Tara of Faye's murder?"

"I don't know about that, but there will be enough evidence to bring charges of kidnapping and attempted murder for what she did to you and Kaitlyn AKA Mila Chambers. I'm still trying to wrap my head around that one," he said. "Seems like she should have been torturing Jimmy."

"She couldn't find him. I'll have to fill you in on the whole sordid story of Jimmy, Vanessa, and Mila. Then it will make more sense."

"That doesn't have to happen now," he said.

"I agree. What do you think will happen to Kaitlyn?"

"She'll probably get out on bail, because she has no record. I'm not sure what charges will be brought."

"I was thinking that what she did to Ashton might be easier to prove. She blackmailed him and that was in writing. Whereas with me, everything was so subtle and yet so terrifying. Although she did tell me she hired someone to mug me. So there's that."

"That will carry a charge, and her friend Jonah will probably turn on her, which will help."

"That's true. Jonah's friend helped with the spyware and the fake audio."

"Kaitlyn will be punished for what she did," Ethan said confidently. "And she won't be allowed to come anywhere near you."

"I'm not worried about her anymore. She can no longer hurt me." I took a moment, then said, "I was taken in by a lot of people, Ethan. I grew up working for a con man, and I let myself get played. That's a strange kind of irony, isn't it? I had no idea Kaitlyn was spying on me. I had no idea Jonah hated me and resented my success. I was completely oblivious."

"It's hard to see betrayal when it comes from people close to you."

"I was blindsided, because I've been so focused on work; I lost track of the people around me. Maybe I didn't give Mitchell enough credit for what he'd done on the film before he got hurt. When I saw Kaitlyn taking away my job, it made me understand him a little better. He was trapped in a hospital bed watching me steal what he thought was his."

"If you hadn't taken over for him, it would have been someone else. That movie was going to get made. And you shouldn't apologize for doing a damn good job of directing it."

"I'm not apologizing. I'm just saying that by protecting myself with secrets and walls, and siphoning off my past, I created a distance that actually wound up hurting me in the end."

"I get it."

"I don't want to live like that anymore. I want to be myself and have real friends. And I'm not talking about Cassie and Alina, although they turned out to be innocent. I asked Kaitlyn about poisoning my dessert, and she had no idea what I was talking about."

"The kiwi was a normal ingredient in that dessert," Ethan agreed.

"There was also a moment when I wondered about Monica,

too, how she had just moved into the condo across the hall three weeks ago. I started thinking maybe that wasn't a coincidence. I never had any real proof she was Delores's granddaughter, either. She just had a key to her unit."

"I wondered about her, too," he agreed. "After you were kidnapped, Peter's assistant looked into Monica as well as Cassie and Alina. All their stories checked out. They were who they said they were."

"I'm glad." I paused again, having things to say but not sure now was the time. "I know you need to leave, Ethan, but I would like to talk about your job. Knowing how fragile the idea of tomorrow is, I'd like to do that now. Why did you lie to me?"

"I only lied to you about the security job. Nothing else, Emily," he said with a desperate sincerity in his gaze. "Everything I told you about my past, my family, Steven...that was all true. I wanted to come clean, but I couldn't risk you blowing my cover. It wouldn't have just put me in danger but others who trusted me to keep them safe. I also didn't want to risk putting you in more danger."

"How long have you been a police officer?"

"Four years."

"When you and Tom were talking in my apartment, it didn't sound like Tom knew you were a cop."

"Tom doesn't know. I started working as a police officer in San Francisco. I moved there after Steven died. I had to get away from San Diego and my past and everyone I knew. It was too painful. Everywhere I went, I would get caught up in a memory. I didn't talk to any of my friends for a couple of years, Tom included. I didn't want to feel the emotional connections. I just wanted to do a job. But as time passed, I started to come out of my funk, and I stumbled onto a case tied to the drug-dealing organization that had taken Steven's life."

I suddenly understood where his story was going. "That's when you went undercover."

"Yes. The organization was in LA, and my best chance at

taking them down was to go undercover. That's what I've been doing the past year and a half. As a cover, I've worked a lot of different jobs—bouncing at bars, being a security guard, driving drug drops. The people I knew in LA never knew I was a cop. They just thought I was still drifting aimlessly after getting out of the Marine Corps and losing my best friend. The only people that did know were Sophia and Peter. Peter was a cop, my partner in fact, before I went under. Then he decided to get out and become a private investigator." Ethan took a breath. "It's been very strange, living a life of secrets. More difficult than I imagined, and I've been feeling conflicted about it. But I was so close to finally nailing key members of the organization who only come to LA from Mexico a few times a year that I couldn't quit."

"And this organization is tied to the jewelry store?"

"Yes. They held a meeting there last night with a key player we've been trying to take down for years. We got him in the store."

"It looked like there was a shootout."

"It was messy."

"I'm glad you weren't hurt."

"Me, too."

"Are you done now?" I asked.

"Yes, I'm done," he said, a certainty to his voice.

"Did you get the men who killed Steven?"

"One of them. The other is still out there."

"Then how are you done?" I queried.

He didn't answer right away. "I have to be done, Emily. I can't live a life based on revenge. I knew that before I met you, but once I got caught up in your life and saw what that kind of obsession can drive people to do, I knew I wasn't that far behind the other Emily."

I smiled doubtfully. "I don't think you were even close. And your revenge was against a criminal. Although, I guess Kaitlyn thought her revenge plan was also against a horrible person—me."

"She was wrong."

"She was," I agreed. "Although, maybe not wrong about Jimmy."

"True. At any rate, the more I got to know you, Emily, the more I also wanted a normal life, to live out in the open. You talked to me about your secrets weighing you down, and I felt the same way. It wasn't just my secrets...it was my desire to avenge Steven's death, as if that would somehow make me feel better. But that was never going to happen. No matter how many people I take down, I still won't get Steven back. I have to let go."

"It's hard to let go of people you love."

"It is." He met my gaze with a look that made my heart race. "But I have to move on. Steven wouldn't want this life for me. I've been living like a ghost since I went undercover. I was losing track of who I was."

"Just like I did," I murmured. "We have more in common than I imagined."

"Hearing you talk about your life and the stories you made up to survive, to fit in, it was like you were holding a mirror up in front of me, and I could see the road I was on. I didn't like where it was going. I haven't had serious relationships, because I haven't wanted to open up, haven't wanted to care that much about anyone. Then I would have to worry about the pain of losing someone. But life isn't about being safe or secretive. That isn't how either one of us should live."

"I agree, Ethan. But I think you knew who you were before Steven died, and then you got lost. Now you've found your way out and you can move forward. I never really knew who I was until tonight, until I faced all those people on that deck and said exactly what I wanted to say. Kaitlyn unknowingly did me a favor, because she broke down my walls, and I couldn't get them back up. I had to face my worst fears. But I'm still here."

"Thank God," he murmured.

"Thank you," I added. "I'm so lucky I met you last Friday. Maybe it was a strange kind of fate that put us in the same place at the same time."

"I didn't want to get involved with you, because I knew you were going to be a distraction, and I had to focus on my real job at the store. You also had a boyfriend, and I was thinking about you in a not-so platonic way."

A tingle shot down my spine at his words. "I had a few of the same thoughts."

"Do you think we could start fresh?" he asked. "Be who we really are? Or did I hurt you too much?"

"I understand why you lied to me, Ethan. You didn't hurt me too much. You saved me."

"You might have saved me, too. And I don't want tonight to be the last time I see you."

"What would seeing me look like?"

"What do you want it to look like?" he questioned.

I thought about that for a moment. "Well, I think you'd be seeing a woman who is working as a film director, either free-lance for herself or for a production company that isn't Holly Roads. A woman who was raised by a con artist and did some shady things when she was a kid but is trying to live a better life." I took a breath. "Who would I be seeing?"

"A former cop turned private investigator," he replied.

"Really?" I was surprised by his answer.

"Yes. Peter has been asking me to team up with him for a while. As soon as this case is completely wrapped up, I'm going to join him. I've worn a lot of uniforms in my life. It's time for me to just be me."

"That sounds like a good plan."

"You'd also be seeing a man who will never use you, Emily. A man who wants nothing to do with your business or any of your connections. A man who knows the real you."

"And I'd be a woman who knows the real you," I said.

"There would be a lot of honesty between us," he agreed. "Can we handle it? We've been living in secrets for a long time."

"I can if you can."

"Then I can," he said with a smile.

I slid closer to him, his face just inches away. "I am a little disappointed that you won't be wearing a uniform, though. I like a man in a uniform."

"I can wear whatever you want."

"How about nothing?" I asked with a wicked smile.

He groaned. "You cannot say things like that when I have to leave in five minutes."

"I just wanted to give you something to think about." I put my arms around his neck. "And maybe think about this, too." I leaned forward and gave him a long, hot kiss. Then I stood up, smiling as he gave me a dark look.

"That was not fair," he said, as he rose.

"Go to work, Ethan. We'll start fresh tomorrow."

"Is that a promise?"

"Yes," I said as we exchanged another quick kiss.

After Ethan left, I locked the door and walked back to the window. I looked out at the dark sea, more than a little relieved that I had not ended up there for eternity.

I would be looking at the beach through new eyes now, but I didn't want to hate the ocean. It might have been the location of my worst nightmare, but it was also the place that still gave me some of the happiest dreams.

My mom's face floated back before my eyes, and she was no longer panicked; she was happy, and so was I.

"I'm back on my feet, Mom," I whispered. "I've made it through everything. I've beaten the bad guys. I've told the truth."

I paused, searching for the right words to express how I was feeling, and after a minute, I knew exactly what those words were.

"I'm me."

WHAT TO READ NEXT...

Looking for another riveting, page-turning mystery to read?

Check out ALL THE PRETTY PEOPLE

Ten years ago, I was seventeen, spending summers with my wealthy family and friends on Hawk Island. One terrible night, I blacked out. The next morning, my best friend, Melanie, was gone—vanished without a trace.

Today, I go back. To the island. To my sister's wedding. To a group of privileged people with whom I've never belonged. To my best friend's brother, a man who hates us all. To secrets that someone will kill to keep.

A storm is coming. A storm that will cut off the island from all hope of help. A storm that could allow a kidnapper to escape or a killer to murder again. A storm that will wash away all the lies and deception and reveal the true faces of *All the Pretty People.*

Will I be the next one to disappear?

For more thrilling reads, check out these titles...

Mystery Thriller Standalones
ALL THE PRETTY PEOPLE
LAST ONE TO KNOW
THE OTHER EMILY

ABOUT THE AUTHOR

Barbara Freethy is a #1 New York Times Bestselling Author of 85 novels ranging from contemporary romance to romantic suspense and women's fiction. With over 13 million copies sold, thirty-three of Barbara's books have appeared on the New York Times and USA Today Bestseller Lists, including SUMMER SECRETS which hit #1 on the New York Times!

Known for her emotional and compelling stories of love, family, mystery and romance, Barbara enjoys writing about ordinary people caught up in extraordinary adventures. Library Journal says, "Freethy has a gift for creating unforgettable characters."

For additional information, please visit Barbara's website at www.barbarafreethy.com.

Made in the USA
Las Vegas, NV
18 October 2023

79329450R00184